FROM A BUICK 8

There is a terrifying secret shrouded in Shed B out at the back of the state police barracks in Statler, Pennsylvania. A secret which lures its victims. For twenty years, curious officers have come to watch the vintage Buick's terrifying displays — from blinding light-shows to feeding time. It is a conduit to a world beyond. Young Ned Wilcox has started coming by the barracks, helping out. It's his way of holding on to his father, recently killed in a strange road accident by another Buick. One day Ned peers through the windows of Shed B and discovers the family secret. And like his father, Ned wants answers. And the secret begins to stir . . .

Books by Stephen King
Published by The House of Ulverscroft:

FIRESTARTER
CUJO
THE DEAD ZONE

EVERYTHING'S EVENTUAL
14 Dark Tales

STEPHEN KING

FROM A BUICK 8

Complete and Unabridged

CHARNWOOD
Leicester

First published in Great Britain in 2002 by
Hodder and Stoughton
London

First Charnwood Edition
published 2003
by arrangement with
Hodder and Stoughton
a division of Hodder Headline
London

The moral right of the author has been asserted

British Library CIP Data

King, Stephen, 1947 –
From a Buick 8.—Large print ed.—
Charnwood library series
1. Buick automobile—Fiction
2. Police stations—Pennsylvania—Fiction
3. Horror tales 4. Large type books
I. Title
813.5'4 [F]

ISBN 0–7089–4960–6

Published by
F. A. Thorpe (Publishing)
Anstey, Leicestershire

Set by Words & Graphics Ltd.
Anstey, Leicestershire
Printed and bound in Great Britain by
T. J. International Ltd., Padstow, Cornwall

This book is printed on acid-free paper

STEPHEN KING

FROM A BUICK 8

Complete and Unabridged

CHARNWOOD
Leicester

First published in Great Britain in 2002 by
Hodder and Stoughton
London

First Charnwood Edition
published 2003
by arrangement with
Hodder and Stoughton
a division of Hodder Headline
London

British Library CIP Data

King, Stephen, *1947* –
    From a Buick 8.—Large print ed.—
Charnwood library series
1. Buick automobile—Fiction
2. Police stations—Pennsylvania—Fiction
3. Horror tales 4. Large type books
I. Title
813.5′4 [F]

ISBN 0–7089–4960–6

Published by
F. A. Thorpe (Publishing)
Anstey, Leicestershire

Set by Words & Graphics Ltd.
Anstey, Leicestershire
Printed and bound in Great Britain by
T. J. International Ltd., Padstow, Cornwall

This book is printed on acid-free paper

This is for Surendra and Geeta Patel

NOW:

Sandy

Curt Wilcox's boy came around the barracks a lot the year after his father died, I mean a lot, but nobody ever told him get out the way or asked him what in *hail* he was doing there again. We understood what he was doing: trying to hold on to the memory of his father. Cops know a lot about the psychology of grief; most of us know more about it than we want to.

That was Ned Wilcox's senior year at Statler High. He must have quit the football team; when it came time for choosing, he picked D Troop instead. Hard to imagine a kid doing that, choosing unpaid choring over all those Friday night games and Saturday night parties, but that's what he did. I don't think any of us talked to him about that choice, but we respected him for it. He had decided the time had come to put the games away, that's all. Grown men are frequently incapable of making such decisions; Ned made his at an age when he still couldn't buy a legal drink. Or a legal pack of smokes, for that matter. I think his dad would have been proud. Know it, actually.

Given how much the boy was around, I suppose it was inevitable he'd see what was out in Shed B, and ask someone what it was and what it was doing there. I was the one he was

1

most likely to ask, because I'd been his father's closest friend. Closest one that was still a Trooper, at least. I think maybe I wanted it to happen. Kill or cure, the oldtimers used to say. Give that curious cat a serious dose of satisfaction.

★ ★ ★

What happened to Curtis Wilcox was simple. A veteran county drunk, one Curt himself knew well and had arrested six or eight times, took his life. The drunk, Bradley Roach, didn't mean to hurt anyone; drunks so rarely do. That doesn't keep you from wanting to kick their numb asses all the way to Rocksburg, of course.

Toward the end of a hot July afternoon in the year oh-one, Curtis pulled over one of those big sixteen-wheelers, an interstate landcruiser that had left the fourlane because its driver was hoping for a home-cooked meal instead of just another dose of I-87 Burger King or Taco Bell. Curt was parked on the tarmac of the abandoned Jenny station at the intersection of Pennsylvania State Road 32 and the Humboldt Road — the very place, in other words, where that damned old Buick Roadmaster showed up in our part of the known universe all those years ago. You can call that a coincidence if you want to, but I'm a cop and don't believe in coincidences, only chains of event which grow longer and ever more fragile until either bad luck or plain old human mean-heartedness breaks them.

Ned's father took out after that semi because it had a flapper. When it went by he saw rubber spinning out from one of the rear tires like a big black pinwheel. A lot of independents run on recaps, with the price of diesel so high they just about have to, and sometimes the tread peels loose. You see curls and hunks of it on the interstate all the time, lying on the highway or pushed off into the breakdown lane like the shed skins of giant blacksnakes. It's dangerous to be behind a flapper, especially on a twolane like SR 32, a pretty but neglected stretch of state highway running between Rocksburg and Statler. A big enough chunk might break some unlucky follow-driver's windshield. Even if it didn't, it could startle the operator into the ditch, or a tree, or over the embankment and into Redfern Stream, which matches 32 twist for twist over a distance of nearly six miles.

Curt lit his bar lights, and the trucker pulled over like a good boy. Curt pulled over right behind him, first calling in his 20 and the nature of his stop and waiting for Shirley to acknowledge. With that done, he got out and walked toward the truck.

If he'd gone directly to where the driver was leaning out and looking back at him, he might still be on Planet Earth today. But he stopped to examine the flapper on the rear outside tire, even gave it a good yank to see if he could pull it off. The trucker saw all of it, and testified to it in court. Curt stopping to do that was the last link save one in the chain that brought his boy to Troop D and eventually made him a part of what

3

we are. The very last link, I'd say, was Bradley Roach leaning over to get another brewski out of the six-pack sitting on the floor in the passenger footwell of his old Buick Regal (not *the* Buick, but *another* Buick, yes — it's funny how, when you look back on disasters and love affairs, things seem to line up like planets on an astrologer's chart). Less than a minute later, Ned Wilcox and his sisters were short a daddy and Michelle Wilcox was short a husband.

* * *

Not very long after the funeral, Curt's boy started showing up at the Troop D House. I'd come in for the three-to-eleven that fall (or maybe just to check on things; when you're the wheeldog, it's hard to stay away) and see the boy before I saw anyone else, like as not. While his friends were over at Floyd B. Clouse Field behind the high school, running plays and hitting the tackling dummies and giving each other high-fives, Ned would be out on the front lawn of the barracks by himself, bundled up in his green and gold high school jacket, making big piles of fallen leaves. He'd give me a wave and I'd return it: right back atcha, kid. Sometimes after I parked, I'd come out front and shoot the shit with him. He'd tell me about the foolishness his sisters were up to just lately, maybe, and laugh, but you could see his love for them even when he was laughing at them. Sometimes I'd just go in the back way and ask Shirley what was up. Law enforcement in western Pennsylvania

4

would fall apart without Shirley Pasternak, and you can take that to the bank.

Come winter, Ned was apt to be around back in the parking lot, where the Troopers keep their personal vehicles, running the snowblower. The Dadier brothers, two local wide boys, are responsible for our lot, but Troop D sits in the Amish country on the edge of the Short Hills, and when there's a big storm the wind blows drifts across the lot again almost as soon as the plow leaves. Those drifts look to me like an enormous white ribcage. Ned was a match for them, though. There he'd be, even if it was only eight degrees and the wind still blowing a gale across the hills, dressed in a snowmobile suit with his green and gold jacket pulled over the top of it, leather-lined police-issue gloves on his hands and a ski-mask pulled down over his face. I'd wave. He'd give me a little right-back-atcha, then go on gobbling up the drifts with the snowblower. Later he might come in for coffee, or maybe a cup of hot chocolate. Folks would drift over and talk to him, ask him about school, ask him if he was keeping the twins in line (the girls were ten in the winter of oh-one, I think). They'd ask if his Mom needed anything. Sometimes that would include me, if no one was hollering too loud or if the paperwork wasn't too heavy. None of the talk was about his father; all of the talk was about his father. You understand.

Raking leaves and making sure the drifts didn't take hold out there in the parking lot was really Arky Arkanian's responsibility. Arky was the custodian. He was one of us as well, though, and he never got shirty or went territorial about his job. Hell, when it came to snowblowing the drifts, I'll bet Arky just about got down on his knees and thanked God for the kid. Arky was sixty by then, had to have been, and his own football-playing days were long behind him. So were the ones when he could spend an hour and a half outside in ten-degree temperatures (twenty-five below, if you factored in the wind chill) and hardly feel it.

And then the kid started in with Shirley, technically Police Communications Officer Pasternak. By the time spring rolled around, Ned was spending more and more time with her in her little dispatch cubicle with the phones, the TDD (telephonic device for the deaf), the Trooper Location Board (also known as the D-map), and the computer console that's the hot center of that high-pressure little world. She showed him the bank of phones (the most important is the red one, which is our end of 911). She explained about how the traceback equipment had to be tested once a week, and how it was done, and how you had to confirm the duty-roster daily, so you'd know who was out patrolling the roads of Statler, Lassburg, and Pogus City, and who was due in court or off-duty.

'My nightmare is losing an officer without knowing he's lost,' I overheard her telling Ned one day.

'Has that ever happened?' Ned asked. 'Just . . . losing a guy?'

'Once,' she said. 'Before my time. Look here,

6

Ned, I made you a copy of the call-codes. We don't have to use them anymore, but all the Troopers still do. If you want to run dispatch, you have to know these.'

Then she went back to the four basics of the job, running them past him yet again: know the location, know the nature of the incident, know what the injuries are, if any, and know the closest available unit. Location, incident, injuries, CAU, that was her mantra.

I thought: *He'll be running it next. She means to have him running it. Never mind that if Colonel Teague or someone from Scranton comes in and sees him doing it she'd lose her job, she means to have him running it.*

And by the good goddam, there he was a week later, sitting at PCO Pasternak's desk in the dispatch cubicle, at first only while she ran to the bathroom but then for longer and longer periods while she went across the room for coffee or even out back for a smoke.

The first time the boy saw me seeing him in there all alone, he jumped and then gave a great big guilty smile, like a kid who is surprised in the rumpus room by his mother while he's still got his hand on his girlfriend's tit. I gave him a nod and went right on about my beeswax. Never thought twice about it, either. Shirley had turned over the dispatch operation of Statler Troop D to a kid who still only needed to shave three times a week, almost a dozen Troopers were out there at the other end of the gear in that cubicle, but I didn't even slow my stride. We were still talking about his father, you see. Shirley and Arky as

7

well as me and the other uniforms Curtis Wilcox had served with for over twenty years. You don't always talk with your mouth. Sometimes what you say with your mouth hardly matters at all. You have to *signify*.

When I was out of his sightline, though, I stopped. Stood there. Listened. Across the room, in front of the highway-side windows, Shirley Pasternak stood looking back at me with a Styrofoam cup of coffee in her hand. Next to her was Phil Candleton, who had just clocked off and was once more dressed in his civvies; he was also staring in my direction.

In the dispatch cubicle, the radio crackled. 'Statler, this is 12,' a voice said. Radio distorts, but I still knew all of my men. That was Eddie Jacubois.

'This is Statler, go ahead,' Ned replied. Perfectly calm. If he was afraid of fucking up, he was keeping it out of his voice.

'Statler, I have a Volkswagen Jetta, tag is 14–0–7–3–9 Foxtrot, that's P-A, stopped County Road 99. I need a 10–28, come back?'

Shirley started across the floor, moving fast. A little coffee sloshed over the rim of the Styrofoam cup in her hand. I took her by the elbow, stopping her. Eddie Jacubois was out there on a county road, he'd just stopped a Jetta for some violation — speeding was the logical assumption — and he wanted to know if there were any red flags on the plate or the plateholder. He wanted to know because he was going to get out of his cruiser and approach the Jetta. He wanted to know because he was going

8

to put his ass out on the line, same today as every day. Was the Jetta maybe stolen? Had it been involved in an accident at any time during the last six months? Had its owner been in court on charges of spousal abuse? Had he shot anyone? Robbed or raped anyone? Were there even outstanding parking tickets?

Eddie had a right to know these things, if they were in the database. But Eddie also had a right to know why it was a high school kid who had just told him *This is Statler, go ahead*. I thought it was Eddie's call. If he came back with *Where the hell is Shirley*, I'd let go of her arm. And if Eddie rolled with it, I wanted to see what the kid would do. *How* the kid would do.

'Unit 12, hold for reply.' If Ned was popping a sweat, it still didn't show in his voice. He turned to the computer monitor and keyed in Uniscope, the search engine used by the Pennsylvania State Police. He hit the keys rapidly but cleanly, then punched ENTER.

There followed a moment of silence in which Shirley and I stood side by side, saying nothing and hoping in perfect unison. Hoping that the kid wouldn't freeze, hoping that he wouldn't suddenly push back the chair and bolt for the door, hoping most of all that he had sent the right code to the right place. It seemed like a long moment. I remember I heard a bird calling outside and, very distant, the drone of a plane. There was time to think about those chains of event some people insist on calling coincidence. One of those chains had broken when Ned's father died on Route 32; here was another, just

9

beginning to form. Eddie Jacubois — never the sharpest knife in the drawer, I'm afraid — was now joined to Ned Wilcox. Beyond him, one link farther down the new chain, was a Volkswagen Jetta. And whoever was driving it.

Then: '12, this is Statler.'

'12.'

'Jetta is registered to William Kirk Frady of Pittsburgh. He is previous . . . uh . . . wait . . . '

It was his only pause, and I could hear the hurried riffle of paper as he looked for the card Shirley had given him, the one with the call-codes on it. He found it, looked at it, tossed it aside with an impatient little grunt. Through all this, Eddie waited patiently in his cruiser twelve miles west. He would be looking at Amish buggies, maybe, or a farmhouse with the curtain in one of the front windows pulled aslant, indicating that the Amish family living inside included a daughter of marriageable age, or over the hazy hills to Ohio. Only he wouldn't really be seeing any of those things. The only thing Eddie was seeing at that moment — seeing clearly — was the Jetta parked on the shoulder in front of him, the driver nothing but a silhouette behind the wheel. And what was he, that driver? Rich man? Poor man? Beggarman? Thief?

Finally Ned just said it, which was exactly the right choice. '12, Frady is DUI times three, do you copy?'

Drunk man, that's what the Jetta's driver was. Maybe not right now, but if he had been speeding, the likelihood was high.

'Copy, Statler.' Perfectly laconic. 'Got a

10

current laminate?' Wanting to know if Frady's license to drive was currently valid.

'Ah . . . ' Ned peered frantically at the white letters on the blue screen. *Right in front of you, kiddo, don't you see it?* I held my breath.

Then: 'Affirmative, 12, he got it back three months ago.'

I let go of my breath. Beside me, Shirley let go of hers. This was good news for Eddie, too. Frady was legal, and thus less likely to be crazy. That was the rule of thumb, anyway.

'12 on approach,' Eddie sent. 'Copy that?'

'Copy, 12 on approach, standing by,' Ned replied. I heard a click and then a large, unsteady sigh. I nodded to Shirley, who got moving again. Then I reached up and wiped my brow, not exactly surprised to find it was wet with sweat.

'How's everything going?' Shirley asked. Voice even and normal, saying that, as far as she was concerned, all was quiet on the western front.

'Eddie Jacubois called in,' Ned told her. 'He's 10-27.' That's an operator check, in plain English. If you're a Trooper, you know that it also means citing the operator for some sort of violation, in nine cases out of ten. Now Ned's voice wasn't quite steady, but so what? Now it was all right for it to jig and jag a little. 'He's got a guy in a Jetta out on Highway 99. I handled it.'

'Tell me how,' Shirley said. 'Go through your procedure. Every step, Ned. Quick's you can.'

I went on my way. Phil Candleton intercepted me at the door to my office. He nodded toward the dispatch cubicle. 'How'd the kid do?'

'Did all right,' I said, and stepped past him

11

into my own cubicle. I didn't realize my legs had gone rubbery until I sat down and felt them trembling.

* * *

His sisters, Joan and Janet, were identicals. They had each other, and their mother had a little bit of her gone man in them: Curtis's blue, slightly uptilted eyes, his blond hair, his full lips (the nickname in Curt's yearbook, under his name, had been 'Elvis'). Michelle had her man in her son, as well, where the resemblance was even more striking. Add a few crow's-feet around the eyes and Ned could have been his own father when Curtis first came on the cops.

That's what they had. What Ned had was us.

* * *

One day in April he came into the barracks with a great big sunny smile on his face. It made him look younger and sweeter. But, I remember thinking, we all of us look younger and sweeter when we smile our real smiles — the ones that come when we are genuinely happy and not just trying to play some dumb social game. It struck me fresh that day because Ned didn't smile much. Certainly not *big*. I don't think I realized it until that day because he was polite and responsive and quick-witted. A pleasure to have around, in other words. You didn't notice how grave he was until that rare day when you saw him brighten up and shine.

He came to the center of the room, and all the little conversations stopped. He had a paper in his hand. There was a complicated-looking gold seal at the top. 'Pitt!' he said, holding the paper up in both hands like an Olympic judge's scorecard. 'I got into Pitt, you guys! And they gave me a scholarship! Almost a full boat!'

Everyone applauded. Shirley kissed him smack on the mouth, and the kid blushed all the way down to his collar. Huddie Royer, who was off-duty that day and just hanging around, stewing about some case in which he had to testify, went out and came back with a bag of L'il Debbie cakes. Arky used his key to open the soda machine, and we had a party. Half an hour or so, no more, but it was good while it lasted. Everyone shook Ned's hand, the acceptance letter from Pitt made its way around the room (twice, I think), and a couple of cops who'd been at home dropped by just to talk to him and pass along their congrats.

Then, of course, the real world got back into the act. It's quiet over here in western Pennsylvania, but not dead. There was a farmhouse fire in Pogus City (which is a city about as much as I'm the Archduke Ferdinand), and an overturned Amish buggy on Highway 20. The Amish keep to themselves, but they'll gladly take a little outside help in a case like that. The horse was okay, which was the big thing. The worst buggy fuckups happen on Friday and Saturday nights, when the younger bucks in black have a tendency to get drunk out behind the barn. Sometimes they get a 'worldly person'

13

to buy them a bottle or a case of Iron City beer, and sometimes they drink their own stuff, a really murderous corn shine you wouldn't wish on your worst enemy. It's just part of the scene; it's our world, and mostly we like it, including the Amish with their big neat farms and the orange triangles on the backs of their small neat buggies.

And there's always paperwork, the usual stacks of duplicate and triplicate in my office. It gets worse every year. Why I ever wanted to be the guy in charge is beyond me now. I took the test that qualified me for Sergeant Commanding when Tony Schoondist suggested it, so I must have had a reason back then, but these days it seems to elude me.

Around six o'clock I went out back to have a smoke. We have a bench there facing the parking lot. Beyond it is a very pretty western view. Ned Wilcox was sitting on the bench with his acceptance letter from Pitt in one hand and tears rolling down his face. He glanced at me, then looked away, scrubbing his eyes with the palm of his hand.

I sat down beside him, thought about putting my arm around his shoulder, didn't do it. If you have to think about a thing like that, doing it usually feels phony. I guess, anyway. I have never married, and what I know about fathering you could write on the head of a pin with room left over for the Lord's Prayer. I lit a cigarette and smoked it awhile. 'It's all right, Ned,' I said eventually. It was the only thing I could think of, and I had no idea what it meant.

'I know,' he replied at once in a muffled, trying-not-to-cry voice, and then, almost as if it was part of the same sentence, a continuation of the same thought: 'No it ain't.'

Hearing him use that word, that *ain't*, made me realize how bad he was hurt. Something had gored him in the stomach. It was the sort of word he would have trained himself out of long ago, just so he wouldn't be lumped with the rest of the Statler County hicks, the pickup-truck-n-snowmobile gomers from towns like Patchin and Pogus City. Even his sisters, eight years younger than he was, had probably given up *ain't* by then, and for much the same reasons. Don't say ain't or your mother will faint and your father will fall in a bucket of paint. Yeah, what father?

I smoked and said nothing. On the far side of the parking lot by one of the county roadsalt piles was a cluster of wooden buildings that needed either sprucing up or tearing down. They were the old Motor Pool buildings. Statler County had moved its plows, graders, 'dozers, and asphalt rollers a mile or so down the road ten years before, into a new brick facility that looked like a prison lockdown unit. All that remained here was the one big pile of salt (which we were using ourselves, little by little — once upon a time, that pile had been a mountain) and a few ramshackle wooden buildings. One of them was Shed B. The black-paint letters over the door — one of those wide garage doors that run up on rails — were faded but still legible. Was I thinking about the Buick Roadmaster inside as I sat there next to the crying boy, wanting to put my arm around him and not knowing how? I don't know. I guess I might have been, but I don't think we know all the things we're thinking. Freud might have been full of shit about a lot of things, but not that one. I don't know about a subconscious, but there's a pulse in our heads, all right, same as there's one in our chests, and it carries unformed, no-language thoughts that most times we can't even read, and they are usually the important ones.

Ned rattled the letter. '*He's* the one I really want to show this to. *He's* the one who wanted to go to Pitt when he was a kid but couldn't afford it. He's the reason I *applied*, for God's sake.' A pause; then, almost too low to hear: 'This is fucked up, Sandy.'

'What did your mother say when you showed her?'

That got a laugh, watery but genuine. 'She didn't *say*. She screamed like a lady who just won a trip to Bermuda on a gameshow. Then she cried.' Ned turned to me. His own tears had stopped, but his eyes were red and swollen. He looked a hell of a lot younger than eighteen just then. The sweet smile resurfaced for a moment. 'Basically, she was great about it. Even the Little J's were great about it. Like you guys. Shirley kissing me . . . man, I got goosebumps.'

I laughed, thinking that Shirley might have raised a few goosebumps of her own. She liked him, he was a handsome kid, and the idea of playing Mrs Robinson might have crossed her mind. Probably not, but it wasn't impossible.

16

Her husband had been out of the picture almost twenty years by then.

Ned's smile faded. He rattled the acceptance letter again. 'I knew this was yes as soon as I took it out of the mailbox. I could just tell, somehow. And I started missing him all over again. I mean *fierce*.'

'I know,' I said, but of course I didn't. My own father was still alive, a hale and genially profane man of seventy-four. At seventy, my mother was all that and a bag of chips.

Ned sighed, looking off at the hills. 'How he went out is just so *dumb*,' he said. 'I can't even tell my kids, if I ever have any, that Grampy went down in a hail of bullets while foiling the bank robbers or the militia guys who were trying to put a bomb in the county courthouse. Nothing like that.'

'No,' I agreed, 'nothing like that.'

'I can't even say it was because he was careless. He was just . . . a drunk just came along and just . . . '

He bent over, wheezing like an old man with a cramp in his belly, and this time I at least put my hand on his back. He was trying so hard not to cry, that's what got to me. Trying so hard to be a man, whatever that means to an eighteen-year-old boy.

'Ned. It's all right.'

He shook his head violently. 'If there was a God, there'd be a reason,' he said. He was looking down at the ground. My hand was still on his back, and I could feel it heaving up and down, like he'd just run a race. 'If there was a

God, there'd be some kind of thread running through it. But there isn't. Not that I can see.'

'If you have kids, Ned, tell them their grandfather died in the line of duty. Then take them here and show them his name on the plaque, with all the others.'

He didn't seem to hear me. 'I have this dream. It's a bad one.' He paused, thinking how to say it, then just plunged ahead. 'I dream it was all a dream. Do you know what I'm saying?'

I nodded.

'I wake up crying, and I look around my room, and it's sunny. Birds are singing. It's morning. I can smell coffee downstairs and I think, 'He's okay. Jesus and thank you God, the old man's okay.' I don't hear him talking or anything, but I just know. And I think what a stupid idea it was, that he could be walking up the side of some guy's rig to give him a warning about a flapper and just get creamed by a drunk, the sort of idea you could only have in a stupid dream where everything seems so *real* . . . and I start to swing my legs out of bed . . . sometimes I see my ankles go into a patch of sun . . . it even feels warm . . . and then I wake up for real, and it's dark, and I've got the blankets pulled up around me but I'm still cold, shivering and cold, and I know that the *dream* was a dream.'

'That's awful,' I said, remembering that as a boy I'd had my own version of the same dream. It was about my dog. I thought to tell him that, then didn't. Grief is grief, but a dog is not a father.

'It wouldn't be so bad if I had it every night.

18

Then I think I'd know, even while I was asleep, that there's no smell of coffee, that it's not even morning. But it doesn't come . . . doesn't come . . . and then when it finally does, I get fooled again. I'm so happy and relieved, I even think of something nice I'll do for him, like buy him that five-iron he wanted for his birthday . . . and then I wake up. I get fooled all over again.' Maybe it was the thought of his father's birthday, not celebrated this year and never to be celebrated again, that started fresh tears running down his cheeks. 'I just hate getting fooled. It's like when Mr Jones came down and got me out of World History class to tell me, but even worse. Because I'm alone when I wake up in the dark. Mr Grenville — he's the guidance counselor at school — says time heals all wounds, but it's been almost a year and I'm still having that dream.'

I nodded. I was remembering Ten-Pound, shot by a hunter one November, growing stiff in his own blood under a white sky when I found him. A white sky promising a winter's worth of snow. In *my* dream it was always another dog when I got close enough to see, not Ten-Pound at all, and I felt that same relief. Until I woke up, at least. And thinking of Ten-Pound made me think, for a moment, of our barracks mascot back in the old days. Mister Dillon, his name had been, after the TV sheriff played by James Arness. A good dog.

'I know that feeling, Ned.'

'Do you?' He looked at me hopefully.

'Yes. And it gets better. Believe me, it does.

But he was your Dad, not a schoolmate or a neighbor from down the road. You may still be having that dream next year at this time. You may even be having it ten years on, every once in awhile.'

'That's horrible.'

'No,' I said. 'That's memory.'

'If there was a reason.' He was looking at me earnestly. 'A damn *reason*. Do you get that?'

'Of course I do.'

'*Is* there one, do you think?'

I thought of telling him I didn't know about reasons, only about chains — how they form themselves, link by link, out of nothing; how they knit themselves into the world. Sometimes you can grab a chain and use it to pull yourself out of a dark place. Mostly, though, I think you get wrapped up in them. Just caught, if you're lucky. Fucking strangled, if you're not.

I found myself gazing across the parking lot at Shed B again. Looking at it, I thought that if I could get used to what was stored in its dark interior, Ned Wilcox could get used to living a fatherless life. People can get used to just about anything. That's the best of our lives, I guess. Of course, it's the horror of them, too.

'Sandy? What do you think?'

'I think that you're asking the wrong guy. I know about work, and hope, and putting a nut away for the GDR.'

He grinned. In Troop D, everyone talked very seriously about the GDR, as though it were some complicated subdivision of law enforcement. It actually stood for 'golden days of retirement'. I

20

think it might have been Huddie Royer who first started talking about the GDR.

'I also know about preserving the chain of evidence so no smart defense attorney can kick your legs out from under you in court and make you look like a fool. Beyond that, I'm just another confused American male.'

'At least you're honest,' he said.

But was I? Or was I begging the goddam question? I didn't *feel* particularly honest right then; I felt like a man who can't swim looking at a boy who is floundering in deep water. And once again Shed B caught my eye. *Is it cold in here?* this boy's father had asked, back in the once-upon-a-time, back in the day. *Is it cold in here, or is it just me?*

No, it hadn't been just him.

'What are you thinking about, Sandy?'

'Nothing worth repeating,' I said. 'What are you doing this summer?'

'Huh?'

'What are you doing this summer?' It wouldn't be golfing in Maine or boating on Lake Tahoe, that was for sure; scholarship or no scholarship, Ned was going to need all of the old folding green he could get.

'County Parks and Rec again, I suppose,' he said with a marked lack of enthusiasm. 'I worked there last summer until . . . you know.'

Until his Dad. I nodded.

'I got a letter from Tom McClannahan last week, saying he was holding a place open for me. He mentioned coaching Little League, but that's just the carrot on the end of the stick. Mostly it'll be swinging a spade and setting out sprinklers, just like last year. I can swing a spade, and I'm not afraid of getting my hands dirty. But Tom . . . ' He shrugged instead of finishing.

I knew what Ned was too discreet to say. There are two kinds of work-functional alcoholics, those who are just too fucking mean to fall down and those so sweet that other people go on covering for them way past the point of insanity. Tom was one of the mean ones, the last sprig on a family tree full of plump county hacks going back to the nineteenth century. The McClannahans had fielded a Senator, two members of the House of Representatives, half a dozen Pennsylvania Representatives, and Statler County trough-hogs beyond counting. Tom was, by all accounts, a mean boss with no ambition to climb the political totem pole. What he liked was telling kids like Ned, the ones who had been raised to be quiet and respectful, where to squat and push. And of course for Tom, they never squatted deep enough or pushed hard enough.

'Don't answer that letter yet,' I said. 'I want to make a call before you do.'

I thought he'd be curious, but he only nodded his head. I looked at him sitting there, holding the letter on his lap, and thought that he looked like a boy who has been denied a place in the college of his choice instead of being offered a fat scholarship incentive to go there.

Then I thought again. Not just denied a place in college, maybe, but in life itself. That wasn't true — the letter he'd gotten from Pitt was only one of the things that proved it — but I've no doubt he felt that way just then. I don't know why success often leaves us feeling lower-spirited than failure, but I know it's true. And remember that he was just eighteen, a Hamlet age if there ever was one.

I looked across the parking lot again at Shed B, thinking about what was inside. Not that any of us really knew.

*   *   *

My call the following morning was to Colonel Teague in Butler, which is our regional headquarters. I explained the situation, and waited while *he* made a call, presumably to Scranton, where the big boys hang their hats. It didn't take long for Teague to get back to me, and the news was good. I then spoke to Shirley, although that was little more than a formality; she had liked the father well enough, but outright doted on the son.

When Ned came in that afternoon after school, I asked him if he'd like to spend the summer learning dispatch — and getting paid for it — instead of listening to Tom McClanna-han bitch and moan down at Parks and Rec. For a moment he looked stunned . . . hammered, almost. Then he broke out in an enormous delighted grin. I thought he was going to hug me. If I'd actually put my arm around him the previous evening instead of just thinking about it, he probably would've. As it was, he settled for clenching his hands into fists, raising them to the sides of his face, and hissing 'Yesssss!'

'Shirley's agreed to take you on as 'prentice, and you've got the official okay from Butler. It ain't swinging a shovel for McClannahan, of course, but — '

This time he *did* hug me, laughing as he did it, and I liked it just fine. I could get used to something like that.

When he turned around, Shirley was standing there with two Troopers flanking her: Huddie Royer and George Stankowski. All of them looking as serious as a heart attack in their gray uniforms. Huddie and George were wearing their lids, making them look approximately nine feet tall.

'You don't mind?' Ned asked Shirley. 'Really?'

'I'll teach you everything I know,' Shirley said.

'Yeah?' Huddie asked. 'What's he going to do after the first week?'

Shirley threw him an elbow; it went in just above the butt of his Beretta and landed on target. Huddie gave an exaggerated *oof!* sound and staggered.

'Got something for you, kid,' George said. He spoke quietly and gave Ned his best you-were-doing-sixty-in-a-hospital-zone stare. One hand was behind his back.

'What?' Ned asked, sounding a little nervous in spite of his obvious happiness. Behind George, Shirley, and Huddie, a bunch of other Troop D's had gathered.

'Don't you *ever* lose it,' Huddie said. Also quietly and seriously.

'What, you guys, what?' More uneasy than ever.

24

From behind his back, George produced a small white box. He gave it to the boy. Ned looked at it, looked at the Troopers gathered around him, then opened the box. Inside was a big plastic star with the words DEPUTY DAWG printed on it.

'Welcome to Troop D, Ned,' George said. He tried to hold on to his solemn face and couldn't. He started to guffaw, and pretty soon they were all laughing and crowding around to shake Ned's hand.

'Pretty funny, you guys,' he said, 'a real belly-buster.' He was smiling, but I thought he was on the verge of tears again. It was nothing you could see, but it was there. I think Shirley Pasternak sensed it, too. And when the kid excused himself to go to the head, I guessed he was going there to regain his composure, or to assure himself he wasn't dreaming again, or both. Sometimes when things go wrong, we get more help than we ever expected. And sometimes it's still not enough.

★   ★   ★

It was great having Ned around that summer. Everyone liked him, and he liked being there. He particularly liked the hours he spent in dispatch with Shirley. Some of it was going over codes, but mostly it was learning the right responses and how to juggle multiple calls. He got good at it fast, shooting back requested information to the road units, playing the computer keys like it was a barrelhouse piano, liaising with other

Troops when it was necessary, as it was after a series of violent thunderstorms whipped through western PA one evening toward the end of June. There were no tornadoes, thank God, but there were high winds, hail, and lightning.

The only time he came close to panic was a day or two later, when a guy taken before the Statler County magistrate suddenly went nuts and started running all over the place, pulling off his clothes and yelling about Jesus Penis. That's what the guy called him; I've got it in a report somewhere. About four different Troopers called in, a couple who were on-scene, a couple who were busting ass to get there. While Ned was trying to figure out how to deal with this, a Trooper from Butler called in, saying he was out on 99, in high-speed pursuit of . . . *blurk!* Transmission ceased. Ned presumed the guy had rolled his cruiser, and he presumed right (the Butler Troop, a rookie, came out all right, but his ride was totaled and the suspect he was chasing got away clean). Ned bawled for Shirley, backing away from the computer, the phones, and the mike as if they had suddenly gotten hot. She took over fast, but still took time to give him a quick hug and a kiss on the cheek before slipping into the seat he had vacated. Nobody was killed or even hurt badly, and Mr Jesus Penis went to Statler Memorial for observation. It was the only time I saw Ned flustered, but he shook it off. And learned from it.

On the whole, I was impressed.

Shirley loved teaching him, too. That was no real surprise; she'd already demonstrated a

26

willingness to risk her job by doing it without official sanction. She *did* know — we all did — that Ned had no intention of making police work his career, he never gave us so much as a hint of that, but it made no difference to Shirley. And he liked being around. We knew that, too. He liked the pressure and the tension, fed on it. There was that one lapse, true, but I was actually glad to see it. It was good to know it wasn't just a computer-game to him; he understood that he was moving real people around on his electronic chessboard. And if Pitt didn't work out, who knew? He was already better than Matt Babicki, Shirley's predecessor.

⋆　⋆　⋆

In early July — it could have been a year to the day since his father had been killed, for all I know — the kid came to me about Shed B. There was a rap on the side of my door, which I mostly leave open, and when I looked up he was standing there in a sleeveless Steelers T-shirt and old bluejeans, a cleaning rag dangling out of each rear pocket. I knew what it was about right away. Maybe it was the rags, or maybe it was something in his eyes.

'Thought it was your day off, Ned.'

'Yeah,' he said, then shrugged. 'There were just some chores I'd been meaning to do. And . . . well . . . when you come out for a smoke, there's something I want to ask you about.' Pretty excited, by the sound of him.

'No time like the present,' I said, getting up.

'You sure? I mean, if you're busy — '
'I'm not busy,' I said, though I was. 'Let's go.'

* * *

It was early afternoon on the sort of day that's common enough in the Short Hills Amish country during midsummer: overcast and hot, the heat magnified by a syrupy humidity that hazed the horizon and made our part of the world, which usually looks big and generous to me, appear small and faded instead, like an old snapshot that's lost most of its color. From the west came the sound of unfocused thunder. By suppertime there might be more storms — we'd been having them three days a week since the middle of June, it seemed — but now there was only the heat and the humidity, wringing the sweat from you as soon as you stepped out of the air conditioning.

Two rubber pails stood in front of the Shed B door, a bucket of suds and a bucket of rinse. Sticking out of one was the handle of a squeegee. Curt's boy was a neat worker. Phil Candleton was currently sitting on the smokers' bench, and he gave me a wise glance as we passed him and walked across the parking lot.

'I was doing the barracks windows,' Ned was explaining, 'and when I finished, I took the buckets over there to dump.' He pointed at the waste ground between Shed B and Shed C, where there were a couple of rusting plow blades, a couple of old tractor tires, and a lot of weeds. 'Then I decided what the heck, I'll give

28

those shed windows a quick once-over before I toss the water. The ones on Shed C were filthy, but the ones on B were actually pretty clean.'

That didn't surprise me. The small windows running across the front of Shed B had been looked through by two (perhaps even three) generations of Troopers, from Jackie O'Hara to Eddie Jacubois. I could remember guys standing at those roll-up doors like kids at some scary sideshow exhibit. Shirley had taken her turns, as had her predecessor, Matt Babicki; come close, darlings, and see the living crocodile. Observe his teeth, how they shine.

Ned's Dad had once gone inside with a rope around his waist. I'd been in there. Huddie, of course, and Tony Schoondist, the old Sergeant Commanding. Tony, whose last name no one could spell on account of the strange way it was pronounced (*Shane*-dinks), was four years in an 'assisted living' institution by the time Ned officially came to work at the barracks. A lot of us had been in Shed B. Not because we wanted to but because from time to time we had to. Curtis Wilcox and Tony Schoondist became scholars (Roadmaster instead of Rhodes), and it was Curt who hung the round thermometer with the big numbers you could read from outside. To see it, all you had to do was lean your brow against one of the glass panes which ran along the roll-up door at a height of about five and a half feet, then cup your hands to the sides of your face to cut the glare. That was the only cleaning those windows would have gotten before Curt's boy showed up; the occasional

29

polishing by the foreheads of those who had come to see the living crocodile. Or, if you want to be literal, the shrouded shape of something that almost looked like a Buick 8-cylinder. It was shrouded because we threw a tarpaulin over it, like a sheet over the body of a corpse. Only every now and then the tarp would slide off. There was no reason for that to happen, but from time to time it did. That was no corpse in there.

'Look at it!' Ned said when we got there. He ran the words all together, like an enthusiastic little kid. 'What a neat old car, huh? Even better than my Dad's Bel Air! It's a Buick, I can tell that much by the portholes and the grille. Must be from the mid-fifties, wouldn't you say?'

Actually it was a '54, according to Tony Schoondist, Curtis Wilcox, and Ennis Rafferty. *Sort* of a '54. When you got right down to it, it wasn't a 1954 at all. Or a Buick. Or even a car. It was something else, as we used to say in the days of my misspent youth.

Meanwhile, Ned was going on, almost babbling.

'But it's in cherry condition, you can see that from here. It was so *weird*, Sandy! I looked in and at first all I saw was this hump. Because the tarp was on it. I started to wash the windows . . . ' Only what he actually said was *warsh the windas*, because that's how we say it in this part of the world, where the Giant Eagle supermarket becomes *Jaunt Iggle*. ' . . . and there was this sound, or two sounds, really, a *wisssshh* and then a thump. The tarp slid off the car while I was washing the windows! Like it

30

wanted me to see it, or something! Now is that weird or is that weird?'

'That's pretty weird, all right,' I said. I leaned my forehead against the glass (as I had done many times before) and cupped my hands to the sides of my face, eliminating what reflection there was on this dirty day. Yes, it looked like an old Buick, all right, but almost cherry, just as the kid had said. That distinctive fifties Buick grille, which looked to me like the mouth of a chrome crocodile. Whitewall tires. Fenderskirts in the back — *yow*, *baby*, we used to say, *too cool for school*. Looking into the gloom of Shed B, you probably would have called it black. It was actually midnight blue.

Buick did make a 1954 Roadmaster in midnight blue — Schoondist checked — but never one of that particular type. The paint had a kind of textured *flaky* look, like a kid's duded-up streetrod.

That's earthquake country in there, Curtis Wilcox said.

I jumped back. Dead a year or not, he spoke directly into my left ear. Or something did.

'What's wrong?' Ned asked. 'You look like you saw a ghost.'

Heard one, I almost said. What I *did* say was 'Nothing.'

'You sure? You jumped.'

'Goose walked over my grave, I guess. I'm okay.'

'So what's the story on the car? Who owns it?'

What a question *that* was. 'I don't know,' I said.

31

'Well, what's it doing just sitting there in the dark? Man, if I had a nice-looking street-custom like that — and vintage! — I'd never keep it sitting in a dirty old shed.' Then an idea hit him. 'Is it, like, some criminal's car? Evidence in a case?'

'Call it a repo, if you want. Theft of services.' It's what *we'd* called it. Not much, but as Curtis himself had once said, you only need one nail to hang your hat on.

'What services?'

'Seven dollars' worth of gas.' I couldn't quite bring myself to tell him who had pumped it.

'Seven *dollars*? That's all?'

'Well,' I said, 'you only need one nail to hang your hat on.'

He looked at me, puzzled. I looked back at him, saying nothing.

'Can we go in?' he asked finally. 'Take a closer look?'

I put my forehead back against the glass and read the thermometer hanging from the beam, as round and bland as the face of the moon. Tony Schoondist had bought it at the Tru-Value in Statler, paying for it out of his own pocket instead of Troop D petty cash. And Ned's father had hung it from the beam. Like a hat on a nail.

Although the temperature out where we were standing had to be at least eighty-five, and everyone knows heat builds up even higher in poorly ventilated sheds and barns, the thermometer's big red needle stood spang between the fives of 55.

'Not just now,' I said.

32

'Why not?' And then, as if he realized that sounded impolite, perhaps even impudent: 'What's wrong with it?'

'Right now it's not safe.'

He studied me for several seconds. The interest and lively curiosity drained out of his face as he did, and he once more became the boy I had seen so often since he started coming by the barracks, the one I'd seen most clearly on the day he'd been accepted at Pitt. The boy sitting on the smokers' bench with tears rolling down his cheeks, wanting to know what every kid in history wants to know when someone they love is suddenly yanked off the stage: why does it happen, why did it happen to me, is there a reason or is it all just some crazy roulette wheel? If it means something, what do I do about it? And if it means nothing, how do I bear it?

'Is this about my father?' he asked. 'Was that my dad's car?'

His intuition was scary. No, it hadn't been his father's car . . . how could it be, when it wasn't really a car at all? Yes, it *had* been his father's car. And mine . . . Huddie Royer's . . . Tony Schoondist's . . . Ennis Rafferty's. Ennis's most of all, maybe. Ennis's in a way the rest of us could never equal. Never *wanted* to equal. Ned had asked who the car belonged to, and I supposed the real answer was Troop D, Pennsylvania State Police. It belonged to all the Troopers, past and present, who had ever known what we were keeping out in Shed B. But for most of the years it had spent in our custody, the Buick had been the special property of Tony and

33

Ned's dad. They were its curators, its Roadmaster Scholars.

'Not exactly your dad's,' I said, knowing I'd hesitated too long. 'But he knew about it.'

'What's to know? And did my Mom know, too?'

'Nobody knows these days except for us,' I said.

'Troop D, you mean.'

'Yes. And that's how it's going to stay.' There was a cigarette in my hand that I barely remembered lighting. I dropped it to the macadam and crushed it out. 'It's our business.'

I took a deep breath.

'But if you really want to know, I'll tell you. You're one of us now . . . close enough for government work, anyway.' His father used to say that, too — all the time, and things like that have a way of sticking. 'You can even go in there and look.'

'When?'

'When the temperature goes up.'

'I don't get you. What's the temperature in there got to do with anything?'

'I get off at three today,' I said, and pointed at the bench. 'Meet me there, if the rain holds off. If it doesn't, we'll go upstairs or down to The Country Way Diner, if you're hungry. I expect your father would want you to know.'

Was that true? I actually had no idea. Yet my impulse to tell him seemed strong enough to qualify as an intuition, maybe even a direct order from beyond. I'm not a religious man, but I sort of believe in such things. And I thought about

34

the oldtimers saying kill or cure, give that curious cat a dose of satisfaction.

Does knowing really satisfy? Rarely, in my experience. But I didn't want Ned leaving for Pitt in September the way he was in July, with his usual sunny nature flickering on and off like a lightbulb that isn't screwed all the way in. I thought he had a right to some answers. Sometimes there are none, I know that, but I felt like trying. Felt I had to try, in spite of the risks.

Earthquake country, Curtis Wilcox said in my ear. *That's earthquake country in there, so be careful.*

'Goose walk over your grave again, Sandy?' the boy asked me.

'I guess it wasn't a goose, after all,' I said. 'But it was something.'

★   ★   ★

The rain held off. When I went out to join Ned on the bench which faces Shed B across the parking lot, Arky Arkanian was there, smoking a cigarette and talking Pirate baseball with the kid. Arky made as if to leave when I showed up, but I told him to stay put. 'I'm going to tell Ned about the Buick we keep over there,' I said, nodding toward the shed across the way. 'If he decides to call for the men in the white coats because the Troop D Sergeant Commanding has lost his shit, you can back me up. After all, you were here.'

Arky's smile faded. His iron-gray hair fluffed around his head in the limp, hot breeze that had sprung up. 'You sure dat a good idear, Sarge?'

'Curiosity killed the cat,' I said, 'but — '

' — satisfaction brought him back,' Shirley finished from behind me. 'A great big dose of it, is what Trooper Curtis Wilcox used to say. Can I join you? Or is this the Boys' Club today?'

'No sex discrimination on the smokers' bench,' I said. 'Join us, please.'

Like me, Shirley had just finished her shift and Steff Colucci had taken her place at dispatch.

She sat next to Ned, gave him a smile, and brought a pack of Parliaments out of her purse. It was two-double-oh-two, we all knew better, had for years, and we went right on killing ourselves. Amazing. Or maybe, considering we live in a world where drunks can crush State Troopers against the sides of eighteen-wheelers and where make-believe Buicks show up from time to time at real gas stations, not so amazing. Anyway, it was nothing to me right then.

Right then I had a story to tell.

THEN

In 1979, the Jenny station at the intersection of SR 32 and the Humboldt Road was still open, but it was staggering badly; OPEC took all the little 'uns out in the end. The mechanic and owner was Herbert 'Hugh' Bossey, and on that particular day he was over in Lassburg, getting his teeth looked after — a bear for his Snickers bars and RC Colas was Hugh Bossey. NO MECH ON DUTY BECAUSE OF TOOTH-AKE, said the sign taped in the window of the garage bay. The pump-jockey was a high school dropout named Bradley Roach, barely out of his teens. This fellow, twenty-two years and untold thousands of beers later, would come along and kill the father of a boy who was not then born, crushing him against the side of a Freuhof box, turning him like a spindle, unrolling him like a noisemaker, spinning him almost skinless into the weeds, and leaving his bloody clothes inside-out on the highway like a magic trick. But all that is in the yet-to-be. We are in the past now, in the magical land of Then.

★　★　★

At around ten o'clock on a morning in July, Brad Roach was sitting in the office of the Jenny station with his feet up, reading *Inside View*. On the front was a picture of a flying saucer hovering ominously over the White House.

The bell in the garage dinged as the tires of a vehicle rolled over the airhose on the tarmac. Brad looked up to see a car — the very one which would spend so many years in the darkness of Shed B — pull up to the second of the station's two pumps. That was the one labeled HI TEST. It was a beautiful midnight-blue Buick, old (it had the big chrome grille and the portholes running up the sides) but in mint condition. The paint sparkled, the windshield sparkled, the chrome side-strike sweeping along the body sparkled, and even before the driver opened the door and got out, Bradley Roach knew there was something wrong with it. He just couldn't put his finger on what it was.

He dropped his newspaper on the desk (he never would have been allowed to take it out of the desk drawer in the first place if the boss hadn't been overtown paying for his sweet tooth) and got up just as the Roadmaster's driver opened his door on the far side of the pumps and got out.

It had rained heavily the night before and the roads were still wet (hell, still *underwater* in some of the low places on the west side of Statler Township) but the sun had come out around eight o'clock and by ten the day was both bright and warm. Nevertheless, the man who got out of the car was dressed in a black trenchcoat and large black hat. 'Looked like a spy in some old movie,' Brad said to Ennis Rafferty an hour or so later, indulging in what was, for him, a flight of poetic fancy. The trenchcoat, in fact, was so long

38

it nearly dragged on the puddly cement tarmac, and it billowed behind the Buick's driver as he strode toward the side of the station and the sound of Redfern Stream, which ran behind it. The stream had swelled wonderfully in the previous night's showers.

Brad, assuming that the man in the black coat and floppy black hat was headed for the seat of convenience, called: 'Bathroom door's open, mister . . . how much of this jetfuel you want?'

'Fill 'er up,' the customer said. He spoke in a voice Brad Roach didn't much like. What he told the responding officers later was that the guy sounded like he was talking through a mouthful of jelly. Brad was in a poetical mood for sure. Maybe Hugh being gone for the day had something to do with it.

'Check the earl?' Brad asked. By this time his customer had reached the corner of the little white station. Judging by how fast he was moving, Brad figured he had to offload some freight in a hurry.

The guy paused, though, and turned toward Brad a little. Just enough for Brad to see a pallid, almost waxy crescent of cheek, a dark, almond-shaped eye with no discernible white in it, and a curl of lank black hair falling beside one oddly made ear. Brad remembered the ear best, remembered it with great clarity. Something about it disturbed him deeply, but he couldn't explain just what it was. At this point, poesy failed him. *Melted, kinda, like he'd been in a fire* seemed to be the best he could do.

'Oil's fine!' the man in the black coat and hat

said in his choked voice, and was gone around the corner in a final batlike swirl of dark cloth. In addition to the quality of the voice — that unpleasant, mucusy sound — the man had an accent that made Brad Roach think of the old *Rocky and Bullwinkle* show, Boris Badinoff telling Natasha *Ve must stop moose und squirrel!*

Brad went to the Buick, ambled down the side closest to the pumps (the driver had parked carelessly, leaving plenty of room between the car and the island), trailing one hand along the chrome swoop and the smooth paintjob as he went. That touch was more admiring than impudent, although it might have had a bit of harmless impudence in it; Bradley was then a young man, with a young man's high spirits. At the back, bending over the fuel hatch, he paused. The fuel hatch was there, but the rear license plate wasn't. There wasn't even a plate*holder*, or screw-holes where a plate would normally go.

This made Bradley realize what had struck him as wrong as soon as he heard the *ding-ding* of the bell and looked up at the car for the first time. There was no inspection sticker. Well, no business of his if there was no plate on the back deck and no inspection sticker on the windshield; either one of the local cops or a Statie from Troop D just up the road would see the guy and nail him for it . . . or they wouldn't. Either way, Brad Roach's job was to pump gas.

He twirled the crank on the side of the hi-test pump to turn back the numbers, stuck the nozzle in the hole, and set the automatic feed.

40

The bell inside the pump started to bing and while it did, Brad walked up the driver's side of the Buick, completing the circuit. He looked through the leftside windows as he went, and the car's interior struck him as singularly stark for what had been almost a luxury car back in the fifties. The seat upholstery was wren-brown, and so was the fabric lining the inside of the roof. The back seat was empty, the front seat was empty, and there was nothing on the floor — not so much as a gum-wrapper, let alone a map or a crumpled cigarette pack. The steering wheel looked like inlaid wood. Bradley wondered if that was the way they had come on this model, or if it was some kind of special option. Looked ritzy. And why was it so *big*? If it had had spokes sticking out of it, you would have thought it belonged on a millionaire's yacht. You'd have to spread your arms almost as wide as your chest just to grip it. Had to be some sort of custom job, and Brad didn't think it would be comfortable to handle on a long drive. Not a bit comfortable.

Also, there was something funny about the dashboard. It looked like burled walnut and the chromed controls and little appliances — heater, radio, clock — looked all right . . . they were in the right *places*, anyway . . . and the ignition key was also in the right place (*trusting soul, ain't he?* Brad thought), yet there was something about the setup that was very much not right. Hard to say what, though.

Brad strolled back around to the front of the car again, admiring the sneering chrome grille (it

41

was all Buick, that grille; that part, at least, was dead on the money) and verifying that there was no inspection sticker, not from PA or anyplace else. There were no stickers on the windshield at all. The Buick's owner was apparently not a member of Triple-A, the Elks, the Lions, or the Kiwanis. He did not support Pitt or Penn State (at least not to the extent of putting a decal on any of the Buick's windows), and his car wasn't protected by Mopar or good old Rusty Jones.

Pretty cool car just the same . . . although the boss would have told him that his job wasn't to admire the rolling stock but just to fill 'em fast.

The Buick drank seven dollars' worth of the good stuff before the feed cut off. That was a lot of gas in those days, when a gallon of hi-test could be purchased for seventy cents. Either the tank had been close to empty when the man in the black coat took the car out, or he'd driven it a far piece.

Then Bradley decided that second idea had to be bullshit. Because the roads were still wet, still brimming over in the dips, for God's sake, but there wasn't a single mudstreak or splatter on the Buick's smooth blue hide. Not so much as a smear on those fat and luxy whitewalls, either. And to Bradley Roach, that seemed flat-out impossible.

It was nothing to him one way or the other, of course, but he could point out the lack of a valid inspection sticker. Might get him a tip. Enough for a six-pack, maybe. He was still six or eight months from being able to buy legally, but there were ways and means if you were dedicated, and even then, in the early going, Bradley was dedicated.

He went back to the office, sat down, picked up his *Inside View*, and waited for the fellow in the black coat to come back. It was a damned hot day for a long coat like that, no doubt about it, but by then Brad thought he had that part figured out. The man was an SKA, just a little different from the ones around Statler. From a sect that allowed car-driving, it seemed. SKAs were what Bradley and his friends called the Amish. It stood for shitkicking assholes.

Fifteen minutes later, when Brad had finished reading 'We *Have* Been Visited!' by UFO expert Richard T. Rumsfeld (US Army Ret.) and had given close attention to a blonde Page Four Girl who appeared to be fly-fishing a mountain stream in her bra and panties, Brad realized he was *still* waiting. The guy hadn't gone to make any nickel-and-dime deposit, it seemed; that guy was clearly a shithouse millionaire.

Snickering, imagining the guy perched on the jakes under the rusty pipes, sitting there in the gloom (the single lightbulb had burned out a month ago and neither Bradley nor Hugh had gotten around to changing it yet) with his black coat puddled all around him and collecting mouse-turds, Brad picked up his newspaper again. He turned to the joke page, which was good for another ten minutes (some of the jokes were so comical Brad read them three and even four times). He dropped the paper back on the desk and looked at the clock over the door. Beyond it, at the pumps, the Buick Roadmaster sparkled in the sun. Almost half an hour had passed since its driver had cried 'Oil's fine!' back over his shoulder in his strangly voice and then disappeared down the side of the building in a fine swirl of black cloth. Was he an SKA? Did any of them drive cars? Brad didn't think so. The SKAs thought anything with an engine was the work of Satan, didn't they?

Okay, so maybe he wasn't. But whatever he was, why wasn't he back?

All at once the image of that guy on the gloomy, discolored throne back there by the diesel pump didn't seem so funny. In his mind's eye, Brad could still see him sitting there with his coat puddled around him on the filthy linoleum and his pants down around his ankles, but now Brad saw him with his head down, his chin resting on his chest, his big hat (which didn't really look like an Amish hat at all) slewed forward over his eyes. Not moving. Not breathing. Not shitting but dead. Heart attack or brain trembolism or something like that. It was possible. If the goddam King of Rock and Roll could croak while doing Number Two, anyone could.

'Naw,' Bradley Roach said softly. 'Naw, that ain't . . . he wudd'n . . . naw!'

He picked up the paper, tried to read about the flying saucers that were keeping an eye on us, and couldn't convert the words into coherent thoughts. He put it down and looked out the door. The Buick was still there, shining in the sun.

No sign of the driver.

44

Half an hour . . . no, thirty-five minutes now. God*dang*. Bradley picked up *Inside View* and tried to read about teenage cultists in Florida. One of the girls had a great rack, but as far as Bradley Roach was concerned, Satan could have the rest of them.

Five more minutes passed and he found himself tearing strips off the newspaper and drifting them down to the wastebasket, where they formed piles of nervous confetti.

'Fuggit,' he said, and got to his feet. He went out the door and around the corner of the little white cinderblock cube where he'd worked since dropping out of high school. The restrooms were down at the back, on the east side. Brad hadn't made up his mind if he should play it straight — *Mister, are you all right?* — or humorous — *Hey Mister, I got a firecracker, if you need one.* As it turned out, he got to deliver neither of these carefully crafted phrases.

The men's room door had a loose latch and was apt to fly open in any strong puff of wind unless bolted shut from the inside, so Brad and Hugh always stuffed a piece of folded cardboard into the crack to keep the door shut when the restroom wasn't in use. If the man from the Buick had been inside the toilet, the fold of cardboard would either have been in there with him (probably left beside one of the sink's faucets while the man tended his business), or it would be lying on the small cement stoop at the foot of the door. This latter was usually the case, Brad later told Ennis Rafferty; he and Hugh were always putting that cardboard wedge back

45

in its place after the customers left. They had to flush the toilet as well, more often than not. People were careless about that when they were away from home. People were as a rule downright *nasty* when they were away from home.

Right now, that cardboard wedge was poking out of the crack between the door and the jamb, just above the latch, exactly where it worked the best. All the same, Brad opened the door to check, catching the little cardboard wedge neatly as it fell — as neatly as he would learn to open a bottle of beer on the driver's-side handle of his own Buick in later years. The little cubicle was empty, just as he'd known in his heart it would be. No sign that the toilet had been used, and there had been no sound of a flush as Brad sat in the office reading his paper. No beads of water on the rust-stained sides of the basin, either.

It occurred to Brad then that the guy hadn't come around the side of the station to use the can but to take a look at Redfern Stream, which was pretty enough to warrant a peek (or even a snap of the old Kodak) from a passerby, running as it did with the Statler Bluffs on its north side and all those willows up on top, spreading out green like a mermaid's hair (there was a poet in the boy, all right, a regular Dylan McYeats). But around back there was no sign of the Buick's driver, either, only discarded auto parts and a couple of ancient tractor-axles lying in the weeds like rusty bones.

The stream was babbling at the top of its lungs, running broad and foamy. Its swelling would be a temporary condition, of course — floods in western PA are spring events, as a rule — but that day the normally sleepy Redfern was quite the torrent.

Seeing how high the water was gave rise to a horrifying possibility in Bradley Roach's mind. He measured the steep slope down to the water. The grass was still wet with rain and probably goddanged slippery, especially if an unsuspecting SKA came thee-ing and thou-ing along in shoes with slippery leather soles. As he considered this, the possibility hardened to a near certainty in his mind. Nothing else explained the unused shithouse and the car still waiting at the hi-test pump, all loaded and ready to go, key still in the ignition. Old Mr Buick Roadmaster had gone around back for a peek at the Redfern, had foolishly dared the embankment slope to get an even better look . . . and then whoops, there goes your ballgame.

Bradley worked his own way down to the water's edge, slipping a couple of times in spite of his Georgia Giants but not falling, always keeping near some hunk of junk he could grab if he did lose his footing. There was no sign of the man at the water's edge, but when Brad looked downstream, he saw something caught in the lee of a fallen birch about two hundred yards from where he stood. Bobbing up and down. Black. It could have been Mr Buick Roadmaster's coat.

'Aw, shit,' he said, and hurried back to the office to call Troop D, which was at least two miles closer to his location than the local cop-shop. And that was how

NOW:

Sandy

'we got into it,' I said. 'Shirley's predecessor was a guy named Matt Babicki. He gave the call to Ennis Rafferty — '

'Why Ennis, Ned?' Shirley asked. 'Quick as you can.'

'CAU,' he said at once. 'Closest available unit.' But his mind wasn't on that, and he never looked at her. His eyes were fixed on me.

'Ennis was fifty-five and looking forward to a retirement he never got to enjoy,' I said.

'And my father was with him, wasn't he? They were partners.'

'Yes,' I said.

There was plenty more to tell, but first he needed to get past this first part. I was quiet, letting him get used to the idea that his father and Roach, the man who had killed him, had once stood face to face and coversed like normal human beings. There Curtis had been, listening to Bradley Roach talk, flipping open his notebook, starting to jot down a time-sequence. By then Ned knew the drill, how we work fresh cases.

I had an idea this was what would stick with the kid no matter what else I had to tell him, no matter how wild and woolly the narrative might get. The image of the manslaughterer and his

48

victim standing together not four minutes' brisk walk from where their lives would again collide, this time with a mortal thud, twenty-two years later.

'How old was he?' Ned almost whispered. 'My Dad, how old was he on the day you're telling me about?'

He could have figured it out for himself, I suppose, but he was just too stunned. 'Twenty-four,' I said. It was easy. Short lives make for simple mathematics. 'He'd been in the Troop about a year. Same deal then as now, two Troopers per cruiser only on the eleven-to-seven, rookies the single exception to the rule. And your Dad was still a rookie. So he was paired with Ennis on days.'

'Ned, are you all right?' Shirley asked. It was a fair question. All of the color had gradually drained out of the kid's face.

'Yes, ma'am,' he said. He looked at her, then at Arky, then at Phil Candleton. The same look directed to all three, half-bewildered and half-accusing. 'How much of this did you know?'

'All of it,' Arky said. He had a little Nordic lilt in his voice that always made me think of Lawrence Welk going ah-one and ah-two, now here's da lovely Lennon Sisters, don't dey look swede. 'It was no secret. Your Dad and Bradley Roach got on all right back den. Even later. Curtis arrested him tree-four times in the eighties — '

'Hell, five or six,' Phil rumbled. 'That was almost always his beat, you know. Five or six at least. One time he drove that dimwit direct to an

49

AA meeting and made him stay, but it didn't do any good.'

'Your dad's job was bein a Statie,' Arky said, 'and by d'middle of d'eighties, Brad's job — his full-time job — was drinkin. Usually while he drove around d'back roads. He loved doin dat. So many of em do.' Arky sighed. 'Anyway, given dem two jobs, boy, dey was almos certain to bump heads from time to time.'

'From time to time,' Ned repeated, fascinated. It was as if the concept of time had gained a new dimension for him.

'But all dat was stric'ly business. Cep maybe for dat Buick. Dey had dat between em all d'years after.' He nodded in the direction of Shed B. 'Dat Buick hung between em like warsh on a close'line. No one's ever kep d'Buick a secret, eider — not edzactly, not on purpose — but I spec it's kinda one, anyway.'

Shirley was nodding. She reached over and took Ned's hand, and he let it be taken.

'People ignore it, mostly,' she said, 'the way they always ignore things they don't understand . . . as long as they can, anyway.'

'Sometimes we can't afford to ignore it,' Phil said. 'We knew that as soon as . . . well, let Sandy tell it.' He looked back at me. They all did. Ned's gaze was the brightest.

I lit a cigarette and started talking again.

THEN

Ennis Rafferty found his binoculars in his tackle box, which went with him from car to car during fishing season. Once he had them, he and Curt Wilcox went down to Redfern Stream for the same reason the bear went over the mountain: to see what they could see.

'Whaddya want *me* to do?' Brad asked as they walked away from him.

'Guard the car and think about your story,' Ennis said.

'*Story?* Why would I need a *story?*' Sounding a little nervous about it. Neither Ennis nor Curt answered.

Easing down the weedy slope, each of them ready to grab the other if he slipped, Ennis said: 'That car isn't right. Even Bradley Roach knows that, and he's pretty short in the IQ department.'

Curt was nodding even before the older man had finished. 'It's like a picture in this activity book I had when I was a kid. FIND TEN THINGS WRONG WITH THIS PICTURE.'

'By God, it is!' Ennis was struck by this idea. He liked the young man he was partnered with, and thought he was going to make a good Trooper once he got a little salt on his skin.

They had reached the edge of the stream by then. Ennis went for his binocs, which he had hung over his neck by the strap. 'No inspection sticker. No damn *license plates*. And the wheel!

51

Curtis, did you see how big that thing is?'

Curt nodded.

'No antenna for the radio,' Ennis continued, 'and no mud on the body. How'd it get up Route 32 without getting some mud on it? We were splashing up puddles everywhere. There's even crud on the windshield.'

'I don't know. Did you see the portholes?'

'Huh? Sure, but all old Buicks have portholes.'

'Yeah, but these are wrong. There's four on the passenger side and only three on the driver's side. Do you think Buick ever rolled a model off the line with a different number of portholes on the sides? Cause I don't.'

Ennis gave his partner a nonplussed look, then raised his binoculars and looked downstream. He quickly found and focused on the black bobbing thing that had sent Brad hurrying to the telephone.

'What is it? Is it a coat?' Curt was shading his eyes, which were considerably better than Bradley Roach's. 'It's not, is it?'

'Nope,' Ennis said, still peering. 'It looks like . . . a garbage can. One of those black plastic garbage cans like they sell down at the Tru-Value in town. Or maybe I'm full of shit. Here. You take a look.'

He handed the binoculars over, and no, he wasn't full of shit. What Curtis saw was indeed a black plastic garbage can, probably washed down from the trailer park on the Bluffs at the height of the previous night's cloudburst. It wasn't a black coat and no black coat was ever found, nor the black hat, nor the man with the white face

52

and the curl of lank black hair beside one strangely made ear. The Troopers might have doubted that there ever *was* such a man — Ennis Rafferty had not failed to notice the copy of *Inside View* on the desk when he took Mr Roach into the office to question him further — but there *was* the Buick. That odd Buick was irrefutable. It was part of the goddam scenery, sitting right there at the pumps. Except by the time the county tow showed up to haul it away, neither Ennis Rafferty nor Curtis Wilcox believed it was a Buick at all.

By then, they didn't know *what* it was.

★ ★ ★

Older cops are entitled to their hunches, and Ennis had one as he and his young partner walked back to Brad Roach. Brad was standing beside the Roadmaster with the three nicely chromed portholes on one side and the four on the other. Ennis's hunch was that the oddities they had so far noticed were only the whipped cream on the sundae. If so, the less Mr Roach saw now, the less he could talk about later. Which was why, although Ennis was extremely curious about the abandoned car and longed for a big dose of satisfaction, he turned it over to Curt while he himself escorted Bradley into the office. Once they were there, Ennis called for a wrecker to haul the Buick up to Troop D, where they could put it in the parking lot out back, at least for the time being. He also wanted to question Bradley while his recollections were relatively fresh. Ennis expected to get his own chance to look over their odd catch, and at his leisure, later on.

'Someone modified it a little, I expect that's all' was what he said to Curt before taking Bradley into the office. Curt looked skeptical. Modifying was one thing, but this was just nuts. Removing one of the portholes, then refinishing the surface so expertly that the scar didn't even show? Replacing the usual Buick steering wheel with something that looked like it belonged in a cabin cruiser? Those were modifications?

'Aw, just look it over while I do some business,' Ennis said.

'Can I check the mill?'

'Be my guest. Only keep your mitts off the steering wheel, so we can get some prints if we need them. And use good sense. Try not to leave your own dabs anywhere.'

They had reached the pumps again. Brad Roach looked eagerly at the two cops, the one he would kill in the twenty-first century and the one who would be gone without a trace that very evening.

'What do you think?' Brad asked. 'Is he dead down there in the stream? Drownded? He is, isn't he?'

'Not unless he crawled into the garbage can floating around in the crotch of that fallen tree and drowned there,' Ennis said.

Brad's face fell. 'Aw, shit. Is that all it is?'

''Fraid so. And it would be a tight fit for a grown man. Trooper Wilcox? Any questions for this young man?'

Because he was still learning and Ennis was still teaching, Curtis did ask a few, mostly to make sure Bradley wasn't drunk and that he was in his right mind. Then he nodded to Ennis, who clapped Bradley on the shoulder as if they were old buddies.

'Step inside with me, what do you say?' Ennis suggested. 'Pour me a slug of mud and we'll see if we can figure this thing out.' And he led Brad away. The friendly arm slung around Bradley Roach's shoulder was very strong, and it just kept hustling Brad along toward the office, Trooper Rafferty talking a mile a minute the whole time.

★   ★   ★

As for Trooper Wilcox, he got about three-quarters of an hour with that Buick before the county tow showed up with its orange light flashing. Forty-five minutes isn't much time, but it was enough to turn Curtis into a lifetime Roadmaster Scholar. True love always happens in a flash, they say.

Ennis drove as they headed back to Troop D behind the tow-truck and the Buick, which rode on the clamp with its nose up and its rear bumper almost dragging on the road. Curt rode shotgun, in his excitement squirming like a little kid who needs to make water. Between them, the Motorola police radio, scuffed and beat-up, the victim of God knew how many coffee- and cola-dousings but still as tough as nails, blatted away on channel 23, Matt Babicki and the

Troopers in the field going through the call-and-response that was the constant background soundtrack of their working lives. It was there, but neither Ennis nor Curt heard it anymore unless their own number came up.

'The first thing's the engine,' Curt said. 'No, I suppose the first thing's the hood-latch. It's way over on the driver's side, and you push it in rather than pulling it out — '

'Never heard of that before,' Ennis grunted.

'You wait, you wait,' his young partner said. 'I found it, anyway, and lifted the hood. The engine . . . man, that *engine* . . . '

Ennis glanced at him with the expression of a man who's just had an idea that's too horribly plausible to deny. The orange glow from the revolving light on the tow-truck's cab pulsed on his face like jaundice. 'Don't you dare tell me it doesn't have one,' he said. 'Don't dare tell me it doesn't have anything but a radioactive crystal or some damn thing like in Dumbwit's flying saucers.'

Curtis laughed. The sound was both cheerful and wild. 'No, no, there's an engine, but it's all wrong. It says BUICK 8 on both sides of the engine block in big chrome letters, as if whoever made it was afraid of forgetting what the damn thing was. There are eight plugs, four on each side, and *that's* right — eight cylinders, eight sparkplugs — but there's no distributor cap and no distributor, not that I can see. No generator or alternator, either.'

'Get out!'

'Ennis, if I'm lyin I'm dyin.'

56

'Where do the sparkplug wires go?'

'Each one makes a big loop and goes right back into the engine block, so far as I can tell.'

'That's nuts!'

'Yes! But listen, Ennis, just listen!' Stop interrupting and let me talk, in other words. Curtis Wilcox squirming in his seat but never taking his eyes off the Buick being towed along in front of him.

'All right, Curt. I'm listening.'

'It's got a radiator, but so far as I can tell, there's nothing inside it. No water and no antifreeze. There's no fanbelt, which sort of makes sense, because there's no fan.'

'Oil?'

'There's a crankcase and a dipstick, but there's no markings on the stick. There's a battery, a Delco, but Ennis, dig this, *it's not hooked up to anything*. There are no battery cables.'

'You're describing a car that couldn't possibly run,' Ennis said flatly.

'Tell me about it. I took the key out of the ignition. It's on an ordinary chain, but the chain's all there is. No fob with initials or anything.'

'Other keys?'

'No. And the ignition key's not really a key. It's just a slot of metal, about so long.' Curt held his thumb and forefinger a key's length apart.

'A blank, is that what you're talking about? Like a keymaker's blank?'

'No. It's nothing like a key at all. It's just a little steel stick.'

'Did you try it?'

Curt, who had been talking almost compulsively, didn't answer that at once.

'Go on,' Ennis said. 'I'm your partner, for Christ's sake. I'm not going to bite you.'

'All right, yeah, I tried it. I wanted to see if that crazy engine worked.'

'Of course it works. Someone drove it in, right?'

'Roach says so, but when I got a good look under that hood, I had to wonder if he was lying or maybe hypnotized. Anyway, it's still an open question. The key-thing won't turn. It's like the ignition's locked.'

'Where's the key now?'

'I put it back in the ignition.'

Ennis nodded. 'Good. When you opened the door, did the dome light come on? Or isn't there one?'

Curtis paused, thinking back. 'Yeah. There was a dome light, and it came on. I should have noticed that. How could it come on, though? How could it, when the battery's not hooked up?'

'There could be a couple of C-cells powering the dome light, for all we know.' But his lack of belief was clear in his voice. 'What else?'

'I saved the best for last,' Curtis told him. 'I had to do some touching inside, but I used a hanky, and I know where I touched, so don't bust my balls.'

Ennis said nothing out loud, but gave the kid a look that said he'd bust Curt's balls if they needed busting.

'The dashboard controls are all fake, just stuck

on there for show. The radio knobs don't turn and neither does the heater control knob. The lever you slide to switch on the defroster doesn't move. Feels like a post set in concrete.'

Ennis followed the tow-truck into the driveway that ran around to the back of Troop D. 'What else? Anything?'

'More like *everything*. It's fucked to the sky.' This impressed Ennis, because Curtis wasn't ordinarily a profane man. 'You know that great big steering wheel? I think that's probably fake, too. I shimmied it — just with the sides of my hands, don't have a hemorrhage — and it turns a little bit, left and right, but only a little bit. Maybe it's just locked, like the ignition, but . . . '

'But you don't think so.'

'No. I don't.'

The tow-truck parked in front of Shed B. There was a hydraulic whine and the Buick came out of its snout-up, tail-down posture, settling back on its whitewalls. The tow driver, old Johnny Parker, came around to unhook it, wheezing around the Pall Mall stuck in his gob. Ennis and Curt sat in Cruiser D-19 meanwhile, looking at each other.

'What the hell we got here?' Ennis asked finally. 'A car that can't drive and can't steer cruises into the Jenny station out on Route 32 and right up to the hi-test pump. No tags. No sticker . . . ' An idea struck him. 'Registration? You check for that?'

'Not on the steering post,' Curt said, opening his door, impatient to get out. The young are always impatient. 'Not in the glove compartment, either, because there *is* no glove compartment. There's a handle for one, and there's a latch-button, but the button doesn't push, the handle doesn't pull, and the little door doesn't open. It's just stage-dressing, like everything else on the dashboard. The dashboard itself is bullshit. Cars didn't come with wooden dashboards in the fifties. Not American ones, at least.'

They got out and stood looking at the orphan Buick's back deck. 'Trunk?' Ennis asked. 'Does *that* open?'

'Yeah. It's not locked. Push the button and it pops open like the trunk of any other car. But it smells lousy.'

'Lousy how?'

'Swampy.'

'Any dead bodies in there?'

'No bodies, no nothing.'

'No spare tire? Not even a jack?'

Curtis shook his head. Johnny Parker came over, pulling off his work gloves. 'Be anything else, men?'

Ennis and Curt shook their heads.

Johnny started away, then stopped. 'What the hell is that, anyway? Someone's idea of a joke?'

'We don't know yet,' Ennis told him.

Johnny nodded. 'Well, if you find out, let me know. Curiosity killed the cat, satisfaction brought him back. You know?'

'Whole lot of satisfaction,' Curt said automatically. The business about curiosity and the cat

60

was a part of Troop D life, not quite an in-joke, just something that had crept into the day-to-day diction of the job.

Ennis and Curt watched the old man go. 'Anything else you want to pass on before we talk to Sergeant Schoondist?' Ennis asked.

'Yeah,' Curtis said. 'It's earthquake country in there.'

'Earthquake country? Just what in the hell does *that* mean?'

So Curtis told Ennis about a show he'd seen on the PBS station out of Pittsburgh just the week before. By then a number of people had drifted over. Among them were Phil Candleton, Arky Arkanian, Sandy Dearborn, and Sergeant Schoondist himself.

The program had been about predicting earthquakes. Scientists were a long way from developing a sure-fire way of doing that, Curtis said, but most of them believed it *could* be done, in time. Because there were forewarnings. Precursors. Animals felt them, and quite often people did, too. Dogs got restless and barked to be let outside. Cattle ran around in their stalls or knocked down the fences of their pastures. Caged chickens sometimes flapped so frantically they broke their wings. Some people claimed to hear a high humming sound from the earth fifteen or twenty minutes before a big temblor (and if some *people* could hear that sound, it stood to reason that most animals would hear it even more clearly). Also, it got cold. Not everyone felt these odd pre-earthquake cold pockets, but a great many people did. There was even some meteorological data to support the subjective reports.

'Are you shitting me?' Tony Schoondist asked.

No indeed, Curt replied. Two hours before the big quake of 1906, temperatures in San Francisco had dropped a full seven degrees; that was a recorded fact. This although all other weather conditions had remained constant.

'Fascinating,' Ennis said, 'but what's it got to do with the Buick?'

By then there were enough Troopers present to form a little circle of listeners. Curtis looked around at them, knowing he might spend the next six months or so tagged the Earthquake Kid on radio calls, but too jazzed to care. He said that while Ennis was in the gas station office questioning Bradley Roach, he himself had been sitting behind that strange oversized steering wheel, still being careful not to touch anything except with the sides of his hands. And as he sat there, he started to hear a humming sound, very high. He told them he had *felt* it, as well.

'It came out of nowhere, this high, steady hum. I could feel it buzzing in my fillings. I think if it had been much stronger, it would've actually jingled the change in my pocket. There's a word for that, we learned it in physics, I think, but I can't for the life of me remember what it is.'

'A harmonic,' Tony said. 'That's when two things start to vibrate together, like tuning forks or wine-glasses.'

Curtis was nodding. 'Yeah, that's it. I don't know what could be causing it, but it's very powerful. It seemed to settle right in the middle of my head, the way the sound of the powerlines up on the Bluff does when you're standing right underneath them. This is going to sound crazy, but after a minute or so, that hum almost sounded like *talking*.'

'I laid a girl up dere on d'Bluffs once,' Arky said sentimentally, sounding more like Lawrence Welk than ever. 'And it was pretty harmonic, all right. Buzz, buzz, buzz.'

'Save it for your memoirs, bub,' Tony said. 'Go on, Curtis.'

'I thought at first it was the radio,' Curt said, 'because it sounded a little bit like that, too: an old vacuum-tube radio that's on and tuned to music coming from a long way off. So I took my hanky and reached over to kill the power. That's when I found out the knobs don't move, either of them. It's no more a real radio than . . . well, than Phil Candleton's a real State Trooper.'

'That's funny, kid,' Phil said. 'At least as funny as a rubber chicken, I guess, or — '

'Shut up, I want to hear this,' Tony said. 'Go on, Curtis. And leave out the comedy.'

'Yes, sir. By the time I tried the radio knobs, I realized it was cold in there. It's a warm day and the car was sitting in the sun, but it was cold inside. Sort of clammy, too. That's when I thought of the show about earthquakes.' Curt shook his head slowly back and forth. 'I got a feeling that I should get out of that car, and fast. By then the hum was quieting down, but it was colder than ever. Like an icebox.'

Tony Schoondist, then Troop D's Sergeant Commanding, walked over to the Buick. He didn't touch it, just leaned in the window. He stayed like that for the best part of a minute, leaning into the dark blue car, back inclined but perfectly straight, hands clasped behind his back. Ennis stood behind him. The rest of the Troopers clustered around Curtis, waiting for Tony to finish with whatever it was he was doing. For most of them, Tony Schoondist was the best SC they'd ever have while wearing the Pennsylvania gray. He was tough; brave; fairminded; crafty when he had to be. By the time a Trooper reached the rank of Sergeant Commanding, the politics kicked in. The monthly meetings. The calls from Scranton. Sergeant Commanding was a long way from the top of the ladder, but it was high enough for the bureaucratic bullshit to hit high gear. Schoondist played the game well enough to keep his seat, but he knew and his men knew he'd never rise higher. Or want to. Because with Tony, his men always came first . . . and when Shirley replaced Matt Babicki, it was his men and his woman. His Troop, in other words. Troop D. They knew this not because he said anything, but because he walked the walk.

At last he came back to where his men were standing. He took off his hat, ran his hand through the bristles of his crewcut, then put the hat back on. Strap in the back, as per summer regulations. In winter, the strap went under the point of the chin. That was the tradition, and as in any organization that's been around for a long time, there was a lot of tradition in the PSP. Until 1962, for instance, Troopers needed permission from the Sergeant Commanding to get married (and the SCs used that power to weed out any number of rookies and young Troopers they felt were unqualified for the job).

'No hum,' Tony said. 'Also, I'd say the temperature inside is about what it should be. Maybe a little cooler than the outside air, but . . . ' He shrugged.

Curtis flushed a deep pink. 'Sarge, I swear — '

'I'm not doubting you,' Tony said. 'If you say the thing was humming like a tuning fork, I believe you. Where would you say this humming sound was coming from? The engine?'

Curtis shook his head.

'The trunk area?'

Another shake.

'Underneath?'

A third shake of the head, and now instead of pink, Curt's cheeks, neck, and forehead were bright red.

'Where, then?'

'Out of the air,' Curt said reluctantly. 'I know it sounds crazy, but . . . yeah. Right out of the air.' He looked around, as if expecting the others to laugh. None of them did.

Just about then Orville Garrett joined the group. He'd been over by the county line, at a building site where several pieces of heavy equipment had been vandalized the night before. Ambling along behind him came Mister Dillon, the Troop D mascot. He was a German Shepherd with maybe a little taste of Collie thrown in. Orville and Huddie Royer had found him as a pup, paddling around in the shallow well of an abandoned farm out on Sawmill Road. The dog might have fallen in by accident, but probably not.

Mister D was no K-9 specialty dog, but only because no one had trained him that way. He was plenty smart, and protective, as well. If a bad boy raised his voice and started shaking his finger at a Troop D guy while Mister Dillon was around, that fellow ran the risk of picking his nose with the tip of a pencil for the rest of his life.

'What's doin, boys?' Orville asked, but before anyone could answer him, Mister Dillon began to howl. Sandy Dearborn, who happened to be standing right beside the dog, had never heard anything quite like that howl in his entire life. Mister D backed up a pace and then hunkered, facing the Buick. His head was up and his hindquarters were down. He looked like a dog does when he's taking a crap, except for his fur. It was bushed out all over his body, every hair standing on end. Sandy's skin went cold.

'Holy God, what's wrong with him?' Phil asked in a low, awed voice, and then Mister D let loose with another long, wavering howl. He took three or four stalk-steps toward the Buick, never coming out of that hunched-over, cramped-up, taking-a-crap stoop, all the time with his muzzle pointing at the sky. It was awful to watch. He made two or three more of those awkward movements, then dropped flat on the macadam, panting and whining.

'What the *hell*?' Orv said.

'Put a leash on him,' Tony said. 'Get him inside.'

Orv did as Tony said, actually running to get Mister Dillon's leash. Phil Candleton, who had always been especially partial to the dog, went with Orv once the leash was on him, walking next to Mister D, occasionally bending down to give him a comforting stroke and a soothing word. Later, he told the others that the dog had been shivering all over.

Nobody said anything. Nobody had to. They were all thinking the same thing, that Mister Dillon had pretty well proved Curt's point. The ground wasn't shaking and Tony hadn't heard anything when he stuck his head in through the Buick's window, but something was wrong with it, all right. A lot more wrong than the size of its steering wheel or its strange notchless ignition key. Something worse.

★ ★ ★

In the seventies and eighties, Pennsylvania State Police forensics investigators were rolling stones, travelling around to the various Troops in a given area from District HQ. In the case of Troop D, HQ was Butler. There were no forensics vans; such big-city luxuries were dreamed of, but wouldn't actually arrive in rural Pennsylvania until almost the end of the century. The forensics guys rode in unmarked police cars, carrying their equipment in trunks and back seats, toting it to various crime scenes in big canvas shoulder-bags with the PSP keystone logo on the sides. There were three guys in most forensics crews: the chief and two technicians. Sometimes there was also a trainee. Most of these looked too young to buy a legal drink.

One such team appeared at Troop D that afternoon. They had ridden over from Shippenville, at Tony Schoondist's personal request. It was a funny informal visit, a vehicle exam not quite in the line of duty. The crew chief was Bibi Roth, one of the oldtimers (men joked that Bibi had learned his trade at the knee of Sherlock Holmes and Dr Watson). He and Tony Schoondist got along well, and Bibi didn't mind doing a solid for the Troop D SC. Not as long as it stayed quiet, that was.

NOW:

Sandy

Ned stopped me at this point to ask why the forensic examination of the Buick was conducted in such an odd (to him, at least) off-the-cuff manner.

'Because,' I told him, 'the only criminal complaint in the matter that any of us could think of was theft of services — seven dollars' worth of hi-test gasoline. That's a misdemeanor, not worth a forensic crew's time.'

'Dey woulda burned almost dat much gas gettin over here from Shippenville,' Arky pointed out.

'Not to mention the man-hours,' Phil added.

I said, 'Tony didn't want to start a paper trail. Remember that there wasn't one at that point. All he had was a car. A very weird car, granted, one with no license plates, no registration, and — Bibi Roth confirmed this — no VIN number, either.'

'But Roach had reason to believe the owner drowned in the stream behind the gas station!'

'Pooh,' Shirley said. 'The driver's overcoat turned out to be a plastic garbage can. So much for Bradley Roach's ideas.'

'Plus,' Phil put in, 'Ennis and your dad observed no tracks going down the slope behind the station, and the grass was still wet. If the guy

69

had gone down there, he would have left a sign.'

'Mostly, Tony wanted to keep it in-house,' Shirley said. 'Would you say that's a fair way to put it, Sandy?'

'Yes. The Buick itself was strange, but our way of dealing with it wasn't much different from the way we'd deal with anything out of the ordinary: a Trooper down — like your father, last year — or one who's used his weapon, or an accident, like when George Morgan was in hot pursuit of that crazy asshole who snatched his kids.'

We were all silent for a moment. Cops have nightmares, any Trooper's wife will tell you that, and in the bad-dream department, George Morgan was one of the worst. He'd been doing ninety, closing in on the crazy asshole, who had a habit of beating the kids he had snatched and claimed to love, when it happened.

George is almost on top of him and all at once here's this senior citizen crossing the road, seventy years old, slower than creeping bullfrog Jesus, and legally blind. The asshole would have been the one to hit her if she'd started across three seconds earlier, but she didn't. No, the asshole blew right by her, the rearview mirror on the passenger side of his vehicle so close it almost took off her nose. Next comes George, and kapow. He had twelve blameless years on the State Police, two citations for bravery, community service awards without number. He was a good father to his own children, a good husband to his wife, and all of that ended when a woman from Lassburg Cut tried to cross the street at the wrong moment and he killed her with PSP

70

cruiser D-27. George was exonerated by the State Board of Review and came back to a desk job on the Troop, rated PLD — permanent light duty — at his own request. He could have gone back full-time as far as the brass was concerned, but there was a problem: George Morgan could no longer drive. Not even the family car to the market. He got the shakes every time he slid behind the wheel. His eyes teared up until he was suffering from a kind of hysterical blindness. That summer he worked nights, on dispatch. In the afternoons he coached the Troop D-sponsored Little League team all the way to the state tournament. When that was over, he gave the kids their trophy and their pins, told them how proud of them he was, then went home (a player's mother drove him), drank two beers, and blew his brains out in the garage. He didn't leave a note; cops rarely do. I wrote a press release in the wake of that. Reading it, you never would have guessed it was written with tears on my face. And it suddenly seemed very important that I communicate some of the reason why to Curtis Wilcox's son.

'We're a family,' I said. 'I know that sounds corny, but it's true. Even Mister Dillon knew that much, and you do, too. Don't you?'

The kid nodded his head. Of course he did. In the year after his father died, we were the family that mattered to him most, the one he sought out and the one that gave him what he needed to get on with his life. His mother and sisters loved him, and he loved them, but they were going on with their lives in a way that Ned could not

71

. . . at least not yet. Some of it was being male instead of female. Some of it was being eighteen. Some of it was all those questions of *why* that wouldn't go away.

I said, 'What families say and how families act when they're in their houses with the doors shut and how they talk and behave when they're out on their lawns and the doors are open . . . those can be very different things. Ennis knew the Buick was wrong, your Dad did, Tony did, I did. Mister D most certainly did. The way that dog howled . . . '

I fell silent for a moment. I've heard that howl in my dreams. Then I pushed on.

'But legally, it was just an object — a *res*, as the lawyers say — with no blame held against it. We couldn't very well hold the *Buick* for theft of services, could we? And the man who ordered the gas that went into its tank was long gone and hard to find. The best we could do was to think of it as an impoundment.'

Ned wore the frown of someone who doesn't understand what he's hearing. I could understand that. I hadn't been as clear as I wanted to be. Or maybe I was just playing that famous old game, the one called It Wasn't Our Fault.

'Listen,' Shirley said. 'Suppose a woman stopped to use the restroom at that station and left her diamond engagement ring on the washstand and Bradley Roach found it there. Okay?'

'Okay . . . ' Ned said. Still frowning.

'And let's say Roach brought it to us instead of just putting it in his pocket and then taking it to a pawnshop in Butler. We'd make a report, maybe put out the make and model of the woman's car to the Troopers in the field, if Roach could give them to us . . . but we wouldn't take the ring. Would we, Sandy?'

'No,' I said. 'We'd advise Roach to put an ad in the paper — *Found, a woman's ring, if you think it may be yours, call this number and describe*. At which point Roach would get pissing and moaning about the cost of putting an ad in the paper — a whole three bucks.'

'And then *we'd* remind him that folks who find valuable property often get rewards,' Phil said, 'and he'd decide maybe he could find three bucks, after all.'

'But if the woman never called or came back,' I said, 'that ring would become Roach's property. It's the oldest law in history: finders-keepers.'

'So Ennis and my dad took the Buick.'

'No,' I said. 'The *Troop* took it.'

'What about theft of services? Did that ever get filed?'

'Oh, well,' I said with an uncomfortable little grin. 'Seven bucks was hardly worth the paperwork. Was it, Phil?'

'Nah,' Phil said. 'But we squared it up with Hugh Bossey.'

A light was dawning on Ned's face. 'You paid for the gas out of petty cash.'

Phil looked both shocked and amused. 'Never in your life, boy! Petty cash is the taxpayers' money, too.'

'We passed the hat,' I said. 'Everybody that

73

was there gave a little. It was easy.'

'If Roach found a ring and nobody claimed it, it would be his,' Ned said. 'So wouldn't the Buick be his?'

'Maybe if he'd kept it,' I said. 'But he turned it over to us, didn't he? And as far as he was concerned, that was the end of it.'

Arky tapped his forehead and gave Ned a wise look. 'Nuttin upstairs, dat one,' he said.

For a moment I thought Ned would turn to brooding on the young man who had grown up to kill his father, but he shook that off. I could almost see him do it.

'Go on,' he said to me. 'What happened next?'

Oh boy. Who can resist that?

THEN

It took Bibi Roth and his children (that's what he called them) only forty-five minutes to go over the Buick from stem to stern, the young people dusting and brushing and snapping pictures, Bibi with a clipboard, walking around and sometimes pointing wordlessly at something with his ballpoint pen.

About twenty minutes into it, Orv Garrett came out with Mister Dillon. The dog was on his leash, which was a rarity around the barracks. Sandy walked over to them. The dog wasn't howling, had quit trembling, and was sitting with his brush of tail curled neatly over his paws, but his dark brown eyes were fixed on the Buick and never moved. From deep in his chest, almost too low to hear, came a steady growl like the rumble of a powerful motor.

'For Chrissake, Orvie, take him back inside,' Sandy Dearborn said.

'Okay. I just thought he might be over it by now.' He paused, then said: 'I've heard bloodhounds act that way sometimes, when they've found a body. I know there's no body, but do you think someone might have died in there?'

'Not that we know of.' Sandy was watching Tony Schoondist come out of the barracks' side door and amble over to Bibi Roth. Ennis was with him. Curt Wilcox was out on patrol again, much against his wishes. Sandy doubted that even pretty girls would be able to talk him into giving them warnings instead of tickets that afternoon. Curt wanted to be at the barracks, watching Bibi and his crew at work, not out on the road; if he couldn't be, lawbreakers in western Pennsylvania would pay.

Mister Dillon opened his mouth and let loose a long, low whine, as if something in him hurt. Sandy supposed something did. Orville took him inside. Five minutes later Sandy himself was rolling again, along with Steve Devoe, to the scene of a two-car collision out on Highway 6.

*   *   *

Bibi Roth made his report to Tony and Ennis as the members of his crew (there were three of them that day) sat at a picnic table in the shade of Shed B, eating sandwiches and drinking the iced tea Matt Babicki had run out to them.

'I appreciate you taking the time to do this,' Tony said.

'Your appreciation is appreciated,' Bibi said, 'and I hope it ends there. I don't want to submit any paperwork on this one, Tony. No one would ever trust me again.' He looked at his crew and clapped his hands like Miss Frances on *Ding-Dong School.* 'Do we want paperwork on this job, children?' One of the children who helped that day was appointed Pennsylvania's Chief Medical Examiner in 1993.

They looked at him, two young men and a young woman of extraordinary beauty. Their

76

sandwiches were raised, their brows creased. None of them was sure what response was required.

'No, Bibi!' he prompted them.

'No, Bibi,' they chorused dutifully.

'No what?' Bibi asked.

'No paperwork,' said young man number one.

'No file copies,' said young man number two.

'No duplicate or triplicate,' said the young woman of extraordinary beauty. 'Not even any singlicate.'

'Good!' he said. 'And with whom are we going to discuss this, *Kinder?*'

This time they needed no prompting. 'No one, Bibi!'

'Exactly,' Bibi agreed. 'I'm proud of you.'

'Got to be a joke, anyway,' said one of the young men. 'Someone's trickin on you, Sarge.'

'I'm keeping that possibility in mind,' Tony said, wondering what any of them would have thought if they had seen Mister Dillon howling and hunching forward like a crippled thing. Mister D hadn't been trickin on nobody.

The children went back to munching and slurping and talking among themselves. Bibi, meanwhile, was looking at Tony and Ennis Rafferty with a slanted little smile.

'They see what they look at with youth's wonderful twenty-twenty vision and don't see it at the same time,' he said. 'Young people are such wonderful idiots. What *is* that thing, Tony? Do you have any idea? From witnesses, perhaps?'

'No.'

Bibi turned his attention to Ennis, who

perhaps thought briefly about telling the man what he knew of the Buick's story and then decided not to. Bibi was a good man . . . but he didn't wear the gray.

'It's not an automobile, that's for sure,' Bibi said. 'But a joke? No, I don't think it's that, either.'

'Is there blood?' Tony asked, not knowing if he wanted there to be or not.

'Only more microscopic examination of the samples we took can determine that for sure, but I think not. Certainly no more than trace amounts, if there is.'

'What did you see?'

'In a word, nothing. We took no samples from the tire treads because there's no dirt or mud or pebbles or glass or grass or anything else in them. I would have said that was impossible. Henry there' — he pointed to young man number one — 'kept trying to wedge a pebble between two of them and it kept falling out. Now what is that? *Why* is that? And could you patent such a thing? If you could, Tony, you could take early retirement.'

Tony was rubbing his cheek with the tips of his fingers, the gesture of a perplexed man.

'Listen to this,' Bibi said. 'We're talking floormats here. Great little dirtcatchers, as a rule. Every one a geological survey. Usually. Not here, though. A few smudges of dirt, a dandelion stalk. That's all.' He looked at Ennis. 'From your partner's shoes, I expect. You say he got behind the wheel?'

'Yes.'

'Driver's-side footwell. And that's where these few artifacts were found.' Bibi patted his palms together, as if to say QED.

'Are there prints?' Tony asked.

'Three sets. I'll want comparison prints from your two officers and the pump-jockey. The prints we lifted from the gas-hatch will almost certainly belong to the pump-jockey. You agree?'

'Most likely,' Tony said. 'You'd run the prints on your own time?'

'Absolutely, my pleasure. The fiber samples, as well. Don't annoy me by asking for anything involving the gas chromatograph in Pittsburgh, there's a good fellow. I will pursue this as far as the equipment in my basement permits. That will be quite far.'

'You're a good guy, Bibi.'

'Yes, and even the best guy will take a free dinner from time to time, if a friend offers.'

'He'll offer. Meantime, is there anything else?'

'The glass is glass. The wood is wood . . . but a wooden dashboard in a car of this vintage — this *purported* vintage — is completely wrong. My older brother had a Buick from the late fifties, a Limited. I learned to drive on it and I remember it well. With fear and affection. The dashboard was padded vinyl. I would say the seatcovers in this one are vinyl, which would be right for this make and model; I will be checking with General Motors to make sure. The odometer . . . very amusing. Did you notice the odometer?'

Ennis shook his head. He looked hypnotized.

'All zeros. Which is fitting, I suppose. That car — that *purported* car — would never drive.' His

79

eyes moved from Ennis to Tony and then back to Ennis again. 'Tell me you haven't seen it drive. That you haven't seen it move a single inch under its own power.'

'Actually, I haven't,' Ennis said. Which was true. There was no need to add that Bradley Roach claimed to have seen it moving under its own power, and that Ennis, a veteran of many interrogations, believed him.

'Good.' Bibi looked relieved. He clapped his hands, once more being Miss Frances. 'Time to go, children! Voice your thanks!'

'Thanks, Sergeant,' they chorused. The young woman of extraordinary beauty finished her iced tea, belched, and followed her white-coated colleagues back to the car in which they had come. Tony was fascinated to note that not one of the three gave the Buick a look. To them it was now a closed case, and new cases lay ahead. To them the Buick was just an old car, getting older by the minute in the summer sun. So what if pebbles fell out when placed between the knuckles of the tread, even when placed so far up along the curve of the tire that gravity should have held them in? So what if there were three portholes on one side instead of four?

They see it and don't see it at the same time, Bibi had said. *Young people are such wonderful idiots.*

Bibi followed his wonderful idiots toward his own car (Bibi liked to ride to crime scenes in solitary splendor, whenever possible), then stopped. 'I said the wood is wood, the vinyl is

80

vinyl, and the glass is glass. You heard me say that?'

Tony and Ennis nodded.

'It appears to me that this purported car's exhaust system is also made of glass. Of course, I was only peering under from one side, but I had a flashlight. Quite a powerful one.' For a few moments he just stood there, staring at the Buick parked in front of Shed B, hands in his pockets, rocking back and forth on the balls of his feet. 'I have never heard of a car with a glass exhaust system,' he said finally, and then walked toward his car. A moment later, he and his children were gone.

★   ★   ★

Tony was uncomfortable with the car out where it was, not just because of possible storms but because anyone who happened to walk out back could see it. Visitors were what he was thinking of, Mr and Mrs John Q. Public. The State Police served John Q and his family as well as they could, in some cases at the cost of their lives. They did not, however, completely trust them. John Q's family was not Troop D's family. The prospect of word getting around — worse, of *rumor* getting around — made Sergeant Schoondist squirm.

He strolled to Johnny Parker's little office (the County Motor Pool was still next door in those days) around quarter to three and sweet-talked Johnny into moving one of the plows out of Shed B and putting the Buick inside. A pint of whiskey sealed the deal, and the Buick was towed into the oil-smelling darkness that became its home. Shed B had garage doors at either end, and Johnny brought the Buick in through the back one. As a result, it faced the Troop D barracks from out there for all the years of its stay. It was something most of the Troopers became aware of as time passed. Not a forebrain thing, nothing like an organized thought, but something that floated at the back of the mind, never quite formed and never quite gone: the pressure of its chrome grin.

★   ★   ★

There were eighteen Troopers assigned to Troop D in 1979, rotating through the usual shifts: seven to three, three to eleven, and the graveyard shift, when they rode two to a cruiser. On Fridays and Saturdays, the eleven-to-seven shift was commonly called Puke Patrol.

By four o'clock on the afternoon the Buick arrived, most of the off-duty Troopers had heard about it and dropped by for a look. Sandy Dearborn, back from the accident on Highway 6 and typing up the paperwork, saw them going out there in murmuring threes and fours, almost like tour groups, Curt Wilcox was off-duty by then and he conducted a good many of the tours himself, pointing out the mismatched portholes and big steering wheel, lifting the hood so they could marvel over the whacked-out mill with BUICK 8 printed on both sides of the engine block.

Orv Garrett conducted other tours, telling the story of Mister D's reaction over and over again. Sergeant Schoondist, already fascinated by the thing (a fascination that would never completely leave him until Alzheimer's erased his mind), came out as often as he could. Sandy remembered him standing just outside the open Shed B door at one point, foot up on the boards behind him, arms crossed. Ennis was beside him, smoking one of those little Tiparillos he liked and talking while Tony nodded. It was after three, and Ennis had changed into jeans and a plain white shirt. After three, and that was the best Sandy could say later on. He wished he could do better, but he couldn't.

The cops came, they looked at the engine (the hood permanently up by that point, gaping like a mouth), they squatted down to look at the exotic glass exhaust system. They looked at everything, they touched nothing. John Q and his family wouldn't have known to keep their mitts off, but these were cops. They understood that while the Buick might not be an evidential *res* as of right then, later on that might change. Especially if the man who had left it at the Jenny station should happen to turn up dead.

'Unless that happens or something else pops, I intend to keep the car here,' Tony told Matt Babicki and Phil Candleton at one point. It was five o'clock or so by then, all three of them had been officially off-duty for a couple of hours, and Tony was finally thinking about going home. Sandy himself had left around four, wanting to mow the grass before sitting down to dinner.

'Why here?' Matt asked. 'What's the big deal, Sarge?'

Tony asked Matt and Phil if they knew about the Cardiff Giant. They said they didn't, and so Tony told them the story. The Giant had been 'discovered' in upstate New York's Onondaga Valley. It was supposed to be the fossilized corpse of a gigantic humanoid, maybe something from another world or the missing link between men and apes. It turned out to be nothing but a hoax perpetrated by a Binghamton cigar-maker named George Hull.

'But before Hull fessed up,' Tony said, 'just about everyone in the whole round world — including P. T. Barnum — dropped by for a look. The crops on the surrounding farms were trampled to mush. Houses were broken into. There was a forest fire started by asshole John Q's camping in the woods. Even after Hull confessed to having the 'petrified man' carved in Chicago and shipped Railway Express to upstate New York, people kept coming. They refused to believe the thing wasn't real. You've heard the saying 'There's a sucker born every minute'? That was coined in 1869, in reference to the Cardiff Giant.'

'What's your point?' Phil asked.

Tony gave him an impatient look. 'The point? The point is that I'm not having any Cardiff fucking Giant on my watch. Not if I can help it. Or the goddam Buick of Turin, for that matter.'

As they moved back toward the barracks, Huddie Royer joined them (with Mister Dillon at his side, now heeling as neatly as a pooch in a dog-show). Huddie caught the Buick of Turin line and snickered. Tony gave him a dour look.

'No Cardiff Giant in western PA; you boys mark what I say and pass the word. Because word of mouth's how it's gonna be done — I'm not tacking any memo up on the bulletin board. I know there'll be some gossip, but it'll die down. I will *not* have a dozen Amish farms overrun by lookie-loos in the middle of the growing season, is that understood?'

It was understood.

By seven o'clock that evening, things had returned to something like normal. Sandy Dearborn knew that for himself, because he'd come back after dinner for his own encore look at the car. He found only three Troopers — two off-duty and one in uniform — strolling around the Buick. Buck Flanders, one of the off-duties, was snapping pictures with his Kodak. That made Sandy a bit uneasy, but what would they show? A Buick, that was all, one not yet old enough to be an official antique.

Sandy got down on his hands and knees and peered under the car, using a flashlight that had been left nearby (and probably for just that purpose). He took a good gander at the exhaust system. To him it looked like Pyrex glass. He leaned in the driver's window for awhile (no hum, no chill), then went back to the barracks to shoot the shit with Brian Cole, who was in the SC chair that shift. The two of them started on the Buick, moved on to their families, and had just gotten to baseball when Orville Garrett stuck his head in the door.

'Either you guys seen Ennis? The Dragon's on the phone, and she's not a happy lady.'

The Dragon was Edith Hyams, Ennis's sister. She was eight or nine years older than Ennis, a longtime widow-lady. There were those in Troop D who opined that she had murdered her husband, simply nagged him into his grave. 'That's not a tongue in her mouth, that's a Ginsu knife,' Dicky-Duck Eliot observed once. Curt, who saw the lady more than the rest of the Troop (Ennis was usually his partner; they got on well despite the difference in their ages), was of the opinion that Edith was the reason Trooper Rafferty had never married. 'I think that deep down he's afraid they're all like her,' he once told Sandy.

Coming back to work after your shift is through is never a good idea, Sandy thought after spending a long ten minutes on the phone with The Dragon. *Where is he, he promised he'd be home by six-thirty at the latest, I got the roast he wanted down at Pepper's, eighty-nine cents a pound, now it's cooked like an old boot, gray as wash-water* (only of course what the lady said was *warsh-warter*), *if he's down at The Country Way or The Tap you tell me right now, Sandy, so I can call and tell him what's what.* She also informed Sandy that she was out of her water-pills, and Ennis was supposed to have brought her a fresh batch. So where the hell was he? Pulling overtime? That would be all right, she reckoned, God knew they could use the money, only he should have called. Or was he drinking? Although she never came right out and said so, Sandy could tell that The Dragon voted for drinking.

Sandy was sitting at the dispatch desk, one hand cupped over his eyes, trying to get a word in edgeways, when Curtis Wilcox bopped in, dressed in his civvies and looking every inch the sport. Like Sandy, he'd come back for another peek at the Roadmaster.

'Hold on, Edith, hold on a second,' Sandy said, and put the telephone against his chest. 'Help me out here, rookie. Do you know where Ennis went after he left?'

'He left?'

'Yeah, but he apparently didn't go home.' Sandy pointed to the phone, which was still held against his chest. 'His sister's on the line.'

'If he left, how come his car's still here?' Curt asked.

Sandy looked at him. Curtis looked back. And then, without a word spoken, the two of them jumped like Jack and Jill to the same conclusion.

★　★　★

Sandy got rid of Edith — told her he'd call her back, or have Ennis call her, if he was around. That taken care of, Sandy went out back with Curt.

There was no mistaking Ennis's car, the American Motors Gremlin they all made fun of. It stood not far from the plow Johnny Parker had moved out of Shed B to make room for the Buick. The shadows of both the car and the plow straggled long in the declining sun of a summer evening, printed on the earth like tattoos.

Sandy and Curt looked inside the Gremlin and saw nothing but the usual road-litter: hamburger wrappers, soda cans, Tiparillo boxes, a couple of maps, an extra uniform shirt hung from the hook in back, an extra citation book on the dusty dashboard, some bits of fishing gear. All that rickrack looked sort of comforting to them after the sterile emptiness of the Buick. The sight of Ennis sitting behind the wheel and snoozing with his old Pirates cap tilted over his eyes would have been even more comforting, but there was no sign of him.

Curt turned and started back toward the barracks. Sandy had to break into a trot in order to catch up and grab his arm. 'Where do you think you're going?' he asked.

'To call Tony.'

'Not yet,' Sandy said. 'Let him have his dinner. We'll call him later if we have to. I hope to God we don't.'

★   ★   ★

Before checking anything else, even the upstairs common room, Curt and Sandy checked Shed B. They walked all around the car, looked inside the car, looked under the car. There was no sign of Ennis Rafferty in any of those places — at least, not that they could see. Of course, looking for signs in and around the Buick that evening was like looking for the track of one particular horse after a stampede has gone by. There was no sign of Ennis *specifically*, but . . .

88

'Is it cold in here, or is it just me?' Curt asked. They were about ready to return to the barracks. Curt had been down on his knees with his head cocked, taking a final look underneath the car. Now he stood up, brushing his knees. 'I mean, I know it's not *freezing* or anything, but it's colder than it should be, wouldn't you say?'

Sandy actually felt too hot — sweat was running down his face — but that might have been nerves rather than room-temperature. He thought Curt's sense of cold was likely just a holdover from what he'd felt, or thought he'd felt, out at the Jenny station.

Curt read that on his face easily enough. 'Maybe it is. Maybe it *is* just me. Fuck, *I* don't know. Let's check the barracks. Maybe he's downstairs in supply, coopin. Wouldn't be the first time.'

The two men hadn't entered Shed B by either of the big roll-up doors but rather through the doorknob-operated, people-sized door that was set into the right side. Curt paused in it instead of going out, looking back over his shoulder at the Buick.

His gaze as he stood beside the wall of pegged hammers, clippers, rakes, shovels, and one posthole digger (the red AA on the handle stood not for Alcoholics Anonymous but for Arky Arkanian) was angry. Almost baleful. 'It wasn't in my mind,' he said, more to himself than to Sandy. 'It was *cold*. It's not now, but it was.'

Sandy said nothing.

'Tell you one thing,' Curt said. 'If that goddam car's going to be around long, I'm getting a thermometer for this place. I'll pay for it out of my own pocket, if I have to. And say! Someone left the damn trunk unlocked. I wonder who — '

He stopped. Their eyes met, and a single thought flashed between them: *Fine pair of cops we are.*

They had looked inside the Buick's cabin, and underneath, but had ignored the place that was — according to the movies, at least — the temporary body-disposal site of choice for murderers both amateur and professional.

The two of them walked over to the Buick and stood by the back deck, peering at the line of darkness where the trunk was unlatched.

'You do it, Sandy,' Curt said. His voice was low, barely above a whisper.

Sandy didn't want to, but decided he had to — Curt was, after all, still a rookie. He took a deep breath and raised the trunk's lid. It went up much faster than he had expected. There was a clunk when it reached the top of its arc, loud enough to make both men jump. Curt grabbed Sandy with one hand, his fingers so cold that Sandy almost cried out.

The mind is a powerful and often unreliable machine. Sandy was so sure they were going to find Ennis Rafferty in the trunk of the Buick that for a moment he saw the body: a curled fetal shape in jeans and a white shirt, looking like something a Mafia hitman might leave in the trunk of a stolen Lincoln.

But it was only overlapped shadows that the two Troopers saw. The Buick's trunk was empty. There was nothing there but plain brown

90

carpeting without a single tool or grease-stain on it. They stood in silence for a moment or two, and then Curt made a sound under his breath, either a snicker or an exasperated snort. 'Come on,' he said. 'Let's get out of here. And shut the damn trunk tight this time. 'Bout scared the life out of me.'

'Me too,' Sandy said, and gave the trunk a good hard slam. He followed Curt to the door beside the wall with the pegged tools on it. Curtis was looking back again.

'Isn't that one hell of a thing,' he said softly.

'Yes,' Sandy agreed.

'It's fucked up, wouldn't you say?'

'I would, rook, I would indeed, but your partner isn't in it. Or anywhere in here. That much is for sure.'

Curt didn't bridle at the word *rook*. Those days were almost over for him, and they both knew it. He was still looking at the car, so smooth and cool and *there*. His eyes were narrow, showing just two thin lines of blue. 'It's almost like it's talking. I mean, I'm sure that's just my imagination — '

'Damn tooting it is.'

' — but I can almost hear it. Mutter-mutter-mutter.'

'Quit it before you give me the willies.'

'You mean you don't already have them?'

Sandy chose not to reply to that. 'Come on, all right?'

They went out, Curt taking one last look before closing the door.

The two of them checked upstairs in the barracks, where there was a living room and, behind a plain blue curtain, a dorm-style bedroom that contained four cots. Andy Colucci was watching a sitcom on television and a couple of Troopers who had the graveyard shift were snoozing; Sandy could hear the snores. He pulled back the curtain to check. Two guys, all right, one of them going *wheek-wheek* through his nose — polite — and the other going *ronk-ronk-ronk* through his open mouth — big and rude. Neither of them was Ennis. Sandy hadn't really expected to find him there; when Ennis cooped, he most commonly did it in the basement supply room, rocked back in the old swivel chair that went perfectly with the World War II-era metal desk down there, the old cracked radio on the shelf playing danceband music soft. He wasn't in the supply room that night, though. The radio was off and the swivel chair with the pillow on the seat was unoccupied. Nor was he in either of the storage cubicles, which were poorly lit and almost as spooky as cells in a dungeon.

There was a total of four toilets in the building, if you included the stainless stell lidless model in the Bad Boy Corner. Ennis wasn't hiding out in any of the three with doors. Not in the kitchenette, not in dispatch, not in the SC's office, which stood temporarily empty, with the doors open and the lights off.

By then, Huddie Royer had joined Sandy and

Curt. Orville Garrett had gone home for the day (probably afraid that Ennis's sister would turn up in person), and had left Mister Dillon in Huddie's care, so the dog was there, too. Curt explained what they were doing and why. Huddie grasped the implications at once. He had a big, open Farmer John face, but Huddie was a long way from stupid. He led Mister D to Ennis's locker and let him smell inside, which the dog did with great interest. Andy Colucci joined them at this point, and a couple of other off-duty guys who had dropped by to sneak a peek at the Buick also joined the party. They went outside, split up into two groups, and walked around the building in opposing circles, calling Ennis's name. There was still plenty of good light, but the day had begun to redden.

Curt, Huddie, Mister D, and Sandy were in one group. Mister Dillon walked slowly, smelling at everything, but the only time he really perked and turned, the scent he'd caught took him on a beeline to Ennis's Gremlin. No help there.

At first yelling Ennis's name felt foolish, but by the time they gave up and went back inside the barracks, it no longer felt that way at all. That was the scary part, how fast yelling for him stopped feeling silly and started feeling serious.

'Let's take Mister D into the shed and see what he smells there,' Curt proposed.

'No way,' Huddie said. 'He doesn't like the car.'

'Come on, man, Ennie's my partner. Besides, maybe ole D will feel different about that car now.'

But ole D felt just the same. He was okay outside the shed, in fact started to pull on his leash as the Troopers approached the side door. His head was down, his nose all but scraping the macadam. He was even more interested when they got to the door itself. The men had no doubt at all that he had caught Ennis's scent, good and strong.

Then Curtis opened the door, and Mister Dillon forgot all about whatever he had been smelling. He started to howl at once, and again hunched over as if struck by bad cramps. His fur bushed out like a peacock's finery, and he squirted urine over the doorstep and on to the shed's concrete floor. A moment later he was yanking at the leash Huddie was holding, still howling, still trying in a crazy, reluctant way to get inside. He hated it and feared it, that was in every line of his body — and in his wild eyes — but he was trying to get at it, just the same.

'Aw, never mind! Just get him out!' Curt shouted. Until then he had kept hold of himself very well, but it had been a long and stressful day for him and he was finally nearing the breaking point.

'It's not his fault,' Huddie said, and before he could say more, Mister Dillon raised his snout and howled again . . . only to Sandy it sounded more like a scream than a howl. The dog took another crippled lurch forward, pulling Huddie's arm out straight like a flag in a high wind. He was inside now, howling and whining, lurching to get forward and pissing everywhere like a pup. Pissing in terror.

94

'I know it's not!' Curt said. 'You were right to begin with, I'll give you a written apology if you want, just get him the fuck out!'

Huddie tried to reel Mister D back in, but he was a big dog, about ninety pounds, and he didn't want to come. Curt had to lay on with him in order to get D going in the right direction. In the end they dragged him out on his side, D fighting and howling and gnashing the air with his teeth the whole way. It was like pulling a sack of polecats, Sandy would say later.

When the dog was at last clear of the door, Curtis slammed it shut. The second he did, Mister Dillon relaxed and stopped fighting. It was as if a switch in his head had been flipped. He continued to lie on his side for a minute or two, getting his breath, then popped to his feet. He gave the Troopers a bewildered look that seemed to say, 'What happened, boys? I was going along good, and then I kind of blanked out.'

'Holy . . . fucking . . . *shit*,' Huddie said in a low voice.

'Take him back to the barracks,' Curt said. 'I was wrong to ask you to let him inside there, but I'm awful worried about Ennis.'

Huddie took the dog back to the barracks, Mister D once again as cool as a strawberry milkshake, just pausing to sniff at the shoes of the Troopers who had helped search the perimeter. These had been joined by others who had heard Mister D freaking out and had come to see what all the fuss was.

'Go on in, guys,' Sandy said, then added what

they always said to the lookie-loos who gathered at accident sites: 'Show's over.'

They went in. Curt and Sandy watched them, standing there by the closed shed door. After awhile Huddie came back without Mister D. Sandy watched Curt reach for the doorknob of the shed door and felt a sense of dread and tension rise in his head like a wave. It was the first time he felt that way about Shed B, but not the last. In the twenty-odd years that followed that day, he would go inside Shed B dozens of times, but never without the rise of that dark mental wave, never without the intuition of almost-glimpsed horrors, of abominations in the corner of the eye.

Not that all of the horrors went unglimpsed. In the end they glimpsed plenty.

★   ★   ★

The three of them walked in, their shoes gritting on the dirty cement. Sandy flipped on the light-switches by the door and in the glare of the naked bulbs the Buick stood like one prop left on a bare stage, or the single piece of art in a gallery that had been dressed like a garage for the showing. What would you call such a thing? Sandy wondered. *From a Buick 8* was what occurred to him, probably because there was a Bob Dylan song with a similar title. The chorus was in his head as they stood there, seeming to illuminate that feeling of dread: *Well, if I go down dyin', you know she's bound to put a blanket on my bed.*

It sat there with its Buick headlights staring and its Buick grille sneering. It sat there on its fat and luxy whitewalls, and inside was a dashboard full of frozen fake controls and a wheel almost big enough to steer a privateer. Inside was something that made the barracks dog simultaneously howl in terror and yank forward as if in the grip of some ecstatic magnetism. If it had been cold in there before, it no longer was; Sandy could see sweat shining on the faces of the other two men and feel it on his own.

It was Huddie who finally said it out loud, and Sandy was glad. He felt it, but never could have put that feeling into words; it was too outrageous.

'Fucking thing ate im,' Huddie said with flat certainty. 'I don't know how that could be, but I think he came in here by himself to take another look and it just . . . somehow . . . ate im.'

Curt said, 'It's watching us. Do you feel it?'

Sandy looked at the glassy headlight eyes. At the downturned, sneering mouth full of chrome teeth. The decorative swoops up the sides, which could almost have been sleek locks of slick hair. He felt *something*, all right. Perhaps it was nothing but childish awe of the unknown, the terror kids feel when standing in front of houses their hearts tell them are haunted. Or perhaps it was really what Curt said. Perhaps it was watching them. Gauging the distance.

They looked at it, hardly breathing. It sat there, as it would sit for all the years to come, while Presidents came and went, while records were replaced by CDs, while the stock market went up and a pair of skyscrapers came down, while movie-stars lived and died and Troopers came and went in the D barracks. It sat there real as rocks and roses. And to some degree they all felt what Mister Dillon had felt: the *draw* of it. In the months that followed, the sight of cops standing there side by side in front of Shed B became common. They would stand with their hands cupped to the sides of their faces to block the light, peering in through the windows running across the front of the big garage door. They looked like sidewalk superintendents at a building site. Sometimes they went inside, too (never alone, though; when it came to Shed B, the buddy system ruled), and they always looked younger when they did, like kids creeping into the local graveyard on a dare.

Curt cleared his throat. The sound made the other two jump, then laugh nervously. 'Let's go inside and call the Sarge,' he said, and this time

NOW:

Sandy

'... and that time I didn't say anything. Just went along like a good boy.'

My throat was as dry as an old chip. I looked at my watch and wasn't exactly surprised to see that over an hour had gone by. Well, that was all right; I was off-duty. The day was murkier than ever, but the faint mutters of thunder had slid away south of us.

'Those old days,' someone said, sounding both sad and amused at the same time — it's a trick only the Jews and the Irish seem to manage with any grace. 'We thought we'd strut forever, didn't we?'

I glanced around and saw Huddie Royer, now dressed in civilian clothes, sitting on Ned's left. I don't know when he joined us. He had the same honest Farmer John face he'd worn through the world back in '79, but now there were lines bracketing the corners of his mouth, his hair was mostly gray, and it had gone out like the tide, revealing a long, bright expanse of brow. He was, I judged, about the same age Ennis Rafferty had been when Ennis pulled his Judge Crater act. Huddie's retirement plans involved a Winnebago and visits to his children and grandchildren. He had them everywhere, so far as I could make out, including the province of Manitoba. If you asked

99

— or even if you didn't — he'd show you a US map with all his proposed routes of travel marked in red.

'Yeah,' I said. 'I guess we did, at that. When did you arrive, Huddie?'

'Oh, I was passing by and heard you talking about Mister Dillon. He was a good old doggie, wasn't he? Remember how he'd roll over on his back if anyone said 'You're under arrest'?'

'Yeah,' I said, and we smiled at each other, the way men do over love or history.

'What happened to him?' Ned asked.

'Punched his card,' Huddie said. 'Eddie Jacubois and I buried him right over there.' He pointed toward the scrubby field that stretched up a hill north of the barracks. 'Must be fifteen years ago. Would you say, Sandy?'

I nodded. It was actually fourteen years, almost to the day.

'I guess he was old, huh?' Ned asked.

Phil Candleton said, 'Getting up there, yes, but — '

'He was poisoned,' Huddie said in a rough, outraged voice, and then said no more.

'If you want to hear the rest of this story — ' I began.

'I do,' Ned replied at once.

' — then I need to wet my whistle.'

I started to get up just as Shirley came out with a tray in her hands. On it was a plate of thick sandwiches — ham and cheese, roast beef, chicken — and a big pitcher of Red Zinger iced tea. 'Sit back down, Sandy,' she said. 'I got you covered.'

'What are you, a mind reader?'

She smiled as she set the tray down on the bench. 'Nope. I just know that men get thirsty when they talk, and that men are always hungry. Even the ladies get hungry and thirsty from time to time, believe it or not. Eat up, you guys, and I expect you to put away at least two of these sandwiches yourself, Ned Wilcox. You're too damn thin.'

Looking at the loaded tray made me think of Bibi Roth, talking with Tony and Ennis while his crew — his children, not much older than Ned was now — drank iced tea and gobbled sandwiches made in the same kitchenette, nothing different except for the color of the tiles on the floor and the microwave oven. Time is also held together by chains, I think.

'Yes, ma'am, okay.'

He gave her a smile, but I thought it was dutiful rather than spontaneous; he kept looking over at Shed B. He was under the spell of the thing now, as so many men had been over the years. Not to mention one good dog. And as I drank my first glass of iced tea, cold and good going down my parched throat, loaded with real sugar rather than that unsatisfying artificial shit, I had time to wonder if I was doing Ned Wilcox any favors. Or if he'd even believe the rest of it. He might just get up, walk away all stiff-shouldered and angry, believing I'd been making a game of him and his grief. It wasn't impossible. Huddie, Arky, and Phil would back me up — so would Shirley, for that matter. She hadn't been around when the Buick came in, but she'd seen plenty — and *done* plenty — since taking the dispatch job in the mid-eighties. The kid still might not believe it, though. It was a lot to swallow.

Too late to back out now, though.

'What happened about Trooper Rafferty?' Ned asked.

'Nothing,' Huddie said. 'He didn't even get his ugly mug on the side of a milk carton.'

Ned gazed at him uncertainly, not sure if Huddie was joking or not.

'Nothing happened,' Huddie repeated, more quietly this time. 'That's the insidious thing about disappearing, son. What happened to your Dad was terrible, and I'd never try to convince you any different. But at least you *know*. That's something, isn't it? There's a place where you can go and visit, where you can lay down flowers. Or take your college acceptance letter.'

'That's just a grave you're talking about,' Ned said. He spoke with a strange patience that made me uneasy. 'There's a piece of ground, and there's a box under it, and there's something in the box that's dressed in my father's uniform, but it's not my father.'

'But you know what happened to him,' Huddie insisted. 'With Ennis . . . ' He spread his hands with the palms down, then turned them up, like a magician at the end of a good trick.

Arky had gone inside, probably to take a leak. Now he came back and sat down.

'All quiet?' I asked.

'Well, yes and no, Sarge Steff tole me to tell

you she's getting dose bursts of interference on d'radio again, dose l'il short ones. You know what I mean. Also, DSS is kaputnik. Jus' dat sign on the TV screen dat say STAND BY SEARCHING FOR SIGNAL.'

Steff was Stephanie Colucci, Shirley's second-shift replacement in dispatch and old Andy Colucci's niece. The DSS was our little satellite dish, paid for out of our own pockets, like the exercise equipment in the corner upstairs (a year or two ago someone tacked a poster to the wall beside the free weights, showing buff biker types working out in the prison yard up at Shabene — THEY *NEVER* TAKE A DAY OFF is the punchline beneath).

Arky and I exchanged a glance, then looked over at Shed B. If the microwave oven in the kitchenette wasn't on the fritz now, it soon would be. We might lose the lights and the phone, too, although it had been awhile since that had happened.

'We took up a collection for that rotten old bitch he was married to,' Huddie said. 'That was mighty big of Troop D, in my view.'

'I thought it was to shut her up,' Phil said.

'Wasn't *nothing* going to shut that one up,' Huddie said. 'She meant to have her say. Anyone who ever met her knew that.'

'It wasn't exactly a collection and he wasn't married to her,' I said. 'The woman was his sister. I thought I made that clear.'

'He was married to her,' Huddie insisted. 'They were like any old couple, with all the yaps and grumps and sore places. They did everything married folks do except for the old in-out, and for all I know — '

'Snip, snip, bite your lip,' Shirley said mildly.

'Yeah,' Huddie said. 'I s'pose.'

'Tony passed the hat, and we all tossed in as much as we could,' I told Ned. 'Then Buck Flanders's brother — he's a stockbroker in Pittsburgh — invested it for her. It was Tony's idea to do it that way rather than just hand her a check.'

Huddie was nodding. 'He brought it up at that meeting he called, the one in the back room at The Country Way. Taking care of The Dragon was just about the last item on the agenda.'

Huddie turned directly to Ned.

'By then we knew nobody was going to find Ennis, and that Ennis wasn't just going to walk into a police station somewhere in Bakersfield, California, or Nome, Alaska, with a case of amnesia from a knock on the head. He was gone. Maybe to the same place the fella in the black coat and hat went off to, maybe to some other place, but gone either way. There was no body, no signs of violence, not even any *clothes*, but Ennie was gone.' Huddie laughed. It was a sour sound. 'Oh, that bad-natured bitch he lived with was so *wild*. Of course she was half-crazy to begin with — '

'More dan half,' Arky said complacently, and helped himself to a ham and cheese sandwich. 'She call all d'time, tree-four times a day, made Matt Babicki in dispatch jus' about tear his hair out. You should count your blessins she's gone,

104

Shirley. Edit' Hyams! What a piece of work!'

'What did she think had happened?' Ned asked.

'Who knows?' I said. 'That we killed him over poker debts, maybe, and buried him in the cellar.'

'You played *poker* in the barracks back then?' Ned looked both fascinated and horrified. 'Did my father play?'

'Oh, please,' I said. 'Tony would have scalped anyone he caught playing poker in the barracks, even for matches. And I'd do exactly the same. I was joking.'

'We're not *firemen*, boy,' Huddie said with such disdain that I had to laugh. Then he returned to the subject at hand. 'That old woman believed we had something to do with it because she hated us. She would have hated anyone that distracted Ennis's attention from her. Is hate too strong a word, Sarge?'

'No,' I said.

Huddie once more turned to Ned. 'We took his time and we took his energy. And I think the part of Ennis's life that was best for him was the part he spent here, or in his cruiser. She knew that, and she hated it — 'The job, the job, the job,' she'd say. 'That's all he cares about, his damned *job*.' As far as she was concerned, we *must* have taken his life. Didn't we take everything else?'

Ned looked bewildered, perhaps because hate of the job had never been a part of his own home life. Not that he'd seen, anyway. Shirley laid a gentle hand on his knee. 'She had to hate *somebody*, don't you see? She had to blame somebody.'

I said, 'Edith called, Edith hectored us, Edith wrote letters to her Congressman and to the State Attorney General, demanding a full investigation. I think Tony knew all that was in the offing, but he went right ahead with the meeting we had a few nights later, and laid out his proposal to take care of her. If we didn't, he said, no one would. Ennis hadn't left much, and without our help she'd be next door to destitute. Ennis had insurance and was eligible for his pension — probably eighty per cent of full by then — but she wouldn't see a penny of either one for a long time. Because — '

' — he just disappeared,' Ned said.

'Right. So we got up a subscription for The Dragon. A couple of thousand dollars, all told, with Troopers from Lawrence, Beaver, and Mercer also chipping in. Buck Flanders's brother put it in computer stocks, which were brand-new then, and she ended up making a small fortune.

'As for Ennis, a story started going around the various Troops over here in western PA that he'd run off to Mexico. He was always talking about Mexico, and reading magazine stories about it. Pretty soon it was being taken as gospel: Ennis had run away from his sister before she could finish the job of cutting him up with that Ginsu knife tongue of hers. Even guys who knew better — or should have — started telling that story after awhile, guys who were in the back room of The Country Way when Tony Schoondist said right out loud that he believed the Buick in Shed

106

B had something to do with Ennis's disappearance.'

'Stopped just short of calling it a transporter unit from Planet X,' Huddie said.

'Sarge was very forceful dat night,' Arky said, sounding so much like Lawrence Welk — *Now here's da lovely Alice-uh Lon* — that I had to raise my hand to cover a smile.

'When she wrote her Congressman, I guess she didn't talk about what you guys had over there in the Twilight Zone, did she?' Ned asked.

'How could she?' I asked. 'She didn't know. That was the main reason Sergeant Schoondist called the meeting. Basically it was to remind us that loose lips sink sh — '

'What's that?' Ned asked, half-rising from the bench. I didn't even have to look to know what he was seeing, but of course I looked anyway. So did Shirley, Arky, and Huddie. You couldn't not look, couldn't not be fascinated. None of us had ever pissed and howled over the Roadmaster like poor old Mister D, but on at least two occasions I had screamed. Oh yes. I had damned near screamed my guts out. And the nightmares afterward. Man oh man.

The storm had gone away to the south of us, except in a way it hadn't. In a way it had been caged up inside of Shed B. From where we sat on the smokers' bench we could see bright, soundless explosions of light going off inside. The row of windows in the roll-up door would be as black as pitch, and then they'd turn blue-white. And with each flash, I knew, the radio in dispatch would give out another bray of static. Instead of showing **5:18 PM**, the clock on the microwave would be reading **ERROR**.

But on the whole, this wasn't a bad one. The flashes of light left afterimages — greenish squares that floated in front of your eyes — but you could look. The first three or four times that pocket storm happened, looking was impossible — it would have fried the eyes right out of your head.

'Holy God,' Ned whispered. His face was long with surprise —

No, that's too timid. It was shock I saw on his face that afternoon. Nor was shock the end of it. When his eyes cleared a little, I saw the same look of fascination I had seen on his father's face. On Tony's. Huddie's. Matt Babicki's and Phil Candleton's. And hadn't I felt it on my own face? It's how we most often appear when we confront the deep and authentic unknown, I think — when we glimpse that place where our familiar universe stops and the real blackness begins.

Ned turned to me. 'Sandy, Jesus Christ, what is it? *What is it?*'

'If you have to call it something, call it a lightquake. A mild one. These days, most of them are mild. Want a closer look?'

He didn't ask if it was safe, didn't ask if it was going to explode in his face or bake the old sperm-factory down below. He just said, '*Yeah!*' Which didn't surprise me in the least.

We walked over, Ned and I in the lead, the others not far behind. The irregular flashes were very clear in the gloom of the late day, but they registered on the eye even in full sunshine. And when we first took possession (that was right around the time Three-Mile Island almost blew, now that I think about it), the Buick Roadmaster in one of its throes literally outshone the sun.

'Do I need shades?' Ned asked as we approached the shed door. I could now hear the humming from inside — the same hum Ned's father had noticed as he sat behind the Buick's oversized wheel out at the Jenny station.

'Nah, just squint,' Huddie said. 'You would have needed shades in '79, though, I can tell you that.'

'You bet your swede ass,' Arky said as Ned put his face to one of the windows, squinting and peering in.

I slotted myself in next to Ned, fascinated as always. Step right up, see the living crocodile.

The Roadmaster stood entirely revealed, the tarp it had somehow shrugged off lying crumpled in a tan drift on the driver's side. To me, it looked more like an *objet d'art* than ever — that big old automotive dinosaur with its curvy lines and hardtop styling, its big wheels and sneermouth grille. Welcome, ladies and gentlemen! Welcome to this evening's viewing of *From a Buick 8*! Just keep a respectful distance, because this is the art that bites!

It sat there moveless and dead . . . moveless and dead . . . and then the cabin lit up a brilliant flashbulb purple. The oversized steering wheel and the rearview mirror stood out with absolute dark clarity, like objects on the horizon during an artillery barrage. Ned gasped and put up a hand to shield his face.

It flashed again and again, each silent detonation printing its leaping shadow across the cement floor and up the board wall, where a few tools still hung from the pegs. Now the humming was very clear. I directed my gaze toward the circular thermometer hanging from the beam which ran above the Buick's hood, and when the light bloomed again, I was able to read the temperature easily: fifty-four degrees Fahrenheit. Not great, but not terrible, either. It was mostly when the temperature in Shed B dropped below fifty that you had to worry; fifty-four wasn't a bad number at all. Still, it was best to play it safe. We had drawn a few conclusions about the Buick over the years — established a few rules — but we knew better than to trust any of them very far.

Another of those bright soundless flashes went off inside the Buick, and then there was nothing for almost a full minute. Ned never budged. I'm not sure he even breathed.

'Is it over?' he asked at last.

'Wait,' I said.

We gave it another two minutes and when there was still nothing I opened my mouth to say we might as well go back and sit down, the Buick had exhausted its supply of fireworks for tonight. Before I could speak, there was a final monstrous flash. A wavering tendril of light, like a spark from some gigantic cyclotron, shot outward and upward from the Buick's rear passenger window. It rose on a jagged diagonal to the back corner of the shed, where there was a high shelf loaded with old boxes, most filled with hardware oddments. These lit up a pallid, somehow eldritch yellow, as if the boxes were filled with lighted candles instead of orphan nuts, bolts, screws, and springs. The hum grew louder, rattling my teeth and actually seeming to vibrate along the bridge of my nose. Then it quit. So did the light. To our dazzled eyes, the interior of the shed now looked pitch-black instead of just gloomy. The Buick was only a hulk with rounded corners and furtive gleams which marked the chrome facings around its headlights.

Shirley let out her breath in a long sigh and stepped back from the window where she had been watching. She was trembling. Arky slipped an arm around her shoulders and gave her a comforting hug.

Phil, who had taken the window to my right, said: 'No matter how many times I see it, boss, I never get used to it.'

'What is it?' Ned asked. His awe seemed to have wound ten or twelve years off his face and turned him into a child younger than his sisters. 'Why does it happen?'

'We don't know,' I said.

'Who else knows about it?'

'Every Trooper who's worked out of Troop D over the last twenty-plus years. Some of the Motor Pool guys know. The County Road Commissioner, I think — '

'Jamieson?' Huddie said. 'Yeah, he knows.'

' — and the Statler Township Chief of Police, Sid Brownell. Beyond that, not many.'

We were walking back to the bench now, most of us lighting up. Ned looked like he could use a cigarette himself. Or something. A big knock of whiskey, maybe. Inside the barracks, things would be going back to normal. Steff Colucci would already be noting an improvement in her radio reception, and soon the DSS dish on the roof would be receiving again — all the scores, all the wars, and six Home Shopping stations. If that wouldn't make you forget about the hole in the ozone layer, by God, nothing would.

'How could folks not know?' Ned asked. 'Something as big as this, how could it not get out?'

'It's not so big,' Phil said. 'I mean, it's a *Buick*, son. A Cadillac, now . . . *that* would be big.'

'Some families can't keep secrets and some families can,' I said. 'Ours can. Tony Schoondist called that meeting in The Country Way, two nights after the Buick came in and Ennis disappeared, mostly to make sure we would. Tony briefed us on any number of things that night. Ennis's sister, of course — how we were going to take care of her and how we were supposed to respond to her until she cooled down — '

'If she ever did, I wasn't aware of it,' Huddie said.

' — and how we were to handle any reporters if she went to the press.'

There had been a dozen Troopers there that night, and with the help of Huddie and Phil, I managed to name most of them. Ned wouldn't have met all of them face to face, but he'd

112

probably heard the names at his dinner table, if his dad talked shop from time to time. Most Troopers do. Not the ugly stuff, of course, not to their families — the spitting and cursing and the bloody messes on the highway — but there's funny stuff, too, like the time we got called out because this Amish kid was roller-skating through downtown Statler, holding on to the tail of a galloping horse and laughing like a loon. Or the time we had to talk to the guy out on the Culverton Road who'd done a snow-sculpture of a naked man and woman in a sexually explicit position. *But it's art!* he kept yelling. We tried to explain that it wasn't art to the neighbors; they were scandalized. If not for a warm spell and a storm of rain, we probably would have wound up in court on that one.

I told Ned about how we'd dragged the tables into a big hollow square without having to be asked, and how Brian Cole and Dicky-Duck Eliot escorted the waitresses out and closed the doors behind them. We served ourselves from the steam tables which had been set up at the front of the room. Later there was beer, the off-duty Troopers pulling their own suds and running their own tabs, and a fug of blue cigarette smoke rising to the ceiling. Peter Quinland, who owned the restaurant in those days, loved The Chairman of the Board, and a steady stream of Frank Sinatra songs rained down on us from the overhead speakers as we ate and drank and smoked and talked: 'Luck Be a Lady', 'Summer Wind', 'New York, New York', and of course 'My Way', maybe the dumbest pop song of the twentieth century. To this day I can't listen to it — or any Sinatra song, really — without thinking of The Country Way and the Buick out in Shed B.

Concerning the Buick's missing driver, we were to say we had no name, no description, and no reason to believe the fellow in question had done anything against the law. Nothing about theft of services, in other words. Queries about Ennis were to be taken seriously and treated honestly — up to a point, anyway. Yes, we were all puzzled. Yes, we were all worried. Yes, we had put out watch-and-want bulletins — what we called W2's. Yes, it was possible that Ennis had just pulled up stakes and moved on. Really, we were instructed to say, *anything* was possible, and Troop D was doing its best to take care of Trooper Rafferty's sister, a dear lady who was so deeply upset she might say anything.

'As for the Buick itself, if anyone asks about it at all, tell them it's an impound,' Tony had said. 'No more than that. If anyone *does* say more than that, I'll find out who and smoke him out like a cigar.' He looked around the room; his men looked back at him, and no one was stupid enough to smile. They'd been around the Sarge long enough to know that when he looked the way he did just then, he was *not* joking. 'Are we clear on this? Everyone got the scoop?'

A general rumble of agreement had temporarily blotted out The Chairman singing 'It was a Very Good Year'. We had the scoop, all right.

★　★　★

114

Ned held up a hand, and I stopped talking, which was actually a pleasure. I hadn't much wanted to revisit that long-gone meeting in the first place.

'What about the tests that guy Bibi Roth did?'

'All inconclusive,' I said. 'The stuff that looked like vinyl wasn't *exactly* vinyl — close, but that was all. The paint-chips didn't match up to any of the automotive paints Bibi had samples of. The wood was wood. 'Likely oak,' Bibi said, but that was all he *would* say, no matter how much Tony pressed him. Something about it bothered him, but he wouldn't say what.'

'Maybe he couldn't,' Shirley said. 'Maybe he didn't know.'

I nodded. 'The glass in the windows and windshield is plain old sandwich safety glass, but not trademarked. Not installed on any Detroit assembly line, in other words.'

'The fingerprints?'

I ticked them off on my own fingers. 'Ennis. Your father. Bradley Roach. End of story. No prints from the man in the black trenchcoat.'

'He must have been wearing gloves,' Ned said.

'You'd think so, yes. Brad couldn't say for sure, but he *thought* he remembered seeing the guy's hands and thinking they were as white as his face.'

'People sometimes make up details like that afterwards, though,' Huddie commented. 'Eye-witnesses aren't as reliable as we'd like them to be.'

'You done philosophizing?' I asked.

Huddie gave me a grand wave of the hand. 'Continue.'

'Bibi found no traces of blood in the car, but fabric samples taken from the interior of the trunk showed microscopic traces of organic matter. Bibi wasn't able to identify any of it, and the stuff — he called it 'soap-scum' — disintegrated. Every slide he took was clear of the stuff in a week. Nothing left but the staining agent he used.'

Huddie raised his hand like a kid in school. I nodded to him.

'A week later you couldn't see the places where those guys chipped the dashboard and the wheel to get their samples. The wood grew back like skin over a grape. Same with the lining in the trunk. If you scratched a fender with a penknife or a key, six or seven hours later the scratch would be gone.'

'It *heals* itself?' Ned said. 'It can do that?'

'Yes,' Shirley said. She'd lit another Parliament and was smoking it in quick, nervous little puffs. 'Your father dragooned me into one of his experiments once — got me to run the video camera. He put a long scratch down the driver's-side door, right under the chrome swoop, and we just let the camera run, came back together every fifteen minutes. It wasn't anything dramatic, like something in a movie, but it was pretty damned amazing. The scratch got shallower and started to darken around the edges, like it was working to match the paintjob. And finally it was just gone. All sign of it.'

'And the tires,' Phil Candleton said, taking a

116

turn. 'You shoved a screwdriver into one of em, the air'd start to whoosh out just like you'd expect. Only then the whoosh'd thin to a whistle and a few seconds later that would stop, too. Then out comes the screwdriver.' Phil pursed his lips and made a *thpp* sound. 'Like spitting out a watermelon seed.'

'Is it alive?' Ned asked me. His voice was so low I could hardly hear it. 'I mean, if it can *heal* itself — '

'Tony always said it wasn't,' I said. 'He was vehement on the subject. 'Just a gadget,' he used to say. 'Just some kind of goddam thingamajig we don't understand.' Your Dad thought just the opposite, and by the end he was just as vehement as Tony had ever been. If Curtis had lived — '

'What? If he'd lived, what?'

'I don't know,' I said. All at once I felt dull and sad. There was a lot more to tell, but suddenly I didn't want to tell it. I didn't feel up to it and my heart was heavy with the prospect of it, the way your heart can grow heavy at the prospect of toil which is necessary but hard and stupid — stumps to pull before sundown, hay to bundle into the barn before afternoon rain. 'I don't know what would have happened if he'd lived, and that's the God's honest truth.'

Huddie came to my rescue. 'Your Dad was bullshit about the car, Ned. I mean bug-eyed bullshit. He was out there every spare minute, walking around it, taking pictures of it . . . touching it. That was what he mostly did. Just touching and touching, like to make sure it was real.'

'Sarge d'same way,' Arky put in.

Not exactly, I thought but didn't say. It had been different for Curt. In the end the Buick had been his in a way it had never been Tony's. And Tony had known it.

'But what about Trooper Rafferty, Sandy? Do you think the Buick — ?'

'Ate im,' Huddie said. He spoke with dead-flat certainty. 'That's what I thought then and it's what I think now. It's what your Dad thought, too.'

'Did he?' Ned asked me.

'Well, yes. Ate him or took him away to someplace else.' Again the image of stupid work came to me — rows of beds to be made, stacks of dishes to be washed, acres of hay to be scythed and carried.

'But you're telling me,' Ned said, 'that no scientist has ever been allowed to study that thing since Trooper Rafferty and my father found it? *Ever*? No physicists, no chemists? No one's ever run a spectrographic analysis?'

'Bibi was back at least once, I think,' Phil said, sounding just the tiniest bit defensive. 'By himself, though, without those kids he used to travel around with. He and Tony and your father wheeled some big machine in there . . . maybe it *was* a spectrograph, but I don't know what it showed. Do you, Sandy?'

I shook my head. There was no one left to answer that question. Or a lot of others. Bibi Roth died of cancer in 1998. Curtis Wilcox, who often walked around the Buick with a Spiral notebook in his hands, writing things down (and

118

sometimes sketching), was also dead. Tony Schoondist, alias the old Sarge, was still alive but now in his late seventies, lost in that confused twilit purgatory reserved for people with Alzheimer's disease. I remembered going to see him, along with Arky Arkanian, at the nursing home where he now lives. Just before Christmas, this was. Arky and I brought him a gold St Christopher's medal, which a bunch of us older fellows had chipped in to buy. It had seemed to me that the old Sarge was having one of his good days. He opened the package without much trouble and seemed delighted by the medallion. Even undid the clasp himself, although Arky had to help him do it up again after he'd slipped it on. When that was finally accomplished, Tony had looked at me closely with his brows knit together, his bleary eyes projecting a parody of his old piercing glare. It was a moment when he really seemed himself. Then his eyes filled with tears, and the illusion was gone. 'Who are you boys?' he'd asked. 'I can almost remember.' Then, as matter-of-factly as someone reporting the weather: 'I'm in hell, you know. This is hell.'

'Ned, listen,' I said. 'What that meeting in The Country Way really boiled down to was just one thing. The cops in California have it written on the sides of some of their cruisers, maybe because their memory is a little bit faulty and they have to write it down. We don't. Do you know what I'm talking about?'

'To serve and protect,' Ned said.

'You got it. Tony thought that thing had come into our hands almost as a result of God's will.

119

He didn't say it that flat-out, but we understood. And your father felt the same way.'

I was telling Ned Wilcox what I thought he needed to hear. What I didn't tell him about was the light in Tony's eyes, and in the eyes of Ned's father. Tony could sermonize about our commitment to serve and protect; he could tell us about how the men of Troop D were the ones best equipped to take care of such a dangerous *res*; he could even allow as how later on we might turn the thing over to a carefully chosen team of scientists, perhaps one led by Bibi Roth. He could spin all those tales, and did. None of it meant jack shit. Tony and Curt wanted the Buick because they just couldn't bear to let it go. That was the cake, and all the rest of it was just icing. The Roadmaster was strange and exotic, unique, and it was *theirs*. They couldn't bear to surrender it.

'Ned,' I asked, 'would you know if your Dad left any notebooks? Spirals, they would have been, like the kind kids take to school.'

Ned's mouth pinched at that. He dropped his head and spoke to a spot somewhere between his knees. 'Yeah, all kinds of them, actually. My Mom said they were probably diaries. Anyway, in his will, he asked that Mom burn all his private papers, and she did.'

'I guess that makes sense,' Huddie said. 'It jibes with what I know about Curt and the old Sarge, at least.'

Ned looked up at him.

Huddie elaborated. 'Those two guys distrusted scientists. You know what Tony called them?

Death's cropdusters. He said their big mission in life was to spread poison everywhere, telling people to go ahead and eat all they wanted, that it was knowledge and it wouldn't hurt them — that it would set them free.' He paused. 'There was another issue, too.'

'What issue?' Ned asked.

'Discretion,' Huddie said. 'Cops can keep secrets, but Curt and Tony didn't believe scientists could. 'Look how fast those idiots cropdusted the atomic bomb all around the world,' I heard Tony say once. 'We fried the Rosenbergs for it, but anyone with half a brain knows the Russians would have had the bomb in two years, anyway. Why? Because scientists like to chat. That thing we've got out in Shed B may not be the equivalent of the A-bomb, but then again it might. One thing's for sure, it isn't *anybody's* A-bomb as long as it's sitting out back under a piece of canvas.' '

I thought that was just part of the truth, not the whole truth. I've wondered from time to time if Tony and Ned's father ever really needed to talk about it — I mean on some late weekday evening when things at the barracks were at their slowest, guys cooping upstairs, other guys watching a movie on the VCR and eating microwave popcorn, just the two of them downstairs from all that, in Tony's office with the door shut. I'm not talking about maybe or kinda or sorta. I mean whether or not they ever spoke the flat-out truth: *There's not anything like this anywhere, and we're keeping it.* I don't think so. Because really, all they would have needed to do was to look into each other's eyes. To see that same eagerness — the desire to touch it and pry into it. Hell, just to walk around it. It was a secret thing, a mystery, a marvel. But I didn't know if the boy could accept that. I knew he wasn't just missing his father; he was angry at him for dying. In that mood, he might have seen what they did as stealing, and that wasn't the truth, either. At least not the whole truth.

'By then we knew about the lightquakes,' I said. 'Tony called them 'dispersal events'. He thought the Buick was getting rid of something, discharging it like static electricity. Issues of discretion and caretaking aside, by the end of the seventies people in Pennsylvania — and not just us but everyone — had one very big reason not to trust the scientists and the techies.'

'Three-Mile,' Ned said.

'Yes. Plus, there's more to that car than self-healing scratches and dust-repellent. Quite a bit more.'

I stopped. It seemed too hard, too much.

'Go on, tell him,' Arky said. He sounded almost angry, a pissed-off bandleader in the gloaming. 'You told him all dis dat don't mean shit, now you tell im da rest.' He looked at Huddie, then Shirley. 'Even 1988. Yeah, even dat part.' He paused, sighed, looked at Shed B. 'Too late to stop now, Sarge.'

I got up and started across the parking lot. Behind me, I heard Phil say: 'No, hunh-unh. Let him go, kid, he'll be back.'

That's one thing about sitting in the big chair; people can say that and almost always be right.

122

Barring strokes, heart attacks, and drunk drivers, I guess. Barring acts of what we mortals hope is God. People who sit in the big chair — who have worked to get there and work to stay there — never say oh fuck it and go fishing. No. Us big-chair folks continue making the beds, washing the dishes, and baling the hay, doing it the best we can. *Ah, man, what would we do without you?* people say. The answer is that most of them would go on doing whatever the hell they want, same as always. Going to hell in the same old handbasket.

I stood at the roll-up door of Shed B, looking through one of the windows at the thermometer. It was down to fifty-two. Still not bad — not *terrible*, anyway — but cold enough for me to think the Buick was going to give another shake or two before settling down for the night. No sense spreading the tarp back over it yet, then; we'd likely just have to do it again later on.

It's winding down: that was the received wisdom concerning the Roadmaster, the gospel according to Schoondist and Wilcox. Slowing like an unwound clock, wobbling like an exhausted top, beeping like a smoke detector that can no longer tell what's hot. Pick your favorite metaphor from the bargain bin. And maybe it was true. Then again, maybe it wasn't. We knew nothing about it, not really. Telling ourselves we did was just a strategy we used so we could continue living next door to it without too many bad dreams.

I walked back to the bench, lighting another

cigarette, and sat down between Shirley and
Ned. I said, 'Do you want to hear about the first
time we saw what we saw tonight?'

The eagerness I saw on his face made it a little
easier to go on.

THEN

Sandy was there when it started, the only one who was. In later years he would say — half-joking — that it was his one claim to fame. The others arrived on the scene soon enough, but to begin with it was only Sander Freemont Dearborn, standing by the gas-pump with his mouth hung open and his eyes squinched shut, sure that in another few seconds the whole bunch of them, not to mention the Amish and the few non-Amish farmers in the area, would be so much radioactive dust in the wind.

It happened a couple of weeks after the Buick came into Troop D's possession, around the first of August in the year 1979. By then the newspaper coverage of Ennis Rafferty's disappearance was dying down. Most of the stories about the missing State Trooper appeared in the Statler County *American*, but the Pittsburgh *Post-Gazette* ran a feature piece on the front page of its Sunday edition at the end of July. **MISSING TROOPER'S SISTER LEFT WITH MANY QUESTIONS**, the headline read, and beneath that: EDITH HYAMS CALLS FOR FULL INVESTIGATION.

Overall, the story played out exactly as Tony Schoondist had hoped it would. Edith believed the men in Troop D knew more than they were telling about her brother's disappearance; she

125

was quoted on that in both papers. What was left between the lines was that the poor woman was half out of her mind with grief (not to mention anger), and looking for someone to blame for what might have been her own fault. None of the Troopers said anything about her sharp tongue and nearly constant fault-finding, but Ennis and Edith had neighbors who weren't so discreet. The reporters from both papers also mentioned that, accusations or no, the men in Ennis's Troop were going ahead with plans to provide the woman with some modest financial support.

The harsh black-and-white photo of Edith in the *Post-Gazette* didn't help her case; it made her look like Lizzie Borden about fifteen minutes before she grabbed the hatchet.

★　★　★

The first lightquake happened at dusk. Sandy had come off patrol around six that evening in order to have a little chat with Mike Sanders, the County Attorney. They had a particularly nasty hit-and-run trial coming up, Sandy the prime witness for the prosecution, the victim a child who had been left a quadriplegic. Mike wanted to be very sure that the coke-snorting Mr Businessman responsible went away. Five years was his goal, but ten wasn't out of the question. Tony Schoondist sat in on part of the meeting, which took place in a corner of the upstairs common room, then went down to his office while Mike and Sandy finished up. When the meeting was over, Sandy decided to top up the

126

tank in his cruiser before hitting the road for another three hours or so.

As he walked past dispatch toward the back door, he heard Matt Babicki say in a low, just-talking-to-myself voice: 'Oh, you fucking thing.' This was followed by a whack. 'Why don't you *behave?*'

Sandy peeped around the corner and asked if Matt was having that delicate time of the month.

Matt wasn't amused. 'Listen to this,' he said, and boosted the gain on his radio. The SQUELCH knob, Sandy saw, was already turned as far as it would go toward +.

Brian Cole checked in from Unit 7, Herb Avery from 5 out on the Sawmill Road, George Stankowski from God knew where. That one was almost entirely lost in a windy burst of static.

'If this gets any worse, I don't know how I'm going to keep track of the guys, let alone shoot them any information,' Matt complained. He slapped the side of his radio again, as if for emphasis. 'And what if someone calls in with a complaint? Is it getting ready to thunderstorm outside, Sandy?'

'It was clear as a bell when I came in,' he said, then looked out the window. 'Clear as a bell now, too . . . as you could see, if your neck had a swivel in it. I was born with one, see?' Sandy turned his head from side to side.

'Very funny. Haven't you got an innocent man to frame, or something?'

'Good one, Matt. That's a very snappy comeback.'

As he went on his way, Sandy heard someone

upstairs wanting to know if the damned TV antenna had fallen down, because the picture had all of a sudden gone to hell during a pretty good *Star Trek* rerun, the one about the Tribbles.

Sandy went out. It was a hot, hazy evening with thunder rumbling off in the distance but no wind and a clear sky overhead. The light was starting to drain away into the west, and a groundmist was rising from the grass; it had gotten to a height of maybe five feet.

He got in his cruiser (D-14 that shift, the one with the busted headrest), drove it across to the Amoco pump, got out, unscrewed the gas cap under the pull-down license plate, then stopped. He had suddenly become aware of how quiet it was — no crickets chirping in the grass, no birds singing anywhere around. The only noise was a low, steady humming, like the sound one hears if one is standing right under the county powerlines, or near an electrical substation.

Sandy started to turn around, and as he did, the whole world went purple-white. His first thought was that, clear sky overhead or no, he had been struck by lightning. Then he saw Shed B lit up like . . .

But there was no way to finish the simile. There *was* nothing like it, not in his experience.

If he had been looking at those first few flashes dead on, he guessed he would have been blinded — maybe temporarily, maybe for good. Luckily for him, the shed's front roll-up door faced away from the gas-pump. Yet still the glare was enough to dazzle his eyes, and to turn that summer

128

twilight as bright as noonday. And it made Shed B, a solid enough wooden structure, seem as insubstantial as a tent made out of gauze. Light shot through every crack and unoccupied nail-hole; it flashed out from beneath the eaves through a small cavity that might have been gnawed by a squirrel; it blazed at ground-level, where a board had fallen off, in a great brilliant bar. There was a ventilator stack on the roof, and it shot the glare skyward in irregular bursts, like smoke-signals made out of pure violet light. The flashes through the rows of windows on the roll-up doors, front and back, turned the rising groundmist into an eerie electric vapor.

Sandy was calm. Startled but calm. He thought: *This is it, motherfucker's blowing, we're all dead.* The thought of running or jumping into his cruiser never entered his head. Run where? Drive where? It was a joke.

What he wanted was crazy: to get closer. It *drew* him. He wasn't terrified of it, as Mister D had been; he felt the fascination but not the fear. Crazy or not, he wanted to get closer. Could almost hear it *calling* him closer.

Feeling like a man in a dream (it crossed his mind that dreaming was a serious possibility), he walked back to the driver's side of D-14, leaned in through the open window, and plucked his sunglasses off the dashboard. He put them on and started walking toward the shed. It was a little better with the sunglasses, but not much. He walked with his hand raised in front of him and his eyes narrowed down to stringent slits. The world boomed silent light all around and

129

throbbed with purple fire. Sandy could see his shadow jumping out from his feet, disappearing, and then jumping out again. He could see the light leaping from the windows in the roll-up door and glaring off the back of the barracks. He could see Troopers starting to spill out, pushing aside Matt Babicki from dispatch, who had been closest and who got outside first. In the flashes from the shed, everyone moved herky-jerky, like actors in a silent film. Those who had sunglasses in their pockets reached to put them on. Some of those who didn't turned and stumbled back in to get them. One Trooper even drew his gun, looked down at it as if to say *What the fuck'm I gonna do with this?* and put it back in his holster. Two of the Troopers without sunglasses groped gamely on toward the shed nevertheless, heads down and eyes shut and hands held out before them like the hands of sleepwalkers, drawn as Sandy had been toward the stuttery flashes and that low, maddening hum. Like bugs to a buglight.

Then Tony Schoondist ran through them, slapping them, shoving them, telling them to get the hell back, to return to the barracks and that was an order. He was trying to get his own sunglasses on and kept missing his face with them. He got them where they belonged only after poking one bow into his mouth and the other into his left eyebrow.

Sandy saw and heard none of that. What he heard was the hum. What he saw were the flashes, turning the groundmist smoke into electric dragons. What he saw was the column of stuttery purple light rising from the conical roof-vent, stabbing up into the darkening air.

Tony grabbed him, shook him. Another silent gunshell of light went off in the shed, turning the lenses of Tony's sunglasses into small blue fireballs. He was shouting, although there was no need to; Sandy could hear him perfectly. There was the humming sound, and someone murmuring *Good God almighty*, and that was all.

'Sandy! Were you here when this started?'

'Yes!' He found himself shouting back in spite of himself. The situation somehow demanded that they shout. The light flared and glared, mute lightning. Each time it went off, the barracks seemed to jump forward like something that was alive, the shadows of the Troopers running up its board side.

'What started it? What set it off?'

'I don't know!'

'Get inside! Call Curtis! Tell him what's happening! Tell him to get his ass over here *now!*'

Sandy resisted the urge to tell his SC that he wanted to stay and see what happened next. In a very elementary way the idea was stupid to begin with: you couldn't actually see anything. It was too bright. Even with sunglasses it was too bright. Besides, he knew an order when he heard it.

He went inside, stumbling over the steps (it was impossible to judge depth or distance in those brilliant stutterflashes), and shuffled his way to dispatch, waving his arms in front of him. In his swimming, dazzled eyesight, the barracks

131

was nothing but overlaid shadows. The only visual reality for him at that moment was the great purple flashes floating in front of him.

Matt Babicki's radio was an endless blare of static with a few voices sticking out of it like the feet or fingers of buried men. Sandy picked up the regular telephone beside the dedicated 911 line, thinking that would be out, too — sure it would — but it was fine. He dialed Curt's number from the list tacked to the bulletin board. Even the telephone seemed to jump with fright each time one of those purple-white flashes lit the room.

Michelle answered the phone and said Curt was out back, mowing the grass before it got dark. She didn't want to call him in, that was clear in her voice. But when Sandy asked her a second time, she said, 'All right, just a minute, don't you guys ever give it a rest?'

The wait seemed interminable to Sandy. The thing in Shed B kept flashing like some crazy neon apocalypse, and the room seemed to waver into a slightly different perspective every time it did. Sandy found it nearly impossible to believe something generating such brilliance could be anything but destructive, yet he was still alive and breathing. He touched his cheeks with the hand not holding the telephone, checking for burns or swelling. There was neither.

For the time being, at least, he told himself. He kept waiting for the cops outside to begin screaming as the thing in the old garage exploded or melted or let something out — something unimaginable with burning electric eyes. Such ideas were a million miles from the usual run of cop-thoughts, but Sandy Dearborn had never felt less like a cop and more like a scared little boy. At last Curt picked up the telephone, sounding both curious and out of breath.

'You have to come right now,' Sandy told him. 'Sarge says so.'

Curt knew what it was about immediately. 'What's it doing, Sandy?'

'Shooting off fireworks. Flashes and sparks. You can't even look at Shed B.'

'Is the building on fire?'

'Don't think so, but there's no way to tell for sure. You can't see inside. It's too bright. Get over here.'

The phone at Curt's end crashed down without another word spoken and Sandy went back outside. If they were going to be nuked, he decided, he wanted to be with his friends when it happened.

* * *

Curt came roaring up the driveway marked TROOPERS ONLY ten minutes later, behind the wheel of his lovingly restored Bel Air, the one his son would inherit twenty-two years later. When he came around the corner he was still moving fast, and Sandy had one horrible moment when he thought Curtis was going to clean out about five guys with his bumper. But Curt was quick on the brake (he still had a kid's reflexes), and brought the Chevy to a nose-dipping halt.

133

He got out of his car, remembering to turn off the engine but not the headlights, tripping over his own eager feet and almost sprawling on the macadam. He caught his balance and went running toward the shed. Sandy had just time to see what was dangling from one hand: a pair of welders' goggles on an elastic strap. Sandy had seen excited men in his time — sure, plenty, almost every guy you stopped for speeding was excited in one way or another — but he had never seen anyone as burning with it as Curt was then. His eyes seemed to be bulging right out of his face, and his hair appeared to be standing on end ... although that might have been an illusion caused by how fast he was running.

Tony reached out and grabbed him on the way by, almost spilling him again. Sandy saw Curt's free hand close into a fist and start to rise. Then it relaxed. Sandy didn't know how close the rookie had come to striking his sergeant and didn't want to know. What mattered was that he recognized Tony (and Tony's authority over him) and stood down.

Tony reached for the goggles.

Curt shook his head.

Tony said something to him.

Curt replied, shaking his head vehemently.

In the still-bright flashes, Sandy saw Tony Schoondist undergo his own brief struggle, wanting to simply order Curt to hand the goggles over. Instead, he swung around and looked at his gathered Troopers. In his haste and excitement, the SC had given them what could have been construed as two orders: to get back

134

and to return to the barracks. Most had chosen to obey the first and ignore the second. Tony took a deep breath, let it out, then spoke to Dicky-Duck Eliot, who listened, nodded, and went back into the barracks.

The rest of them watched Curt run toward Shed B, dropping his baseball cap on the pavement as he went and slipping the goggles over his eyes. Much as Sandy liked and respected the newest member of Troop D, he did not see anything heroic in this advance, not even while it was happening. Heroism is the act of going forward in the face of fear. Curt Wilcox felt no fear that night, not the slightest twinge of it. He was simply bugshit with excitement and a curiosity so deep it was a compulsion. Much later, Sandy would decide the Old Sarge had let Curtis go because he saw there was no chance of holding him back.

Curt stopped about ten feet in front of the roll-up door, raising his hands to block his eyes as a particularly brilliant flash erupted from inside the shed. Sandy saw the light shining through Curt's fingers in purple-white spokes. At the same time, Curt's shadow appeared on the mist like the figure of a giant. Then the light died and through a blot of afterimage Sandy saw Curt advance again. He reached the door and looked inside. He stood that way until the next flash came. He recoiled when it did, then at once went back to the window.

Meanwhile, here came Dicky-Duck Eliot back from his errand, whatever it had been. Sandy saw what he was holding as Dicky-Duck went past.

135

The Sarge insisted that all of his D-cars should go out equipped with Polaroid cameras, and Dicky-Duck had run to fetch one of them. He handed it to Tony, cringing involuntarily as the shed lit up in another silent fusillade of light.

Tony took the camera and jogged across to Curtis, who was still peering into the shed and recoiling at each new flash (or series of them). Even the welders' goggles weren't enough protection from what was going on in there, it seemed.

Something nuzzled Sandy's hand and he almost screamed before looking down and seeing the barracks dog. Mister Dillon had likely slept through the whole thing until then, snoring on the linoleum between the sink and the stove, his favorite spot. Now he'd emerged to see what all the excitement was about. It was clear to Sandy from the brilliance of his eyes, the peak of his ears, and the high set of his head that he knew *something* was going on, but his previous terror wasn't in evidence. The flashing lights didn't seem to bother him in the slightest.

Curtis tried to grab the Polaroid, but Tony wouldn't let it go. They stood there in front of the Shed B door, turned into flinching silhouettes by each new flash from the shed. Arguing? Sandy didn't think so. Not quite, anyway. It looked to him like they were having the sort of heated discussion any two scientists might have while observing some new phenomenon. *Or maybe it's not a phenomenon at all,* Sandy thought. *Maybe it's an experiment, and we're the guinea pigs.*

136

He began to measure the length of the dark intervals as he and the others stood watching the two men in front of the shed, one wearing an oversized pair of goggles and the other holding a boxy Polaroid camera, both of them outlined like figures on a laser-lit dancefloor. The flashes had been like chain lightning when they began, but now there were significant pauses. Sandy counted six seconds between . . . ten seconds . . seven . . . fourteen . . . twenty.

Beside him, Buck Flanders said: 'I think it's ending.'

Mister D barked and made as if to start forward. Sandy grabbed him by the collar and held him back. Maybe the dog just wanted to go to Curt and Tony, but maybe it was the thing in the shed he wanted to go to. Maybe it was calling him again. Sandy didn't care which; he liked Mister Dillon right where he was.

Tony and Curt went around to the walk-in door. There they engaged in another warm discussion. At last Tony nodded — reluctantly, Sandy thought — and handed over the camera. Curt opened the door, and as he did the thing flashed out again, burying him in a glare of brilliant light. Sandy fully expected him to be gone when it died out, disintegrated or perhaps teleported to a galaxy far, far away, where he'd spend the rest of his life lubing X-wing fighters or maybe polishing Darth Vader's shiny black ass.

He had time just to register Curt still standing there, one hand upraised to shield his goggled eyes. To his right and slightly behind him, Tony

Schoondist was caught in the act of turning away from the glare, hands upraised to shield his face. Sunglasses were simply no protection; Sandy was wearing his own and knew that. When he could see again, Curt had gone into the shed.

At that moment, all of Sandy's attention switched to Mister Dillon, who was lunging forward in spite of the hold Sandy had on his collar. The dog's former calm was gone. He was growling and whining, ears flat against his skull, muzzle wrinkled back to show the white wink of teeth.

'Help me, help me out here!' Sandy shouted.

Buck Flanders and Phil Candleton also grabbed Mister D's collar, but at first it made no difference. The dog went motoring on, coughing and dripping slobber on the pavement, eyes fixed on the side door. He was ordinarily the sweetest mutt in creation, but right then Sandy wished for a leash and a muzzle. If D turned to bite, one of them was apt to wind up a finger or two shy.

'Shut the door!' Sandy bawled at the Sergeant. 'If you don't want D in there with him, *shut the damn door!*'

Tony looked startled, then saw what was wrong and closed the door. Almost at once Mister Dillon relaxed. The growling stopped, then the whining. He gave out a couple of puzzled barks, as if he couldn't remember exactly what had been bugging him. Sandy wondered if it was the hum, which was appreciably louder with the door open, or some smell. He thought the latter, but there was no way of telling for sure. The Buick wasn't about

138

what you knew but what you didn't.

Tony saw a couple of men moving forward and told them to stay back. Hearing his normal speaking voice so clearly was calming, but it still seemed wrong. Sandy couldn't help feeling there should have been whoops and screams in the background, movie-soundtrack explosions, perhaps rumbles from the outraged earth itself.

Tony turned back to the windows running along the roll-up door and peered in.

'What's he doing, Sarge?' Matt Babicki asked. 'He all right?'

'He's fine,' Tony said. 'Walking around the car taking pictures. What are you doing out here, Matt? Get in on dispatch, for Christ's sake.'

'The radio's FUBAR, boss. Static.'

'Well, maybe it's getting better. Because *this* is getting better.' To Sandy he sounded normal on top — like the Sergeant — but underneath, that excitement still throbbed in his voice. And as Matt turned away, Tony added: 'Not a word about this goes out over the air, you hear me? Not in the clear, anyway. Now or ever. If you have to talk about the Buick, it's . . . it's Code D. You understand?'

'Yessir,' Matt said, and went up the back steps with his shoulders slumped, as if he had been spanked.

'Sandy!' Tony called. 'What's up with the dog?'

'Dog's fine. Now. What's up with the car?'

'The car also appears to be fine. Nothing's burning and there's no sign anything exploded. The thermometer says fifty-four degrees. It's cold in there, if anything.'

'If the car's fine, why's he taking pictures of it?' Buck asked.

'Y's a crooked letter that can't be made straight,' Sergeant Schoondist replied, as if this explained everything. He kept his eye on Curtis, who went on circling the car like a fashion photographer circling a model, snapping photos, tucking each Polaroid as it came out of the slot into the waistband of the old khaki shorts he was wearing. While this was going on, Tony allowed the rest of those present to approach by fours and take a look. When Sandy's turn came, he was struck by how Curtis's ankles lit up green each time the Buick flashed out. *Radiation!* he thought. *Jesus Christ, he's got radiation burns!* Then he remembered what Curt had been doing earlier and had to laugh. Michelle hadn't wanted to call him in to the phone because he was mowing the grass. And that was what was on his ankles — grass-stains.

'Come outta there,' Phil muttered from Sandy's left. He still had the dog by the collar, although now Mister D seemed quite docile. 'Come on out, don't be pressing your luck.'

Curt started backing toward the door as if he'd heard Phil — or all of them — thinking that same thing. More likely he was just out of film.

As soon as he came through the door, Tony put an arm around his shoulders and pulled him aside. As they stood talking, a final weak pulse of purple light came. It was really no more than a twitch. Sandy looked at his watch. It was ten minutes of nine. The entire event had lasted not quite an hour.

140

Tony and Curt were looking at the Polaroids with an intensity Sandy couldn't understand. If, that was, Tony had been telling the truth when he said the Buick and the other stuff in the shed were unchanged. And to Sandy, all of it *did* look unchanged.

At last Tony nodded as if something was settled and walked back to the rest of the Troopers. Curt, meanwhile, went to the roll-up door for a final peek. The welders' goggles were pushed up on his forehead by then. Tony ordered everyone back into the barracks except for George Stankowski and Herb Avery. Herb had come in from patrol while the lightshow was still going on, probably to take a dump. Herb would drive five miles out of his way to take a dump at the barracks; he was famous for it, and took all ribbing stoically. He said you could get diseases from strange toilet seats, and anyone who didn't believe that deserved what he got. Sandy thought Herb was simply partial to the magazines in the upstairs crapper. Trooper Avery, who would be killed in a rollover car crash ten years later, was an *American Heritage* man.

'You two have got the first watch,' Tony said. 'Sing out if you see anything peculiar. Even if you only *think* it's peculiar.'

Herb groaned at getting sentry duty and started to protest.

'Put a sock in it,' Tony said, pointing at him. 'Not one more word.'

Herb noted the red spots on his SC's cheeks and closed his mouth at once. Sandy thought that showed excellent sense.

141

Matt Babicki was talking on the radio as the rest of them crossed the ready-room behind Sergeant Schoondist. When Matt told Unit 6 to state his twenty, Andy Colucci's response was strong and perfectly clear. The static had cleared out again.

They filled the seats in the little living room upstairs, those last in line having to content themselves with grabbing patches of rug. The ready-room downstairs was bigger and had more chairs, but Sandy thought Tony's decision to bring the crew up here was a good one. This was family business, not police business.

Not *strictly* police business, at least.

Curtis Wilcox came last, holding his Polaroids in one hand, goggles still pushed up on his forehead, rubber flip-flops on his green feet. His T-shirt read HORLICKS UNIVERSITY ATHLETIC DEPARTMENT.

He went to the Sergeant and the two of them conferred in murmurs while the rest waited. Then Tony turned back to the others. 'There was no explosion, and neither Curt nor I think there was any sort of radiation leak, either.'

Big sighs of relief greeted this, but several of the Troopers still looked doubtful. Sandy didn't know how he looked, there was no mirror handy, but he still *felt* doubtful.

'Pass these around, if you want,' Curt said, and handed out his stack of Polaroids by twos and threes. Some had been taken during the flashes and showed almost nothing: a glimmer of grillework, a piece of the Buick's roof. Others were much clearer. The best had that odd, flat, declamatory quality which is the sole property of Polaroid photographs. *I see a world where there's only cause and effect*, they seem to say. *A world where every object is an avatar and no gods move behind the scenes.*

'Like conventional film, or the badges workers in radiation-intensive environments have to wear,' Tony said, 'Polaroid stock fogs when it's exposed to strong gamma radiation. Some of these photos are overexposed, but none of them are fogged. We're not hot, in other words.'

Phil Candleton said, 'No offense to you, Sarge, but I'm not crazy about trusting my 'nads to the Polaroid Corporation of America.'

'I'll go up to The Burg tomorrow, first thing, and buy a Geiger counter,' Curt said. He spoke calmly and reasonably, but they could still hear the pulse of excitement in his voice. Under the cool will-you-please-step-out-of-your-car-sir voice, Curt Wilcox was close to blowing his top. 'They sell them at the Army Surplus store on Grand. I think they go for around three hundred bucks. I'll take the money out of the contingency fund, if no one objects.'

No one did.

'In the meantime,' Tony said, 'it's more important than ever that we keep this quiet. I believe that, either by luck or providence, that thing has fallen into the hands of men who can actually do that. Will you?'

There were murmurs of agreement.

Dicky-Duck was sitting cross-legged on the floor, stroking Mister Dillon's head. D was asleep with his muzzle on his paws. For the barracks mascot, the excitement was definitely over. 'I'm all right with that as long as the needle on the old Geiger doesn't move out of the green,' Dicky-Duck said. 'If it does, I vote we call the feds.'

'Do you think they can take care of it any better than we can?' Curt asked hotly. 'Jesus Christ, Dicky! The Feebs can't get out of their own way, and — '

'Unless you have plans to lead-line Shed B out of the contingency fund — ' someone else began.

'That's a pretty stupid — ' Curt began, and then Tony put a hand on his shoulder, stilling the kid before he could go any farther and maybe hurt himself.

'If it's hot,' Tony promised them, 'we'll get rid of it. That's a promise.'

Curt gave him a betrayed look. Tony stared back calmly. *We* know *it's not radioactive*, that gaze said, *the film proves it, so why do you want to start chasing your own tail?*

'I sort of think we ought to turn it over to the government anyway,' Buck said. 'They might be able to help us . . . you know . . . or find stuff out . . . defense stuff . . . ' His voice getting smaller and smaller as he sensed the silent disapproval all around him. PSP officers worked with the federal government in one form or another every day — FBI, IRS, DEA, OSHA, and, most of all, the Interstate Commerce Commission. It didn't take many years on the job to learn most of those federal boys were *not* smarter than the average bear. Sandy's opinion was that when the feds *did* show the occasional flash of intelligence, it tended to be self-serving and sometimes downright malicious. Mostly they were slaves to the grind, worshippers at the altar of Routine Procedure. Before joining the PSP, Sandy had seen the same sort of dull go-through-the-proper-channels thinking in the Army. Also, he wasn't much older than Curtis himself, which made him young enough to hate the idea of giving the Roadmaster up. Better to hand it over to scientists in the private sector, though, if it came to that — perhaps even a bunch from the college advertised on the front of Curtis's lawn-mowing shirt.

But best of all, the Troop. The gray family.

Buck had petered out into silence. 'Not a good idea, I guess,' he said.

'Don't worry,' someone said. 'You *do* win the *Grolier Encyclopedia*, and our exciting home game.'

Tony waited for a few chuckles to ripple across the room and die away before going on. 'I want everyone who works out of this barracks to know what went on tonight, so they'll know what to expect if it happens again. Spread the word. Spread the code for the Buick, as well — D as in dog. Just D. Right? And I'll let you all know what happens next, starting with the Geiger counter. That test will be made before second shift tomorrow, I guarantee it. We're not going to tell our wives or sisters or brothers or best friends off the force what we have here, gentlemen, but we are going to keep each other *exquisitely* well informed. That's my promise to you. We're going

145

to do it the old-fashioned way, by verbal report. There has been no paperwork directly concerning the vehicle out there — if it *is* a vehicle — and that's how it's going to stay. All understood?'

There was another murmur of agreement.

'I won't tolerate a blabbermouth in Troop D, gentlemen; no gossip and no pillow-talk. Is *that* understood?'

It seemed it was.

'Look at this one,' Phil said suddenly, holding up one of the Polaroids. 'The trunk's open.'

Curt nodded. 'Closed again now, though. It opened during one of the flashes, and I think it closed during the next one.'

Sandy thought of Ennis and had an image, very brief but very clear, of the Buick's trunk-lid opening and closing like a hungry mouth. See the living crocodile, take a good look, but for God's sake don't stick your fingers there.

Curt went on, 'I also believe the windshield wipers ran briefly, although my eyes were too dazzled by then for me to be sure, and none of the pictures show it.'

'Why?' Phil asked. 'Why would stuff like that happen?'

'Electrical surge,' Sandy guessed. 'The same thing that screwed up the radio in dispatch.'

'Maybe the wipers, but the trunk of a car doesn't run on electricity. When you want to open the trunk, you just push the button and lift the lid.'

Sandy had no answer for that.

'The temperature in the shed has gone down

146

another couple of degrees,' Curt said. 'That'll bear watching.'

The meeting ended, and Sandy went back out on patrol. Every now and then, when radioing back to Base, he'd ask Matt Babicki if D was 5-by. The response was always *Roger, D is 5-by-5.* In later years, it would become a standard call-and-response in the Short Hills area surrounding Statler, Pogus City, and Patchin. A few other barracks eventually picked it up, even a couple over the Ohio state line. They took it to mean *Is everything cool back home?* This amused the men working out of Troop D, because that was what *Is D still 5-by?* did mean.

★ ★ ★

By the next morning, everyone in Troop D was indeed in the picture, but it was business as usual. Curt and Tony went to Pittsburgh to get a Geiger counter. Sandy was off-shift but stopped by two or three times to check on the Buick just the same. It was quiet in there, the car simply sitting on the concrete and looking like an art exhibit, but the needle on the big red thermometer hung from the beam continued to ease down. That struck everyone as extremely eerie, silent confirmation that something was going on in there. Something beyond the ability of mere State Troopers to understand, let alone control.

No one actually went inside the shed until Curt and Tony got back in Curt's Bel Air

147

— SC's orders. Huddie Royer was looking through the shed windows at the Buick when the two of them turned up. He strolled over as Curt opened the carton sitting on the hood of his car and took the Geiger counter out. 'Where's your *Andromeda Strain* suits?' Huddie asked.

Curt looked at him, not smiling. 'That's a riot,' he said.

Curt and the Sergeant spent an hour in there, running the Geiger counter all over the Buick's hull, cruising the pickup over the engine, taking it into the cabin, checking the seats and dashboard and weird oversized wheel. Curt went underneath on a crawly gator, and the Sergeant checked the trunk, being especially careful about that; they propped the lid up with one of the rakes on the wall. The counter's needle hardly stirred during any of this. The only time the steady cluck-cluck-cluck coming from its little speaker intensified was when Tony held the pickup close to the radium dial of his wristwatch, wanting to make sure the gadget was working. It was, but the Roadmaster had nothing to tell it.

They broke only once, to go inside and get sweaters. It was a hot day outside, but in Shed B the needle of the thermometer had settled just a hair below 48. Sandy didn't like it, and when the two of them came out, he suggested that they roll up the doors and let in some of the day's heat. Mister Dillon was snoozing in the kitchenette, Sandy said; they could close him in there.

'No,' Tony said, and Sandy could see that Curtis went along with that call.

148

'Why not?'

'I don't know. Just a feeling.'

By three that afternoon, while Sandy was dutifully printing his name in the duty-book under **2nd Shift/3P-11P** and getting ready to head out on patrol, the temperature in Shed B had dropped to 47. That was forty degrees colder than the summer day on the other side of those thin wooden walls.

It must have been around six o'clock, while Sandy was parked around the side of Jimmy's Diner on the old Statler Pike, drinking coffee and watching for speeders, that the Roadmaster gave birth for the first time.

★   ★   ★

Arky Arkanian was the first person to see the thing that came out of the Buick, although he didn't know what he was seeing. Things were quiet at the Troop D barracks. Not serene, exactly, but quiet. This was due in large measure to Curt and Tony's report of zero radiation emanating from Shed B. Arky had come in from his trailer in Dreamland Park on top of the Bluffs, wanting his own little off-duty peek at the impounded car. He had it to himself; Shed B was for the time being entirely deserted. Forty yards away, the barracks was midshift quiet, which was about as quiet as it ever got. Matt Babicki had clocked out for the night and one of the younger cops was running dispatch. The Sarge had gone home at five o'clock. Curt, who had given his wife some cock-and-bull story about his call-out the night before, was presumably back in his flip-flop sandals and finishing his lawn like a good boy.

At five minutes past seven, the Troop D custodian (by then very pale, very thoughtful, and very scared) went past the kid in the dispatch cubby and into the kitchenette, to see who he could find. He wanted someone who wasn't a rookie, someone who knew the score. He found Huddie Royer, just putting the finishing touches on a big pot of Kraft Macaroni and Cheese.

NOW:

Arky

'Well?' the kid ask, and there was so much of his Daddy in him just then — the way he sat there on the bench, the way his eyes stared into yours, the way his eyebrows quirk, most of all the headlong impatience. That impatience was his Dad all over. '*Well?*'

'This isn't my part of the story,' Sandy tell him. 'I wasn't there. These other two were, though.'

So then, sure, the kid switch over from Sandy to me and Huddie.

'You do it, Hud,' I say. 'You're used to makin reports.'

'Shit on that,' he tell me right back, 'you were there first. You saw it first. You start.'

'Aw — '

'Well *one* of you start!' the boy tell us, and wham! He hit his forehead with the butt of his palm, right between the eyes. I had to laugh at that.

'Go on, Arky,' the Sarge tell me.

'Ah, nuts,' I say. 'I ain't never told it, you know, like a story. Don't know how it'll come out.'

'Give it your best shot,' Sarge say, and so I do. It was pretty hard going at first — seemed I could feel the kid's eyes boring into me like nails

151

and I kept thinking, *He ain't gonna believe this, who would?* But it got easier after a little bit. If you talk about something that happened long ago, you find it open up to you all over again. It open up like a flower. That can be a good thing or a bad thing, I guess. Sitting there that night, talking to Curtis Wilcox's boy, it felt like both.

Huddie join in after awhile and started to help. He remembered all sorts of things, even the part about how it was Joan Baez on the radio. 'Redemption's in the details,' old Sarge used to say (usually when someone left something out of a report that should have been in). And all through it the kid sittin there on the bench, looking at us, his eyes gettin bigger and bigger as the evening darkened and give up its smells like it does in the summer and the bats flew overhead and thunder rumbled all the way in the south. It made me sad to see how much he looked like his father. I don't know why.

He only broke in once. Turned to Sandy, wanting to know if we still had the —

'Yes,' Sandy tell him right off. 'Oh yes. We certainly do. Plus tons of pictures. Polaroids, mostly. If there's one thing cops know about, kiddo, it's preserving the chain of evidence. Now be quiet. You wanted to know; let the man tell you.'

I know by that he mean me, so I started talkin again.

THEN

Arky had an old Ford pickup in those days, a standard threeshifter (*But I got four if you count d'reverse*, he used to joke) with a squeaky clutch. He parked it where he would still be parking twenty-three years later, although by then he would have traded up to a Dodge Ram with the automatic transmission *and* the four-wheel drive.

In 1979 there was an ancient Statler County schoolbus at the far end of the parking lot, a rust-rotten yellow barge that had been there since the Korean War at least, sinking deeper and deeper into the weeds and the dirt with each passing year. Why no one ever took it away was just another of life's mysteries. Arky nestled his truck in beside it, then crossed to Shed B and looked through one of the windows in the roll-up door, cupping his hands to block the light of the sun, which was on the wester.

There was a light on overhead and the Buick sat beneath it, looking to Arky like a display model, the kind of unit that shows up so pretty under the lights that anyone in his right mind would want to sign on the line and drive that honey home. Everything looked 5-by except for the trunk-lid. It was up again.

I ought to report that to the duty officer, Arky thought. He wasn't a cop, just a custodian, but in his case Trooper gray rubbed off. He stepped back from the window, then happened to glance

153

up at the thermometer Curt had mounted from one of the overhead beams. The temperature in the shed had gone up again, and by quite a lot. Sixty-one degrees in there. It occurred to Arky that the Buick was like some sort of weird refrigerator coil that had now turned itself off (or perhaps burnt itself out during the fireworks show).

The sudden rise in temperature was something else no one knew, and Arky was excited. He started to swing away from the door, meaning to hurry directly across to the barracks. That was when he saw the thing in the corner of the shed.

Nothing but an old bunch of rags, he thought, but something else suggested . . . well, something else. He went back to the glass, once more cupping his hands to the sides of his face. And no, by God, that thing in the corner was *not* just a bunch of rags.

Arky felt a flu-like weakness in the joints of his knees and the muscles of his thighs. The feeling spread upward into his stomach, dropping it, and then to his heart, speeding it up. There was an alarming moment when he was almost certain he was going to drop to the ground in a faint.

Hey, y'big dumb Swede — why don't you try breathing again? See if that helps any.

Arky took two big dry gasps of air, not caring much for the sound of them. His old man had sounded like that when he was having his heart attack, lying on the sofa and waiting for the ambulance to come.

He stepped away from the roll-up door,

154

patting the center of his chest with the side of a closed fist. 'Come on, honey. Take up d'slack, now.'

The sun, going down in a cauldron of blood, glared in his eyes. His stomach had continued to drop, making him feel on the verge of vomiting. The barracks all at once looked two, maybe even three miles away. He set off in that direction, reminding himself to breathe and concentrating on taking big, even steps. Part of him wanted to break into a run, and part of him understood that if he tried doing that, he really *might* faint.

'Guys'd never let you hear the end of *dat*, and you know it.'

But it wasn't really teasing he was concerned about. Mostly he didn't want to go in looking all wild-eyed and pushing the panic-button like any John Q. in off the road with a tale to tell.

And by the time he got inside, Arky actually did feel a little better. Still scared, but no longer like he was going to puke or just go bolting away from Shed B any old whichway. By then he'd also had an idea which had eased his mind a bit. Maybe it was just a trick. A prank. Troopers were always pulling stuff on him, and hadn't he told Orville Garrett he might come back that evening for a little lookie-see at that old Buick? He had. And maybe Orv had decided to give him the business. Bunch of comedians he worked with, someone was *always* giving him the business.

The thought served to calm him, but in his heart of hearts, Arky didn't believe it. Orv Garrett was a practical joker, all right, liked to have his fun just like the next guy, but he

155

wouldn't make that thing in the shed part of a gag. None of them would. Not with Sergeant Schoondist so hopped up about it.

Ah, but the Sarge wasn't there. His door was shut and the frosted glass panel was dark. The light was on in the kitchenette, though, and music was coming out through the door: Joan Baez, singing about the night they drove old Dixie down. Arky went in and there was Huddie Royer, just dropping a monster chunk of oleo into a pot of noodles. *Your heart ain't gonna thank you for* dat *shit*, Arky thought. Huddie's radio — a little one on a strap that he took everyplace — was sitting on the counter next to the toaster.

'Hey, Arky!' he said. 'What're you doing here? As if I didn't know.'

'Is Orv around?' Arky asked.

'Nope. He's got three days off, starting tomorrow. Lucky sucker went fishing. You want a bowl of this?' Huddie held the pot out, took a really good look at him, and realized he was looking at a man who was scared just about to death. 'Arky? What the hell's wrong with you?'

Arky sat down heavily in one of the kitchen chairs, hands dangling between his thighs. He looked up at Huddie and opened his mouth, but at first nothing came out.

'What is it?' Huddie slung the pot of macaroni on to the counter without a second look. 'The Buick?'

'Youda d-o tonight, Hud?'

'Yeah. Until eleven.'

'Who else here?'

156

'Couple of guys upstairs. Maybe. If you're thinking about the brass, you can stop. I'm the closest you're going to get tonight. So spill it.'

'You come out back,' Arky told him. 'Take a look for yourself. And bring some binoculars.'

★ ★ ★

Huddie snagged a pair of binocs from the supply room, but they turned out to be no help. The thing in the corner of Shed B was actually too close — in the glasses it was just a blur. After two or three minutes of fiddling with the focus-knob, Huddie gave up. 'I'm going in there.'

Arky gripped his wrist. 'Cheesus, no! Call the Sarge! Let him decide!'

Huddie, who could be stubborn, shook his head. 'Sarge is sleeping. His wife called and said so. You know what it means when she does that — no one hadn't ought to wake him up unless it's World War III.'

'What if dat t'ing in dere *is* World War III?'

'I'm not worried,' Huddie said. Which was, judging from his face, the lie of the decade, if not the century. He looked in again, hands cupped to the sides of his face, the useless binoculars standing on the pavement beside his left foot. 'It's dead.'

'Maybe,' Arky said. 'And maybe it's just playin possum.'

Huddie looked around at him. 'You don't mean that.' A pause. 'Do you?'

'I dunno what I mean and what I don't mean. I dunno if dat t'ing's over for good or just restin

157

up. Neither do you. What if it *wants* someone t'go in dere? You t'ought about dat? What if it's waitin for you?'

Huddie thought it over, then said: 'I guess in that case, it'll get what it wants.'

He stepped back from the door, looking every bit as scared as Arky had looked when he came into the kitchen, but also looking set. Meaning it. Just a stubborn old Dutchman.

'Arky, listen to me.'

'Yeah.'

'Carl Brundage is upstairs in the common room. Also Mark Rushing — I think, anyway. Don't bother Loving in dispatch, I don't trust him. Too wet behind the ears. But you go on and tell the other two what's up. And get that look off your face. This is probably nothing, but a little backup wouldn't hurt.'

'Just in case it ain't nothin.'

'Right.'

'Cause it might be *sumpin*.'

Huddie nodded.

'You sure?'

'Uh-huh.'

'Okay.'

Huddie walked along the front of the roll-up door, turned the corner, and stood in front of the smaller door on the side. He took a deep breath, held it in for a five-count, let it out. Then he unsnapped the strap over the butt of his pistol — a .357 Ruger, back in those days.

'Huddie?'

Huddie jumped. If his finger had been on the trigger instead of outside the guard, he might

158

have blown off his own foot. He spun around and saw Arky standing there at the corner of the shed, his big dark eyes swimming in his pinched face.

'Lord Jesus Christ!' Huddie cried. 'Why the fuck're you creeping after me?'

'I wasn't creepin, Troop — just walkin like normal.'

'Go inside! Get Carl and Mark, like I told you.'

Arky shook his head. Scared or not, he had decided he wanted to be a part of what was going down. Huddie supposed he could understand. Trooper gray *did* have a way of rubbing off.

'All right, ya dumb Swede. Let's go.'

★ ★ ★

Huddie opened the door and stepped into the shed, which was still cooler than the outside . . . although just *how* cool it might have been was impossible for either man to tell, because they were both sweating like pigs. Huddie was holding his gun up beside his right cheekbone. Arky grabbed a rake from the pegs close by the door. It clanged against a shovel and both of them jumped. To Arky, the look of their shadows on the wall was even worse than the sound: they seemed to *leap* from place to place, like the shadows of nimble goblins.

'Huddie — ' he began.

'Shhh!'

'If it's dead, why you go shhh?'

159

'Don't be a smartass!' Huddie whispered back.

He started across the cement floor toward the Buick. Arky followed with the rake-handle gripped tight in his sweaty hands, his heart pounding. His mouth tasted dry and somehow burnt. He had never been so scared in his life, and the fact that he didn't know exactly what he was scared *of* only made it worse.

Huddie got to the rear of the Buick and peeped into the open trunk. His back was so broad Arky couldn't see around it. 'What's in there, Hud?'

'Nothing. It's clean.'

Huddie reached for the trunk-lid, hesitated, then shrugged and slammed it down. They both jumped at the sound and looked at the thing in the corner. It didn't stir. Huddie started toward it, gun once more held up by the side of his head. The sound of his feet shuffling on the concrete was very loud.

The thing was indeed dead, the two men became more and more sure of it as they approached, but that didn't make things better, because neither of them had ever seen anything like it. Not in the woods of western Pennsylvania, not in a zoo, not in a wildlife magazine. It was just *different*. So goddam *different*. Huddie found himself thinking of horror movies he'd seen, but the thing huddled up in the angle where the shed walls met wasn't really like something from those, either.

Goddam different was what he kept coming back to. What they both kept coming back to.

Everything about it screamed that it wasn't from here, *here* meaning not just the Short Hills but all of Planet Earth. Maybe the entire universe, at least as C-students in science such as themselves understood that concept. It was as if some warning circuit buried deep in their heads had suddenly awakened and begun to wail.

Arky was thinking of spiders. Not because the thing in the corner *looked* like a spider, but because . . . well . . . spiders were different. All those legs — and you had no idea what they might be thinking, or how they could even exist. This thing was like that, only worse. It made him sick just to look at it, to try to make sense of what his eyes said they were seeing. His skin had gone clammy, his heart was missing beats, and his guts seemed to have gained weight. He wanted to run. To just turn tail and stampede out of there.

'Christ,' Huddie said in a little moan of a voice. 'Ohhhh, *Christ.*' It was as if he were pleading for it to go away. His gun sagged downward and outward until the barrel was pointed at the floor. It was only three pounds, but his arm could no longer support even that paltry weight. The muscles of his face also sagged, pulling his eyes wide and dropping his jaw down until his mouth opened. Arky never forgot the way Huddie's teeth gleamed in the shadows. At the same time he began to shiver all over, and Arky became aware he was shivering, too.

★ ★ ★

161

The thing in the corner was the size of a very large bat, like the ones that roosted in Miracle Caves over in Lassburg or the so-called Wonder Cavern (guided tours three dollars a head, special family rates available) in Pogus City. Its wings hid most of its body. They weren't folded but lay in messy overlapping crumples, as if it had *tried* to fold them — and failed — before it died. The wings were either black or a very dark mottled green. What they could see of the creature's back was a lighter green. The stomach area was a cheesy whitish shade, like the gut of a rotted stump or the throat of a decaying swamp-lily. The triangular head was cocked to one side. A bony thing that might have been a nose or a beak jutted from the eyeless face. Below it, the creature's mouth hung open. A yellowish rope of tissue dangled from it, as if the thing had been regurgitating its last meal as it died. Huddie took one look and knew he wouldn't be eating any more macaroni and cheese for awhile.

Beneath the corpse, spread around its hindquarters, was a thin puddle of congealing black goo. The idea that any such substance could serve as blood made Huddie feel like crying out. He thought: *I won't touch it. I'd kill my own mother before I'd touch that thing.*

He was still thinking that when a long wooden rod slid into his peripheral vision. He gave a little shriek and flinched back. 'Arky, don't!' he yelled, but it was too late.

Later on, Arky was unable to say just why he had prodded the thing in the corner — it was

162

simply some strong urge to which he had given in before he was completely aware of what he was doing.

When the end of the rake-handle touched the place where the wings were crumpled across each other, there was a sound like rustling paper and a bad smell, like old stewed cabbage. The two of them barely noticed. The top of the thing's face seemed to peel back, revealing a dead and glassy eye that looked as big as a factory ball bearing.

Arky backed away, dropping the rake with a clatter and putting both hands over his mouth. Above the spread fingers, his eyes had begun to ooze terrified tears. Huddie simply stood where he was, locked in place.

'It was an eyelid,' he said in a low, hoarse voice. 'Just an eyelid, that's all. You joggled it with the rake, you goddam fool. You joggled it and it rolled back.'

'Christ, Huddie!'

'It's dead.'

'Christ, Jesus God — '

'It's *dead*, okay?'

'Ho . . . Ho-kay,' Arky said in that crazy Swedish accent of his. It was thicker than it had ever been. 'Less get oudda here.'

'You're pretty smart for a janitor.'

The two of them headed back for the door — slowly, backing up, not wanting to lose sight of the thing. Also because both of them knew they would lose control and bolt if they actually *saw* the door. The safety of the door. The promise of a sane world beyond the door.

Getting there seemed to take forever.

Arky backed out first and began taking huge gasps of the fresh evening air. Huddie came out behind him and slammed the door. Then for a moment the two of them just looked at each other. Arky had gone past white and directly to yellow. To Huddie he looked like a cheese sandwich without the bread.

'What-choo laughin about?' Arky asked him. 'What's so funny?'

'Nothing,' Huddie said. 'I'm just trying not to be hysterical.'

'You gonna call Sergeant Schoondist now?'

Huddie nodded. He kept thinking about how the whole top half of the thing's head had seemed to peel back when Arky prodded it. He had an idea he'd be revisiting that moment in his dreams later on, and that turned out to be absolutely correct.

'What about Curtis?'

Huddie thought about it and shook his head. Curt had a young wife. Young wives liked to have their husbands home, and when they didn't get what they wanted for at least a few nights in a row, they were apt to get hurt feelings and ask questions. It was natural. As it was natural for young husbands to sometimes answer their questions, even when they knew they weren't supposed to.

'Just the Sarge, then?'

'No,' Huddie said. 'Let's get Sandy Dearborn in on this, too. Sandy's got a good head.'

★   ★   ★

164

Sandy was still in the parking lot at Jimmy's Diner with his radar gun in his lap when his radio spoke up. 'Unit 14, Unit 14.'

'14.' As always, Sandy had glanced at his watch when he heard his unit number. It was twenty past seven.

'Ah, could you return to base, 14? We have a D-code, say again a D-code, copy?'

'3?' Sandy asked. In most American police forces, 3 means emergency.

'No, negative, but we sure could use some help.'

'Roger.'

He got back about ten minutes before the Sarge arrived in his personal, which happened to be an International Harvester pickup even older than Arky's Ford. By then the word had already started to spread and Sandy saw a regular Trooper convention in front of Shed B — lots of guys at the windows, all of them peering in. Brundage and Rushing, Cole and Devoe, Huddie Royer. Arky Arkanian was pacing around in little circles behind them with his hands stuffed forearm-deep in his pants pockets and lines climbing his forehead like the rungs of a ladder. He wasn't waiting for a window, though. Arky had seen all he wanted to, at least for one night.

Huddie filled Sandy in on what had happened and then Sandy had his own good long look at the thing in the corner. He also tried to guess what the Sergeant might want when he arrived, and put the items in a cardboard box near the side door.

Tony pulled in, parked askew behind the old schoolbus, and came jogging across to Shed B. He elbowed Carl Brundage unceremoniously away from the window that was closest to the dead creature and stared at it while Huddie made his report. When Huddie was done, Tony called Arky over and listened to Arky's version of the story.

Sandy thought that Tony's methods of handling the Roadmaster were put to the test that evening and proved sound. All through his debriefing of Huddie and Arky, Troop D personnel were showing up. Most of the men were off-duty. Those few in uniform had been close enough to come in for a look-see when they heard Huddie give the code for the Buick. Yet there was no loud cross-talk, no jostling for position, no men getting in the way of Tony's investigation or gumming things up with a lot of stupid questions. Above all, there were no flaring tempers and no panic. If reporters had been there and experienced the atavistic power of that thing — a thing which remained awful and somehow threatening even though it was obviously dead — Sandy dreaded to think about what the consequences might have been. When he mentioned that to Schoondist the next day, the Sarge had laughed. 'The Cardiff Giant in hell,' he said. '*That* would have been your consequence, Sandy.'

Both of them, the Sarge who was and the Sarge who would be, knew what the press called such information-management, at least when the managers were cops: fascism. That was a little

166

heavy, no doubt, but neither of them actually questioned the fact that all sorts of abuses lay a turn or two down that road. ('You want to see cops out of control, look at LA,' Tony said once. 'For every three good ones, you've got two Hitler Youth dingbats on motorcycles.') The business of the Buick was a bona fide Special Case, however. Neither of them questioned that, either.

Huddie wanted to know if he'd been right not to call Curtis. He was worried Curt would feel left out, passed over. If the Sarge wanted, Huddie said, he could go in the barracks that very second and make a telephone call. Happy to do it.

'Curtis is fine right where he is,' Tony said, 'and when it's explained to him why he wasn't called, he'll understand. As for the rest of you fellows . . . '

Tony stepped away from the roll-up door. His posture was easy and relaxed, but his face was very pale. The sight of that thing in the corner had affected him, too, even through a pane of glass. Sandy felt the same way himself. But he could also sense Sergeant Schoondist's excitement, the balls-to-the-wall curiosity he shared with Curt. The throbbing undertone that said *Holy shit, do you fuckin BELIEVE it!* Sandy heard it and recognized it for what it was, although he felt none of it himself, not a single iota. He didn't think any of the others did, either. Certainly Huddie's curiosity — and Arky's — had faded quickly enough. 'Gone the way of the blue suede shoe,' as Curtis might have said.

167

'You men on duty listen up to me, now,' Tony said. He was wearing his slanted little grin, but to Sandy it looked a bit forced that night. 'There's fires in Statler, floods in Leesburg, and a rash of Piggly Wiggly robberies down in Pogus County; we suspect the Amish.'

There was some laughter at this.

'So what are you waiting for?'

There was a general exodus of Troopers on duty followed by the sound of Chevrolet V-8 engines starting up. The off-duty fellows hung around for awhile, but nobody had to tell them to move along, move along, come on, boys, show's over. Sandy asked the Sarge if he should also saddle up and ride.

'No, Trooper,' he said. 'You're with me.' And he started briskly toward the walk-in door, pausing only long enough to examine the items Sandy had put into the carton: one of the evidence-documenting Polaroids, extra film, a yardstick, an evidence-collection kit. Sandy had also grabbed a couple of green plastic garbage bags from the kitchenette.

'Good job, Sandy.'

'Thanks, sir.'

'Ready to go in?'

'Yes, sir.'

'Scared?'

'Yes, sir.'

'Scared as me, or not quite that scared?'

'I don't know.'

'Me, either. But I'm scared, all right. If I faint, you catch me.'

'Just fall in my direction, sir.'

He laughed. 'Come on. Step into my parlor,' said the spider to the fly.'

★   ★   ★

Scared or not, the two of them made a pretty thorough investigation. They collaborated on a diagram of the shed's interior, and when Curt later complimented Sandy on it, Sandy nodded and agreed that it had been a good one. Good enough to take into court, actually. Still, a lot of the lines on it were wavery. Their hands began to shake almost from the moment they entered the shed, and didn't stop until they were back out again.

They opened the trunk because it had been open when Arky first looked in, and although it was as empty as ever, they took Polaroids of it. They likewise photo'd the thermometer (which by then had gotten all the way up to seventy degrees), mostly because Tony thought Curt would want them to. And they took pictures of the corpse in the corner, took them from every angle they could think of. Every Polaroid showed that unspeakable single eye. It was shiny, like fresh tar. Seeing himself reflected in it made Sandy Dearborn feel like screaming. And every two or three seconds, one of them would look back over his shoulder at the Buick Roadmaster.

When they were done with the photos, some of which they took with the yardstick lying beside the corpse, Tony shook out one of the garbage bags. 'Get a shovel,' he said.

169

'Don't you want to leave it where it is until Curt — '

'Probationary Trooper Wilcox can look at it down in the supply closet,' Tony said. His voice was oddly tight — strangled, almost — and Sandy realized he was working very hard not to be sick. Sandy's own stomach took a queasy little lurch, perhaps in sympathy. 'He can look at it there to his heart's content. For once we don't have to worry about breaking the chain of evidence, because no district attorney is ever going to be involved. Meantime, we're scooping this shit *up*.' He wasn't shouting, but a raw little edge had come into his voice.

Sandy took a shovel from where it hung on the wall and slid the blade beneath the dead creature. The wings made a papery and somehow terrible crackling sound. Then one of them fell back, revealing a black and hairless side. For the second time since the two of them had stepped in, Sandy felt like screaming. He could not have told why, exactly, but there was something deep down in his head begging not to be shown any more.

And all the time they were smelling it. That sour, cabbagey reek.

Sandy observed sweat standing out all over Tony Schoondist's forehead in fine little dots. Some of these had broken and run down his cheeks, leaving tracks like tears.

'Go on,' he said, holding the bag open. 'Go on, now, Sandy. Drop it in there before I lose my groceries.'

Sandy tilted it into the bag and felt a little bit

170

better when the weight slid off the shovel. After Tony had gotten a sack of the liquid-absorbing red sawdust they kept for oil-spills and sprinkled it over the gooey stain in the corner, both of them felt better. Tony twirled the top of the garbage bag with the creature inside, then knotted it. Once that was done, the two of them started backing toward the door.

Tony stopped just before they reached it. 'Photo that,' he said, pointing to a place high on the roll-up door behind the Buick — the door through which Johnny Parker had towed the car in the first place. To Tony Schoondist and Sandy Dearborn, that already seemed like a long time ago. 'And that, and there, and over there.'

At first Sandy didn't see what the Sarge was pointing at. He looked away, blinked his eyes once or twice, then looked back. And there it was, three or four dark green smudges that made Sandy think of the dust that rubs off a moth's wings. As kids they had solemnly assured each other that mothdust was deadly poison, it would blind you if you got some on your fingers and then rubbed your eyes.

'You see what happened, don't you?' Tony asked as Sandy raised the Polaroid and sighted in on the first mark. The camera seemed very heavy and his hands were still shivering, but he got it done.

'No, Sarge, I, ah . . . don't guess I do.'

'Whatever that thing is — bird, bat, some kind of robot drone — it flew out of the trunk when the lid came open. It hit the back door, that's the first smudge, and then it started bouncing off the

171

walls. Ever seen a bird that gets caught in a shed or a barn?'

Sandy nodded.

'Like that.' Tony wiped sweat off his forehead and looked at Sandy. It was a look the younger man never forgot. He had never seen the Sarge's eyes so naked. It was, he thought, the look you sometimes saw on the faces of small children when you came to break up a domestic disturbance.

'Man,' Tony said heavily. '*Fuck*.'

Sandy nodded.

Tony looked down at the bag. 'You think it looks like a bat?'

'Yeah,' Sandy said, then, 'No.' After another pause he added, 'Bullshit.'

Tony barked a laugh that sounded somehow haggard. 'That's very definitive. If you were on the witness stand, no defense attorney could peel *that* back.'

'I don't know, Tony.' What Sandy *did* know was that he wanted to stop shooting the shit and get back out into the open air. 'What do you think?'

'Well, if I drew it, it'd look like a bat,' Tony said. 'The Polaroids we took also make it look like a bat. But . . . I don't know exactly how to say it, but . . . '

'It doesn't *feel* like a bat,' Sandy said.

Tony smiled bleakly and pointed a finger at Sandy like a gun. 'Very Zen, Grasshoppah. But those marks on the wall suggest it at least *acted* like a bat, or a trapped bird. Flew around in here until it dropped dead in the corner. Shit, for all we know, it died of fright.'

Sandy recalled the glaring dead eye, a thing almost too alien to look at, and thought that for the first time in his life he could really understand the concept Sergeant Schoondist had articulated. Die of fright? Yes, it could be done. It really could. Then, because the Sarge seemed to be waiting for something, he said: 'Or maybe it hit the wall so hard it broke its neck.' Another idea came to him. 'Or — listen, Tony — maybe the *air* killed it.'

'Say what?'

'Maybe — '

But Tony's eyes had lit up and he was nodding. 'Sure,' he said. 'Maybe the air on the other side of the Buick's trunk is different air. Maybe it'd taste like poison gas to us . . . rupture our lungs . . . '

For Sandy, that was enough. 'I have to get out of here, Tony, or *I'm* gonna be the one who throws up.' But what he really felt in danger of was choking, not vomiting. All at once the normally broad avenue of his windpipe was down to a pinhole.

★ ★ ★

Once they were back outside (it was nearly dark by then and an incredibly sweet summer breeze had sprung up), Sandy felt better. He had an idea Tony did, too; certainly some of the color had come back into the Sarge's cheeks. Huddie and a few other Troopers came over to the two of them as Tony shut the walk-in side door, but nobody said anything. An outsider with no context upon which to draw might have looked at those faces and thought that the President had died or war had been declared.

'Sandy?' Tony asked. 'Any better now?'

'Yeah.' He nodded at the garbage bag, hanging like a dead pendulum with its strange weight at the bottom. 'You really think it might have been our air that killed it?'

'It's possible. Or maybe just the shock of finding itself in our world. I don't think I could live for long in the world this thing came from, tell you that much. Even if I *could* breathe the — ' Tony stopped, because all at once Sandy looked bad again. Terrible, in fact. 'Sandy, what is it? What's wrong?'

Sandy wasn't sure he wanted to tell his SC what was wrong, wasn't even sure he could. What he'd thought of was Ennis Rafferty. The idea of the missing Trooper added to what they had just discovered in Shed B suggested a conclusion that Sandy didn't want to consider. Once it had come into his mind, though, it was hard to get it back out. If the Buick was a conduit to some other world, and the bat-thing had gone through it in one direction, then Ennis Rafferty had almost certainly gone through in the other.

'Sandy, talk to me.'

'Nothing wrong, boss,' Sandy replied, then had to bend over and grip his shins in both hands. It was a good way to stop yourself from fainting, always assuming you had enough time to use it. The others stood around watching him,

174

still saying nothing, still wearing those long faces that said the King is dead, long live the King.

At last the world steadied again, and Sandy straightened up. 'I'm okay,' he said. 'Really.'

Tony considered his face, then nodded. He lifted the green bag slightly. 'This is going into the storage closet off the supply room, the little one where Andy Colucci keeps his stroke-books.'

A few nervous titters greeted this.

'That room is going to be off-limits except for myself, Curtis Wilcox, and Sandy Dearborn. BPO, people, got it?'

By permission only. They nodded.

'Sandy, Curtis, and me — this is now our investigation, so designated.' He stood straight in the gathering gloom, almost at attention, holding the garbage bag in one hand and the Polaroids in the other. 'This stuff is evidence. Of what I have no current idea. If any of *you* come up with any ideas, bring them to me. If they seem like crazy ideas to you, bring them to me even quicker. It's a crazy situation. But, crazy or not, we *will* roll this case. Roll it as we would any other. Questions?'

There were no questions. Or, if you wanted to look at it the other way, Sandy reflected, there was nothing *but* questions.

'We ought to have a man on that shed as much as we can,' Tony said.

'Guard duty, Sarge?' Steve Devoe asked.

'Let's call it surveillance,' Tony said. 'Come on, Sandy, stick with me until I get this thing stowed. I don't want to take it downstairs by myself, and that's the God's truth.'

As they started across the parking lot, Sandy heard Arky Arkanian saying that Curt was gonna get mad he dint get called, wait and see, dat boy was gonna be madder'n a wet hen.

★ ★ ★

But Curtis was too excited to be mad, too busy trying to prioritize the things he wanted to do, too full of questions. He asked only one of those before pelting down to look at the corpse of the creature they'd found in Shed B: where had Mister Dillon been last evening? With Orville, he was told. Orville Garrett often took Mister D when he had a few days off.

Sandy Dearborn was the one who brought Curtis up to speed (with occasional help from Arky). Curt listened silently, brows lifting when Arky described how the whole top of the thing's head had appeared to roll back, disclosing the eye. They lifted again when Sandy told him about the smudges on the door and the walls, and how they had reminded him of mothdust. He asked his question about Mister D, got his answer, then grabbed a pair of surgical gloves out of an evidence kit and headed downstairs at what was nearly a run. Sandy went with him. That much seemed to be his duty, somehow, since Tony had appointed him a co-investigator, but he stayed in the supply room while Curt went into the closet where Tony had left the garbage bag. Sandy heard it rustling as Curt undid the knot in the top; his skin prickled and went cold at the sound.

Rustle, rustle, rustle. Pause. Another rustle. Then, very low: 'Christ almighty.'

A moment later Curt came running out with his hand over his mouth. There was a toilet halfway down the hall leading to the stairs. Trooper Wilcox made it just in time.

Sandy Dearborn sat at the cluttered worktable in the supply room, listening to him vomit and knowing that the vomiting probably meant nothing in the larger scheme of things. Curtis wasn't going to back off. The corpse of the bat-thing had revolted him as much as it had Arky or Huddie or any of them, but he'd come back to examine it more fully, revulsion or no revulsion. The Buick — and the things *of the Buick* — had become his passion. Even coming out of the storage closet with his throat working and his cheeks pale and his hand pressed to his mouth, Sandy had seen the helpless excitement in his eyes, dimmed only a little by his physical distress. Passion is the hardest taskmaster.

From down the hall came the sound of running water. It stopped, and then Curt came back into the supply room, blotting his mouth with a paper towel.

'Pretty awful, isn't it?' Sandy asked. 'Even dead.'

'Pretty awful,' he agreed, but he was heading back in there even as he spoke. 'I thought I understood, but it caught me by surprise.'

Sandy got up and went to the doorway. Curt was looking into the bag again but not *reaching* in. Not yet, at least. That was a relief. Sandy didn't want to be around when the kid touched

177

it, even wearing gloves. Didn't even want to *think* about him touching it.

'Was it a trade, do you think?' Curt asked.

'Huh?'

'A trade. Ennis for this thing.'

For a moment Sandy didn't reply. *Couldn't* reply. Not because the idea was horrible (although it was), but because the kid had gotten to it so fast.

'I don't know.'

Curt was rocking back and forth on the heels of his shoes and frowning down at the plastic garbage bag. 'I don't think so,' he said after awhile. 'When you make a swap, you usually do the whole deal at the same time. Right?'

'Usually, yeah.'

He closed the bag and (with obvious reluctance) reknotted the top. 'I'm going to dissect it,' he said.

'Curtis, no! *Christ!*'

'Yes.' He turned to Sandy, his face drawn and white, his eyes brilliant. '*Someone* has to, and I can't very well take it up to the Biology Department at Horlicks. Sarge says we keep this strictly in-house, and that's the right call, but who does that leave to do this? Just me. Unless I'm missing something.'

Sandy thought, *You wouldn't take it up to Horlicks even if Tony hadn't said a goddam word about keeping it in-house. You can bear to have us in on it, probably because nobody but Tony really wants anything to do with it, but share it with someone else? Someone who doesn't wear Pennsylvania gray and know when*

178

to shift the hat-strap from the back of the head to under the chin? Someone who might first get ahead of you and then take it away from you? I don't think so.

Curt stripped off the gloves. 'The problem is that I haven't cut anything up since Chauncey, my fetal pig in high school biology. That was nine years ago and I got a C in the course. I don't want to fuck this up, Sandy.'

Then don't touch it in the first place.

Sandy thought it but didn't say it. There would have been no point in saying it.

'Oh well.' The kid talking to himself now. Nobody but himself. 'I'll bone up. Get ready. I've got time. No sense being impatient. Curiosity killed the cat, but satisfaction — '

'What if that's a lie?' Sandy asked. He was surprised at how tired of that little jingle-jangle he had grown. 'What if there's no satisfaction? What if you're never able to solve for x?'

Curt looked up at him, almost shocked. Then he grinned. 'What do you think Ennis would say? If we could ask him, that is?'

Sandy found the question both patronizing and insensitive. He opened his mouth to say so — to say *something*, anyway — and then didn't. Curtis Wilcox didn't mean any harm; he was just flying high on adrenaline and possibility, as hyped as any junkie. And he really *was* a kid. Even Sandy recognized that, although they were much of an age.

'Ennis would tell you to be careful,' Sandy said. 'I'm sure of that much.'

'I will,' Curt agreed, starting up the stairs. 'Oh

179

yeah, of course I will.' But those were just words, like the Doxology you rush through in order to get free of church on Sunday morning. Sandy knew it even if Probationary Trooper Wilcox did not.

★ ★ ★

In the weeks that followed, it became obvious to Tony Schoondist (not to mention the rest of the Troop D personnel) that there wasn't enough manpower to institute twenty-four-hour surveillance of the Buick in the shed out back. Nor did the weather cooperate; the second half of that August was rainy and unseasonably cold.

Visitors added another headache. Troop D didn't live in a vacuum on top of its hill, after all; the Motor Pool was next door, the County Attorney (plus his staff) was just down the road, there were lawyers, there were perps cooling their heels in the Bad Boy Corner, the occasional Boy Scout tour, the steady trickle of folks who wanted to lodge complaints (against their neighbors, against their spouses, against Amish buggy-drivers taking too much of the road, against the State Troopers themselves), wives bringing forgotten lunches or sometimes boxes of fudge, and sometimes just interested John Q.'s who wanted a look at what their tax dollars were buying. These latter were usually surprised and disappointed by the calmness of the barracks, the ho-hum sense of bureaucracy at work. It didn't feel like their favorite TV shows.

One day toward the end of that month,

Statler's member of the United States House of Representatives dropped by, along with ten or twelve of his closest media friends, to do a meet-and-greet and to make a statement about the Police Aid, Science, and Infrastructure bill then pending before the House, a bill this fellow just happened to be co-sponsoring. Like many US Representatives from rural districts, this fellow looked like a small-town barber who had had a lucky day at the dog-track and hoped for a blowjob before bedtime. Standing beside one of the cruisers (Sandy thought it was the one with the busted headrest), he told his media friends how important the police were, especially the fine men and women of the Pennsylvania State Police, most especially the fine men and women of Troop D (that was a bit of information shortfall, there being no female Troopers or PCOs in D at that time, but none of the Troopers offered a correction, at least not while the cameras were rolling). They were, the Representative said, a thin gray line dividing Mr and Mrs John Q Taxpayer from the evil of the Chaos Gang, and so on and so on, God bless America, may all your children grow up to play the violin. Captain Diment came down from Butler, presumably because someone felt his stripes would lend a little extra tone to the event, and he later told Tony Schoondist in a low growl: 'That toupee-wearing touchhole asked me to fix his wife's speeding ticket.'

And all the time the Representative was blathering and the entourage was touring and the reporters were reporting and the cameras were rolling, the Buick Roadmaster was sitting just fifty yards away, blue as deep dusk on its fat and luxy whitewalls. It sat under the big round thermometer Curt had mounted on one of the beams. It sat there with its zeroed odometer and dirt wouldn't stick to it. To the Troopers who knew about it, the damned thing felt like an itch between the shoulderblades, the one place you can't . . . quite . . . reach.

There was bad weather to contend with, there were all kinds of John Q's to contend with — many who came to praise the family but who weren't of the family — and there were also visiting police officers and Troopers from other barracks. These last were in some ways the most dangerous, because cops had sharp eyes and nosy minds. What might they have thought if they'd seen a Trooper in a rain-slicker (or a certain janitor with a Swedish accent) standing out there by Shed B like one of those tall-hat soldiers guarding the gate at Buckingham Palace? Occasionally walking over to the roll-up door and peering inside? Might a visiting policeman seeing this have been curious about what was in there? Does a bear shit in the woods?

Curt solved this as well as it could be solved. He sent Tony a memo that said it was a shame the way the raccoons kept getting into our garbage and scattering it around, and that Phil Candleton and Brian Cole had agreed to build a little hutch to store the garbage cans in. Curt thought that out behind Shed B would be a good place for it, if the SC agreed. SC Schoondist wrote OK across the top of the memo, and that one *did* get filed. What the memo neglected to mention was that the Troop hadn't had any real problems with coons since Arky bought a couple of plastic garbage cans from Sears, the kind with the snap-down tops.

The hutch was built, painted (PSP gray, of course), and ready for action three days after the memo landed in Tony's in-basket. Prefab and purely functional, it was just big enough for two garbage cans, three shelves, and one State Trooper sitting on a kitchen chair. It served the dual purpose of keeping the Trooper on watch (a) out of the weather and (b) out of sight. Every ten or fifteen minutes the man on duty would get up, leave the hutch, and look through one of the windows in Shed B's rear roll-up door. The hutch was stocked with soda, munchies, magazines, and a galvanized pail. The pail had a paper strip reading I COULD NOT HOLD IT ANY LONGER taped to the side. That was Jackie O'Hara's touch. The others called him The Irish Wonder Boy, and he never failed to make them laugh. He was making them laugh even three years later as he lay in his bedroom, dying of esophageal cancer, eyes glassy with morphine, telling stories about Padeen the bogtrotter in a hoarse whisper while his old mates visited and sometimes held his hand when the pain was especially bad.

Later on, there would be plenty of video cameras at Troop D — at all the PSP barracks — because by the nineties, all the cruisers were equipped with dashboard-mounted Panasonic

Eyewitness models. These were made specially for law enforcement organizations, and came without mikes. Video of road-stops was legal; because of existing wiretap laws, audio was not. But all of that was later. In the late summer of 1979, they had to make do with a videocam Huddie Royer had gotten for his birthday. They kept it on one of the shelves out in the hutch, stored in its box and wrapped in plastic to make sure it stayed dry. Another box contained extra batteries and a dozen blank tapes with the Cellophane stripped off so they'd be ready to go. There was also a slate with a number chalked on it: the current temperature inside the shed. If the person on duty noticed a change, he erased the last observation, wrote in the current one, and added a chalk arrow pointing either up or down. It was the closest thing to a written record Sergeant Schoondist would allow.

Tony seemed delighted with this jury-rig. Curt tried to emulate him, but sometimes his worry and frustration broke through. 'There won't be anyone on watch the next time something happens,' he said. 'You wait and see if I'm not right — it's always the way. Nobody'll volunteer for midnight to four some night, and whoever comes on next will look in and see the trunk-lid up and another dead bat on the floor. You wait and see.'

Curt tried persuading Tony to at least keep a surveillance sign-up sheet. There was no shortage of volunteers, he argued; what they were short on was organization and scheduling, things that would be easy to change. Tony remained adamant: no paper trail. When Curt volunteered to take over more of the sentry duty himself (many of the Troopers took to calling it Hutch Patrol), Tony refused and told him to ease off. 'You've got other responsibilities,' he said. 'Not the least of them is your wife.'

Curt had the good sense to keep quiet while in the SC's office. Later, however, he unburdened himself to Sandy, speaking with surprising bitterness as the two of them stood outside at the far corner of the barracks. 'If I'd wanted a marriage counselor, I would have consulted the goddam Yellow Pages,' he said.

Sandy offered him a smile, one without much humor in it. 'I think you better start listening for the pop,' he said.

'What are you talking about?'

'The pop. Very distinctive sound. You hear it when your head finally comes out of your ass.'

Curtis stared at him, hard little roses of color burning high up on his cheekbones. 'Am I missing something here, Sandy?'

'Yes.'

'What? For God's sake, *what*?'

'Your job and your life,' Sandy said. 'Not necessarily in that order. You are experiencing a problem of perspective. That Buick is starting to look too big to you.'

'Too . . . ' Curt hit his forehead with the palm of his hand in that way he had. Then he turned and looked out at the Short Hills. At last he swung back to Sandy. 'It's something from another world, Sandy — *from another world*. How *can* a thing like that look too big?'

'That's exactly your problem,' Sandy replied. 'Your problem of perspective.'

He had an idea that the next thing Curtis said would be the beginning of an argument, possibly a bitter one. So before Curt could say anything, Sandy went inside. And perhaps that talk did some good, because as August gave way to September, Curt's all but constant requests for more surveillance time stopped. Sandy Dearborn never tried to tell himself that the kid had seen the light, but he did seem to understand that he'd gone as far as he could, at least for the time being. Which was good, but maybe not quite good enough. Sandy thought that the Buick was always going to look too big to Curtis. But then, there have always been two sorts of people in the world. Curt was of the sort who believed satisfaction actually did bring felines back from the other side of the great divide.

* * *

He began to show up at the barracks with biology books instead of *Field and Stream*. The one most commonly observed under his arm or lying on the toilet tank in the crapper was Dr John H. Maturin's *Twenty Elementary Dissections*, Harvard University Press, 1968. When Buck Flanders and his wife went over to Curt's for dinner one evening, Michelle Wilcox complained about her husband's 'gross new hobby'. He had started getting specimens from a medical supply house, she said, and the area of the basement which he had designated as his

186

darkroom-to-be only the year before now smelled of mortuary chemicals.

Curt started with mice and a guinea pig, then moved on to birds, eventually working his way up to a horned owl. Sometimes he brought specimens to work. 'You haven't really lived,' Matt Babicki told Orville Garrett and Steve Devoe one day, 'until you go downstairs for a fresh box of ballpoint pens and find a jar of formaldehyde with an owl-eye in it sitting on top of the Xerox machine. Man, that wakes you up.'

Once the owl had been conquered, Curtis moved on to bats. He did eight or nine of those, each specimen from a different species. A couple he caught himself in his back yard; the rest he ordered from a biological supply house in The Burg. Sandy never forgot the day Curtis showed him a South American vampire bat pinned to a board. The thing was furry, brownish on the belly, and velvet-black on the membranous wings. Its tiny pointed teeth were bared in a psychotic smile. Its guts were laid open in a teardrop shape by Curt's increasingly skilled technique. Sandy believed Curt's high school biology teacher — the one who had given him the C — would have been surprised at how fast his old student was learning.

Of course when desire drives, any fool can be a professor.

* * *

It was while Curt Wilcox was learning the fine art of dissection from Dr Maturin that Jimmy

187

and Rosalynn took up residence in the Buick 8. They were Tony's brainstorm. He had it one day at the Tri-Town Mall, while his wife tried on clothes in Country Casuals. An improbable sign in the window of My Pet caught his eye: **COME ON IN AND JOIN OUR GERBIL RIOT!**

Tony didn't join the gerbil riot just then — his wife would have had a thousand questions — but he sent big George Stankowski back the very next day with more cash from the contingency fund and orders to buy a pair of gerbils. Also a plastic habitat for them to live in.

'Should I get them some food, too?' George asked.

'No,' Tony answered. 'Absolutely not. We're going to buy a couple of gerbils and then let them starve to death out in the shed.'

'Really? That seems sort of mean to — '

Tony sighed. 'Get them food, George, yes. By all means get them food.'

The only specification Tony made concerning the habitat was that it fit comfortably on the Buick's front seat. George got a nice one, not top-of-the-line but almost. It was made of a yellow see-through plastic and consisted of a long corridor with a boxy room at either end. One was the gerbil dining room and the other was the gerbil version of Gold's Gym. The dining room had a food-trough and a water-bottle clipped to the side; the gym had an exercise wheel.

'They live better than some people,' Orvie Garrett said.

Phil, who was watching Rosalynn take a shit in

188

the food-trough, said: 'Speak for yourself.'

Dicky-Duck Eliot, perhaps not the swiftest horse ever to canter around life's great racetrack, wanted to know why they were keeping gerbils in the Buick. Wasn't that sort of dangerous?

'Well, we'll see about that, won't we?' Tony asked in an oddly gentle voice. 'We'll just see if it is or not.'

★ ★ ★

On a day not long after Troop D acquired Jimmy and Rosalynn, Tony Schoondist crossed his own personal Rubicon and lied to the press.

Not that the representative of the Fourth Estate in this case was very impressive, just a weedy redheaded boy of twenty or so, a summer intern at The Statler County *American* who would be going back to Ohio State in another week or so. He had a way of listening to you with his mouth hung partway open that made him look, in Arky's words, like a stark raving natural-born fool. But he *wasn't* a fool, and he'd spent most of one golden September afternoon listening to Mr Bradley Roach. Brad gave the young reporter quite an earful about the man with the Russian accent (by this time Brad was positive the guy had been Russian) and the car the man had left behind. The weedy redhead, Homer Oosler by name, wanted to do a feature story on all of this and go back to college with a bang. Sandy thought the young man could imagine a front-page headline with the words **MYSTERY CAR** in it. Perhaps even **RUSSIAN**

189

SPY'S MYSTERY CAR.

Tony never hesitated, just went ahead and lied. He undoubtedly would have done the same thing even if the reporter presenting himself that day had been case-hardened old Trevor Ronnick, who owned the County *American* and had forgotten more stories than the redhead would ever write.

'Car's gone,' Tony said, and there it was: lie told, Rubicon crossed.

'Gone?' Homer Oosler asked, clearly disappointed. He had a big old Minolta camera on his lap. PROPERTY OF COUNTY AMERICAN was Dymotaped across the back of the case. 'Gone where?'

'State Impound Bureau,' Tony said, creating this impressive-sounding organization on the spot. 'In Philly.'

'Why?'

'They auction unclaimed rolling iron. After they search em for drugs, of course.'

'Course. Do you have any paperwork on it?'

'Must have,' Tony said. 'Got it on everything else. I'll look for it, give you a ring.'

'How long do you think that'll take, Sergeant Schoondist?'

'Awhile, son.' Tony waved his hand at his in/out basket, which was stacked high with papers. Oosler didn't need to know that most of them were the week's junkalogue from Scranton — everything from updates on retirement benefits to the schedule for autumn softball — and would be in the wastebasket before the Sarge went home. That weary wave of the hand

190

suggested that there were similar piles of paper everywhere. 'Hard keeping up with all this stuff, you know. They say things'll change when we start getting computerized, but that won't be this year.'

'I go back to school next week.'

Tony leaned forward in his chair and looked at Oosler keenly. 'And I hope you work hard,' he said. 'It's a tough world out there, son, but if you work hard you can make it.'

*   ★   ★

A couple of days after Homer Oosler's visit, the Buick fired up another of its lightstorms. This time it happened on a day that was filled with bright sun, but it was still pretty spectacular. And all Curtis's worries about missing the next manifestation proved groundless.

The shed's temperature made it clear the Buick was building up to something again, dropping from the mid-seventies to the upper fifties over a course of five days. Everyone became anxious to take a turn out in the hutch; everyone wanted to be the one on duty when it happened, whatever 'it' turned out to be this time.

Brian Cole won the lottery, but all the Troopers at the barracks shared the experience at least to some extent. Brian went into Shed B at around two P.M. to check on Jimmy and Rosalynn. They were fine as paint, Rosalynn in the habitat's dining room and Jimmy busting heavies on the exercise wheel in the gym. But as

Brian leaned farther into the Buick to check the water reservoir, he heard a humming noise. It was deep and steady, the kind of sound that vibrates your eyes in their sockets and rattles your fillings. Below it (or entwined with it) was something a lot more disturbing, a kind of scaly, wordless whispering. A purple glow, very dim, was spreading slowly across the dashboard and the steering wheel.

Mindful of Ennis Rafferty, gone with no forwarding address for well over a month by then, Trooper Cole vacated the Buick's vicinity in a hurry. He proceeded without panic, however, taking the video camera from the hutch, screwing it on to its tripod, loading in a fresh tape, checking the time-code (it was correct) and the battery level (all the way in the green). He turned on the overheads before going back out, then placed the tripod in front of one of the windows, hit the RECORD button, and double-checked to make sure the Buick was centered in the viewfinder. It was. He started toward the barracks, then snapped his fingers and went back to the hutch. There was a little bag filled with camera accessories in there. One of them was a brightness filter. Brian attached this to the video camera's lens without bothering to hit the PAUSE button (for one moment the big dark shapes of his hands blot out the image of the Buick, and when they leave the frame again the Buick reappears as if in a deep twilight). If there had been anyone there watching him go about his business — one of those visiting John Q.'s curious about how his tax dollars were spent, perhaps — he never would have guessed how fast Trooper Cole's heart was beating. He was afraid as well as excited, but he did okay. When it comes to dealing with the unknown, there's a great deal to be said for a good shot of police training. All in all, he forgot only one thing.

He poked his head into Tony's office at about seven minutes past two and said, 'Sarge, I'm pretty sure something's happening with the Buick.'

Tony looked up from his yellow legal pad, where he was scribbling the first draft of a speech he was supposed to give at a law enforcement symposium that fall, and said: 'What's that in your hand, Bri?'

Brian looked down and saw he was holding the gerbils' water reservoir. 'Ah, what the hell,' he said. 'They may not need it anymore, anyway.'

★ ★ ★

By twenty after two, Troopers in the barracks could hear the humming clearly. Not that there were many in there; most were lined up at the windows in Shed B's two roll-up doors, hip to hip and shoulder to shoulder. Tony saw this, debated whether or not to order them away, and finally decided to let them stay where they were. With one exception.

'Arky.'

'Yessir, Sarge?'

'I want you to go on out front and mow the lawn.'

193

'I just mow it on Monday!'

'I know. Seemed like you spent the last hour doing the part under my office window. I want you to do it again just the same. With this in your back pocket.' He handed Arky a walkie-talkie. 'And if anyone comes calling who shouldn't see ten Pennsylvania State Troopers lined up in front of that shed like there was a big-money cockfight going on inside, shoot me the word. Got it?'

'Yeah, you betcha.'

'Good. Matt! Matt Babicki, front and center!'

Matt rushed up, puffing and red-faced with excitement. Tony asked him where Curt was. Matt said he was on patrol.

'Tell him to return to base, code D and ride quiet, got that?'

'Code D and ride quiet, roger.'

To ride quiet is to travel *sans* flashers and siren. Curt presumably obeyed this injunction, but he was still back at the barracks by quarter to three. No one dared ask him how far he'd come in half an hour. However many miles it might have been, he arrived alive and before the silent fireworks started up again. The first thing he did was to remove the videocam from the tripod. Until the fireworks were over, the visual record would be Curtis Wilcox's baby.

The tape (one of many squirreled away in the storage closet) preserves what there was to see and hear. The Buick's hum is very audible, sounding like a loose wire in a stereo speaker, and it gets appreciably louder as time passes. Curt got footage of the big thermometer with its red needle standing at just a hair past 54. There's

Curt's voice, asking permission to go in and check on Jimmy and Rosalynn, and Sergeant Schoondist's voice coming back with 'Permission denied' almost at once, brisk and sure, brooking no argument.

At 3:08:41P, according to the time-code on the bottom of the screen, a blush like a violet sunrise begins to rise on the Buick's windshield. At first a viewer might pass this phenomenon off as a technical glitch or an optical illusion or perhaps some sort of reflection.

Andy Colucci: 'What's that?'

Unknown speaker: 'A power surge or a — '

Curtis Wilcox: 'Those of you with goggles better put them on. Those of you without them, this is risky, I'd back the hell off. We have — '

Jackie O'Hara (probably): 'Who took — '

Phil Candleton (probably): 'My *God*!'

Huddie Royer: 'I don't think we should — '

Sergeant Commanding Schoondist, sounding as calm as an Audubon guide on a nature hike: 'Get those goggles down, fellas, I would. Chop-chop.'

At 3:09:24, that violet light took an auroral leap in all the Buick's windows, turning them into brilliant purple mirrors. If one slows the tape down and then advances it frame by frame, one can see actual reflections appearing in the formerly clear window-glass: the tools hung on their pegs, the orange plow-blade stored against one wall, the men outside, peering in. Most are wearing goggles and look like aliens in a cheap science fiction movie. One can isolate Curt because of the video camera blocking the left side of his face. The hum gets louder and louder. Then, about five seconds before the Buick starts shooting off those flashes, the sound stops. A viewer of this tape can hear an excited babble of voices, none identifiable, all seeming to ask questions.

Then the image disappears for the first time. The Buick and the shed are both gone, lost in the white.

'*Jesus Christ, did you guys see that?*' Huddie Royer screams.

There are cries of *Get back, Holy fuck*, and everyone's favorite in times of trouble, *Oh shit*. Someone says *Don't look at it* and someone else says *It's pissing lightning* in that weirdly matter-of-fact tone one can sometimes hear on cockpit flight recorders, a pilot who's talking without realizing it, who only knows that he's down to the last ten or twelve seconds of his life.

Then the Buick returns from the land of overexposure, looking first like a meaningless clot, then taking back its actual form. Three seconds later it flashes out again. The glare shoots thick rays from every window and then whites out the image once more. During this one Curt says *We need a better filter* and Tony replies *Maybe next time*.

The phenomenon continues for the next forty-six minutes, every bit of it captured on tape. At first the Buick whites out and disappears with every flash. Then, as the phenomenon starts to weaken, the viewer can see a vague car-shape sunk deep in soundless lightbursts that are more purple than white. Sometimes the image joggles and there's a fast, blurry pan of human faces as Curtis hurries to a different observation point, hoping for a revelation (or perhaps just a better view).

At 3:28:17, one can observe a jagged line of fire burst up from (or maybe it's through) the Buick's closed trunk. It shoots all the way to the ceiling, where it seems to splash outward like water from a fountain.

Unidentified voice: 'Holy shit, high voltage, high voltage!'

Tony: 'The hell it is.' Then, presumably to Curt: 'Keep taping.'

Curt: 'Oh yeah. You better believe it.'

There are several more of the lightning bolts, some shooting out of the Buick's windows, some rising from the roof or the trunk. One leaps out from beneath the car and fires itself directly at the rear roll-up door. There are surprised yells as the men back away from that one, but the camera stays steady. Curt was basically too excited to be afraid.

At 3:55:03 there's a final weak blip — it comes from the back seat, behind the driver's position — and then there's no more. You can hear Tony Schoondist say, 'Why don't you save the battery, Curt? The show seems to be over.' At that point the tape goes momentarily black.

When the picture resumes at 4:08:16, Curt is onscreen. There's something yellow wrapped around his midsection. He waves jauntily and says, 'I'll be right back.'

Tony Schoondist — he's the one running the

camera at that point — replies, 'You better be.' And he doesn't sound jaunty in the least.

★ ★ ★

Curt wanted to go in and check on the gerbils — to see how they were, assuming they were still there at all. Tony refused permission adamantly and at once. No one was going in Shed B for quite awhile, he said, not until they were sure it was safe to do so. He hesitated, maybe replaying that remark in his head and realizing the absurdity of it — as long as the Buick Roadmaster was in Shed B it was never going to be safe — and changed it to: 'Everyone stays out until the temperature's back over sixty-five.'

'Someone's *gotta* go,' Brian Cole said. He spoke patiently, as if discussing a simple addition problem with a person of limited intelligence.

'I fail to see why, Trooper,' Tony said.

Brian reached into his pocket and pulled out Jimmy and Rosalynn's water-reservoir. 'They got plenty of those pellets they eat, but without this, they'll die of thirst.'

'No, they won't. Not right away.'

'It might be a couple of *days* before the temperature in there goes up to sixty-five, Sarge. Would you want to go forty-eight hours without a drink?'

'I know *I* wouldn't,' Curt said. Trying not to smile (and smiling a little anyway), he took the calibrated plastic tube from Brian. Then Tony took it from *him* before it could start to feel at home in Curt's hand. The SC did not look at his

198

fellow scholar as he did this; he kept his eyes fixed on Trooper Brian Cole.

'I'm supposed to allow one of the men under my command to risk his life in order to bring water to a pair of pedigreed mice. Is that what you're telling me, Trooper? I just want to be clear on this.'

If he expected Brian to blush or scuffle, he was disappointed. Brian just kept looking at him in that patient way, as if to say *Yes, yes, get it out of your system, boss — the sooner you get it out of your system, the sooner you'll be able to relax and do the right thing.*

'I can't believe it,' Tony said. 'One of us has lost his mind. Probably it's me.'

'They're just little guys,' Brian said. His voice was as patient as his face. 'And we're the ones who put them in there, Sarge, they didn't exactly volunteer. We're responsible. Now I'll do it if you want, I'm the one who forgot — '

Tony raised his hands to the sky, as if to ask for divine intervention, then dropped them back to his sides. Red was creeping out of his collar, up his neck, and over his jaw. It met the red patches on his cheeks: howdy-do, neighbor. '*Hair pie!*' he muttered.

The men had heard him say this before, and knew better than to crack a smile. It is at this point that many people — perhaps even a majority — would be apt to yell, 'Oh, screw it! Do what you want!' and stamp away. But when you're in the big chair, getting the big bucks for making the big decisions, you can't do that. The D Troopers gathered in front of the shed knew

199

this, and so, of course, did Tony. He stood there, looking down at his shoes. From out front of the barracks came the steady blat of Arky's old red Briggs & Stratton mower.

'Sarge — ' Curtis began.

'Kid, do us all a favor and shut up.'

Curt shut up.

After a moment, Tony raised his head. 'The rope I asked you to pick up — did you get it?'

'Yes, sir. It's the good stuff. You could take it mountain-climbing. At least that's what the guy at Calling All Sports said.'

'Is it in there?' Tony nodded at the shed.

'No, in the trunk of my car.'

'Well, thank God for small favors. Bring it over here. And I hope we never have to find out how good it is.' He looked at Brian Cole. 'Maybe you'd like to go down to The Agway or The Giant Eagle, Trooper Cole. Get those mice a few bottles of Evian or Poland Spring Water. Hell, Perrier! How about some Perrier?'

Brian said nothing, just gave the Sergeant a little more of that patient look. Tony couldn't stand it and looked away. 'Mice with pedigrees! *Hair* pie!'

⋆   ⋆   ⋆

Curt brought the rope, a length of triple-braided yellow nylon at least a hundred feet long. He made a sliding loop, cinched it around his waist, then gave the coil to Huddie Royer, who weighed two-fifty and always anchored when D Troop played tug-of-war against the other PSP octets

200

during the Fourth of July picnic.

'If I give you the word,' Tony told Huddie, 'you yank him back like he just caught fire. And don't worry about breaking his collarbone or his thick skull pulling him through the door. Do you understand that?'

'Yes, Sarge.'

'If you see him fall down, or just start swaying on his feet like he's lightheaded, don't wait for the word. Just yank. Got it?'

'Yes, Sarge.'

'Good. I'm very glad that someone understands what's going on here. Fucking hair-pie summer-camp snipe-hunt is what it is.' He ran his hand through the short bristles of his hair, then turned to Curt again. 'Do I need to tell you to turn around and come out of there if you sense anything — *any slightest thing* — wrong?'

'No.'

'And if the trunk of that car comes open, Curtis, you *fly*. Got it? Fly out of there like a bigass bird.'

'I will.'

'Give me the video camera.'

Curtis held it out and Tony took it. Sandy wasn't there — missed the whole thing — but when Huddie later told him it was the only time he had ever seen the Sarge looking scared, Sandy was just as glad he spent that afternoon out on patrol. There were some things you just didn't want to see.

'You have one minute in the shed, Trooper Wilcox. After that I drag you out whether you're

201

fainting, farting, or singing 'Columbia, the Gem of the Ocean'.'

'Ninety seconds.'

'No. And if you try one more time to bargain with me, your time goes down to thirty seconds.'

⋆ ⋆ ⋆

Curtis Wilcox is standing in the sun outside the walk-in door on the side of Shed B. The rope is tied around his waist. He looks young on the tape, younger with each passing year. He looked at that tape himself from time to time and probably felt the same, although he never said. And he doesn't look scared. Not a bit. Only excited. He waves to the camera and says, 'I'll be right back.'

'You better be,' Tony replies.

Curt turns and goes into the shed. For a moment he looks ghostly, hardly there, then Tony moves the camera forward to get it out of the bright sun and you can see Curt clearly again. He crosses directly to the car and starts around to the back.

'No!' Tony shouts. 'No, you dummy, you want to foul the rope? Check the gerbils, give em their goddam water, and get the hell out of there!'

Curt raises one hand without turning, giving him a thumbs-up. The picture jiggles as Tony uses the zoom to get in tighter on him.

Curtis looks in the driver's-side window, then stiffens and calls: 'Holy *shit*!'

'Sarge, should I pull — ' Huddie begins, and then Curt looks back over his shoulder. Tony's juggling the picture again — he doesn't have Curt's light touch with the camera and the image is going everywhere — but it's still easy enough to read the wide-eyed expression of shock on Curtis's face.

'Don't you pull me back!' Curt shouts. 'Don't do it! I'm five-by-five!' And with that, he opens the door of the Roadmaster.

'Stay out of there!' Tony calls from behind the madly jiggling camera.

Curt ignores him and pulls the plastic gerbil condo out of the car, waggling it gently back and forth to get it past the big steering wheel. He uses his knee to shut the Buick's door and then comes back to the shed door with the habitat cradled in his arms. With a square room at either end, the thing looks like some strange sort of plastic dumbbell.

'Get it on tape!' Curt is shouting, all but *frying* with excitement. 'Get it on tape!'

Tony did. The picture zooms in on the left end of the environment just as soon as Curt steps out of the shed and back into the sun. And here is Rosalynn, no longer eating but scurrying about cheerfully enough. She becomes aware of the men gathered around her and turns directly toward the camera, sniffing at the yellow plastic, whiskers quivering, eyes bright and interested. It was cute, but the Troopers from Statler D weren't interested in cute just then.

The camera makes a herky-jerky pan away from her, traveling along the empty corridor to the empty gerbil gym at the far end. Both of the environment's hatches are latched tight, and

203

nothing bigger than a gnat could get through the hole for the water-tube, but Jimmy the gerbil is gone, just the same — just as gone as Ennis Rafferty or the man with the Boris Badinoff accent, who had driven the Buick Roadmaster into their lives to begin with.

NOW:

Sandy

I came to a stop and swallowed a glass of Shirley's iced tea in four long gulps That planted an icepick in the center of my forehead, and I had to wait for it to melt.

At some point Eddie Jacubois had joined us. He was dressed in his civvies and sitting at the end of the bench, looking both sorry to be there and reluctant to leave. I had no such divided feelings; I was delighted to see him. He could tell his part. Huddie would help him along, if he needed helping; Shirley, too. By 1988 she'd been with us two years, Matt Babicki nothing but a memory refreshed by an occasional postcard showing palm trees in sunny Sarasota, where Matt and his wife own a learn-to-drive school. A very successful one, at least according to Matt.

'Sandy?' Ned asked. 'Are you all right?'

'I'm fine. I was just thinking about how clumsy Tony was with that video camera,' I said. 'Your dad was great, Ned, a regular Steven Spielberg, but — '

'Could I watch those tapes if I wanted to?' Ned asked.

I looked at Huddie ... Arky ... Phil ... Eddie. In each set of eyes I saw the same thing: *It's your call.* As of course it was. When you sit in the big chair, you make all the big calls.

And mostly I like that. Might as well tell the truth.

'Don't see why not,' I said. 'As long as it's here. I wouldn't be comfortable with you taking them out of the barracks — you'd have to call them Troop D property — but here? Sure. You can run em on the VCR in the upstairs lounge. You ought to take a Dramamine before you look at the stuff Tony shot, though. Right, Eddie?'

For a moment Eddie looked across the parking lot, but not toward where the Roadmaster was stored. His gaze seemed to rest on the place where Shed A had been until 1982 or thereabouts. 'I dunno much about that,' he said. 'Don't remember much. Most of the big stuff was over by the time I got here, you know.'

Even Ned must have known the man was lying; Eddie was spectacularly bad at it.

'I just came out to tell you I put in those three hours I owed from last May, Sarge — you know, when I took off to help my brother-in-law build his new studio?'

'Ah,' I said.

Eddie bobbed his head up and down rapidly. 'Uh-huh. I'm all clocked out, and I put the report on those marijuana plants we found in Robbie Rennerts's back field on your desk. So I'll just be heading on home, if it's all the same to you.'

Heading down to The Tap was what he meant. His home away from home. Once he was out of uniform, Eddie J.'s life was a George Jones song. He started to get up and I put a hand on his wrist. 'Actually, Eddie, it's not.'

'Huh?'

'It's not all the same to me. I want you to stick around awhile.'

'Boss, I really ought to — '

'Stick around,' I repeated. 'You might owe this kid a little something.'

'I don't know what — '

'His father saved your life, remember?'

Eddie's shoulders came up in a kind of defensive hunch. 'I don't know if I'd say he exactly — '

'Come on, get off it,' Huddie said. 'I was *there*.'

Suddenly Ned wasn't so interested in videotapes. 'My father saved your life, Eddie? How?'

Eddie hesitated, then gave in. 'Pulled me down behind a John Deere tractor. The O'Day brothers, they — '

'The spine-tingling saga of the O'Day brothers is a story for another time,' I said. 'The point is, Eddie, we're having us a little exhumation party here, and you know where one of the bodies is buried. And I mean quite literally.'

'Huddie and Shirley were there, they can — '

'Yeah, they were. George Morgan was there, too, I think — '

'He was,' Shirley said quietly.

' — but so what?' I still had my hand on Eddie's wrist, and had to fight a desire to squeeze it again. Hard. I liked Eddie, always had, and he could be brave, but he also had a yellow streak. I don't know how those two things can exist side by side in the same man, but they can;

207

I've seen it more than once. Eddie froze back in '96, on the day Travis and Tracy O'Day started firing their fancy militia machine-guns out of their farmhouse windows. Curt had to break cover and yank him to safety by the back of his jacket. And now here he was trying to squiggle out of his part in the other story, the one in which Ned's father had played such a key role. Not because he'd done anything wrong — he hadn't — but because the memories were painful and frightening.

'Sandy, I really ought to get toddling. I've got a lot of chores I've been putting off, and — '

'We've been telling this boy about his father,' I said. 'And what I think you ought to do, Eddie, is sit there quiet, maybe have a sandwich and a glass of iced tea, and wait until you have something to say.'

He settled back on the end of the bench and looked at us. I know what he saw in the eyes of Curt's boy: puzzlement and curiosity. We'd become quite a little Council of Elders, though, surrounding the young fellow, singing him our warrior-songs of the past. And what about when the songs were done? If Ned had been a young Indian brave, he might have been sent out on some sort of dream quest — kill the right animal, have the right vision while the blood of the animal's heart was still smeared around his mouth, come back a man. If there could be some sort of test at the end of this, I reflected, some way in which Ned could demonstrate new maturity and understanding, things might have been a lot simpler. But that's not the way things

208

work nowadays. At least not by and large. These days it's lot more about how you feel than what you do. And I think that's wrong.

And what did Eddie see in our eyes? Resentment? A touch of contempt? Perhaps even the wish that it had been him who had flagged down the truck with the flapper rather than Curtis Wilcox, that it had been him who had gotten turned inside-out by Bradley Roach? Always-almost-overweight Eddie Jacubois, who drank too much and would probably be making a little trip to Scranton for a two-week stay in the Member Assistance Program if he didn't get a handle on his drinking soon? The guy who was always slow filing his reports and who almost never got the punchline of a joke unless it was explained to him? I hope he didn't see any of those things, because there was another side to him — a better side — but I can't say for sure he didn't see at least some of them. Maybe even all of them.

' — about the big picture?'

I turned to Ned, glad to be diverted from the uncomfortable run of my own thoughts. 'Come again?'

'I asked if you ever talked about what the Buick really was, where it came from, what it meant. If you ever discussed, you know, the big picture.'

'Well . . . there was the meeting at The Country Way,' I said. I didn't quite see where he was going. 'I told you about that — '

'Yeah, but that one sounded, you know, more administrative than anything else — '

'You do okay in college,' Arky said, and patted him on the knee. 'Any kid can say a word like dat, jus' roll it out, he bound t'do okay in college.'

Ned grinned. 'Administrative. Organizational. Bureaucratized. Compartmentalized.'

'Quit showing off, kiddo,' Huddie said. 'You're giving me a headache.'

'Anyway, the thing at The Country Way's not the kind of meeting I'm talking about. You guys must've . . . I mean, as time went on you *must* have . . . '

I knew what he was trying so say, and I knew something else at the same time: the boy would *never* quite understand the way it had really been. How *mundane* it had been, at least on most days. On most days we had just gone on. The way people go on after seeing a beautiful sunset, or tasting a wonderful champagne, or getting bad news from home. We had the miracle of the world out behind our workplace, but that didn't change the amount of paperwork we had to do or the way we brushed our teeth or how we made love to our spouses. It didn't lift us to new realms of existence or planes of perception. Our asses still itched, and we still scratched them when they did.

'I imagine Tony and your father talked it over a lot,' I said, 'but at work, at least for the rest of us, the Buick gradually slipped into the background like any other inactive case. It — '

'*Inactive!*' He nearly shouted it, and sounded so much like his father it was frightening. It was

210

another chain, I thought, this resemblance between father and son. The chain had been mangled, but it wasn't broken.

'For long periods of time, it was,' I said. 'Meantime, there were fender-benders and hit-and-runs and burglaries and dope and the occasional homicide.'

The look of disappointment on Ned's face made me feel bad, as if I'd let him down. Ridiculous, I suppose, but true. Then something occurred to me. 'I *can* remember one bull-session about it. It was at — '

' — the picnic,' Phil Candleton finished. 'Labor Day picnic. That's what you're thinking about, right?'

I nodded. Nineteen seventy-nine. The old Academy soccer field, down by Redfern Stream. We all liked the Labor Day picnic a lot better than the one on the Fourth of July, partly because it was a lot closer to home and the men who had families could bring them, but mostly because it was just us — just Troop D. The Labor Day picnic really *was* a picnic.

Phil put his head back against the boards of the barracks and laughed. 'Man, I'd almost forgotten about it. We talked about that damn yonder Buick, kid, and just about nothing else. More we talked, the more we drank. My head ached for two days after.'

Huddie said: 'That picnic's always a good time. You were there last summer, weren't you, Ned?'

'Summer before last,' Ned said. 'Before Dad died.' He was smiling. 'That tire swing that goes

211

out over the water? Paul Loving fell out of it and sprained his knee.'

We all laughed at that, Eddie as loud as the rest of us.

'A lot of talk and not one single conclusion,' I said. 'But what conclusions could we draw? Only one, really: when the temperature goes down inside that shed, things happen. Except even that turned out not to be a hard-and-fast rule. Sometimes — especially as the years went by — the temperature would go down a little, then rebound. Sometimes that humming noise would start . . . and then it would stop again, just cut out as if someone had pulled the plug on a piece of electrical equipment. Ennis disappeared with no lightshow and Jimmy the gerbil disappeared after a *humongous* lightshow and Rosalynn didn't disappear at all.'

'Did you put her back into the Buick?' Ned asked.

'Nah,' Phil said. 'This is America, kid — no double jeopardy.'

'Rosalynn lived the rest of her life upstairs in the common room,' I said. 'She was three or four when she died. Tony said that was a fairly normal lifespan for a gerbil.'

'Did more things come out of it? Out of the Buick?'

'Yes. But you couldn't correlate the appearance of those things with — '

'What sort of things? And what about the bat? Did my father ever get around to dissecting it? Can I see it? Are there pictures, at least? Was it — '

212

'Whoa, hold on,' I said, raising my hand. 'Eat a sandwich or something. Chill out.'

He picked up a sandwich and began to nibble, his eyes looking at me over the top. For just a moment he made me think of Rosalynn the gerbil turning to look into the lens of the video camera, eyes bright and whiskers twitching.

'Things appeared from time to time,' I said, 'and from time to time things — living things would disappear. Frogs. A butterfly. A tulip right out of the pot it was growing in. But you couldn't correlate the chill, the hum, or the lightshows with either the disappearances or what your Dad called the Buick's miscarriages. Nothing really correlates. The chill is pretty reliable, there's never been one of those fireworks displays without a preceding temperature-drop — but not every temperature-drop means a display. Do you see what I mean?'

'I think so,' Ned said. 'Clouds don't always mean rain, but you don't get rain without them.'

'I couldn't have put it more neatly,' I said.

Huddie tapped Ned on the knee. 'You know how folks say, 'There's an exception to every rule'? Well, in the case of the Buick, we've got about one rule and a dozen exceptions. The driver himself is one — you know, the guy in the black coat and black hat. *He* disappeared, but not from the vicinity of the Buick.'

'Can you say that for sure?' Ned asked.

It startled me. For a boy to look like his father is natural. To sound like his father, too. But for a moment there, Ned's voice and looks combined to make something more than a resemblance.

Nor was I the only one who felt that. Shirley and Arky exchanged an uneasy glance.

'What do you mean?' I asked him.

'Roach was reading a newspaper, wasn't he? And from the way you described him, that probably took most of his concentration. So how do you know the guy didn't come back to his car?'

I'd had something like twenty years to think about that day and the consequences of that day. Twenty years, and the idea of the Roadmaster's driver coming back (perhaps even *sneaking* back) had never once occurred to me. Or, so far as I knew, to anyone else. Brad Roach said the guy hadn't returned, and we'd simply accepted that. Why? Because cops have built-in bullshit detectors, and in that case none of the needles swung into the red. Never even twitched, really. Why would they? Brad Roach at least *thought* he was telling the truth. That didn't mean he knew what he was talking about, though.

'I guess that it's possible,' I said.

Ned shrugged as if to say, *Well, there you go.*

'We never had Sherlock Holmes or Lieutenant Columbo working out of D Troop,' I said. I thought I sounded rather defensive. I *felt* rather defensive. 'When you get right down to it, we're just the mechanics of the legal system. Blue-collar guys who actually wear gray collars and have a slightly better-than-average education. We can work the phones, compile evidence if there's evidence to compile, make the occasional deduction. On good days we can make fairly *brilliant* deductions. But with the

214

Buick there was no consistency, hence no basis for deduction, brilliant or otherwise.'

'Some of the guys thought it came from space,' Huddie said. 'That it was . . . oh, I don't know, a disguised scout-ship, or something. They had the idea Ennis was abducted by an E.T. disguised to look at least passably human in his — *its* — black coat and hat. This talk was at the picnic — the Labor Day picnic, okay?'

'Yeah,' Ned said.

'That was one seriously weird get-together, kiddo,' Huddie said. 'It seems to me that everyone got a lot drunker'n usual, and a lot faster, but no one got rowdy, not even the usual suspects like Jackie O'Hara and Christian Soder. It was very quiet, especially once the shirts-and-skins touch football game was over.

'I remember sitting on a bench under an elm tree with a bunch of guys, all of us moderately toasted, listening to Brian Cole tell about these flying saucer sightings around the powerlines in New Hampshire — only a few years before, that was — and how some woman claimed to have been abducted and had all these probes stuck up inside her, entrance ramps and exit ramps both.'

'Is that what my father believed? That aliens abducted his partner?'

'No,' Shirley said. 'Something happened here in 1988 that was so . . . so outrageous and beyond belief . . . so fucking *awful* . . . '

'What?' Ned asked. 'For God's sake, *what*?'

Shirley ignored the question. I don't think she even heard it. 'A few days afterward, I asked your father flat-out what he believed. He said it didn't matter.'

Ned looked as if he hadn't heard her correctly. 'It didn't *matter*?'

'That's what he said. He believed that, whatever the Buick was, it didn't matter in the great scheme of things. In that big picture you were talking about. I asked him if he thought someone was using it, maybe to watch us . . . if it was some sort of television . . . and he said, 'I think it's forgotten.' I still remember the flat, certain way he said it, as if he was talking about . . . I don't know . . . something as important as a king's treasure buried under the desert since before the time of Christ or something as *un*important as a postcard with the wrong address sitting in a Dead Letter file somewhere. 'Having a wonderful time, wish you were here,' and who cares, because all that was long, long ago. It comforted me and at the same time it chilled me to think anything so strange and awful could just be forgotten . . . misplaced . . . overlooked. I said that, and your Dad, he laughed. Then he flapped his arm at the western horizon and he said, 'Shirley, tell me something. How many nuclear weapons do you think this great nation of ours has got stored out there in various places between the Pennsylvania — Ohio line and the Pacific Ocean? And how many of them do you think will be left behind and forgotten over the next two or three centuries?''

We were all silent for a moment, thinking about this.

'I was considering quitting the job,' Shirley

said at last. 'I couldn't sleep. I kept thinking about poor old Mister Dillon, and in my mind quitting was almost a done deal. It was Curt who talked me into staying, and he did it without even knowing he was doing it. 'I think it's forgotten,' he said, and that was good enough for me. I stayed, and I've never been sorry, either. This is a good place, and most of the guys who work here are good Troops. That goes for the ones who are gone, too. Like Tony.'

'I love you, Shirley, marry me,' Huddie said. He put an arm around her and puckered his lips. Not a pretty sight, all in all.

She elbowed him. 'You're married already, foolish.'

Eddie J. spoke up then. 'If your Dad believed anything, it was that yonder machine came from some other dimension.'

'Another *dimension*? You're kidding.' He looked at Eddie closely. 'No. You're *not* kidding.'

'And he didn't think it was planned at all,' Eddie went on. 'Not, you know, like you'd plan to send a ship across the ocean or a satellite into space. In some ways, I'm not even sure he thought it was real.'

'You lost me,' the kid said.

'Me, too,' Shirley agreed.

'He said . . . ' Eddie shifted on the bench. He looked out again at the grassy place where Shed A had once stood. 'This was at the O'Day farm, if you want to know the truth. That day. You hafta realize we were out there almost seven goddam hours, parked in the corn and waiting for those two dirtbags to come back. Cold.

Couldn't run the engine, couldn't run the heater. We talked about everything — hunting, fishing, bowling, our wives, our plans. Curt said he was going to get out of the PSP in another five years — '

'He said that?' Ned was round-eyed.

Eddie gave him an indulgent look. 'From time to time we all say that, kid. Just like all the junkies say they're going to quit the spike. I told him how I'd like to open my own security business in The Burg, also how I'd like to get me a brand-new Winnebago. He told me about how he wanted to take some science courses at Horlicks and how he was getting resistance from your Mom. She said it was their job to put the *kids* through school, not him. He caught a lot of flak from her but never blamed her. Because she didn't know why he wanted to take those courses, what had got him interested, and he couldn't tell her. That's how we got around to the Buick. And what he said — I remember this clear as the sky on a summer morning — was that we saw it as a Buick because we had to see it as *something*.'

'Have to see it as something,' Ned muttered. He was leaning forward and rubbing the center of his forehead with two fingers, like a man with a headache.

'You look as confused as I felt, but I *did* sort of understand what he meant. In here.' Eddie tapped his chest, above his heart.

Ned turned back to me. 'Sandy, that day at the picnic, did any of you talk about . . . ' He trailed off without finishing.

218

'Talk about what?' I asked him.

He shook his head, looked down at the remains of his sandwich, and popped the last bite into his mouth. 'Never mind. Isn't important. Did my Dad really dissect the bat-thing you guys found?'

'Yep. After the second lightshow but before the Labor Day picnic. He — '

'Tell the kid about the leaves,' Phil said. 'You forgot that part.'

And I had. Hell, I hadn't even *thought* about the leaves in six or eight years. '*You* tell him,' I said. 'You're the one who had your hands on them.'

Phil nodded, sat silent for a few moments, and then began to speak staccato, as if giving a report to a superior officer.

NOW:

Phil

'The second lightshow happened midafternoon. Okay? Curt goes into the shed with the rope on when it's over and brings out the gerbil whatchacallit. We see one of the critters is gone. There's some more talk. Some more picture-taking. Sergeant Schoondist says okay, okay, everyone as you were, who's on duty out in the hutch. Brian Cole says 'Me, Sarge.'

'The rest of us go back in the barracks. Okay? And I hear Curtis say to the Sarge, 'I'm gonna dissect that thing before it disappears like everything else. Will you help me?' And the Sarge says he will — that night, if Curt wants. Curt says 'Why not right now?' and the Sarge says, 'Because you got a patrol to finish. Shift-and-a-half. John Q. is depending on you, boy, and lawbreakers tremble at the sound of your engyne.' That's the way he talked, sometimes, like a piney-woods preacher. And he never said *engine*, always *engyne*.

'Curt, he don't argue. Knows better. Goes off. Around five o'clock Brian Cole comes in and gets me. Asks will I cover the shed for him while he goes to the can. I say sure. I go out there. Take a look inside. Situation normal, fi'-by. Thermometer's gone up a degree. I go into the hutch. Decide the hutch is too hot, okay? There's an

220

L.L. Bean catalogue on the chair. I go to grab that. Just as I put my fingers on it, I hear this *creak-thump* sound. Only one sound like it, when you unlatch the trunk of your car and it springs up hard. I go rushing out of the hutch. Over to the shed windows. Buick's trunk's open. All this what I thought at first was paper, charred bits of paper, is whooshing up out of the trunk. Spinning around like they were caught in a cyclone. But the dust on the floor wasn't moving. Not at all. The only moving air was coming out of the trunk. And then I saw all the pieces of paper looked pretty much the same and I decided they were leaves. Turned out that was what they were.'

I took my notebook out of my breast pocket. Clicked out the tip of my ballpoint and drew this:

'It looks sort of like a smile,' the kid said.

'Like a goddam *grin*,' I said. 'Only there wasn't just one of them. Was hundreds. Hundreds of black grins swirling and spinning around. Some landed on the Buick's roof. Some dropped back into the trunk. Most of em went on the floor. I ran to get Tony. He came out with the video camera. He was all red in the face and muttering, 'What now, what next, what the hell, what now?' Like that. It was sort of funny, but only later on, okay? Wasn't funny at the time, believe me.

'We looked in the window. Saw the leaves scattered all across the cement floor. There were almost as many as you might have on your lawn after a big October windstorm blows through. Only by then they were curling up at the corners. Made em look a little less like grins and a little more like leaves. Thank God. And they weren't staying black. They were turning whitish-gray right in front of our eyes. And *thinning*. Sandy was there by then. Didn't make it in time for the lightshow, but turned up in time for the leafshow.'

Sandy said, 'Tony called me at home and asked if I could come in that evening around seven. He said that he and Curt were going to do something I might want to be in on. Anyway, I didn't wait for seven. I came in right away. I was curious.'

'It killed the cat,' Ned said, and sounded so much like his pa that I almost shivered. Then he was looking at me. 'Tell the rest.'

'Not much to tell,' I said. 'The leaves were thinning. I might be wrong, but I think we could actually see it happening.'

'You're not wrong,' Sandy said.

'I was excited. Not thinking. Ran around to the side door of the shed. And Tony, man, Tony was on me like white on rice. He grabs me around the neck in a choke-hold. 'Hey,' I says. 'Leggo me, leggo me, police brutality!' And he tells me to save it for my gig at the Comedy Shop over in Statesboro. 'This is no joke, Phil,' he says. 'I have good reason to believe I've lost one officer to that goddamned thing.

222

I'm not losing another.'

'I told him I'd wear the rope. I was hot to trot. Can't remember exactly why, but I was. He said he wasn't going back to get the goddam rope. I said *I'd* go back and get the goddam rope. He said, 'You can forget the goddam rope, permission denied.' So I says, 'Just hold my feet, Sarge. I want to get a few of those leaves. There's some not five feet from the door. Not even close to the car. What do you say?'

''I say you must have lost your friggin mind, *everything in there* is close to the car,' he says, but since that wasn't exactly no, I went ahead and opened the door. You could smell it right away. Something like peppermint, only not nice. Some smell underneath it, making the one on top even worse. That cabbagey smell. Made your stomach turn over, but I was almost too excited to notice. I was younger then, okay? I got down on my stomach. Wormed my way in. Sarge has got me by the calves, and when I'm just a little way inside the shed he says, 'That's far enough, Phil. If you can grab some, grab away. If you can't, get out.'

'There were all kinds that had turned white, and I got about a dozen of those. They were smooth and soft, but in a bad way. Made me think of how tomatoes get when they've gone rotten under the skin. A little farther away there was a couple that were still black. I stretched out and got hold of em, only the very second I touched em, they turned white like the others. There was this very faint stinging sensation in my fingertips. Got a stronger whiff

223

of peppermint and I heard a sound. Think I did, anyway. A kind of sigh, like the sound a soda can makes when you break the seal on the poptop.

'I started wiggling out, and at first I was doing all right, but then I . . . something about the feel of those things in my hands . . . all sleek and smooth like they were . . .'

For a few seconds I couldn't go on. It was like I was feeling it all over again. But the kid was looking at me and I knew he wouldn't let it go, not for love or money, so I pushed ahead. Now just wanting to get it over with.

'I panicked. Okay? Started to push backward with my elbows and kick with my feet. Summer. Me in short sleeves. One of my elbows kind of winged out and touched one of the black leaves and it hissed like . . . like I don't know what. Just hissed, you know? And sent up a puff of that peppermint-cabbage stink. Turned white. Like me touching it had given it frostbite and killed it. Thought of that later. Right then I didn't think about anything except getting the righteous fuck out of there. Scuse me, Shirley.'

'Not at all,' Shirley said, and patted my arm. Good girl. Always was. Better in dispatch than Babicki — by a country mile — and a whole lot easier on the eyes. I put my hand over hers and gave a little squeeze. Then I went on and it was easier than I thought it would be. Funny how things come back when you talk about them. How they get clearer and clearer as you go along.

'I looked up at that old Buick. And even though it was in the middle of the shed, had to be twelve feet away from me easy, all at once it seemed a lot closer than that. Big as Mount Everest. Shiny as the side of a diamond. I got the idea that the headlights were eyes and the eyes were looking at me. And I could hear it whispering. Don't look so surprised, kid. We've all heard it whispering. No idea what it's saying — if it's really saying anything — but sure, I could hear it. Only inside my head, going from the inside out. Like telepathy. Might have been imagination, but I don't think so. All of a sudden it was like I was six again. Scared of the thing under my bed. It meant to take me away, I was sure of it. Take me to wherever it had taken Ennis. So I panicked. I yelled, 'Pull me, pull me, hurry up!' and they sure did. The Sarge and some other guy — '

'The other guy was me,' Sandy said. 'You scared the living crap out of us, Phil. You seemed all right at first, then you started to yell and twist and buck. I sort of expected to see you bleeding somewhere, or turning blue in the face. But all you had was . . . well.' And he made a little gesture at me to go on.

'I had the leaves. What was left of them, anyway. When I freaked out, I must have made fists, okay? Clenched down on them. And once I was back outside, I realized my hands were all wet. People were yelling *Are you all right?* and *What happened in there, Phil?* Me up on my knees, with most of my shirt around my neck and a damn floorburn on my gut from being dragged, and I'm thinking *My hands are bleeding. That's why they're wet.* Then I see this

225

white goo. Looked like the kind of paste the teacher gives you in the first grade. It was all that was left of the leaves.'

I stopped, thought about it.

'And now I'm gonna tell you the truth, okay? It didn't look like paste at all. It was like I had two fistfuls of warm bull-jizz. And the smell was awful. I don't know why. You could say *A little peppermint and cabbage, what's the big deal?* and you'd be right, but at the same time you'd be wrong. Because really that smell was like nothing on earth. Not that I ever smelled before, anyway.

'I wiped my hands on my pants and went back to the barracks. Went downstairs. Brian Cole is just coming out of the crapper down there. He thought he heard some yelling, wants to know what's going on. I pay him absolutely no mind. Almost knock him over getting into the can, matter of fact. I start washing my hands. I'm still washing away when all at once I think of how I looked with that cummy-white leaf-gunk dripping out of my fists and how it was so warm and soft and somehow *sleek* and how it made strings when I opened up my fingers. And that was it. Thinking of how it made strings between my palms and the tips of my fingers, I upchucked. It wasn't like having your guts send your supper back by Western Union, either. It was like my actual stomach making a personal appearance, coming right up my throat and tipping everything I'd swallowed down lately right back out my mouth. The way my ma used to throw her dirty wash-water over the back porch railing.

I don't mean to go on about it, but you need to know. It's another way of trying to understand. It wasn't like puking, it was like dying. Only other time I had anything like that was my first road fatality. I get there and the first thing I see is a loaf of Wonder bread on the yellow line of the old Statler Pike and the next thing I see is the top half of a kid. A little boy with blond hair. Next thing I see is there's a fly on the kid's tongue. Washing its legs. That set me off. I thought I was going to puke myself to death.'

'It happened to me, too,' Huddie said. 'Nothing to be ashamed of.'

'Not ashamed,' I said. 'Trying to make him see, is all. Okay?' I took in a deep breath, smelling the sweet air, and then it hit me that the kid's father was also a road kill. I gave the kid a smile. 'Oh well, thank God for small favors — the commode was right next to the basin, and I didn't get hardly any on my shoes or the floor.'

'And in the end,' Sandy said, 'the leaves came to nothing. And I mean that literally. They melted like the witch in *The Wizard of Oz*. You could see traces of them in Shed B for awhile, but after a week there was nothing but some little stains on the concrete. Yellowish, very pale.'

'Yeah, and for the next couple of months I turned into one of those compulsive hand-washers,' I said. 'There were days when I couldn't bring myself to touch food. If my wife packed me sandwiches, I picked em up with a napkin and ate them that way, dropping the last piece out of the napkin and into my mouth so I never had to touch any of it with my fingers. If I was by myself in my cruiser, I was apt to eat with my gloves on. And I kept thinking I'd get sick just the same. What I kept imagining was that gum disease where all your teeth fall out. But I got over it.' I looked at Ned and waited until he met my eyes. 'I got over it, son.'

He met my eyes, but there was nothing in them. It was funny. Like they were painted on, or something.

Okay?

NOW:

Sandy

Ned was looking at Phil. The boy's face was calm enough, but I sensed rejection in his gaze, and I think Phil sensed it, too. He sighed, folded his arms across his chest, and looked down as if to say he was done talking, his testimony was finished.

Ned turned to me. 'What happened that night? When you dissected the bat?'

He kept calling it a bat and it *hadn't* been a bat. That was just a word I'd used, what Curtis would have called a nail to hang my hat on. And all at once I was mad at him. More than mad — pissed like a bear. And I was also angry at myself for feeling that way, for daring to feel that way. You see, mostly what I was angry at was the kid raising his head. Raising his eyes to mine. Asking his questions. Making his foolish assumptions, one of which happened to be that when I said bat I meant bat, and not some unspeakable, indescribable thing that crept out of a crack in the floor of the universe and then died. But mostly it was him raising his head and his eyes. I know that doesn't exactly make me out to be the prince of the world, but I'm not going to lie about it.

Up until then, what I'd mostly felt was sorry for him. Everything I'd done since he started

229

showing up at the barracks had been based on that comfortable pity. Because all that time when he'd been washing windows and raking leaves and snowblowing his way through the drifts in the back parking lot, all that time he'd kept his head down. Meekly down. You didn't have to contend with his eyes. You didn't have to ask yourself any questions, because pity is comfortable. Isn't it? Pity puts you right up on top. Now he had lifted his head, he was using my own words back at me, and there was nothing meek in his eyes. He thought he had a right, that made me mad. He thought I had a responsibility — that what was being said out here wasn't a gift being given but a debt being repaid — and that made me madder. That he was right made me maddest of all. I felt like shoving the heel of my hand up into the shelf of his chin and knocking him spang off the bench. He thought he had a right and I wanted to make him sorry.

Our feelings toward the young never much change in this regard, I suppose. I don't have kids of my own. I've never been married — like Shirley, I guess I married Troop D. But I've got plenty of experience when it comes to the young, both inside and outside the barracks. I've had them in my face plenty of times. It seems to me that when we can no longer pity them, when they reject our pity (not with indignation but with impatience), we pity ourselves instead. We want to know where they went, our comfy little ones, our baby buntings. Didn't we give them piano lessons and show them how to throw the curveball? Didn't we read them *Where the Wild*

Things Are and help them search for Waldo? How dare they raise their eyes to ours and ask their rash and stupid questions? How dare they want more than we want to give?

'Sandy? What happened when you guys dissected the — '

'Not what *you* want to hear,' I said, and when his eyes widened a little at the coldness he heard in my voice, I was not exactly displeased. 'Not what your father wanted to see. Or Tony, either. Not some answer. There never was an answer. Everything to do with the Buick was a shimmer-mirage, like the ones you see on I-87 when it's hot and bright. Except that's not quite true, either. If it had been, I think we could have dismissed the Buick eventually. The way you dismiss a murder when six months go by and you all just kind of realize you're not going to catch whoever did it, that the guy is going to slide. With the Buick and the things that came out of the Buick, there was always something you could catch hold of. Something you could touch or hear. Or something you could

THEN

'Oi,' Sandy Dearborn said. 'That *smell*.'

He put his hand up to his face but couldn't actually touch his skin because of the plastic breathing cup he was wearing over his mouth and nose — the kind dentists put on before going prospecting. Sandy didn't know how it was on germs, but the mask did nothing to stop the smell. It was that cabbagey aroma, and it choked the air of the storage closet as soon as Curt opened the stomach of the bat-thing.

'We'll get used to it,' Curt said, his own breathing cup bobbing up and down on his face. His and Sandy's were blue; the Sergeant's was a rather cute shade of candy-pink. Curtis Wilcox was a smart guy, right about a lot of things, but he was wrong about the smell. They didn't get used to it. No one ever did.

Sandy couldn't fault Trooper Wilcox's preparation, however; it seemed perfect. Curt had swung home at the end of his shift and picked up his dissection kit. To this he had added a good microscope (borrowed from a friend at the university), several packets of surgical gloves, and a pair of extremely bright Tensor lamps. He told his wife he intended to examine a fox someone had shot behind the barracks.

'You be careful,' she said. 'They can have rabies.'

Curt promised her he'd glove up, and it was a

232

promise he meant to keep. Meant for all three of them to keep. Because the bat-thing might have something a lot worse than rabies, something which remained virulent long after its original host was dead. If Tony Schoondist and Sandy Dearborn had needed a reminder of this (they probably didn't), they got it when Curt first closed the door at the foot of the stairs and then bolted it.

'I'm in charge as long as that door's locked,' Curt said. His voice was flat and absolutely sure of itself. It was mostly Tony he was speaking to, because Tony was twice his age, and if anyone was his partner in this, it was the SC. Sandy was just along for the ride, and knew it. 'Is that understood and agreed? Because if it isn't, we can stop right n — '

'It's understood,' Tony said. 'In here you're the general. Sandy and I are just a couple of buck privates. I have no problem with that. Just for Chrissake let's get it over with.'

Curt opened his kit, which was almost the size of an Army footlocker. The interior was packed with stainless steel instruments wrapped in chamois. On top of them were the dental masks, each in its own sealed plastic bag.

'You really think these are necessary?' Sandy asked.

Curt shrugged. 'Better safe than sorry. Not that those things are worth much. We should probably be wearing respirators.'

'I sort of wish we had Bibi Roth here,' Tony said.

Curt made no verbal reply to that, but the

flash of his eyes suggested that was the last thing in the world *he* wanted. The Buick belonged to the Troop. And anything that came out of it belonged to the Troop.

Curt opened the door of the storage closet and went in, pulling the chain that turned on the little room's green-shaded hanging lamp. Tony followed. There was a table not much bigger than a grade-schooler's desk under the light. Small as the closet was, there was barely room for two, let alone three. That was fine with Sandy; he never stepped over the threshold at all that night.

Shelves heaped with old files crowded in on three sides. Curt put his microscope on the little desk and plugged its light-source into the closet's one outlet. Sandy, meanwhile, was setting up Huddie Royer's videocam on its sticks. In the video of that peculiar postmortem, one can sometimes see a hand reach into the picture, holding out whatever instrument Curt has called for. It's Sandy Dearborn's hand. And one can hear the sound of vomiting at the end of the tape, loud and clear. That is also Sandy Dearborn.

'Let's see the leaves first,' Curt said, snapping on a pair of the surgical gloves.

Tony had a bunch of them in a small evidence bag. He handed it over. Curt opened it and took out the remains of the leaves with a small pair of tongs. There was no way to get just one; by now they were all semi-transparent and stuck together like clumps of Saran Wrap. They were seeping little trickles of fluid, and the men could smell their aroma — that uneasy mix of cabbage and peppermint — immediately. It was not nice, but it was a long way from unbearable. Unbearable was at that point still ten minutes in the future.

Sandy used the zoom in order to get a good image of Curt separating a fragment of the mass from the whole, using the pincers deftly. He'd treated himself to a lot of practice over the last few weeks, and here was the payoff.

He transferred the fragment directly to the stage of the microscope, not attempting to make a slide. Phil Candleton's leaves were just the Coming Attractions reel. Curtis wanted to get to the feature presentation as soon as possible.

He bent over the twin eyepieces for a good long time nevertheless, then beckoned Tony for a look.

'What're the black things that look like threads?' Tony asked after several seconds of study. His voice was slightly muffled by his pink mask.

'I don't know,' Curt said. 'Sandy, give me that gadget that looks like a Viewmaster. It has a couple of cords wrapped around it and PROPERTY H. U. BIOLOGY DEPARTMENT Dymo-taped on the side.'

Sandy passed it to him over the top of the videocam, which was pretty much blocking the doorway. Curt plugged one of the cords into the wall and the other into the base of the microscope. He checked something, nodded, and pushed a button on the side of the Viewmaster-thing three times, presumably taking

pictures of the leaf fragments on the microscope's stage.

'Those black things aren't moving,' Tony said.
He was still peering into the microscope.

'No.'

Tony finally raised his head. His eyes had a
dazed, slightly awed look. 'Is it . . . could it be
like, I don't know, DNA?'

Curt's mask bobbed slightly on his face as he
smiled. 'This is a great scope, Sarge, but we
couldn't see DNA with it. Now, if you wanted to
go up to Horlicks with me after midnight and
pull a bag-job, they've got this really beautiful
electron microscope in the Evelyn Silver Physics
Building, never been driven except by a little old
lady on her way to church and her weekly — '

'What's the white stuff?' Tony asked. 'The stuff
the black threads are floating in?'

'Nutrient, maybe.'

'But you don't know.'

'Of *course* I don't know.'

'The black threads, the white goo, why the
leaves are melting, what that smell is. We don't
know dick about any of those things.'

'No.'

Tony gave him a level look. 'We're crazy to be
fucking with this, aren't we?'

'No,' Curt said. 'Curiosity killed the cat,
satisfaction made him fat. You want to squeeze in
and take a peek, Sandy?'

'You took photos, right?'

'I did if this thing worked the way it's s'posed
to.'

'Then I'll take a pass.'

'Okay, let's move on to the main event,' Curt said. 'Maybe we'll actually find something.'

The gobbet of leaves went back into the evidence bag and the evidence bag went back into a file cabinet in the corner. That battered green cabinet would become quite the repository of the weird and strange over the next two decades.

In another corner of the closet was an orange Eskimo cooler. Inside, under two of those blue chemical ice packets people sometimes take on camping trips, was a green garbage bag. Tony lifted it out and then waited while Curt finished getting ready. It didn't take long. The only real delay was finding an extension cord so they could plug in both of the Tensor lamps without disturbing the microscope or the attached still camera. Sandy went to get a cord from the cabinet of odds and ends at the far end of the hall. While he was doing that, Curt placed his borrowed microscope on a nearby shelf (of course, in those close quarters, everything was nearby) and set up an easel on the desktop. On this he mounted a square of tan corkboard. Beneath it he placed a small metal trough of the sort found on the more elaborate barbecue setups, where they are used to catch drippings. Off to one side he put a jar-top filled with Push-pins.

Sandy came back with the extension cord. Curt plugged in the lamps so they shone on the corkboard from either side, illuminating his work-surface with a fierce, even glow that eliminated every shadow. It was obvious he'd thought all of this out, step by step. Sandy wondered how many nights he'd lain awake long after Michelle had gone to sleep beside him. Just lying there and looking up at the ceiling and going over the procedure in his mind. Reminding himself he'd just have the one shot. Or how many afternoons there had been, Curt parked a little way up some farmer's lane with the Genesis radar gun pointed at an empty stretch of highway, calculating how many practice bats he'd have to go through before he dared tackle the real thing.

'Sandy, are you getting glare from these lights?'

He checked the viewfinder. 'No. With white I probably would, but tan is great.'

'Okay.'

Tony unwound the yellow tie holding the neck of the garbage bag shut. The moment he opened it, the smell got stronger. 'Whew, Jesus!' he said, waving a gloved hand. Then he reached in and pulled out another evidence bag, this one a large.

Sandy was watching over the top of the camera. The thing in the bag looked like a shopworn freakshow monstrosity. One of the dark wings was folded over the lower body, the other pressed against the clear plastic of the evidence bag, making him think of a hand pressed against a pane of glass. Sometimes when you collared a drunk and shut him in the back of the cruiser he'd put his hands on the glass and look out at the world from between them, a dazed dark face framed by starfish. This was a little like that, somehow.

'Seal's open in the middle,' Curt said, and nodded disapprovingly at the evidence bag. 'That explains the smell.'

Nothing explained it, in Sandy's opinion.

Curt opened the bag completely and reached inside. Sandy felt his stomach knot into a sick ball and wondered if he could have forced himself to do what Curt was doing. He didn't think so. Trooper Wilcox never hesitated, however. When his gloved fingers touched the corpse in the bag, Tony recoiled a little. His feet stayed put but his upper body swayed backward, as if to avoid a punch. And he made an involuntary sound of disgust behind his cute pink mask.

'You okay?' Curt asked.

'Yes,' Tony said.

'Good. I'll mount it. You pin it.'

'Okay.'

'Are you sure you're all right?'

'Yes, goddammit.'

'Because I feel queasy, too.' Sandy could see sweat running down the side of Curt's face, dampening the elastic that held his mask.

'Let's save the sensitivity-training session for later and just get it done, what do you say?'

Curt lifted the bat-thing to the corkboard. Sandy could hear an odd and rather terrible sound as he did so. It might have been only the combination of overstrained ears and the quiet rustle of clothes and gloves, but Sandy didn't actually believe that. It was dead skin rubbing against dead skin, creating a sound that was somehow like words spoken very low in an alien

239

tongue. It made Sandy want to cover his ears.

At the same time he became aware of that tenebrous rustling, his eyes seemed to sharpen. The world took on a preternatural clarity. He could see the rosy pink of Curtis's skin through the thin gloves he was wearing, and the matted whorls that were the hairs on the backs of his fingers. The glove's white was very bright against the creature's midsection, which had gone a matted, listless gray. The thing's mouth hung open. Its single black eye stared at nothing, its surface dull and glazed. To Sandy that eye looked as big as a teacup.

The smell was getting worse, but Sandy said nothing. Curt and the Sergeant were right in there with it, next to the source. He guessed if they could stand it, he could.

Curt peeled up the wing lying across the creature's middle, revealing sallow green fur and a small puckered cavity that might have held the thing's genitals. He held the wing against the corkboard. 'Pin,' he said.

Tony pinned the wing. It was dark gray and all membrane. There was no sign of bone or blood vessels that Sandy could see. Curt shifted his hand on the thing's midsection so he could raise the other wing. Sandy heard that liquid squelching sound again. It was getting hot in the supply room and had to be even worse in the closet. Those Tensor lamps.

'Pin, boss.'

Tony pinned the other wing and now the creature hung on the board like something out of a Bela Lugosi film. Except, once you could see all of it, it didn't really look much like a bat at all, or a flying squirrel, or certainly any kind of bird. It didn't look like *anything*. That yellow prong sticking out from the center of its face, for instance — was it a bone? A beak? A nose? If it was a nose, where were the nostrils? To Sandy it looked more like a claw than a nose, and more like a thorn than a claw. And what about that single eye? Sandy tried to think of any earthly creature that had only one eye and couldn't. There had to be such a creature, didn't there? Somewhere? In the jungles of South America, or maybe at the bottom of the ocean?

And the thing had no feet; its body simply ended in a butt like a green-black thumb. Curt pinned this part of the specimen's anatomy to the board himself, pinching the furry hide away from its body and then impaling a loose fold. Tony finished the job by driving pins into the corkboard through the thing's armpits. *Or maybe you call them wingpits*, Sandy thought. This time it was Curtis who made an involuntary sound of disgust behind his mask, and he wiped his brow with his forearm. 'I wish we'd thought to bring in the fan,' he said. Sandy, whose head was beginning to swim, agreed. Either the stench was getting worse or it had a cumulative effect.

'Plug in one more thing and we'd probably trip the breaker,' Tony said. 'Then we could be in the dark with this ugly motherfucker. Also trapped, on account of Cecil B. DeMille's got his camera set up in the doorway. Go on, Curt. I'm okay if you are.'

Curt stepped back, snatched a breath of

slightly cleaner air, tried to compose himself, then stepped forward to the table again. 'I'm not measuring,' he said. 'We got all that done out in the shed, right?'

'Yeah,' Sandy replied. 'Fourteen inches long. Thirty-six centimeters, if you like that better. Body's about a handspan across at the widest. Maybe a little less. Go on, for God's sake, so we can get out of here.'

'Give me both scalpels, plus retractors.'

'How many retractors?'

Curt gave him a look that said *Don't be a bozo.* 'All of them.' Another quick swipe of the forehead. And after Sandy had handed the stuff over the top of the camera and Curt had arranged it as best he could: 'Watch through the viewfinder, okay? Zoom the shit out of the mother. Let's get the best record we can.'

'People'd still say it's a fake,' Tony told him. 'You know that, don't you?'

Curtis then said something Sandy never forgot. He believed that Curtis, already under severe mental strain and in increasingly severe physical distress, spoke the truth of his mind in baldly simple terms people rarely dare to use, because they reveal too much about the speaker's real heart. 'Fuck the John Q's,' was what Curtis said. 'This is for us.'

'I've got a good tight shot,' Sandy told him. 'The smell may be bad, but the light's heavenly.' The time-code at the bottom of the little interior TV screen read 7:49:01P.

'Cutting now,' Curt said, and slid his larger scalpel into the pinned creature's midsection.

242

His hands didn't tremble; any stage-fright accompanying the arrival of the big moment must have come and gone quickly. There was a wet popping sound, like a bubble of some thick liquid breaking, and all at once drops of black goo began to patter into the trough under the easel.

'Oh man,' Sandy said. 'Oh, that really stinks.'

'Fucking *foul*,' Tony added. His voice was thin and dismayed.

Curt took no notice. He opened the thing's abdomen and made the standard branching incisions up to the pinned wingpits, creating the Y-cut used in any human postmortem. He then used his pincers to pull back the hide over the thoracic area, more clearly revealing a spongy dark green mass beneath a narrow arch of bone.

'Jesus God, where's its *lungs*?' Tony asked. Sandy could hear him breathing in harsh little sips.

'This green thing could be a lung,' Curt said. 'Looks more like a — '

'Like a brain, yeah, I know it does. A green brain. Let's take a look.'

Curt turned his scalpel and used the blunt side to tap the white arch above the crenellated green organ. 'If the green thing's a brain, then its particular evolution gave it a chastity belt for protection instead of a safety deposit box. Give me the shears, Sandy. The smaller pair.'

Sandy handed them over, then bent back to the video camera's viewfinder. He was zoomed to the max, as per instructions, and had a nice clear picture.

'Cutting . . . now.'

Curt slipped the lower blade of the shears under the arch of bone and snipped it as neatly as the cord on a package. It sprang back on both sides like a rib, and the moment it did the surface of the green sponge in the thing's chest turned white and began to hiss like a radiator. A strong aroma of peppermint and clove filled the air. A bubbling sound joined the hissing. It was like the sound of a straw prospecting the bottom of a nearly empty milkshake glass.

'Think we should get out of here?' Tony asked.

'Too late.' Curt was bent over the opened chest, where the spongy thing had now begun to sweat droplets and runnels of whitish-green liquid. He was more than interested; he was rapt. Looking at him, Sandy could understand about the fellow who deliberately infected himself with yellow fever or the Curie woman, who gave herself cancer fiddling around with radiation. 'I am made the destroyer of worlds,' Robert Oppenheimer muttered during the first successful detonation of an atomic bomb in the New Mexico desert, and then went on to start work on the H-bomb with hardly a pause for tea and scones. *Because stuff gets you,* Sandy thought. *And because, while curiosity is a provable fact, satisfaction is more like a rumor.*

'What's it doing?' Tony asked. Sandy thought that from what he could see above the pink mask, the Sarge already had a pretty good idea.

'Decomposing,' Curt replied. 'Getting a good picture, Sandy? My head not in your way?'

'It's fine, five-by,' Sandy replied in a slightly

244

strangled voice. At first the peppermint-clove variation had seemed almost refreshing, but now it sat in the back of his throat like the taste of machine-oil. And the cabbagey reek was creeping back. Sandy's head was swimming more strenuously than ever, and his guts had begun to slosh. 'I wouldn't take too long about this, though, or we're going to choke in here.'

'Open the door at the end of the hall,' Curt said.

'You told me — '

'Go on, do what he says,' Tony told him, and so Sandy did. When he came back, Tony was asking Curt if Curt thought snipping the bone arch had sped up the decomposition process.

'No,' Curt said. 'I think touching the spongy stuff with the tip of the shears is what did it. The things that come out of that car don't seem to get along with us very well, do they?'

Neither Tony nor Sandy had any wish to argue that. The green sponge didn't look like a brain or a lung or anything else recognizable by then; it was just a pustulant, decomposing sac in the corpse's open chest.

Curt glanced toward Sandy. 'If that green thing was its brain, what do you suppose is in its head? Inquiring minds want to know.' And before either of them completely realized what he was doing, Curt reached out with the smaller of his scalpels and poked the blade into the thing's glazed eye.

There was a sound like a man popping his finger in his cheek. The eye collapsed and slid out of its socket whole, like a hideous shed tear.

Tony gave an involuntary shout of horror. Sandy uttered a low scream. The collapsed eye struck the thing's furry shoulder and then plopped into the drip-gutter. A moment later it began to hiss and turn white.

'Stop it,' Sandy heard himself saying. 'This is pointless. We're not going to learn anything from it, Curtis. There's nothing to learn.'

Curtis, so far as Sandy could tell, didn't even hear him. 'Holy shit,' he was whispering. 'Holy fucking shit.'

Fibrous pink stuff began to bulge from the vacant eyesocket. It looked like cotton candy, or the insulation people use in their attics. It came out, formed an amorphous node, then turned white and began to liquefy, like the green thing.

'Was that shit alive?' Tony asked. 'Was that shit alive when it — '

'No, that was only depressurization,' Curt said. 'I'm sure of it. It's no more alive than shaving cream when it comes out of the can. Did you get it on tape, Sandy?'

'Oh yeah. For what it's worth.'

'Okay. Let's look in the lower gut and then we're done.'

What came out next killed any real sleep for at least a month. Sandy was left with those short dozes from which one wakes, gasping, sure that something one can't quite see has been crouching on one's chest and stealing one's breath.

Curt retracted the hide from the abdominal area and asked Tony to pin it, first on the left and then on the right. Tony managed, although not without difficulty; the work had become very fine and both of them had their faces close to the incision. The reek in that close must have been tremendous, Sandy thought.

Without turning his head, Curt groped out, found one of the Tensor lamps, and turned it slightly, intensifying the light pouring into the incision. Sandy saw a folded rope of dark liverish red stuff — intestines — piled on top of a bluish-gray sac.

'Cutting,' Curt murmured, and caressed the edge of his scalpel down the sac's lumpy, bulging surface. It split open and black ichor shot out directly into Curt's face, painting his cheeks and splashing his mask. More of it splattered Tony's gloves. Both men recoiled, crying out, while Sandy stood frozen behind the video camera with his jaw hung down. Pouring out of the rapidly deflating sac was a flood of rough black pellets, each of them wrapped in a swaddle of gray membrane. To Sandy they looked like spider-snacks which had been put up in cobweb shrouds. Then he saw that each pellet had an open glazed eye and that each eye seemed to be staring at *him*, marking him, and that was when his nerve broke. He backed away from the camera, screaming. The screams were replaced by a gagging sound. A moment later he vomited down the front of his shirt. Sandy himself remembered almost none of that; the five minutes or so following Curt's final incision were pretty much burned out of his memory, and he counted that a mercy.

The first thing he remembered on the other side of that cigarette-burn in the surface of his memory was Tony saying, 'Go on, now, you hear? You guys go on back upstairs. Everything here is under control.' And, close to his left ear, Curt was murmuring another version of the same thing, telling Sandy he was all right, totally cool, fi'-by-fi'.

Five-by-five: that was what lured Sandy back from his brief vacation in the land of hysteria. But if everything was five-by, why was Curt breathing so fast? And why was the hand on Sandy's arm so cold? Even through the rubber membrane of the glove (which he had so far neglected to take off), Curt's hand was cold.

'I threw up,' Sandy said, and felt the dull heat hit his cheeks as the blood rose there. He couldn't remember ever feeling so ashamed and demoralized. 'Christ Jesus, I threw up all over myself.'

'Yeah,' Curt said, 'you hurled like a hero. Don't worry about it.'

Sandy took a breath and then grimaced as his stomach knotted and almost betrayed him again. They were in the corridor, but even out here that cabbagey reek was almost overpowering. At the same time he realized exactly where in the hallway he was: standing in front of the rickrack cabinet from which he had scrounged the extension cord. The cabinet's door was open. Sandy wasn't sure, but he had an idea he'd fled down here from the supply room, perhaps with the idea of crawling into the cabinet, pulling the door shut behind him, and just curling up in the dark. This struck him funny and he voiced a single shrill chuckle.

'There, that's better,' Curt said. He gave Sandy a pat and looked shocked when Sandy shrank away from his touch.

'Not you,' Sandy said. 'That mung . . . that goo — '

He couldn't finish; his throat had locked up. He pointed at Curt's hand, instead. The slime which had come out of the bat-thing's pregnant dead uterus was smeared all over Curt's gloves, and some of it was now on Sandy's arm as well. Curt's mask, pulled down so it hung against his neck, was also streaked and stained. There was a black crust like a scab on his cheek.

At the other end of the hall, past the open supply room door, Tony stood at the foot of the stairs, talking to four or five gawking, nervous State Troopers. He was making shooing gestures, trying to get them to go back up, but they weren't quite ready to do that.

Sandy walked back down the hall as far as the supply room door, stopping where they could all get a good look at him. 'I'm okay, fellas — I'm okay, you're okay, everybody's okay. Go upstairs and chill out. After we get squared away, you can all look at the video.'

'Will we want to?' Orville Garrett asked.

'Probably not,' Sandy said.

The Troopers went upstairs. Tony, his cheeks as pale as glass, turned to Sandy and gave him a little nod. 'Thanks.'

'Least I could do. I panicked, boss. I'm sorry as hell.'

Curtis clapped him on the shoulder this time instead of just patting. Sandy almost shrank away again before seeing that the kid had pulled off his stained gloves. So that was all right. Better, anyway.

'You weren't alone,' Curt said. 'Tony and I were right behind you. You were just too freaked to notice. We knocked over Huddie's videocam in the stampede. Hope it's okay. If it's not, I guess we'll be passing the hat to buy him a replacement. Come on, let's look.'

The three of them returned to the supply room resolutely enough, but at first none of them was able to go inside. Part of it was the smell, like rotten soup. Most of it was just knowing the bat-thing was still in there, pinned to the corkboard, flayed open and needing to be cleaned up like the weekend road accidents where when you got there the smell of blood and busted guts and spilled gasoline and boiled rubber was like some hideous old acquaintance who would never move out of town; you smelled it and knew that somebody was dead or almost dead, that somebody else would be crying and screaming, that you were going to find a shoe — hopefully not a child's, but all too often it was — lying in the road. For Sandy it was like that. You found them in the road or on the side of the road with the bodies God gave them saying *Here, get through life with it just as best you can* tortured into new shapes: bones bursting out through pants and shirts, heads twisted halfway

around the neck but still talking (and screaming), eyes hanging loose, a bleeding mother
holding out a bleeding child like a broken doll
and saying *Is she still alive? Please, would you
check? I can't, I don't dare.* There was always
blood on the seats in pools and fingerprints of
blood on what remained of the windows. When
the blood was on the road it was also in pools
and it turned purple in the pulse of the red
bubblegum lights and you needed to clean it up,
the blood and the shit and the broken glass, oh
yes, because John Q. and his family didn't want
to be looking at it on their way to church come
Sunday morning. And John Q. paid the bills.

'We have to take care of this,' the Sarge said.
'You boys know that.'

They knew it. And still none of them moved.

What if some of them are still alive? That was
what Sandy was thinking. It was a ridiculous
idea, the bat-thing had been in a plastic evidence
bag which had been in a sealed Eskimo cooler
for six weeks or more, but knowing such an idea
was ridiculous wasn't enough. Logic had lost its
power, at least for awhile. When you were dealing
with a one-eyed thing that had its brain (its
green brain) in its chest, the very idea of logic
seemed laughable. Sandy could all too easily
imagine those black pellets in their gauzy
overwrappings starting to pulse and move about
like lethargic jumping-beans on the little desk as
the fierce glow from the Tensor lamps warmed
them back to vitality. Sure, that was easy to
imagine. And sounds coming from them. High
little mewling noises. The sounds of baby birds

251

or baby rats working to be born. But he had been the first one out, goddammit. He could be the first one back in, at least he could do that much.

'Come on,' Sandy said, and stepped over the threshold. 'Let's get this done. Then I'm going to spend the rest of the night in the shower.'

'You'll have to wait in line,' Tony said.

⋆　⋆　⋆

So they cleaned the mess up as they had cleaned up so many on the highway. It took about an hour, all told, and although getting started was hard, they were almost themselves by the time the job was finished. The biggest help in getting back on an even keel was the fan. With the Tensor lamps turned off, they could run it with no worries about popping a breaker. Curt never said another word about keeping the supply room's door shut, either. Sandy guessed he'd figured any poor quarantine they might have managed had been breached to a faretheewell.

The fan couldn't clear that sallow stench of cabbage and bitter peppermint entirely, but it drove enough of it out into the hall so that their stomachs settled. Tony checked the videocam and said it appeared to be fine.

'I remember when Japanese stuff used to break,' he said. 'Curt, do you want to look at anything under the microscope? We can hang in a little longer if you do. Right, Sandy?'

Although not enthusiastic, Sandy nodded his head. He was still deeply ashamed of the way he had puked and run; felt he hadn't made up for that yet, not quite.

'No,' Curt said. He sounded tired and dispirited. 'The damn Gummi Bears that fell out of it were its litter. The black stuff was probably its blood. As for the rest? I wouldn't know what I was seeing.'

Not just dispirit but something close to despair, although neither Tony nor Sandy would realize that until later. It came to Sandy on one of those sleepless nights he had just bought and paid for. Lying in the bedroom of his small home in East Statler Heights with his hands behind his head and the lamp on the nighttable burning and the radio on low, sleep a thousand miles away. Realizing what Curt had come face to face with for the first time since the Buick showed up, and maybe for the first time in his life: that he was almost certainly never going to know what he wanted to know. What he'd told himself he *needed* to know. His ambition had been to discover and uncover, but so what? Spit on that, Jack, as they used to say when they were kids. All over the United States there were scrambling shirttail grammar school kids who'd tell you their ambition was to play in the NBA. Their futures in almost all cases would turn out to be more mundane. There comes a time when most folks see the big picture and realize they're puckered up not to kiss smiling fate on the mouth because life just slipped them a pill, and it tastes bitter. Wasn't that where Curtis Wilcox was now? Sandy thought yeah. His interest in the Buick was likely to continue, but with each passing year that interest would look more and more like what it really was — ordinary police work. Stakeout and surveillance, writing reports (in journals his wife would later burn), cleaning up the occasional mess when the Buick gave birth to another monstrosity which would struggle briefly and then die.

Oh, and living through the occasional sleepless night. But they came with the territory, didn't they?

★ ★ ★

Curt and Tony unpinned the monstrosity from the corkboard. They put it back in the evidence bag. All but two of the black pellets followed, swept into the evidence bag with a fingerprint brush. This time Curt made sure the seal on the bag was tight all the way across the top. 'Is Arky still around?' he asked.

Tony said, 'No. He wanted to stay, but I sent him home.'

'Then would one of you go upstairs and ask Orv or Buck to start a fire in the incinerator out back? Also, someone needs to put a pot of water on the stove. A big one.'

'I'll do it,' Sandy said, and after ejecting the tape from Huddie's videocam, he did.

While he was gone, Curt took swabs of the viscid black stuff which had come out of the thing's gut and uterus; he also swabbed the thinner white fluid from the chest organ. He covered each swab with Saran Wrap and put them into another evidence bag. The two remaining unborn creatures with their tiny wings wrapped around them (and their unsettling one-eyed stares) went into a third evidence bag. Curt worked competently, but with no zest, much as he would have worked a cold crime-scene.

The specimens and the bat-thing's flayed body eventually wound up in the battered green cabinet, which George Morgan took to calling 'the Troop D sideshow'. Tony allowed two of the Troopers from upstairs to come down when the pot of water on the stove had reached a boil. The five men donned heavy rubber kitchen gloves and scrubbed down everything they could reach. The unwanted organic leftovers went into a plastic bag, along with the scrub-rags, surgical gloves, dental masks, and shirts. The bag went into the incinerator and the smoke went up to the sky, God the Father, ever and ever, amen.

Sandy, Curtis, and Tony took showers — long enough and hot enough to exhaust the tank downstairs not once but twice. After that, rosy-cheeked and freshly combed, dressed in clean clothes, they ended up on the smokers' bench.

'I'm so clean I almost squeak,' Sandy said.

'Squeak this,' Curt replied, but amiably enough.

They sat and just looked at the shed for awhile, not talking.

'A lot of that shit got on us,' Tony said at last. '*Lot* of that shit.' Overhead, a three-quarter moon hung in the sky like a polished rock. Sandy could feel a tremble in the air. He thought maybe it was the seasons getting ready to change. 'If we get sick — '

'I think if we were going to get sick, we'd be sick already,' Curt said. 'We were lucky. *Damn* lucky. Did you boys get a good look at your peepers in the bathroom mirror?'

They had, of course. Their eyes were red-rimmed and bloodshot, the eyes of men who have spent a long day fighting a brushfire.

'I think that'll go away,' Curt said, 'but I believe wearing those masks was probably a damn good idea, after all. They're no protection against germs, but at least none of that black crap got in our mouths. I think the results of something like that might have been quite nasty.'

He was right.

NOW:

Sandy

The sandwiches were gone. So was the iced tea. I told Arky to get ten bucks out of the contingency fund (which was kept in a jar in the upstairs closet) and go down to Finn's Cash and Carry. I thought two six-packs of Coke and one of root beer would probably carry us through to the end.

'I do dat, I miss d'part about d'fish,' Arky said.

'Arky, you *know* the part about the fish. You know *all* the parts of this story. Go on and get us some cold drinks. Please.'

He went, firing up his old truck and driving out of the parking lot too fast. A man driving that way was apt to get a ticket.

'Go on,' Ned said. 'What happened next?'

'Well,' I said, 'let's see. The old Sarge became a grandfather, that was one thing. It probably happened a lot sooner than he wanted it to, baby girl born out of wedlock, big hooraw in the family, but everyone eventually calmed down and that girl has gone on to Smith, which is not a bad place for a young lady to get her diploma, or so I understand. George Morgan's boy hit a home run in tee-ball and George went around just about busting his buttons, he was so proud. This was I think two years before he killed the woman in the road and then killed himself.

Orvie Garrett's wife got blood poisoning in her foot and lost a couple of toes. Shirley Pasternak came to work with us in 1984 — '

'1986,' she murmured.

''86 it was,' I said, and patted her knee. 'There was a bad fire in Lassburg around that same time, kids playing with matches in the basement of an apartment house. Just goofing. No supervision. When someone says to me that the Amish are crazy to live like they do, I think about that fire in Lassburg. Nine people killed, including all but one of the kids in the basement. The one who got out probably wishes he hadn't. He'd be sixteen now, right around the age boys are generally getting good and interested in girls, and this kid probably looks like the lead actor in a burn-ward production of *Beauty and the Beast*. It didn't make the national news — I have theory that multiple-fatality apartment-house fires only make the news if they happen at Christmas — but it was bad enough for these parts, thank you very much, and Jackie O'Hara got some terrible burns on his hands, helping out. Oh, and we had a Trooper — James Dockery, his name was — '

'Docker-*ty*,' Phil Candleton said. '*T*. But you're forgiven, Sarge, he wasn't here more than a month or two, then he transferred over to Lycoming.'

I nodded. 'Anyhow, this Dockerty won a third prize in the Betty Crocker Bakeoff for a recipe called Golden Sausage Puffs. He got ribbed like a motherfucker, but he took it well.'

'*Very* well,' Eddie J. agreed. 'He shoulda

258

stayed. He woulda fit in here.'

'We won the tug-of-war that year at the Fourth of July picnic, and — '

I saw the look on the kid's face and smiled at him.

'You think I'm teasing you, Ned, but I'm not. Honest. What I'm doing is trying to make you understand. The Buick was not the only thing happening around here, okay? *Not.* In fact, there were times when we forgot it entirely. Most of us, anyway. For long stretches of time it was easy to forget. For long stretches of time all it did was sit out back and be quiet. Cops came and went while it did. Dockerty stayed just long enough to get nicknamed Chef Prudhomme. Young Paul Loving, the one who sprained his knee last Labor Day, got transferred out and then got transferred back in three years later. This job isn't the revolving door that some jobs are, but the door turns, all right. There's probably been seventy Troopers through here since the summer of 1979 — '

'Oh, that's way low,' Huddie said. 'Make it a hundred, counting the transfers and the Troops who are on duty here currently. Plus a few bad eggs.'

'Yeah, a few bad eggs, but most of us did our jobs. And Ned, listen — your father and Tony Schoondist learned a lesson the night your father opened up that bat-thing. I did, too. Sometimes there's nothing to learn, or no way to learn it, or no reason to even try. I saw a movie once where this fellow explained why he lit a candle in church even though he wasn't a very good

Catholic anymore. 'You don't fuck around with the infinite,' he said. Maybe that was the lesson we learned.

'Every now and then there was another lightquake in Shed B. Sometimes just a little temblor, sometimes a great-gosh-a'mighty. But people have a really amazing capacity to get used to stuff, even stuff they don't understand. A comet shows up in the sky and half the world goes around bawling about the Last Days and the Four Horsemen, but let the comet stay there six months and no one even notices. It's a big ho-hum. Same thing happened at the end of the twentieth century, remember? Everyone ran around screaming that the sky was falling and all the computers were going to freeze up; a week goes by and it's business as usual. What I'm doing is trying to keep things in perspective for you. To — '

'Tell me about the fish,' he said, and I felt that anger again. He wasn't going to hear all I had to say, no matter how much I wanted him to or how hard I tried. He'd hear the parts he wanted to hear and call it good. Think of it as the Teenage Disease. And the light in his eyes was like the light in his father's when Curt bent over the bat-thing with his scalpel in his gloved hand. (*Cutting now*: I sometimes still hear Curtis Wilcox saying that in my dreams.) Not *exactly* like it, though. Because the boy wasn't just curious. He was angry, as well. Pissed like a bear.

My own anger rose out of his refusal to take everything I wanted to give, for having the gall to pick and choose. But where did his come from?

260

What was its center? That his mother had been lied to, not just once but over and over as the years passed? That he himself had been lied to, if only by omission? Was he mad at his father for holding on to a secret? Mad at us? *Us?* Surely he didn't believe the Buick had killed his father, why would he? Bradley Roach was safely on the hook for that, Roach had unspooled him up the side of a pulled-over sixteen-wheeler, leaving a bloodsmear ten feet long and as tall as a State Trooper, about six-feet-two in the case of Curtis Wilcox, pulling his clothes not just off but inside out as well in the scream of brakes and all the while the radio playing WPND, which billed itself Western Pennsylvania's Country-Fried Radio, what else would it be but country with a half-drunk low rider like Bradley? Daddy sang bass and Momma sang tenor as the coins were ripped out of Curt Wilcox's pants and his penis was torn off like a weed and his balls were reduced to strawberry jelly and his comb and wallet landed on the yellow line; Bradley Roach responsible for all that, or maybe you wanted to save some blame for Dicky's Convenience in Statler that sold him the beer, or maybe for the beer company itself with its goodtime ads about cute talking frogs and funny ballpark beer-men instead of dead people lying by the highway with their guts hanging out, or maybe you want to blame it on Bradley's DNA, little twists of cellular rope that had been whispering *Drink more, drink more* ever since Bradley's first sip (because some people are just wired up that way, which is to say like suitcase bombs ready to

261

explode, which is absolutely zero comfort to the dead and wounded). Or maybe God was to blame, God's always a popular whipping boy because He doesn't talk back and never writes a column for the Op-Ed page. Not the Buick, though. Right? He couldn't find the Buick in Curt's death no matter how he traced it out. The Buick had been sitting miles away in Shed B, fat and luxy and blameless on whitewall tires that wouldn't take dirt or even the slightest pebble in the treads but repudiated them each and every one, right down to (as far as we could tell) the finest grain of sand. It was just sitting there and minding its business when Trooper Wilcox bled out on the side of Pennsylvania State Road 32. And if it was sitting there all the while in the faintest baleful reek of cabbage, what of that? Did this boy think —

'Ned, it didn't reach out for him, if that's what you're thinking,' I said. 'It doesn't do that.' I had to laugh at myself a little, sounding so sure. Sounding as if I knew that for a fact. Or anything else for a fact, when it came to the Roadmaster. 'It has pull, maybe even a kind of voice, when it's in one of its . . . I don't know . . . '

'Active phases,' Shirley suggested.

'Yes. When it's in one of its active phases. You can hear the hum, and sometimes you can hear it in your head, as well . . . kind of calling . . . but could it reach all the way out to Highway 32 by the old Jenny station? No way.'

Shirley was looking at me as if I'd gone slightly loopy, and I *felt* slightly loopy. What, exactly, was I doing? Trying to talk myself out of being angry at this unlucky, father-lost boy?

'Sandy? I just want to hear about the fish.'

I looked at Huddie, then Phil and Eddie. All three offered variations of the same rueful shrug. *Kids! What are you gonna do?*

Finish it. That was what I was going to do. Set aside my anger and finish it. I had spilled the beans (I hadn't known how many beans there were in the bag when I started, I'll grant you that much), and now I was going to clean them up.

'All right, Ned. I'll tell you what you want to hear. But will you at least bear in mind that this place stayed a barracks? Will you try to remember that, whether you believe it or not, whether you *like* it or not, the Buick eventually became just another part of our day, like writing reports or testifying in court or cleaning puke off the floormats of a cruiser or Steve Devoe's Polish jokes? Because it's important.'

'Sure. Tell me about the fish.'

I leaned back against the wall and raised my eyes to the moon. I wanted to give him his life back if I could. Or stars in a paper cup. All the poetry. All *he* wanted to hear about was the goddamned fish.

So fuck it, I told him.

THEN

No paper trail: that was Tony Schoondist's decree, and it was followed. People still knew how matters pertaining to the Buick were to be handled, though, what the proper channels were. It wasn't tough. One either reported to Curt, the Sarge, or to Sandy Dearborn. They were the Buick guys. Sandy supposed he'd become part of that triumvirate simply by virtue of having been present at the infamous autopsy. Certainly it wasn't because he had any special curiosity about the thing.

Tony's no-paper edict notwithstanding, Sandy was quite sure that Curt kept his own records — notes and speculations — about the Buick. If so, he was discreet about it. Meanwhile, the temperature drops and the energy discharges — the lightquakes — seemed to be slowing down. The life was draining out of the thing.

Or so they all hoped.

Sandy kept no notes and could never have provided a reliable sequence of events. The videotapes made over the years would have helped do that (if it ever needed doing), but there would still be gaps and questions. Not every lightquake was taped, and so what if they had been? They were all pretty much the same. There were probably a dozen between 1979 and 1983. Most were small. A couple were as big as the first one, and one was even bigger. That big one — the all-time champ — came in 1983. Those who were there sometimes still called '83 The Year of the Fish, as if they were Chinese.

Curtis made a number of experiments between '79 and '83, leaving various plants and animals in and around the Buick when the temperature dropped, but all the results were essentially reruns of what happened with Jimmy and Rosalynn. Which is to say sometimes things disappeared, and sometimes they didn't. There was no way of predicting in advance; it all seemed as random as a coin-toss.

During one temperature drop, Curt left a guinea pig by the Roadmaster's left front tire. Put it in a plastic bucket. Twenty-four hours after the purple fireworks were over and the temperature in the shed had gone back to normal, the guinea pig was still in his bucket, hopping and reasonably happy. Before another lightshow, Curt put a cage with two frogs in it directly under the Buick. There were still two frogs in the cage after the lightshow ended. A day later, however, there was only *one* frog in the cage.

A day after that, the cage was empty.

Then there was the Famous Trunk Experiment of 1982. That one was Tony's idea. He and Curt put six cockroaches in a clear plastic box, then put the box in the Buick's trunk. This was directly after one of the fireworks shows had ended, and it was still cold enough in the Buick so that they could see vapor coming out of their mouths when they bent into the trunk. Three days went by, with one of them checking the trunk every day (always with a rope tied around the waist of the one doing the checking, and everyone wondering what good a damn rope would do against something that had been able to snatch Jimmy out of his gerbil-condo without opening either of the hatches . . . or the frogs out of their latched cage, for that matter). The roaches were fine the first day, and the second, and the third. Curt and Tony went out on the fourth day to retrieve them, another failed experiment, back to the old drawing board. Only the roaches were gone, or so it seemed when they first opened the trunk.

'No, wait!' Curt yelled. 'There they are! I see em! Running around like mad bastards!'

'How many?' Tony called back. He was standing outside the door on the side of the shed, holding the end of the rope. 'Are they all there? How'd they get out of the damn *box*, Curtis?'

Curtis counted only four instead of six, but that didn't mean much. Cockroaches don't need a bewitched automobile to help them disappear; they are quite good at that on their own, as anybody who's ever chased one with a slipper knows. As for how they'd gotten out of the plastic box, that much was obvious. It was still latched shut, but now there was a small round hole in one side of it. The hole was three-quarters of an inch across. To Curt and the Sarge, it looked like a large-caliber bullet-hole. There were no cracks radiating out from around it, which might also indicate that something had punched through at an extremely high velocity.

Or perhaps *burned* through. No answers. Only mirages. Same as it ever was. And then the fish came, in June of 1983.

★   ★   ★

It had been at least two and a half years since Troop D had kept a day-in-and-out watch on the Buick, because by late 1979 or early 1980 they had decided that, with reasonable precautions, there wasn't much to worry about. A loaded gun is dangerous, no argument, but you don't have to post an around-the-clock guard on one to make sure it won't shoot by itself. If you put it up on a high shelf and keep the kiddies away, that's usually enough to do the trick.

Tony bought a vehicle tarp so anyone who came out back and happened to look in the shed wouldn't see the car and ask questions (a new fellow from the Motor Pool, a Buick-fancier, had once offered to buy it). The video camera stayed out in the hutch, mounted on its tripod and with a plastic bag pulled over it to keep it free of moisture, and the chair was still there (plus a good high stack of magazines beneath it), but Arky began to use the place more and more as a gardening shed. Bags of peat and fertilizer, pallets of sod, and flower-planters first began to crowd the Buick-watching stuff and then to crowd it out. The only time the hutch reverted to its original purpose was just before, during, and after one of the lightquakes.

June in The Year of the Fish was one of the most beautiful early summer months in Sandy's memory — the grass lush, the birds all in tune, the air filled with a kind of delicate heat, like a teenage couple's first real kiss. Tony Schoondist was on vacation, visiting his daughter on the west coast (she was the one whose baby had caused all that trouble). The Sarge and his wife were trying to mend a few fences before they got broken down entirely. Probably not a bad plan. Sandy Dearborn and Huddie Royer were in charge while he was gone, but Curtis Wilcox — no longer a rookie — was boss of the Buick, no doubt about that. And one day in that marvelous June, Buck Flanders came to see him in that capacity.

'Temp's down in Shed B,' he said.

Curtis raised his eyebrows. 'Not exactly the first time, is it?'

'No,' Buck admitted, 'but I've never seen it go down so fast. Ten degrees since this morning.'

That got Curt out to the shed in a hurry, with the old excited light in his eyes. When he put his face to one of the windows in the roll-up front door, the first thing he noticed was the tarp Tony had bought. It was crumpled along the driver's side of the Buick like a scuffed-up rug. It wasn't the first time for that, either; it was as if the Buick sometimes trembled (or shrugged) and slid the nylon cover off like a lady shrugging off an evening wrap by lifting her shoulders. The needle on the round thermometer stood at 61.

'It's seventy-four out here,' Buck said. He was standing at Curt's elbow. 'I checked the thermometer over by the bird-feeder before coming in to see you.'

268

'So it's actually gone down *thirteen* degrees, not ten.'

'Well, it was sixty-four in there when I came to get you. That's how fast it's going down. Like a . . . a cold front setting in, or something. Want me to get Huddie?'

'Let's not bother him. Make up a watch-roster. Get Matt Babicki to help you. Mark it . . . um, 'Car Wash Detail.' Let's get two guys watching the Buick the rest of the day, and tonight, as well. Unless Huddie says no or the temp bounces back up.'

'Okay,' Buck said. 'Do you want to be on the first stand?'

Curt did, and quite badly — he sensed something was going to happen — but he shook his head. 'Can't. I have court, then there's that truck-trap over in Cambria.' Tony would have screamed and clutched his head if he had heard Curt call the weigh-in on Highway 9 a truck-trap, but essentially that was what it was. Because someone was moving heroin and cocaine from New Jersey over that way, and the thinking was that it was moving in some of the independent truckers' loads. 'Truth is, I'm busier'n a one-legged man in an ass-kicking contest. Damn!'

He struck his thigh with his fist, then cupped his hands to the sides of his face and peered in through the glass again. There was nothing to see but the Roadmaster, sitting in two bars of sunlight that crisscrossed on the long dark blue hood like the contending beams of spotlights.

'Get Randy Santerre. And didn't I see Chris

Soder mooning around?'

'Yeah. He's technically off-duty, but his wife's two sisters are still visiting from over Ohio and he came here to watch TV.' Buck lowered his voice. 'Don't want to tell you your business, Curt, but I think both those guys are jagoffs.'

'They'll do for this. They'll have to. Tell them I want regular reports, too. Standard Code D. And I'll call in by landline before I leave court.'

Curt took a final, almost anguished look at the Buick, then started back to the barracks, where he would shave and get ready for the witness stand. In the afternoon he'd be poking in the backs of trucks along with some boys from Troop G, looking for coke and hoping nobody decided to unlimber an automatic weapon. He would have found someone to swap with if there had been time, but there wasn't.

Soder and Santerre got Buick-watching duty instead, and they didn't mind. Jagoffs never do. They stood beside the hutch, smoking, shooting the shit, taking the occasional look in at the Buick (Santerre too young to know what to expect, and he never lasted long in the PSP, anyway), telling jokes and enjoying the day. It was a June day so simple and so simply beautiful that even a jagoff couldn't help but enjoy it. At some point Buck Flanders spelled Randy Santerre; a little later on, Orville Garrett spelled Chris Soder. Huddie came out for the occasional peek. At three o'clock, when Sandy came in to drop his ass in the SC's chair, Curtis Wilcox finally got back and spelled Buck out by Shed B. Far from rebounding, the shed's temperature had rolled off another ten degrees by then, and off-duty Troopers began to clog the lot out back with their personal vehicles. Word had spread. Code D.

★　★　★

Around four P.M., Matt Babicki stuck his head into the SC's office and told Sandy he was losing the radio. 'Bad static, boss. Worst ever.'

'Shit.' Sandy closed his eyes, rubbed his knuckles against them, and wished for Tony. This was his first time as acting Sergeant Commanding, and while the temporary bump in his paycheck at the end of the month would no doubt be satisfying, this aggravation was not. 'Trouble with that goddam car. Just what I wanted.'

'Don't take it to heart,' Matt said. 'It'll shoot off a few sparks and then everything'll go back to normal. Including the radio. Isn't that the way it usually goes?'

Yes, that was the way it usually went. Sandy was not, in truth, especially worried about the Buick. But what if someone out on patrol found trouble while communications were FUBAR? Someone who had to call in a 33 — *Help me quick* — or a 47 — *Send an ambulance* — or, worst of all, a 10 — 99: *Officer down.* Sandy had well over a dozen guys out there, and at that moment it felt as if every one of them was riding him piggyback.

'Listen to me, Matt. Get in my ride — it's Unit 17 — and take it down to the bottom of the

271

hill. You should be clear of interference there. Call every one of ours currently running the roads and tell them base dispatch is temporarily 17. Code D.'

'Aw, Sandy, Jesus! Isn't that a little — '

'I don't have time to listen to your imitation of *Siskel and Ebert at the Movies* just now,' Sandy said. He had never felt more impatient with Police Communications Officer Babicki's whiny brand of foot-dragging bullshit than he did then. 'Just do it.'

'But I won't be here to see — '

'No, probably you won't.' Sandy's voice rising a little now. 'That's one you'll absolutely have to put on your TS list before you send it to the chaplain.'

Matt started to say something else, took a closer look at Sandy's face, and wisely decided to keep his mouth shut. Two minutes later, Sandy saw him headed down the hill, behind the wheel of Unit 17.

'Good,' Sandy muttered. 'Stay there awhile, you little backtalking pissant.'

Sandy went out to Shed B, where there was quite a little crowd. Most of them were Troopers, but some were Motor Pool guys in the grease-stained green Dickies that were their unofficial uniform. After four years of living with the Buick, none of them was afraid, exactly, but they were a rather nervy group that day, just the same. When you saw twenty degrees roll off the thermometer on a warm summer day, in a room where the air conditioning consisted of an occasionally opened door, it was hard not to

272

believe that something large was in the works.

Curt had been back long enough to set up a number of experiments — all he had time to arrange, Sandy guessed. On the Buick's front seat he'd placed a Nike sneaker box with some crickets in it. The frog cage was on the back seat. There was only one frog in it this time, but it was a whopper, one of those marsh bullfrogs with the bulgy yellow-black eyes. He had also taken the windowbox of flowers which had been outside Matt Babicki's office window and stuck them in the Buick's trunk. Last but not least, he took Mister Dillon for a promenade out there, toured him all around the car on his leash, the full three-sixty, just to see what would happen. Orvie Garrett didn't like that much, but Curt talked him into it. In most respects Curt was still a little rough around the edges and a little wet behind the ears, but when it came to the Buick, he could be as smooth as a riverboat gambler.

Nothing happened during D's walk — not that time — but it was clear the Troop mascot would rather have been just about anywhere else. He hung at the end of his leash so hard it choked him a little, and he walked with his head down and his tail lowered, giving the occasional dry cough. He looked at the Buick, but he looked at everything else out there as well, as if whatever it was he didn't like had spread out from the bogus car until it contaminated the whole shed.

When Curt brought him outside again and handed the leash back to Orville, he said, 'There's something going on, he feels it and so do I. But it's not like before.' He saw Sandy and

273

repeated it: not like before.

'No,' Sandy said, then nodded at Mister D. 'At least he's not howling.'

'Not yet,' Orville said. 'Come on, D, let's go back in the barracks. You did good. I'll give you a Bonz.' What Orvie gave Curt was a final reproachful look. Mister Dillon trotted neatly at Trooper Garrett's right knee, no longer needing the leash to keep him at heel.

At four-twenty or so, the TV upstairs in the common room suddenly went goofy. By four-forty, the temperature in Shed B had dropped to forty-nine degrees. At four-fifty, Curtis Wilcox shouted: 'It's starting! I hear it!'

Sandy had been inside to check on dispatch (and what a snafu it was by then, nothing but one big balls-to-the-wall roar of static), and when Curt yelled he was returning across the parking lot, where there were now so many personals you would have thought it was the Police Benefit Rummage Sale or the Muscular Dystrophy Kids' Carnival they put on each July. Sandy broke into a run, cutting through the knot of spectators craning to look in through the side door, which was still, unbelievably, standing wide open. And Curt was there, standing in it. Waves of cold were rolling out, but he seemed not to feel them. His eyes were huge, and when he turned to Sandy he was like a man dreaming. 'Do you see it? Sandy, *do you see it?*'

Of course he did: a waxing violet glow that was spilling out of the car's windows and seeping up through the crack which outlined the trunk-lid and went spilling down the Buick's sides like some thin radioactive fluid. Inside the car Sandy could clearly see the shapes of the seats and the oversized steering wheel. They were outlines, silhouettes. The rest of the cabin was swallowed in a cold purple glare, brighter than any furnace. The hum was loud and getting louder. It made Sandy's skull ache, made his ears almost wish they were deaf. Not that being deaf would do any good, because you seemed to hear that sound not just with your ears but with your whole body.

Sandy yanked Curt out on to the pavement, then grabbed the knob, meaning to shut the door. Curt took hold of his wrist. 'No, Sandy, no! I want to see it! I want — '

Sandy peeled his hand off, not gently. 'Are you crazy? There's a procedure we follow on this, a goddam *procedure*. No one should know that better than you! You helped think it up, for God's sake!'

When Sandy slammed the door shut, cutting off any direct view of the Buick, Curt's eyelids fluttered and he twitched like a man waking out of a deep sleep. 'Okay,' he said. 'Okay, boss. I'm sorry.'

'It's all right.' Not really believing it was. Because the damned fool would have stood right there in the doorway. No question about it in Sandy's mind. Would have stood there and been fried, if frying was on that thing's agenda.

'I need to get my goggles,' Curt said. 'They're in the trunk of my car. I have extras, and they're extra dark. A whole box of them. Do you want a pair?' Sandy still got the feeling that Curt wasn't fully awake, that he was only pretending, like you did when the telephone rang in the middle of the night.

'Sure, why not? But we're going to be cautious, right? Because this is looking like a bad one.'

'Looking like a *great* one!' Curt said, and the exuberance in his voice, although slightly scary, made Sandy feel a little better. At least Curt didn't sound as if he was sleepwalking any longer. 'But yes, Mother — we'll follow procedure and be as cautious as hell.'

He ran for his car — not his cruiser but his personal, the restored Bel Air — and opened the trunk. He was still rummaging in the boxes of stuff he kept back there when the Buick exploded.

★   ★   ★

It did not literally explode, but there seemed to be no other word for what it *did* do. Those who were there that day never forgot it, but they talked about it remarkably little, even among themselves, because there seemed no way to express the terrifying magnificence of it. The *power* of it. The best they could say was that it darkened the June sun and seemed to turn the shed transparent, into a ghost of itself. It was impossible to comprehend how mere glass could stand between that light and the outside world. The throbbing brilliance poured through the boards of the shed like water through cheese-cloth; the shapes of the nails stood out like the dots in a newspaper photograph or purple beads of blood on top of a fresh tattoo. Sandy heard Carl Brundage shout *She's gonna blow this time, she most surely will!* From behind him, in the barracks, he could hear Mister Dillon howling in terror.

'But he still wanted to get out and get at it,' Orville told Sandy later. 'I had im in the upstairs lounge, as far from that goddam shed as I could get him, but it didn't make any difference. He knew it was there. Heard it, I imagine — heard it humming. And then he saw the window. Holy Christ! If I hadn't been quick, hadn't grabbed him right off, I think he would have jumped right through it, second story or not. He pissed all over me and I never realized it until half an hour later, that's how scared *I* was.'

Orville shook his head, his face heavy and thoughtful.

'Never seen a dog like that. *Never.* His fur was all bushed out, he was foamin at the mouth, and his eyeballs looked like they were poppin right out of his head. *Christ.*'

* * *

Curt, meanwhile, came running back with a dozen pairs of protective goggles. The Troopers put them on but there was still no way of looking in at the Buick; it was impossible to even approach the windows. And again there was that weird silence when they all felt they should have been standing at the center of a cacophony, hearing thunder and landslides and erupting

277

volcanoes. With the shed's doors shut, they (unlike Mister D) couldn't even hear the humming noise. There was the shuffle of feet and someone clearing his throat and Mister Dillon howling in the barracks and Orvie Garrett telling him to calm down and the sound of Matt Babicki's static-drowned radio from dispatch, where the window (now denuded of its flower box, thanks to Curt) had been left open. Nothing else.

Curt walked to the roll-up door, head bent and hands raised. Twice he tried to lift his face and look inside Shed B, but he couldn't. It was too bright. Sandy grabbed his shoulder.

'Quit trying to look. You can't do it. Not yet, anyway. It'll knock the eyes right out of your head.'

'What is it, Sandy?' Curt whispered. 'What in God's name is it?'

Sandy could only shake his head.

★   ★   ★

For the next half hour the Buick put on the lightshow to end all lightshows, turning Shed B into a kind of fireball, shooting parallel lines of brilliance through all the windows, flashing and flashing, a gaudy neon furnace without heat or sound. If anyone from John Q. Public's family had turned up during that time, God knew what they might have thought or who they would have told or how much those they told might have believed, but no outsiders *did* turn up. And by five-thirty, the D Troopers had started to see individual flashes of light again, as if the power-source driving the phenomenon had begun to wobble. It made Sandy think of the way a motorcycle will lurch and spurt when the gas-tank is almost dry.

Curt edged up to the windows again, and although he had to duck down each time one of those bolts of light shot out, he could take little peeks in between. Sandy joined him, ducking away from the brighter pulses (*We probably look like we're practicing some weird drill routine*, he thought), squinting, eyes dazzled in spite of the triple layer of polarized glass in the goggles.

The Buick was still perfectly intact and apparently unchanged. The tarp lay in its same draped dune, unsinged by any fire. Arky's tools hung undisturbed on their pegs, and the stacks of old County *American* newspapers were still in the far corner, bundled and tied with twine. A single kitchen match would have been enough to turn those dry piles of old news into pillars of flame, but all that brilliant purple light hadn't charred so much as a single corner of a single Bradlee's circular.

'Sandy — can you see any of the specimens?'

Sandy shook his head, stood back, and took off the goggles Curt had loaned him. He passed them on to Andy Colucci, who was wild for a look into the shed. Sandy himself headed back to the barracks. Shed B was not going to blow up after all, it seemed. And he was the acting SC, with a job to do.

On the back step, he paused and looked back. Even wearing goggles, Andy Colucci and the others were reluctant to approach the row of windows. There was only one exception, and that was Curtis Wilcox. He stood right there — big as Billy-be-damned, Sandy's mother might have said — as close as he could get and leaning forward to get even closer, goggles actually pressed to the glass, only turning his head aside slightly each time the thing flashed out an especially bright bolt, which it was still doing every twenty seconds or so.

Sandy thought, *He's apt to put his eyes out, or at least go snowblind from it.* Except he wouldn't. He seemed to have almost timed the flashes, to have gotten in rhythm with them. From where Sandy was, it looked as if Curtis was actually turning his face aside a second or two before each flash came. And when it did come he would for a moment become his own exclamatory shadow, an exotic frozen dancer caught against a great sheet of purple light. Looking at him that way was scary. To Sandy it was like watching something that was there and not there at the same time, real but not real, both solid and mirage. Sandy would later think that when it came to the Buick 8, Curt was oddly like Mister Dillon. He wasn't howling like the dog was, upstairs in the common room, but he seemed in touch with the thing just the same, in sync with it. *Dancing* with it: then and later, that was how it would come back to Sandy.

Dancing with it.

★   ★   ★

280

At ten minutes of six that evening, Sandy radioed down the hill to Matt and asked what was up. Matt said nothing (*Nothing, Gramma* was what Sandy heard in his tone), and Sandy told him to come on back to base. When he did, Sandy said he was free to step across the parking lot and have a look at Old '54, if he still wanted one. Matt was gone like a shot. When he came back a few minutes later, he looked disappointed.

'I've seen it do *that* before,' he said, leaving Sandy to reflect on how dense and thankless human beings were, for the most part; how quickly their senses dulled, rendering the marvelous mundane. 'All the guys said it really blew its stack an hour ago, but none of them could describe it.' This was said with a contempt Sandy didn't find surprising. In the world of the police communications officer, *everything* is describable; the world's cartography must and can be laid out in ten-codes.

'Well, don't look at *me*,' Sandy said. 'I can tell you one thing, though. It was bright.'

'Oh. Bright.' Matt gave him a look that said *Not just a gramma but a loser gramma.* Then he went back inside.

* * *

By seven o'clock, Troop D's TV reception (always an important consideration when you were off the road) had returned to normal. Dispatch communications were back to normal. Mister Dillon had eaten his usual big bowl of

Gravy Train and then hung out in the kitchen, trolling for scraps, so *he* was back to normal. And when Curt poked his head into the SC's office at seven forty-five to tell Sandy he wanted to go into the shed and check on his specimens, Sandy could think of no way to stop him. Sandy was in charge of Troop D that evening, no argument there, but when it came to the Buick, Curt had as much authority as he did, maybe even a little more. Also, Curt was already wearing the damn yellow rope around his waist. The rest was looped over his forearm in a coil.

'Not a good idea,' Sandy told him. That was about as close to no as he could get.

'Bosh.' It was Curtis's favorite word in 1983. Sandy hated it. He thought it was a snotty word.

He looked over Curt's shoulder and saw they were alone. 'Curtis,' he said, 'you've got a wife at home, and the last time we talked about her, you said she might be pregnant. Has that changed?'

'No, but she hasn't been to the — '

'So you've got a wife for sure and a maybe baby. And if she's not preg this time, she probably will be next time. That's nice. It's just the way it should be. What I don't understand is why you'd put all that on the line for that goddam Buick.'

'Come on, Sandy — I put it on the line every time I get into a cruiser and go out on the road. Every time I step out and approach. It's true of everyone who works the job.'

'This is different and we both know it, so you can quit the high school debate crap. Don't you remember what happened to Ennis?'

282

'I remember,' Curt said, and Sandy supposed he did, but Ennis Rafferty had been gone almost four years by then. He was, in a way, as out-of-date as the stacks of County *Americans* in Shed B. And as for more recent developments? Well, the frogs had just been frogs. Jimmy might have been named after a President, but he was really just a gerbil. And Curtis was wearing the rope. The rope was supposed to make everything all right. *Sure,* Sandy thought, *and no toddler wearing a pair of water-wings ever drowned in a swimming pool.* If he said that to Curt, would Curtis laugh? No. Because Sandy was sitting in the big chair that night, the acting SC, the visible symbol of the PSP. But Sandy thought he would see laughter in Curt's eyes, just the same. Curtis had forgotten the rope had never been tested, that if the force hiding inside the Buick decided it wanted him, there might be a single last flash of purple light and then nothing but a length of yellow line lying on the cement floor with an empty loop at the end of it; so long, partner, happy trails to you, one more curious cat off hunting satisfaction in the big nowhere. But Sandy couldn't order him to stand down as he'd ordered Matt Babicki to drive down the hill. All he could do was get into an argument with him, and it was no good arguing with a man who had that bright and twirly let's-play-Bingo look in his eyes. You could cause plenty of hard feelings, but you could never convince the other guy that you had the right side of the argument.

'You want me to hold the other end of the rope?' Sandy asked him. 'You came in here wanting something, and it surely wasn't my opinion.'

'Would you?' Curt grinned. 'I'd like that.'

Sandy went out with him, and he held the rope with most of the coil snubbed around his elbow and Dicky-Duck Eliot standing behind him, ready to grab his belt loops if something happened and Sandy started to slide. The acting SC, standing in the side doorway of Shed B, not braced but ready to brace if something funny happened, biting his lower lip and breathing just a little too fast. His pulse felt like maybe a hundred and twenty beats a minute. He could still feel the chill in the shed even though the thermometer was by then easing its way back up; in Shed B, early summer had been revoked and what one met at the door was the dank cold of a hunting camp when you arrive in November, the stove in the middle of the room as dead as an unchurched god. Time slowed to a crawl. Sandy opened his mouth to ask Curt if he was going to stay in there forever, then glanced down at his watch and saw only forty seconds had passed. He did tell Curt not to go around to the far side of the Buick. Too much chance of snagging the rope.

'And Curtis? When you open the trunk, stand clear!'

'Roger that.' He sounded almost amused, indulgent, like a kid promising Mother and Dad that no, he *won't* speed, he *won't* take a drink at the party, he *will* watch out for the other guy, oh gosh yes, of course, you bet. Anything to keep them happy long enough to get the Christ out of the house, and then . . . *yeeeeeee-HAW!*

He opened the driver's door of the Buick and leaned in past the steering wheel. Sandy braced again for the pull he more than half-expected, the *yank*. He must have communicated the feeling backward, because he felt Dicky grab his belt loops. Curt reached, reached, and then stood up holding the shoebox with the crickets inside. He peered through the holes. 'Looks like they're all still there,' he said, sounding a little disappointed.

'You'd think they'd be roasted,' Dicky-Duck said. 'All that fire.'

But there had been no fire, just light. There wasn't a single scorch-mark on the shed's walls, they could see the thermometer's needle standing in the fifties, and electing not to believe that number wasn't much of an option, not with the shed's dank chill pushing into their faces. Still, Sandy knew how Dicky-Duck Eliot felt. When your head was still pounding from the dazzle and the last of the afterimages still seemed to be dancing in front of your eyes, it was hard to believe that a bunch of crickets sitting on ground zero could come through unscathed.

Yet they had. Every single one of them, as it turned out. So did the bullfrog, except its yellow-black eyes had gone cloudy and dull. It was present and accounted for, but when it hopped, it hopped right into the wall of its cage. It had gone blind.

Curt opened the trunk and moved back from it all in the same gesture, a move almost like ballet and one most policemen know. Sandy

285

braced in the doorway again, hands fisted on the slack rope, ready for it to go taut. Dicky-Duck once more snagged a tight hold on his belt loops. And again there was nothing.

Curt leaned into the trunk.

'Cold in here,' he called. His voice sounded hollow, oddly distant. 'And I'm getting that smell — the cabbage smell. Also peppermint. And . . . wait . . . '

Sandy waited. When nothing came, he called Curt's name.

'I think it's salt,' Curt said. 'Like the ocean, almost. This is the center of it, the vortex, right here in the trunk. I'm sure of it.'

'I don't care if it's the Lost Dutchman Mine,' Sandy told him. 'I want you out of there. Now.'

'Just a second more.' He leaned deep into the trunk. Sandy almost expected him to jerk forward as if something was pulling him, Curt Wilcox's idea of a knee-slapper. Perhaps he thought of it, but in the end he knew better. He simply got Matt Babicki's windowbox and pulled it out. He turned and held it up so Sandy and Dicky could see. The flowers looked fine and blooming. They were dead a couple of days later, but there was nothing very supernatural about that; they had been frozen in the trunk of the car as surely as they would have been if Curtis had put them in the freezer for awhile.

'Are you done yet?' Sandy was even starting to sound like Old Gammer Dearborn to himself, but he couldn't help it.

'Yeah. Guess so.' Curtis sounding disappointed. Sandy jumped when he slammed the

Buick's trunk-lid back down, and Dick's fingers tightened on the back of his pants. Sandy had an idea ole Dicky-Duck had come pretty close to yanking him right out the doorway and on to his ass in the parking lot. Curt, meantime, walked slowly toward them with the frog cage, the sneaker box, and the windowbox stacked up in his arms. Sandy kept coiling up the rope as he came so Curt wouldn't trip over it.

When they were all outside again, Dicky took the cage and looked wonderingly at the blind bullfrog. 'That beats everything,' he said.

Curt slipped out of the loop around his waist, then knelt on the macadam and opened the shoebox. Four or five other Troopers had gathered around by then. The crickets hopped out almost as soon as Curt took the lid off the box, but not before both Curtis and Sandy had a chance to take attendance. Eight, the number of cylinders in yonder Buick's useless engine. Eight, the same number of crickets that had gone in.

Curt looked disgusted and disappointed. 'Nothing,' he said. 'In the end, that's what it always comes to. If there's a formula — some binomial theorem or quadratic equation or something like that — I don't see it.'

'Then maybe you better give it a pass,' Sandy said.

Curt lowered his head and watched the crickets go hopping across the parking lot, widening out from each other, going their separate ways, and no equation or theorem ever invented by any mathematician who ever breathed could predict where any single one of them might end up. They were Chaos Theory hopping. The goggles were still hung around Curt's neck on their elastic strap. He fingered them for a few moments, then glanced at Sandy. His mouth was set. The disappointed look had gone out of his eyes. The other one, the half-crazed let's-play-Bingo-until-the-money's-all-gone look, had come back to take its place.

'Don't think I'm ready to do that,' he said. 'There must be . . . '

Sandy gave him a chance, and when Curtis didn't finish, he asked: 'There must be what?'

But Curtis only shook his head, as if he could not say. Or would not.

★ ★ ★

Three days went by. They waited for another bat-thing or another cyclone of leaves, but there was nothing immediate in the wake of the lightshow; the Buick just sat there. Troop D's piece of Pennsylvania was quiet, especially on the second shift, which suited Sandy Dearborn right down to the ground. One more day and he'd be off for two. Huddie's turn to run the show again. Then, when Sandy came back, Tony Schoondist would be in the big chair, where he belonged. The temperature in Shed B still hadn't equalized with the temperature of the outside world, but was getting there. It had risen into the low sixties, and Troop D had come to think of the sixties as safe territory.

For the first forty-eight hours after the monster lightquake, they'd kept someone out there around the clock. After twentyfour uneventful hours, some of the men had started grumbling about putting in the extra time, and Sandy couldn't much blame them. It was uncompensated time, of course. Had to be. How could they have sent Overtime Reports for Shed B-watching to Scranton? What would they have put in the space marked REASON FOR OVER-TIME ACTIVITY (SPECIFY IN FULL)?

Curt Wilcox wasn't crazy about dropping the full-time surveillance, but he understood the realities of the situation. In a brief conference, they decided on a week's worth of spot checks, most to be performed by Troopers Dearborn and Wilcox. And if Tony didn't like that when he got back from sunny California, he could change it.

So now comes eight o'clock of a summer evening right around the time of the solstice, the sun not down but sitting red and bloated on the Short Hills, casting the last of its long and longing light. Sandy was in the office, beavering away at the weekend duty roster, that big chair fitting him pretty well just then. There were times when he could imagine himself sitting in it more or less permanently, and that summer evening was one of them. *I think I could do this job*: that was what was going through his mind as George Morgan rolled up the driveway in Unit D-11. Sandy raised his hand to George and grinned when George ticked a little salute off the brim of his big hat in return: right-back-atcha.

George was on patrol that shift, but happened to be close by and so came in to gas up. By the nineties, Pennsylvania State Troopers would no longer have that option, but in 1983 you could still pump your go-juice at home and save the state a few pennies. He put the pump on slow automatic and strolled over to Shed B for a peek.

There was a light on inside (they always left it on) and there it was, the Troop D bonus baby, Old '54, sitting quiet with its chrome gleaming, looking as if it had never eaten a State Trooper, blinded a frog, or produced a freak bat. George, still a few years from his personal finish-line (two cans of beer and then the pistol in the mouth, jammed way up in back past the soft palate, not taking any chances, when a cop decides to do it he or she almost always gets it right), stood at the roll-up door as they all did from time to time, adopting the stance they all seemed to adopt, kind of loose and spraddle-legged like a sidewalk superintendent at a city building site, hands on hips (Pose A) or crossed on the chest (Pose B) or cupped to the sides of the face if the day was especially bright (Pose C). It's a stance that says the sidewalk superintendent in question is a man with more than a few of the answers, an expert gent with plenty of time to discuss taxes or politics or the haircuts of the young.

George had his look and was just about to turn away when all at once there was a thud from in there, toneless and heavy. This was followed by a pause (long enough, he told Sandy later, for him to think he'd imagined the sound in the first place) and then there was a second thud. George saw the Buick's trunk-lid move up and down in the middle, just once, quick. He started for the side door, meaning to go in and

290

investigate. Then he recalled what he was dealing with, a car that sometimes ate people. He stopped, looked around for someone else — for backup — and saw no one. There's never a cop around when you need one. He considered going into the shed by himself anyway, thought of Ennis — four years and still not home for lunch — and ran for the barracks instead.

★ ★ ★

'Sandy, you better come.' George standing in the doorway, looking scared and out of breath. 'I think maybe one of these idiots may have locked some other idiot in the trunk of that fucking nuisance in Shed B. Like for a joke.'

Sandy stared at him, thunderstruck. Unable (or perhaps unwilling) to believe that *anyone*, even that dope Santerre, could do such a thing. Except people could, he knew it. He knew something else, as well — incredible as it might seem, in many cases they meant no harm.

George mistook the acting SC's surprise for disbelief. 'I might be wrong, but honest-to-God I'm not pulling your chain. Something's thumping the lid of the trunk. *From the inside.* Sounds like with his fist. I started to go in on my own, then changed my mind.'

'That was the right call,' Sandy said. 'Come on.'

They hurried out, stopping just long enough so Sandy could look in the kitchen and then bawl upstairs to the common room. No one. The barracks was never deserted, but it was deserted now, and why? Because there was never a cop around when you needed one, that was why. Herb Avery was running dispatch that night, at least that was one, and he joined them.

'Want me to call someone in off the road, Sandy? I can, if you want.'

'No.' Sandy was looking around, trying to remember where he'd last seen the coil of rope. In the hutch, probably. Unless some yo-yo had taken it home to haul something upstairs with, which would be just about par for the course. 'Come on, George.'

The two of them crossed the parking lot in the red sunset light, their trailing shadows all but infinite, going first to the roll-up door for a little look-see. The Buick sat there as it had ever since old Johnny Parker dragged it in behind his tow-truck (Johnny now retired and getting through his nights with an oxygen tank beside his bed — but still smoking). It cast its own shadow on the concrete floor.

Sandy started to turn away, meaning to check the hutch for the rope, and just as he did there came another thump. It was strong and flat and unemphatic. The trunk-lid shivered, dimpled up in the middle for a moment, then went back down. It looked to Sandy as if the Roadmaster actually rocked a little bit on its springs.

'There! You see?' George said. He started to add something else, and that was when the Buick's trunk came unlatched and the lid sprang up on its hinges and the fish fell out.

Of course, it was a fish no more than the bat-thing was a bat, but they both knew at once it was nothing made to live on land; it had not one gill on the side they could see but four of them in a line, parallel slashes in its skin, which was the color of dark tarnished silver. It had a ragged and membranous tail. It unfolded out of the trunk with a last convulsive, dying shiver. Its bottom half curved and flexed, and Sandy could see how it might have made that thumping sound. Yes, that was clear enough, but how a thing of such size could ever have fit into the closed trunk of the Buick in the first place was beyond both of them. What hit the concrete floor of Shed B with a flat wet slap was the size of a sofa.

George and Sandy clutched each other like children and screamed. For a moment they *were* children, with every adult thought driven out of their heads. Somewhere inside the barracks, Mister Dillon began to bark.

It lay there on the floor, no more a fish than a wolf is a housepet, although it may look quite a bit like a dog. And in any case, *this* fish was only a fish up to the purple slashes of its gills. Where a fish's head would have been — something that at least had the steadying sanity of eyes and a mouth — there was a knotted, naked mass of pink things, too thin and stiff to be tentacles, too thick to be hair. Each was tipped with a black node and Sandy's first coherent thought was *A shrimp, the top half of it's some kind of shrimp and those black things are its eyes.*

'What's wrong?' someone bawled. 'What is it?'

Sandy turned and saw Herb Avery on the back step. His eyes were wild and he had his Ruger in

293

his hand. Sandy opened his mouth and at first nothing came out but a phlegmy little wheeze. Beside him, George hadn't even turned; he was still looking through the window, mouth hanging slack in an idiot's gape.

Sandy took a deep breath and tried again. What was meant for a shout emerged as a faint punched-in-the-belly wheeze, but at least it was something. 'Everything's okay, Herb — five-by-five. Go back inside.'

'Then why did you — '

'Go inside!' *There, that's a little better*, Sandy thought. 'Go on, now, Herb. And holster that piece.'

Herb looked down at the gun as if unaware until then that he had drawn it. He put it back in his holster, looked at Sandy as if to ask was he sure. Sandy made little flapping gestures with his hands and thought, *Granny Dearborn says go back inside, dad-rattit!*

Herb went, yelling for Mister D to shut up that foolish barking as he did.

Sandy turned back to George, who had gone white. 'It was breathing, Sandy — or trying to. The gills were moving and the side was going up and down. Now it's stopped.' His eyes were huge, like the eyes of a child who has been in a car accident. 'I think it's dead.' His lips were quivering. 'Man, I *hope* it's dead.'

Sandy looked in. At first he was sure George was wrong: the thing was still alive. Still breathing, or trying to breathe. Then he realized what he was seeing and told George to get the videocam out of the hutch.

'What about the r — '

'We won't need the rope, because we're not going in there — not yet, we're not — but get the camera. Fast as you can.'

George went around the side of the garage, not moving very well. Shock had made him gawky. Sandy looked back into the shed, cupping his eyes to the sides of his face to cut the red sunset glare. There was motion in the shed, all right, but not life's motion. It was mist rising from the thing's silver side and also from the purple slashes of its gills. The bat-thing hadn't decomposed, but the leaves had, and quickly. This thing was starting to rot like the leaves, and Sandy had the feeling that once the process really got going, it would go fast.

Even standing outside, with the closed door between him and it, he could smell it. An acrid, watery reek of mixed cabbage and cucumber and salt, the smell of a broth you might feed to someone if you wanted to make them sicker instead of well.

More mist was rising from its side; it dribbled up from the nest of tangled pink ropes that seemed to serve as its head, as well. Sandy thought he could hear a faint hissing noise, but knew he could just as well be imagining it. Then a black slit appeared in the grayish-silver scales, running north from the tattered nylon of its tail to the rearmost gill. Black fluid, probably the same stuff Huddie and Arky had found around the bat-thing's corpse, began to trickle out — listlessly at first, then with a little more spirit. Sandy could see an ominous bulge developing behind the split in the skin. It was no hallucination, and neither was the hissing sound. The fish was doing something more radical than decomposing; it was *giving in*. Yielding to the change in pressure or perhaps the change in everything, its whole environment. He thought of something he'd read once (or maybe seen in a *National Geographic* TV special), about how when some deep-sea creatures were brought up from their dwelling places, they simply exploded.

'*George!*' Bawling at the top of his lungs. '*Hurry the hell up!*'

George flew back around the corner of the shed, holding the tripod way up high, where the aluminum legs came together. The lens of the videocam glared above his fist, looking like a drunk's eyeball in the day's declining red light.

'I couldn't get it off the tripod,' he panted. 'There's some kind of latch or lock and if I'd had time to figure it out — or maybe I was trying to turn the Christly thing backward — '

'Never mind.' Sandy snatched the videocam from him. There was no problem with the tripod, anyway; the legs had been adjusted to the height of the windows in the shed's two roll-up doors for years. The problem came when Sandy pushed the ON button and looked through the viewfinder. Instead of a picture, there were just red letters reading LO BAT.

'Judas-fucking-Iscariot on a chariot-driven crutch! Go back, George. Look on the shelf by the box of blank tapes, there's another battery there. Get it.'

'But I want to see — '

296

'I don't care! Go on!'

He went, running hard. His hat had gone askew on his head, giving him a weirdly jaunty look. Sandy pushed the RECORD button on the side of the camera's housing, not knowing what he'd get but hoping for something. When he looked into the viewfinder again, however, even the letters reading LO BAT were fading.

Curt's going to kill me, he thought.

He looked back through the shed window just in time to catch the nightmare. The thing ruptured all the way up its side, spilling out that black ichor not in trickles but in a flood. It spread across the floor like backflow from a clogged drain. Following it came a noisome spew of guts: flabby bags of yellowish-red jelly. Most of them split and began to steam as soon as the air hit them.

Sandy turned, the back of his hand pressed hard against his mouth until he was sure he wasn't going to vomit, and then he yelled: 'Herb! If you still want a look, now's your chance! Quick as you can!'

Why getting Herb Avery on-scene should have been the first thing he thought of, Sandy could not later say. At the time, however, it seemed perfectly reasonable. If he had called his dead mother's name, he would have been equally unsurprised. Sometimes one's mind simply passes beyond one's rational and logical control. Right then he wanted Herb. Dispatch is never to be left unattended, it's a rule anyone in rural law enforcement knows, the Fabled Automatic. But rules were made to be broken, and Herb would

297

never see anything like this again in his life, none of them would, and if Sandy couldn't have videotape, he would at least have a witness. Two, if George got back in time.

Herb came out fast, as if he had been standing right inside the back door and watching through the screen all along, and sprinted across the nearly empty parking lot in the red light. His face was both scared and avid. Just as he arrived, George steamed back around the corner, waving a fresh battery for the video camera. He looked like a game show contestant who has just won the grand prize.

'Oh Mother, what's that smell?' Herb asked, clapping his hand over his mouth and nose so that everything after *Mother* came out muffled.

'The smell isn't the worst,' Sandy said. 'You better get a look while you still can.'

They both looked, and uttered almost identical cries of revulsion. The fish was blown out all down its length by then, and deflating — sinking into the black liquor of its own strange blood. White billows rose from its body and the innards which had already spilled from that gaping flayment. The vapor was as thick as smoke rising from a pile of smoldering damp mulch. It obscured the Buick from its open trunk forward until Old '54 was nothing but a ghost-car.

If there had been more to see, Sandy might actually have fumbled longer with the camera, perhaps getting the battery in wrongways on the first try or even knocking the whole works over and breaking it in his fumble-fingered haste. The

298

fact that there was going to be damned little to tape no matter how fast he worked had a calming effect, and he snapped the battery home on the first try. When he looked into the viewfinder again, he had a clear, bright view of not much: a disappearing amphibious thing that might have been a fabulous landlocked sea monster or just a fishy version of the Cardiff Giant sitting on a concealed block of dry ice. On the tape one can see the pink tangle that served as the amphibian's head quite clearly for perhaps ten seconds, and a number of rapidly liquefying red lumps strewn along its length; one can see what appears to be filthy seafoam sweating out of the thing's tail and running across the concrete in a sluggish rill. Then the creature that convulsed its bulk out of the Roadmaster's trunk is mostly gone, no more than a shadow in the mist. The car itself is hardly there. Even in the mist, however, the open trunk is visible, and it looks like a gaping mouth. Come closer, all good little children, come closer, see the living crocodile.

George stepped away, gagging and shaking his head.

Sandy thought again of Curtis, who for a change had left as soon as his shift was over. He and Michelle had big plans — dinner at The Cracked Platter in Harrison, followed by a movie. The meal would be over by now and they'd be at the show. Which one? There were three within striking distance. If there had been kids instead of just a maybe baby, Sandy could have called the house and asked the sitter. But would he have made that call? Maybe not. Probably not, in fact. Curt had begun to settle a bit over the last eighteen months or so, and Sandy hoped that settling would continue. He had heard Tony say on more than one occasion that when it came to the PSP (or any law enforcement agency worth its salt), one could best assess a man's worth by the truthful answer to a single question: How are things at home? It wasn't just that the job was dangerous; it was also a *crazy* job, full of opportunities to see people at their absolute worst. To do it well over a long period of time, to do it *fairly*, a cop needed an anchor. Curt had Michelle, and now he had the baby (maybe). It would be better if he didn't go bolting off to the barracks unless he absolutely had to, especially when he had to lie about the reason. A wife could swallow only so many rabid fox-tales and unexpected changes in the duty roster. He'd be angry that he hadn't been called, angrier still when he saw the bitched-up videotape, but Sandy would deal with that. He'd have to. And Tony would be back. Tony would help him deal with it.

★　★　★

The following day was cool, with a fresh breeze. They rolled up Shed B's big doors and let the place air out for six hours or so. Then four Troopers, led by Sandy and a stony-faced Trooper Wilcox, went in with hoses. They cleaned off the concrete and washed the final decaying lumps of the fish out into the tall grass

300

behind the shed. It was really the story of the bat all over again, only with more mess and less to show at the end of the day. In the end it was more about Curtis Wilcox and Sandy Dearborn than it was about the ruins of that great unknown fish.

Curt was indeed furious at not having been called, and the two law enforcement officers had an extremely lively discussion on that subject — and others — when they had gotten to a place where no one else on the roster could possibly overhear. This turned out to be the parking lot behind The Tap, where they had gone for a beer after the clean-up operation was finished. In the bar it was just talking, but once outside, their voices started to climb. Pretty soon they were both trying to talk at the same time, and of course that led to shouting. It almost always does.

Man, I can't believe you didn't call me.

You were off-duty, you were out with your wife, and besides, there was nothing to see.

I wish you'd let me decide —

There wasn't —

— decide that, Sandy —

— any time! It all happened —

Least you could have done was get some half-decent video for the file —

Whose file are we talking about, Curtis? Huh? Whose goddam file?

By then the two of them were standing nose to nose, fists clenched, almost down to it. Yes, really on the verge of getting down to it. There are moments in a life that don't matter and moments that do and some — maybe a dozen — when everything is on a hinge. Standing there in the parking lot, wanting to sock the kid who was no longer a kid, the rookie who was no longer a rookie, Sandy realized he had come to one of those moments. He liked Curt, and Curt liked him. They had worked together well over the last years. But if this went any farther, all that would change. It depended on what he said next.

'It smelled like a basket of minks.' That was what he said. It was a remark that came from nowhere at all, at least nowhere he could pinpoint. 'Even from the outside.'

'How would you know what a basket of minks smelled like?' Curt starting to smile. Just a little.

'Call it poetic license.' Sandy also starting to smile, but also only a little. They had turned in the right direction, but they weren't out of the woods.

Then Curtis asked: 'Did it smell worse than that whore's shoes? The one from Rocksburg?'

Sandy started laughing. Curt joined him. And they were off the hinge, just like that.

'Come on in,' Curt said. 'I'll buy you another beer.'

Sandy didn't want another beer, but he said okay. Because now it wasn't about beer; it was about putting the crap behind them.

Back inside, sitting in a corner booth, Curt said: 'I've had my hands in that trunk, Sandy. I've knocked on the bottom of it.'

'Me too.'

'And I've been under it on a crawler. It's not a magician's trick, like a box with a false bottom.'

'Even if it was, that was no white rabbit that came out of there yesterday.'

Curtis said, 'For things to disappear, they only have to be in the *vicinity*. But when things show up, they always come out of the trunk. Do you agree?'

Sandy thought it over. None of them had actually seen the bat-thing emerge from the Buick's trunk, but the trunk had been open, all right. As for the leaves, yes — Phil Candleton had seen them swirling out.

'Do you agree?' Impatient now, his voice saying Sandy *had* to agree, it was so goddam obvious.

'It seems likely, but I don't think we have enough evidence to be a hundred per cent sure yet,' Sandy replied at last. He knew saying that made him hopelessly stodgy in Curtis's eyes, but it was what he believed. ' 'One swallow doesn't make a summer.' Ever heard that one?'

Curt stuck out his lower lip and blew an exasperated breath up his face. ' 'Plain as the nose on your face', ever heard *that* one?'

'Curt — '

Curt raised his hands as if to say no, no, they didn't have to go back out into the parking lot and pick up where they had left off. 'I see your point. Okay? I don't agree, but I see it.'

'Okay.'

'Just tell me one thing: when'll we have enough to draw some conclusions? Not about everything, mind you, but maybe a few of the bigger things. Like where the bat and the fish came from, for instance. If I had to settle for just one answer, it'd probably be that one.'

'Probably never.'

Curt raised his hands to the smoke-stained tin ceiling, then dropped them back to the table with a clump. '*Gahh*! I *knew* you'd say that! I could *strangle* you, Dearborn!'

They looked at each other across the table, across the tops of beers neither one of them wanted, and Curt started to laugh. Sandy smiled. And then he was laughing, too.

NOW:

Sandy

Ned stopped me there. He wanted to go inside and call his mother, he said. Tell her he was okay, just eating dinner at the barracks with Sandy and Shirley and a couple of the other guys. Tell her lies, in other words. As his father had before him.

'Don't you guys move,' he said from the doorway. 'Don't you move a red inch.'

When he was gone, Huddie looked at me. His broad face was thoughtful. 'You think telling him all this stuff is a good idea, Sarge?'

'He gonna want to see all dose ole tapes, nex' t'ing,' Arky said dolefully. He was drinking a root beer. 'Hell's own movie-show.'

'I don't know if it's a good idea or a bad one,' I said, rather peevishly. 'I only know that it's a little late to back out now.' Then I got up and went inside myself.

Ned was just hanging up the phone. 'Where are *you* going?' he asked. His brows had drawn together, and I thought of standing nose to nose with his father outside The Tap, the scurgy little bar that had become Eddie J.'s home away from home. That night Curt's brows had drawn together in that exact same way.

'Just to the toilet,' I said. 'Take it easy, Ned, you'll get what you want. What there is to get,

305

anyway. But you have to stop waiting for the punchline.'

I went into the can and shut the door before he had a chance to reply. And the next fifteen seconds or so were pure relief. Like beer, iced tea is something you can't buy, only rent. When I got back outside, the smokers' bench was empty. They had stepped across to Shed B and were looking in, each with his own window in the roll-up door facing the rear of the barracks, each in that sidewalk superintendent posture I knew so well. Only now it's changed around in my mind. It's exactly backwards. Whenever I pass men lined up at a board fence or at sawhorses blocking off an excavation hole, the first things I think of are Shed B and the Buick 8.

'You guys see anything in there you like better than yourselves?' I called across to them.

It seemed they didn't. Arky came back first, closely followed by Huddie and Shirley. Phil and Eddie lingered a bit longer, and Curt's boy returned last to the barracks side of the parking lot. Like father like son in this, too. Curtis had also always lingered longest at the window. If, that was, he had time to linger. He wouldn't *make* time, though, because the Buick never took precedence. If it had, he and I almost certainly *would* have come to blows that night at The Tap instead of finding a way to laugh and back off. We found a way because us getting into a scrape would have been bad for the Troop, and he kept the Troop ahead of everything — the Buick, his wife, his family when the family came. I once asked him what he was proudest of in his life.

This was around 1986, and I imagined he'd say his son. His response was *The uniform.* I understood that and responded to it, but I'd be wrong not to add that the answer horrified me a little, as well. But it saved him, you know. His pride in the job he did and the uniform he wore held him steady when the Buick might otherwise have unbalanced him, driven him into an obsessional madness. Didn't the job also get him killed? I suppose. But there were years in between, a lot of good years. And now there was this kid, who was troubling because he didn't have the job to balance him. All he had was a lot of questions, and the naïve belief that, just because he felt he needed the answers, those answers would come. *Bosh,* his father might have said.

'Temp in there's gone down another tick,' Huddie said as we all sat down again. 'Probably nothing, but she might have another surprise or two left in her. We'd best watch out.'

'What happened after you and my dad almost got into that fight?' Ned asked. 'And don't start telling me about calls and codes, either. I *know* about calls and codes. I'm learning dispatch, remember.'

What *was* the kid learning, though? After spending a month of officially sanctioned time in the cubicle with the radio and the computers and the modems, what did he really know? The calls and codes, yes, he was a quick study and he sounded as professional as hell when he answered the red phone with *State Police Statler, Troop D, this is PCO Wilcox, how can I*

307

help?, but did he know that each call and each code is a link in a chain? That there are chains everywhere, each link in each one a little bit stronger or weaker than the last? How could you expect a kid, even a smart one, to know that? These are the chains we forge in life, to misquote Jacob Marley. We make them, we wear them, and sometimes we share them. George Morgan didn't really shoot himself in his garage; he just got tangled in one of those chains and hanged himself. Not, however, until after he'd helped us dig Mister Dillon's grave on one brutally hot summer day after the tanker-truck blew over in Poteenville.

There was no call or code for Eddie Jacubois spending more and more of his time in The Tap; there was none for Andy Colucci cheating on his wife and getting caught at it and begging her for a second chance and not getting it; no code for Matt Babicki leaving; no call for Shirley Pasternak coming. There are just things you can't explain unless you admit a knowledge of those chains, some made of love and some of pure happenstance. Like Orville Garrett down on one knee at the foot of Mister Dillon's fresh grave, crying, putting D's collar on the earth and saying *Sorry, partner, sorry.*

And was all that important to my story? I thought so. The kid, obviously, thought different. I kept trying to give him a context and he kept repudiating it, just as the Buick's tires repudiated any invasion — yes, right down to the smallest sliver of a pebble that would simply not stay caught between the treads. You could put that

308

sliver of pebble in, but five or ten or fifteen seconds later it would fall back out again. Tony had tried this experiment; I had tried it; this boy's father had tried it time and time and time again, often with videotape rolling. And now here sat the boy himself, dressed in civvies, no gray uniform to balance *his* interest in the Buick, here he sat repudiating even in the face of his father's undoubtedly dangerous eight-cylinder miracle, wanting to hear the story out of context and out of history, chainless and immaculate. He wanted what suited him. In his anger, he thought he had a right to that. I thought he was wrong, and I was sort of pissed at him myself, but I tell you with all the truth in my heart that I loved him, too. He was so much like his father then, you see. Right down to the let's-play-Bingo-with-the-paycheck look in his eyes.

'I can't tell you this next part,' I said. 'I wasn't there.'

I turned to Huddie, Shirley, Eddie J. None of them looked comfortable. Eddie wouldn't meet my gaze at all.

'What do you say, guys?' I asked them. 'PCO Wilcox doesn't want any calls or codes, he just wants the story.' I gave Ned a satiric look he either didn't understand or chose not to understand.

'Sandy, what — ' Ned began, but I held up my palm like a traffic cop. I had opened the door to this. Probably opened it the first time I'd gotten to the barracks and seen him out mowing the lawn and hadn't sent him home. He wanted the story. Fine. Let him have it and be done.

'This boy is waiting. Which of you will help him out? And I want to have *all* of it. Eddie.'

He jumped as if I'd goosed him, and gave me a nervous look.

'What was the guy's name? The guy with the cowboy boots and the Nazi necklace?'

Eddie blinked, shocked. His eyes asked if I was sure. No one talked about that guy. Not, at least, until now. Sometimes we talked about the day of the tanker-truck, laughed about how Herb and that other guy had tried to make up with Shirley by picking her a bouquet of flowers out back (just before the shit hit the fan, that was), but not about the guy in the cowboy boots. Not him. Never. But we were going to talk about him now, by God.

'Leppler? Lippman? Lippier? It was something like that, wasn't it?'

'His name was Brian Lippy,' Eddie said at last. 'Him and me, we went back a little.'

'Did you?' I asked. 'I didn't know that.'

I began the next part, but Shirley Pasternak told quite a bit of the tale (once she came into it, that was), speaking warmly, eyes fixed on Ned's and one of her hands lying on top of his. It didn't surprise me that she should be the one, and it didn't surprise me when Huddie chimed in and began telling it with her, turn and turn about. What surprised me was when Eddie J. began to add first sidelights . . . then footlights . . . and finally spotlights. I had told him to stick around until he had something to say, but it still surprised me when his time came and he started talking. His voice was low and tentative at first, but by the time he got to the part about discovering that asshole Lippy had kicked out the window, he was speaking strongly and steadily, his voice that of a man who remembers everything and has made up his mind to hide nothing. He spoke without looking at Ned or me or any of us. It was the shed he looked at, the one that sometimes gave birth to monsters.

THEN:

Sandy

By the summer of 1988, the Buick 8 had become an accepted part of Troop D's life, no more or less a part of it than any other. And why not? Given time and a fair amount of goodwill, any freak can become a part of any family. That was what had happened in the nine years since the disappearance of the man in the black coat ('Oil's fine!') and Ennis Rafferty.

The thing still put on its lightshows from time to time, and both Curt and Tony continued to run experiments from time to time. In 1984, Curtis tried a videocam which could be activated by remote control inside the Buick (nothing happened). In '85, Tony tried much the same thing with a top-of-the-line Wollensak audio recorder (he got a faint off-and-on humming and the distant calling of some crows, nothing more). There were a few other experiments with live test animals. A couple died, but none disappeared.

On the whole, things were settling down. When the lightshows *did* happen, they were nowhere near as powerful as the first few (and the whopper in '83, of course). Troop D's biggest problem in those days was caused by someone who knew absolutely nothing about the Buick. Edith Hyams (aka The Dragon) continued to talk to the press (whenever the press

312

would listen, that was) about her brother's disappearance. She continued to insist it was no ordinary disappearance (which once caused Sandy and Curt to muse on just what an 'ordinary disappearance' might be). She also continued to insist that Ennis's fellow officers Knew More Than They Were Telling. She was absolutely right on that score, of course. Curt Wilcox said on more than one occasion that if Troop D ever came to grief over the Buick, it would be that woman's doing. As a matter of public policy, however, Ennis's Troop-mates continued to support her. It was their best insurance, and they all knew it. After one of her forays in the press Tony said, 'Never mind, boys — time's on our side. Just remember that and keep smilin.' And he was right. By the mid-eighties, the representatives of the press were for the most part no longer returning her calls. Even WKML, the tri-country indie station whose Action News at Five broadcasts frequently featured stories about sightings of Sasquatch in the Lassburg Forest and such thoughtful medical briefings as **CANCER IN THE WATER SUPPLY! IS YOUR TOWN NEXT?**, had begun to lose interest in Edith.

On three more occasions, things appeared in the Buick's trunk. Once it was half a dozen large green beetles which looked like no beetles anyone in Troop D had ever seen. Curt and Tony spent an afternoon at Horlicks University, looking through stacks of entomology texts, and there was nothing like those green bugs in the books, either. In fact, the very shade of green was

313

like nothing anyone in Troop D had ever seen before, although none could have explained exactly how it was different. Carl Brundage dubbed it Headache Green. Because, he said, the bugs were the color of the migraines he sometimes got. They were dead when they showed up, the whole half-dozen. Tapping their carapaces with the barrel of a screwdriver produced the sort of noise you would have gotten by tapping a piece of metal on a block of wood.

'Do you want to try a dissection?' Tony asked Curt.

'Do *you* want to try one?' Curt replied.

'Not particularly, no.'

Curt looked at the bugs in the trunk — most of them on their backs with their feet up — and sighed. 'Neither do I. What would be the point?'

So, instead of being pinned to a piece of corkboard and dissected while the video camera ran, the bugs were bagged, tagged with the date (the line on the tag for NAME/RANK OF OIC was left blank, of course), and stored away downstairs in that battered green file-cabinet. Allowing the alien bugs to make their journey from the Buick's trunk to the green file-cabinet unexamined was another step down Curt's road to acceptance. Yet the old look of fascination still came into his eyes sometimes. Tony or Sandy would see him standing at the roll-up door, peering in, and that light would be there, more often than not. Sandy came to think of it as his Kurtis the Krazy Kat look, although he never told anyone that, not even the old Sarge. The rest of them lost interest in the Buick's misbegotten stillbirths, but Trooper Wilcox never did.

In Curtis, familiarity never bred contempt.

★ ★ ★

On a cold February day in 1984, five months or so after the appearance of the bugs, Brian Cole stuck his head into the SC's office. Tony Schoondist was in Scranton, trying to explain why he hadn't spent his entire budget appropriation for 1983 (there was nothing like one or two scrimpy SCs to make everyone else look bad), and Sandy Dearborn was holding down the big chair.

'Think you better take a little amble out to the back shed, boss,' Brian said. 'Code D.'

'What kind of Code D we talking about, Bri?'

'Trunk's up.'

'Are you sure it didn't just pop open? There haven't been any fireworks since just before Christmas. Usually — '

'Usually there's fireworks, I know. But the temperature's been too low in there for the last week. Besides, I can see something.'

That got Sandy on his feet. He could feel the old dread stealing its fat fingers around his heart and starting to squeeze. Another mess to clean up, maybe. Probably. *Please God don't let it be another fish*, he thought. *Nothing that has to be hosed out of there by men wearing masks*.

'Do you think it might be alive?' Sandy asked. He thought he sounded calm enough, but he did not feel particularly calm. 'The thing you saw, does it look — '

'It looks like some sort of uprooted plant,' Brian said. 'Part of it's hanging down over the back bumper. Tell you what, boss, it looks a little bit like an Easter lily.'

'Have Matt call Curtis in off the road. His shift's almost over, anyway.'

Curt rogered the Code D, told Matt he was out on Sawmill Road, and said he'd be back at base in fifteen minutes. That gave Sandy time to get the coil of yellow rope out of the hutch and to have a good long look into Shed B with the pair of cheap low-power binoculars that were also kept in the hutch. He agreed with Brian. The thing hanging out of the trunk, a draggled and membranous white shading to dark green, looked as much like an Easter lily as anything else. The kind you see about five days after the holiday, half-past drooping and going on dead.

Curt showed up, parked sloppily in front of the gas-pump, and came on the trot to where Sandy, Brian, Huddie, Arky Arkanian, and a few others were standing at the shed windows in those sidewalk superintendent poses. Sandy held the binoculars out and Curt took them. He stood for nearly a full minute, at first making tiny adjustments to the focus-knob, then just looking.

'Well?' Sandy asked when he was finally finished.

'I'm going in,' Curt replied, a response that didn't surprise Sandy in the slightest; why else had he bothered to get the rope? 'And if it doesn't rear up and try to bite me, I'll

316

photograph it, video it, and bag it. Just give me five minutes to get ready.'

It didn't take him even that. He came out of the barracks wearing surgical gloves — what were already coming to be known in the PSP as 'AIDS mittens' — a barber's smock, rubber galoshes, and a bathing cap over his hair. Hung around his neck was a Puff-Pak, a little plastic breathing mask with its own air supply that was good for about five minutes. In one of his gloved hands he had a Polaroid camera. There was a green plastic garbage bag tucked into his belt.

Huddie had unlimbered the videocam and now he trained it on Curt, who looked *très fantastique* as he strode manfully across the parking lot in his blue bathing cap and red galoshes (and even more so when Sandy had knotted the yellow rope around his middle).

'You're beautiful!' Huddie cried, peering through the video camera. 'Wave to your adoring fans!'

Curtis Wilcox waved dutifully. Some of his fans would look at this tape in the days after his sudden death seventeen years later, trying not to cry even as they laughed at the foolish, amiable look of him.

From the open dispatch window, Matt sang after him in a surprisingly strong tenor voice: '*Hug me . . . you sexy thing! Kiss me . . . you sexy thing!*'

Curt took all the ribbing well, but it was secondary to him, his mates' laughter like something overheard in another room. That light was in his eyes.

317

'This really isn't very bright,' Sandy said as he cinched the loop of the rope snugly around Curt's waist. Not with any real hope of changing Curt's mind, however. 'We should probably wait and see what develops. Make sure this is all, that there's nothing else coming through.'

'I'll be okay,' Curt said. His tone was absent; he was barely listening. Most of him was inside his own head, running over a checklist of things to do.

'Maybe,' Sandy said, 'and maybe we're starting to get a little careless with that thing.' Not knowing if it was really true, but wanting to say it out loud, try it on for size. 'We're starting to really believe that if nothing's happened to any of us so far, nothing ever will. That's how cops and lion-tamers get hurt.'

'We're fine,' Curt said, and then — appearing not to sense any contradiction — he told the other men to stand back. When they had, he took the video camera from Huddie, put it on the tripod, and told Arky to open the door. Arky pushed the remote clipped to his belt and the door rattled up on its tracks.

Curt let the Polaroid's strap slip to his elbow, so he could pick up the videocam tripod, and went into Shed B. He stood for a moment on the concrete halfway between the door and the Buick, one gloved hand touching the Puff-Pak's mask under his chin, ready to pull it up at once if the air was as foul as it had been on the day of the fish.

'Not bad,' he said. 'Just a little whiff of

something sweet. Maybe it really *is* an Easter lily.'

It wasn't. The trumpet-shaped flowers — three of them — were as pallid as the palms of a corpse, and almost translucent. Within each was a dab of dark blue stuff that looked like jelly. Hanging in the jelly were little pips. The stalks looked more like treebark than parts of a flowering plant, their green surfaces covered with a network of cracks and crenellations. There were brown spots that looked like some sort of fungoid growth, and these were spreading. The stems came together in a rooty clod of black soil. When he leaned toward this (none of them liked seeing Curt lean into the trunk that way, it was too much like watching a man stick his stupid head into a bear's mouth), Curt said he could smell that cabbagey aroma again. It was faint but unmistakable.

'And I tell you, Sandy, there's the smell of salt, as well. I know there is. I spent a lot of summers on Cape Cod, and you can't miss that smell.'

'I don't care if it smells like truffles and caviar,' Sandy replied. 'Get the hell out of there.'

Curt laughed — *Silly old Gramma Dearborn!* — but he pulled back. He set the video camera pointing down into the trunk from its tripod, got it running, then took some Polaroids for good measure.

'Come on in, Sandy — check it out.'

Sandy thought it over. Bad idea, very bad idea. *Stupid* idea. No doubt about it. And once he had that clear in his head, Sandy handed the coil of rope to Huddie and went on in. He looked at the deflated flowers lying in the Buick's trunk (and the one hanging over the lip, the one Brian Cole had seen) and couldn't suppress a little shiver.

'I know,' Curt said, lowering his voice so the Troopers outside wouldn't hear. 'Hurts just to look, doesn't it? It's the visual equivalent of hearing someone scrape a blackboard with his fingernails.'

Sandy nodded. Hole in one.

'But what triggers that reaction?' Curt asked. 'I can't put my finger on any one thing. Can you?'

'No.' Sandy licked his lips, which had gone dry. 'And I think that's because it's everything together. A lot of it's the white.'

'The white. The color.'

'Yeah. Nasty. Like a toad's belly.'

'Like cobwebs spun into flowers,' Curt said.

They looked at each other for a moment, trying to smile and not doing a very good job of it. State Police poets, Trooper Frost and Trooper Sandburg. Next they'd be comparing the goddam thing to a summer's day. But you had to try doing that, because it seemed you could only grasp what you were seeing by an act of mental reflection that was like poetry.

Other similes, less coherent, were banging and swerving in Sandy's head. White like a Communion wafer in a dead woman's mouth. White like a thrush infection under your tongue. White like the foam of creation just beyond the edge of the universe, maybe.

'This stuff comes from a place we can't even begin to comprehend,' Curt said. 'Our senses can't grasp any of it, not really. Talking about it's a joke — you might as well try to describe a four-sided triangle. Look there, Sandy. Do you see?' He pointed the tip of a gloved finger at a dry brown patch just below one of the corpse-lily flowers.

'Yeah, I see it. Looks like a burn.'

'And it's getting bigger. All the spots are. And look there on the flower.' It was another brown patch, spreading as they looked at it, gobbling an ever-widening hole in the flower's fragile white skin. 'That's decomposition. It's not going in quite the same way as the bat and the fish, but it's going, just the same. Isn't it?'

Sandy nodded.

'Pull the garbage bag out of my belt and open it, would you?'

Sandy did as he was asked. Curt reached into the trunk and grasped the plant just above its rooty bulb. When he did, a fresh whiff of that watery cabbage/spoiled cucumber stench drifted up to them. Sandy took a step back, hand pressed against his mouth, trying not to gag and gagging anyway.

'Hold that bag open, goddammit!' Curt cried in a choked voice. To Sandy he sounded like someone who has just taken a long hit off a primo blunt and wants to hold the smoke down as long as possible. 'Jesus, it feels nasty! Even through the gloves!'

Sandy held the bag open and shook the top. 'Hurry up, then!'

Curt dropped the decaying corpse-lily plant inside, and even the sound it made going down the bag's plastic throat was somehow wrong — like a harsh whispered cry, something being pressed relentlessly between two boards and almost silently choking. None of the similes was right, yet each seemed to flash a momentary light on what was basically unknowable. Sandy Dearborn could not express even to himself how fundamentally revolting and dismaying the corpse-lilies were. Them and all the Buick's miscarried children. If you thought about them too long, the chances were good that you really would go mad.

Curt made as if to wipe his gloved hands on his shirt, then thought better of it. He bent into the Buick's trunk instead, and rubbed them briskly on the brown trunk-mat. Then he stripped the gloves off, motioned for Sandy to open the plastic bag again, and threw them inside on top of the corpse-lily. That smell puffed out again and Sandy thought of once when his mother, eaten up by cancer and with less than a week to live, had belched in his face. His instinctive but feeble effort to block that memory before it could rise fully into his consciousness was useless.

Please don't let me be sick, Sandy thought. *Oh please, no.*

Curt checked to make sure the Polaroids he had taken were still tucked into his belt, then slammed the Buick's trunk. 'Let's get out of here, Sandy. What do you say?'

'I say that's the best idea you've had all year.'

Curt winked at him. It was the perfect wiseguy wink, spoiled only by his pallor and the sweat running down his cheeks and forehead. 'Since it's only February, that's not saying much. Come on.'

★ ★ ★

Fourteen months later, in April of 1985, the Buick threw a lightquake that was brief but extremely vicious — the biggest and brightest since The Year of the Fish. The force of the event mitigated against Curt and Tony's idea that the energy flowing from or through the Roadmaster was dissipating. The brevity of the event, on the other hand, seemed to argue *for* the idea. In the end, it was a case of you pays your money and you takes your choice. Same as it ever was, in other words.

Two days after the lightquake, with the temperature in Shed B standing at an even sixty degrees, the Buick's trunk flew open and a red stick came sailing up and out of it, as if driven by a jet of compressed air. Arky Arkanian was actually in the shed when this happened, putting his posthole digger back on its pegs, and it scared the hell out of him. The red stick clunked against one of the shed's overhead beams, came down on the Buick's roof with a bang, then rolled off and landed on the floor. Hello, stranger.

The new arrival was about nine inches long, irregular, the thickness of a man's wrist, with a couple of knotholes in one end. It was Andy Colucci, looking in at it through the binoculars five or ten minutes later, who determined that

323

the knotholes were eyes, and what looked like grooves or cracks on one side of the thing was actually a leg, perhaps drawn up in its final death-agony. Not a stick, Andy thought, but some kind of red lizard. Like the fish, the bat, and the lily, it was a goner.

Tony Schoondist was the one to go in and collect the specimen that time, and that night at The Tap he told several Troopers he could barely bring himself to touch it. 'The goddamned thing was staring at me,' he said. 'That's what it felt like, anyway. Dead or not.' He poured himself a glass of beer and drank it down at a single draught. 'I hope that's the end of it,' he said. 'I really, really do.'

But of course it wasn't.

THEN:

Shirley

It's funny how little things can mark a day in your mind. That Friday in 1988 was probably the most horrible one in my life — I didn't sleep well for six months after, and I lost twenty-five pounds because for awhile I couldn't eat — but the way I mark it in time is by something nice. That was the day Herb Avery and Justin Islington brought me the bouquet of field-flowers. Just before everything went crazy, that was.

They were in my bad books, those two. They'd ruined a brand-new linen skirt, horsing around in the kitchen. I was no part of it, just a gal minding her own business, getting a cup of coffee. Not paying attention, and isn't that mostly when they get you? Men, I mean. They'll be all right for awhile, so you relax, even get lulled into thinking they might be basically sane after all, and then they just break out. Herb and that Islington came galloping into the kitchen like a couple of horses yelling about some bet. Justin is thumping Herb all around the head and shoulders and hollering *Pay up, you son of a buck, pay up!* and Herb is like *We were just kidding around, you know I don't bet when I play cards, let loose of me!* But laughing, both of them. Like loons. Justin was half up on Herb's

325

back, hands around his neck, pretending to choke him. Herb was trying to shake him off, neither of them looking at me or even knowing I was there, standing by the Mr Coffee in my brand-new skirt. Just PCO Pasternak, you know — part of the furniture.

'Look out, you two galoots!' I yelled, but it was too late. They ran smack into me before I could put my cup down and there went the coffee, all down my front. Getting it on the blouse didn't bother me, it was just an old thing, but the skirt was brand-new. And *nice*. I'd spent half an hour the night before, fixing the hem.

I gave a yell and they finally stopped pushing and thumping. Justin still had one leg around Herb's hip and his hands around his neck. Herb was looking at me with his mouth hung wide open. He was a nice enough fellow (about Islington I couldn't say one way or the other; he was transferred over to Troop K in Media before I really got to know him), but with his mouth hung open that way, Herb Avery looked as dumb as a bag of hammers.

'Shirley, oh jeez,' he said. You know, he sounded like Arky, now that I think back, same accent, just not quite as thick. 'I never sar' you dere.'

'I'm not surprised,' I said, 'with that other one trying to ride you like you were a horse in the goddam Kentucky Derby.'

'Are you burned?' Justin asked.

'You bet I'm burned,' I said. 'This skirt was thirty-five dollars at JC Penney and it's the first time I wore it to work and it's ruined. You want

326

to believe I'm burned.'

'Jeepers, calm down, we're sorry,' Justin said. He even had the gall to sound offended. And that's also men as I've come to know them, pardon the philosophy. If they say they're sorry, you're supposed to go all mellow, because that takes care of everything. Doesn't matter if they broke a window, blew up the powerboat, or lost the kids' college fund playing blackjack in Atlantic City. It's like *Hey, I said I was sorry, do you have to make a federal case of it?*

'Shirley — ' Herb started.

'Not now, honeychile, not now,' I said. 'Just get out of here. Right out of my sight.'

Trooper Islington, meanwhile, had grabbed a handful of napkins off the counter and started mopping the front of my skirt.

'Stop that!' I said, grabbing his wrist. 'What do you think this is, Free Feel Friday?'

'I just thought . . . if it hasn't set in yet . . . '

I asked him if his mother had any kids that lived and he started in with *Well Jesus, if* that's *the way you feel*, all huffy and offended.

'Do yourself a favor,' I said, 'and go right now. Before you end up wearing this goddam coffee pot for a necklace.'

Out they went, more slinking than walking, and for quite awhile afterward they steered wide around me, Herb shamefaced and Justin Islington still wearing that puzzled, offended look — *I* said *I was sorry, what do you want, egg in your beer?*

Then, a week later — on the day the shit hit the fan, in other words — they showed up in dispatch at two in the afternoon, Justin first, with the bouquet, and Herb behind him. Almost *hiding* behind him, it looked like, in case I should decide to start hucking paperweights at them.

Thing is, I'm not much good at holding a grudge. Anyone who knows me will tell you that. I do all right with them for a day or two, and then they just kind of melt through my fingers. And the pair of them looked cute, like little boys who want to apologize to Teacher for cutting up dickens in the back of the room during social studies. That's another thing about men that gets you, how in almost the blink of a damned eye they can go from being loudmouth galoots who cut each other in the bars over the least little thing — *baseball scores*, for the love of God — to sweeties right out of a Norman Rockwell picture. And the next thing you know, they're in your pants or trying to get there.

Justin held out the bouquet. It was just stuff they'd picked in the field behind the barracks. Daisies, black-eyed Susans, things of that nature. Even a few dandelions, as I recall. But that was part of what made it so cute and disarming. If it had been hothouse roses they'd bought downtown instead of that kid's bouquet, I might have been able to stay mad a little longer. That was a *good* skirt, and I hate hemming the damned things, anyway.

Justin Islington out in front because he had those blue-eyed football-player good looks, complete with the one curl of dark hair tumbled over his forehead. Supposed to make me melt,

328

and sort of did. Holding the flowers out. Shucks, oh gorsh, Teacher. There was even a little white envelope stuck in with the flowers.

'Shirley,' Justin said — solemn enough, but with that cute little twinkle in his eyes — 'We want to make up with you.'

'That's right,' Herb said. 'I hate having you mad at us.'

'I do, too,' Justin said. I wasn't so sure that one meant it, but I thought Herb really did, and that was good enough for me.

'Okay,' I said, and took the flowers. 'But if you do it again — '

'We won't!' Herb said. 'No way! Never!' Which is what they all say, of course. And don't accuse me of being a hardass, either. I'm just being realistic.

'If you do, I'll thump you crosseyed.' I cocked an eyebrow at Islington. 'Here's something your mother probably never told you, you being a pointer instead of a setter: sorry won't take a coffee stain out of a linen skirt.'

'Be sure to look in the envelope,' Justin said, still trying to slay me with those bright blue eyes of his.

I put the vase down on my desk and plucked the envelope out of the daisies. 'This isn't going to puff sneezing powder in my face or anything like that, is it?' I asked Herb. I was joking, but he shook his head earnestly. Looking at him that way, you had to wonder how he could ever stop anyone and give them a ticket for speeding or reckless driving without getting a ration of grief. But Troopers are different on the highway, of course. They have to be.

I opened the envelope, expecting a little Hallmark card with another version of *I'm sorry* on it, this one written in flowery rhymes, but instead there was a folded piece of paper. I took it out, unfolded it, and saw it was a JC Penney gift certificate, made out to me in the amount of fifty dollars.

'Hey, no,' I said. All at once I felt like crying. And while I'm at it, that's the other thing about men — just when you're at your most disgusted with them, they can lay you out with some gratuitous act of generosity and all at once, stupid but true, instead of being mad you feel ashamed of yourself for ever having had a mean and cynical thought about them. 'Fellas, you didn't need to — '

'We *did* need to,' Justin said. 'That was double dumb, horsing around in the kitchen like that.'

'*Triple* dumb,' Herb said. He was bobbing his head up and down, never taking his eyes off me.

'But this is too much!'

Islington said, 'Not according to our calculations. We had to figure in the annoyance factor, you see, as well as the pain and suffering — '

'I didn't get burned, that coffee was only luke — '

'You're taking it, Shirley,' Herb said, very firmly. He hadn't gotten all the way back to being Mr State Cop Marlboro Man, but he was well on his way. 'It's a done deal.'

I'm really glad they did that, and I'll never forget it. What happened later was so horrible, you see. It's nice to have something that can balance out a little bit of that horror, some act of ordinary kindness like two goofs paying not just for the skirt they spoiled but for the inconvenience and exasperation. And giving me flowers on top of that. When I remember the other part, I try to remember those guys, too. Especially the flowers they picked out back.

I thanked them and they headed upstairs, probably to play chess. There used to be a tournament here toward the end of every summer, with the winner getting this little bronze toilet seat called The Scranton Cup. All that kind of got left behind when Lieutenant Schoondist retired. The two of them left me with the look of men who've done their duty. I suppose that in a way they had. *I* felt that they had, anyway, and I could do my part by getting them a big box of chocolates or some winter hand-warmers with what was left over from the gift certificate after I'd bought a new skirt. Hand-warmers would be more practical, but maybe a little too domestic. I was their dispatcher, not their den mother, after all. They had wives to buy them hand-warmers.

Their silly little peace bouquet had been nicely arranged, there were even a few springs of green to give it that all-important town florist's feel, but they hadn't thought to add water. Arrange the flowers, then forget the water: it's a guy thing. I picked up the vase and started toward the kitchen and that was when George Stankowski came on the radio, coughing and sounding scared to death. Let me tell you something you can file away with whatever else you consider to be the great truths of life: only one thing scares a police communications officer more than hearing a Trooper in the field actually sounding scared on the radio, and that's one calling in a 29–99. Code 99 is *General response required*. Code 29 . . . you look in the book and you see only one word under 29. The word is *catastrophe*.

★　★　★

'Base, this is 14. Code 29–99, do you copy? Two-niner-niner-niner.'

I put the vase with the wildflowers in it back down on my desk, very carefully. As I did, I had a very vivid memory: hearing on the radio that John Lennon had died. I was making breakfast for my Dad that day. I was going to serve him and then just dash, because I was late for school. I had a glass bowl with eggs in it curled against my stomach. I was beating them with a whisk. When the man on the radio said that Lennon had been shot in New York City, I set the glass bowl down in the same careful way I now set down the vase.

'Tony!' I called across the barracks, and at the sound of my voice (or the sound of what was *in* my voice), everyone stopped what they were doing. The talk stopped upstairs, as well. 'Tony, George Stankowski is 29–99!' And without waiting, I scooped up the microphone and told George that I copied, five-by, and come on back.

'My 20 is County Road 46, Poteenville,' he said. I could hear an uneven crackling sound

332

behind his transmission. It sounded like fire. Tony was standing in my doorway by then, and Sandy Dearborn in his civvies, with his cop-shoes hung from the fingers of one hand. 'A tanker-truck has collided with a schoolbus and is on fire. That's the *tanker* that's on fire, but the front half of the schoolbus is involved, copy that?'

'Copy,' I said. I sounded okay, but my lips had gone numb.

'This is a chemical tanker, Norco West, copy?'

'I copy Norco West, 14.' Writing it on the pad beside the red telephone in large capital letters. 'Placks?' Short for *placards*, the little diamonds with icons for fire, gas, radiation, and a few other fun things.

'Ah, can't make out the placks, too much smoke, but there's white stuff coming out and it's catching fire as it runs down the ditch and across the highway, copy that?' George had started coughing into his mike again.

'Copy,' I said. 'Are you breathing fumes, 14? You don't sound so good, over?'

'Ah, roger that, roger fumes, but I'm okay. The problem — ' But before he could finish, he started coughing again.

Tony took the mike from me. He patted my shoulder to say I'd been doing all right, he just couldn't bear to stand there listening anymore. Sandy was putting on his shoes. Everyone else was drifting toward dispatch. There were quite a few guys there, with the shift change coming up. Even Mister Dillon had come out of the kitchen to see what all the excitement was about.

'The problem's the *school*,' George went on when he could. 'Poteenville Grammar is only two hundred yards away.'

'School's not in for almost another month, 14. You — '

'Break, break. Maybe not, but I see kids.'

Behind me someone murmured, 'August is Crafts Month out there. My sister's teaching pottery to nine- and ten-year-olds.' I remember the terrible sinking feeling I got in my chest when I heard that.

'Whatever the spill is, I'm upwind of it,' George went on when he could. 'The school isn't, I repeat the school is not. Copy?'

'Copy, 14,' Tony said. 'Do you have FD support?'

'Negative, but I hear sirens.' More coughing. 'I was practically on top of this when it happened, close enough to hear the crash, so I got here first. Grass is on fire, fire's headed toward the school. I see kids on the playground, standing around and watching. I can hear the alarm inside, so I have to guess they've been evacked. Can't tell if the fumes have gotten that far, but if they haven't, they will. Send the works, boss. Send the farm. This is a legitimate 29.'

Tony: 'Are there casualties on the bus, 14? Do you see casualties, over?'

I looked at the clock. It was quarter till two. If we were lucky, the bus would've been coming, not going — arriving to take the kids home from making their pots and jars.

'Bus appears empty except for the driver. I can see him — or maybe it's her — slumped over the

334

wheel. That's the half in the fire and I'd have to say the driver is DRT, copy?'

DRT is a slang abbreviation the PSP picked up in the ER's back in the seventies. It stands for 'dead right there'.

'Copy, 14,' Tony said. 'Can you get to where the kids are?'

Cough-cough-cough. He sounded bad. 'Roger, base, there's an access road runs alongside the soccer field. Goes right to the building, over.'

'Then get in gear,' Tony said. He was the best I ever saw him that day, as decisive as a general on the field of battle. The fumes turned out not to be all that toxic after all, and most of the burning was leaking gasoline, but of course none of us knew that then. For all George Stankowski knew, Tony had just signed his death warrant. And sometimes that's the job, yes.

'Roger, base, rolling.'

'If they're getting gassed, stuff them in your cruiser, sit them on the hood and the trunk, put them on the roof hanging on to the lightbars. Get as many as you can, copy that?'

'Copy, base, 14 out.'

Click. That last click seemed very loud.

Tony looked around. '29–99, you all heard it. Assigned units, all rolling. Those of you waiting for switch-over rides at three, get Kojak lights out of the supply room and run your personals. Shirley, bend every duty-officer you can raise.'

'Yes, sir. Should I start calling OD's?'

'Not yet. Huddie Royer, where are you?'

'Here, Sarge.'

'You're anchoring.'

There were no movie-show protests about this from Huddie, nothing about how he wanted to be out there with the rest of the crew, fighting fire and poison gas, rescuing children. He just said yessir.

'Check Pogus County FD, find out what they're rolling, find out what Lassburg and Statler's rolling, call Pittsburgh OER, anyone else you can think of.'

'How about Norco West?'

Tony didn't quite slap his forehead, but almost. 'Oh you bet.' Then he headed for the door, Curt beside him, the others right behind them, Mister Dillon bringing up the rear.

Huddie grabbed his collar. 'Not today, boy. You're here with me and Shirley.' Mister D sat down at once; he was well-trained. He watched the departing men with longing eyes, just the same.

All at once the place seemed very empty with just the two of us there — the three of us, if you counted D. Not that we had time to dwell on it; there was plenty to do. I might have noticed Mister Dillon getting up and going to the back door, sniffing at the screen and whining way back low in his throat. I think I did, actually, but maybe that's only hindsight at work. If I *did* notice, I probably put it down to disappointment at being left behind. What I think now is that he sensed something starting to happen out in Shed B. I think he might even have been trying to let us know.

I had no time to mess with the dog, though

— not even time enough to get up and shut him in the kitchen, where he might have had a drink from his water bowl and then settled down. I wish I'd made time; poor old Mister D might have lived another few years. But of course I didn't know. All I knew right then was that I had to find out who was on the road and where. I had to bend them west, if I could and they could. And while I worked on that, Huddie was in the SC's office, hunched over the desk and talking into the phone with the intensity of a man who's making the biggest deal of his life.

I got all my active officers except for Unit 6, which was almost here ('20-base in a tick' had been my last word from them). George Morgan and Eddie Jacubois had a delivery to make before heading over to Poteenville. Except, of course, 6 never *did* get to Poteenville that day. No, Eddie and George never got to Poteenville at all.

THEN:

Eddie

It's funny how a person's memory works. I didn't recognize the guy who got out of that custom Ford pickup, not to begin with. To me he was just a red-eyed punk with an inverted crucifix for an earring and a silver swastika hung around his neck on a chain. I remember the stickers. You learn to read the stickers people put on their rides; they can tell you a lot. Ask any motor patrol cop. I DO WHATEVER THE LITTLE VOICES TELL ME TO on the left side of this guy's back bumper, I EAT AMISH on the right. He was unsteady on his feet, and probably not just because he was wearing a pair of fancy-stitched cowboy boots with those stacked heels. The red eyes peeking out from under his scraggle of black hair suggested to me that he was high on something. The blood on his right hand and spattered on the right sleeve of his T-shirt suggested it might be something mean. Angel dust would have been my guess. It was big in our part of the world back then. Crank came next. Now it's ex, and I'd give that shit away myself, if they'd let me. At least it's mellow. I suppose it's also possible that he was gazzing — what the current crop of kids calls huffing. But I didn't think I knew him until he said, 'Hey, I be goddam, it's Fat Eddie.'

338

Bingo, just like that I knew. Brian Lippy. He and I went back to Statler High, where he'd been a year ahead of me. Already majoring in Dope Sales & Service. Now here he was again, standing on the edge of the highway and swaying on the high heels of his fancy cowboy boots, head-down Christ hanging from his ear, Nazi twisted cross around his neck, numbfuck stickers on the bumper of his ride.

'Hi there, Brian, want to step away from the truck?' I said.

When I say the truck was a custom, I mean it was one of those bigfoot jobs. It was parked on the soft shoulder of the Humboldt Road, not a mile and a half from the intersection where the Jenny station stood . . . only by that summer, the Jenny'd been closed two or three years. In truth, the truck was almost in the ditch. My old pal Brian Lippy had swerved *way* over when George hit the lights, another sign that he wasn't exactly straight.

I was glad to have George Morgan with me that day. Mostly riding single is all right, but when you happen on a guy who's all over the road because he's whaling on the person sitting next to him in the cab of the truck he's driving, it's nice to have a partner. As for the punching, we could see it. First as Lippy drove past our 20 and then as we pulled out behind him, this silhouette driver pistoning out his right arm, his right fist connecting again and again with the side of the passenger's silhouette head, too busy-busy-busy to realize the fuzz was crawling right up his tailpipe until George hit the reds.

Fuck me til I cry, I think, ain't that prime. Next thing my old pal Brian's over on the shoulder and half in the ditch like he's been expecting it all his life, which on some level he probably has been.

If it's pot or tranks, I don't worry as much. It's like ex. They go, 'Hey, man, what's up? Did I do something wrong? I love you.' But stuff like angel dust and PCP makes people crazy. Even glueheads can go bonkers. I've seen it. For another thing, there was the passenger. It was a woman, and that could make things a lot worse. He might have been punching the crap out of her, but that didn't mean she might not be dangerous if she saw us slapping the cuffs on her favorite Martian.

Meantime, my old pal Brian wasn't stepping away from the truck as he'd been asked. He was just standing there, grinning at me, and how in God's name I hadn't recognized him right off the bat was a mystery, because at Statler High he'd been one of those kids who makes your life hell if he notices you. Especially if you're a little pudgy or pimply, and I was both. The Army took the weight off — it's the only diet program I know where they pay you to participate — and the pimples took care of themselves in time like they almost always do, but in SHS I'd been this guy's afternoon snack any day he wanted. That was another reason to be happy George was with me. If I'd been alone, my old pal Bri might have gotten the idea that if he put the evil eye on me, I'd still shrivel. The more stoned he was, the more apt he was to think that.

'Step away from the truck, sir,' George said in his flat and colorless Trooper voice. You'd never believe, hearing him talk to some John Q. at the side of the road, that he could scream himself hoarse on the Little League field, yelling at kids to bunt the damn ball and to keep their heads down while they were running the bases. Or kidding with them on the bench before their games to loosen them up.

Lippy had never torn the Fruit Loops off any of *George's* shirts in study hall period four, and maybe that's why he stepped away from the truck when George told him to. Looking down at his boots as he did it, losing the grin. When guys like Brian Lippy lose the grin, what comes in to take its place is this kind of dopey sullenness.

'Are you going to be trouble, sir?' George asked. He hadn't drawn his gun, but his hand was on the butt of it. 'If you are, tell me now. Save us both some grief.'

Lippy didn't say anything. Just looked down at his boots.

'His name is Brian?' George asked me.

'Brian Lippy.' I was looking at the truck. Through the back window I could see the passenger, still sitting in the middle, not looking at us. Head dropped. I thought maybe he'd beaten her unconscious. Then one hand went up to her mouth and out of the mouth came a plume of cigarette smoke.

'Brian, I want to know if we're going to have trouble. Answer up so I can hear you, now, just like a big boy.'

'Depends,' Brian said, lifting his upper lip to

341

get a good sneer on the word. I started toward the truck to do my share of the job. When my shadow passed over the toes of his boots, Brian kind of recoiled and took a step backward, as if it had been a snake instead of a shadow. He was high, all right, and to me it was seeming more like PCP or angel dust all the time.

'Let me have your driver's license and registration,' George said.

Brian paid no immediate attention. He was looking at me again. 'ED-die JACK-you-BOYS,' he said, chanting it the way he and his friends always had back in high school, making a joke out of it. He hadn't worn any head-down Christs or Nazi swastikas back at Statler High, though; they would have sent him home if he'd tried that shit. Anyway, him saying my name like that got to me. It was like he'd found an old electrical switch, dusty and forgotten behind a door but still wired up. Still hot.

He knew it, too. Saw it and started grinning. 'Fat Eddie JACK-you-BOYS. How many boys *did* you jack, Eddie? How many boys did you jack in the shower room? Or did you just get right down on your knees and suck em off? Straight to the main event. Mister Takin Care of Business.'

'Want to close your mouth, Brian?' George asked. 'You'll catch a fly.' He took his handcuffs off his belt.

Brian Lippy saw them and started to lose the grin again. 'What you think you gonna do with those?'

'If you don't hand me your operating papers

342

right now, I'm going to put them on you, Brian. And if you resist, I can guarantee you two things: a broken nose and eighteen months in Castlemora for resisting arrest. Could be more, depending on which judge you draw. Now what do you think?'

Brian took his wallet out of his back pocket. It was a greasy old thing with the logo of some rock group — Judas Priest, I think — inexpertly burned into it. Probably with the tip of a soldering iron. He started thumbing through the various compartments.

'Brian,' I said.

He looked up.

'The name is Jacubois, Brian. Nice French name. And I haven't been fat for quite awhile now.'

'You'll gain it back,' he said, 'fat boys always do.'

I burst out laughing. I couldn't help it. He sounded like some halfbaked guest on a talkshow. He glowered at me, but there was something uncertain in it. He'd lost the advantage and he knew it.

'Little secret,' I said. 'High school's over, my friend. This is your actual, real life. I know that's hard for you to believe, but you better get used to it. It's not just detention anymore. This *actually counts.*'

What I got was a kind of stupid gape. He wasn't getting it. They so rarely do.

'Brian, I want to see your paperwork with no more delay,' George said. 'You put it right in my hand.' And he held his hand out, palm up. Not very wise, you might say, but George Morgan had been a State Trooper for a long time, and in his judgment, this situation was now going in the right direction. Right enough, anyway, for him to decide he didn't need to put the cuffs on my old friend Brian just to show him who was in charge.

I went over to the truck, glancing at my watch as I did. It was just about one-thirty in the afternoon. Hot. Crickets singing dry songs in the roadside grass. The occasional car passing by, the drivers slowing down for a good look. It's always nice when the cops have someone pulled over and it's not you. That's a real daymaker.

The woman in the truck was sitting with her left knee pressed against the chrome post of Brian's Hurst shifter. Guys like Brian put them in just so they can stick a Hurst decal in the window, that's what I think. Next to the ones saying Fram and Pennzoil. She looked about twenty years old with long ironed brownette hair, not particularly clean, hanging to her shoulders. Jeans and a white tank top. No bra. Fat red pimples on her shoulders. A tat on one arm that said AC ⚡ DC and one on the other saying BRIAN MY LUV. Nails painted candycane pink but all bitten down and ragged. And yes, there was blood. Blood and snot hanging out of her nose. More blood spattered up her cheeks like little birthmarks. Still more on her split lips and chin and tank top. Head down so the wings of her hair hid some of her face. Cigarette going up and down, tick-tock, either a Marlboro or a Winston, in those days before the prices went up

344

and all the fringe people went to the cheap brands, you could count on it. And if it's Marlboro, it's always the hard pack. I have seen so many of them. Sometimes there's a baby and it straightens the guy up, but usually it's just bad luck for the baby.

'Here,' she said, and lifted her right thigh a little. Under it was a slip of paper, canary yellow. 'The registration. I tell him to keep his ticket in his wallet or the glove compartment, but it's always floppin around in here someplace with the Mickey Dee wrappers and the rest of the trash.'

She didn't sound stoned and there were no beer cans or liquor bottles floating around in the cab of the truck. That didn't make her sober, of course, but it was a step in the right direction. She also didn't seem like she was going to turn abusive, but of course that can change. In a hurry.

'What's your name, ma'am?'

'Sandra?'

'Sandra what?'

'McCracken?'

'Do you have any ID, Ms McCracken?'

'Yeah.'

'Show me, please.'

There was a little Leatherette clutch purse on the seat beside her. She opened it and started pawing through it. She worked slowly, and with her head bent over her purse, her face disappeared completely. You could still see the blood on her tank top but not on her face; you couldn't see the swollen lips that turned her mouth into a cut plum, or the old mouse fading around one eye.

And from behind me: 'Fuck no, I ain't getting in there. What makes you think you got a right to put me in there?'

I looked around. George was holding the back door of the cruiser open. A limo driver couldn't have done it more courteously. Except the back seat of a limo doesn't have doors you can't open and windows you can't unroll from the inside, or mesh between the front and the back. Plus, of course, that faint smell of puke. I've never driven a cruiser — well, except for a week or so after we got the new Caprices — that didn't have that smell.

'What makes me think I have the right is you're *busted*, Brian. Did you just hear me read you your rights?'

'The fuck *for*, man? I wasn't speedin!'

'That's true, you were too busy tuning up on your girlfriend to really get the pedal to the metal, but you were driving recklessly, driving to endanger. Plus assault. Let's not forget that. So get in.'

'Man, you can't — '

'Get in, Brian, or I'll put you up against the car and cuff you. Hard, so it hurts.'

'Like to see you try it.'

'Would you?' George asked, his voice almost too low to hear even in that dozy afternoon quiet.

Brian Lippy saw two things. The first was that George could do it. The second was that George sort of *wanted* to do it. And Sandra McCracken would see it happen. Not a good thing, letting your bitch see you get cuffed. Bad enough she saw you getting busted.

'You'll be hearing from my lawyer,' said Brian Lippy, and got into the back of the cruiser.

George slammed the door and looked at me. 'We're gonna hear from his lawyer.'

'Don't you hate that,' I said.

The woman poked my arm with something. I turned and saw it was the corner of her driver's license laminate. 'Here,' she said. She was looking at me. It was only a moment before she turned away and began rummaging in her bag again, this time coming out with a couple of tissues, but it was long enough for me to decide she really was straight. Dead inside, but straight.

'Trooper Jacubois, the vehicle operator states his registration is in his truck,' George said.

'Yeah, I have it.'

George and I met at the pickup's ridiculous jacked rear bumper — I DO WHATEVER THE LITTLE VOICES TELL ME TO, I EAT AMISH — and I handed him the registration.

'Will she?' he asked in a low voice.

'No,' I said.

'Sure?'

'Pretty.'

'Try,' George said, and went back to the cruiser. My old schoolmate started yelling at him the second George leaned through the driver's-side window to snag the mike. George ignored him and stretched the cord to its full length, so he could stand in the sun. 'Base, this is 6, copy-back?'

347

I returned to the open door of the pickup. The woman had snubbed her cigarette out in the overflowing ashtray and lit a fresh one. Up and down went the fresh cigarette. Out from between the mostly closed wings of her hair came the plumes of used smoke.

'Ms McCracken, we're going to take Mr Lippy to our barracks — Troop D, on the hill? Like you to follow us.'

She shook her head and began to work with the Kleenex. Bending her head to it rather than raising the tissue to her face, closing the curtains of her hair even farther. The hand with the cigarette in it now resting on the leg of her jeans, the smoke rising straight up.

'Like you to follow us, Ms McCracken.' Speaking just as softly as I could. Trying to make it caring and knowing and just between us. That's how the shrinks and family therapists say to handle it, but what do they know? I kind of hate those SOBs, that's the ugly truth. They come out of the middle class smelling of hairspray and deodorant and they talk to us about spousal abuse and low self-esteem, but they don't have a clue about places like Lassburg County, which played out once when the coal finished up and then again when big steel went away to Japan and China. Does a woman like Sandra McCracken even hear soft and caring and nonthreatening? Once upon a time, maybe. I didn't think anymore. If, on the other hand, I'd grabbed all that hair out of her face so she had to look at me and then shouted, 'YOU'RE COMING! YOU'RE COMING AND YOU'RE GOING TO MAKE

348

AN ASSAULT CHARGE AGAINST HIM! YOU'RE COMING, YOU DUMB BEATEN BITCH! YOU ALLOWING CUNT! YOU ARE! *YOU FUCKING WELL ARE!*', that might have made a difference. That might have worked. You have to speak their language. The shrinks and the therapists, they don't want to hear that. They don't want to believe there is a language that's not their language.

She shook her head again. Not looking at me. Smoking and not looking at me.

'Like you to come on up and swear out an assault complaint on Mr Lippy there. You pretty much have to, you know. I mean, we saw him hitting you, my partner and I were right behind you, and we got a real good look.'

'I *don't* have to,' she said, 'and you can't make me.' She was still using that clumpy, greasy old mop of brownette to hide her face, but she spoke with a certain quiet authority, all the same. She knew we couldn't force her to press charges because she'd been down this road before.

'So how long do you want to take it?' I asked her.

Nothing. The head down. The face hidden. The way she'd lowered her head and hidden her face at twelve when her teacher asked her a hard question in class or when the other girls made fun of her because she was getting tits before they did and that made her a chunky-fuck. That's what girls like her grow that hair for, to hide behind. But knowing didn't give me any more patience with her. Less, if anything. Because, see, you have to take care of yourself in this world. Especially if you ain't purty.

'Sandra.'

A little movement of her shoulders when I switched over to her first name. No more than that. And boy, they make me mad. It's how easy they give up. They're like birds on the ground.

'Sandra, look at me.'

She didn't want to, but she would. She was used to doing what men said. Doing what men said had pretty much become her life's work.

'Turn your head and look at me.'

She turned her head but kept her eyes down. Most of the blood was still on her face. It wasn't a bad face. She probably *was* a little bit purty when someone wasn't tuning up on her. Nor did she look as stupid as you'd think she must be. As stupid as she wanted to be.

'I'd like to go home,' she said in a faint child's voice. 'I had a nosebleed and I need to clean up.'

'Yeah, I know you do. Why? You run into a door? I bet that was it, wasn't it?'

'That's right. A door.' There wasn't even defiance in her face. No trace of her boyfriend's I EAT AMISH 'tude. She was just waiting for it to be over. This roadside chatter wasn't real life. Getting hit, that was real life. Hawking back the snot and the blood and the tears all together and swallowing it like cough syrup. 'I was comin down the hall to use the bat'room, and Bri, I dittun know he was in there and he come out all at once, fast, and the door — '

'How long, Sandra?'

'How long what?'

'How long you going to go on eating his shit?'

350

Her eyes widened a little. That was all.

'Until he knocks all your teeth out?'

'I'd like to go home.'

'If I check at Statler Memorial, how many times am I going to find your name? Cause you run into a lot of doors, don't you?'

'Why don't you leave me alone? I ain't bothering you.'

'Until he fractures your skull? Until he kills your ass?'

'I want to go home, Officer.'

I want to say *That was when I knew I'd lost her* but it would be a lie because you can't lose what you never had. She'd sit there until hell froze over or until I got pissed enough to do something that would get me in trouble later. Like hit her. Because I wanted to hit her. If I hit her, at least she'd know I was there.

I keep a card case in my back pocket. I took it out, riffled through the cards, and found the one I wanted. 'This woman's in Statler Village. She's talked to hundreds of young women like you, and helped a lot of them. If you need *pro bono*, which means free counseling, that'll happen. She'll work it out with you. Okay?'

I held the card in front of her face, between the first two fingers of my right hand. When she didn't take it, I dropped it on to the seat. Then I went back to the cruiser to get the registration. Brian Lippy was sitting in the middle of the back seat with his chin lowered to the neck of his T-shirt, staring up at me from under his brows. He looked like some fucked-up hotrod Napoleon.

'Any luck?' George asked.

'Nah,' I said. 'She ain't had enough fun yet.'

I took the registration back to the truck. She'd moved over behind the wheel. The truck's big V-8 was rumbling. She had pushed the clutch in, and her right hand was on the shifter-knob. Bitten pink nails against chrome. If places like rural Pennsylvania had flags, you could put that on it. Or maybe a six-pack of Iron City Beer and a pack of Winstons.

'Drive safely, Ms McCracken,' I said, handing her the yellow.

'Yeah,' she said, and pulled out. Wanting to give me some lip and not daring because she was well-trained. The truck did some jerking at first — she wasn't as good with his manual transmission as she maybe thought she was — and she jerked with it. Back and forth, hair flying. All at once I could see it again, him all over the road, driving his one piece of property with his one hand and punching the piss out of his other piece of property with the other one, and I felt sick to my stomach. Just before she finally achieved second gear, something white fluttered out of the driver's-side window. It was the card I'd given her.

I went back to the cruiser. Brian was still sitting with his chin down on his chest, giving me his fucked-up Napoleon look from beneath his brows. Or maybe it was Rasputin. I got in on the passenger side, feeling very hot and tired. Just to make things complete, Brian started chanting from behind me. 'Fat ED-die JACK-you-BOYS. How many boys — '

352

'Oh shut up,' I said.

'Come on back here and shut me up, Fat Eddie. Why don't you come on back here and try it?'

Just another wonderful day in the PSP, in other words. This guy was going to be back in whatever shithole he called home by seven o'clock, drinking a beer while Vanna spun the Wheel of Fortune. I glanced at my watch — 1.44 p.m. — and then picked up the microphone. 'Base, this is 6.'

'Copy, 6.' Shirley right back at me, calm as a cool breeze. Shirley just about to get her flowers from Islington and Avery. Out on CR 46 in Poteenville, about twenty miles from our 20, a Norco West tanker had just collided with a schoolbus, killing the schoolbus's driver, Mrs Esther Mayhew. George Stankowski had been close enough to hear the bang of the collision, so who says there's never a cop around when you need one?

'We are Code 15 and 17-base, copy?' Asshole in custody and headed home, in other words.

'Roger, 6, you have one subject in custody or what, over?'

'One subject, roger.'

'This is Fat Fuck One, over and out,' Brian said from the back seat. He began to laugh — the high, chortling laugh of the veteran stoner. He also began to stomp his cowboy boots up and down. We'd be half an hour getting back to the barracks. I had an idea it was going to be a long ride.

THEN:

Huddie

I dropped the SC's phone into the cradle and almost trotted across to dispatch, where Shirley was still working hard, bending active Troopers west. 'Norco says it's chlorine liquid,' I told her. 'That's a break. Chlorine's nasty, but it's not usually fatal.'

'Are they sure that's what it is?' Shirley asked.

'Ninety per cent. It's what they have out that way. You see those trucks headed up to the water-treatment plant all the time. Pass it on, starting with George S. And what in the name of God's wrong with the dog?'

Mister Dillon was at the back door, nose down to the base of the screen, going back and forth. Almost *bouncing* back and forth, and whining way down in his throat. His ears were laid back. While I was watching, he bumped the screen with his muzzle hard enough to bell it out. Then gave a kind of yelp, as if to say *Man, that hurts*.

'No idea,' Shirley said in a voice that told me she had no time for Mister Dillon. Neither, strictly speaking, did I. Yet I looked at him a moment longer. I'd seen hunting dogs behave that way when they ran across the scent of something big in the woods nearby — a bear, or maybe a timberwolf. But there hadn't been any wolves in the Short Hills since before Vietnam,

354

and precious few bears. There was nothing beyond that screen but the parking lot. And Shed B, of course. I looked up at the clock over the kitchen door. It was 2.12 p.m. I couldn't remember ever having been in the barracks when the barracks was so empty.

'Unit 14, Unit 14, this is base, copy?'

George came back to her, still coughing. 'Unit 14.'

'It's chlorine, 14, Norco West says it's pretty confident of that. Chlorine liquid.' She looked at me and I gave her a thumb up. 'Irritating but not — '

'Break, break.' And cough, cough.

'Standing by, 14.'

'Maybe it's chlorine, maybe it's not, base. It's on fire, whatever it is, and there are big white clouds of it rolling this way. My 20 is at the end of the access road, the one by the soccer field. Those kids're coughing worse'n me and I see several people down, including one adult female. There are two schoolbuses parked off to the side. I'm gonna try and take those folks out in one. Over.'

I took the mike from Shirley. 'Goerge, this is Huddie. Norco says the fire's probably just fuel running out on top of the chlorine. You ought to be safe moving the kids on foot, over?'

What came next was a classic George S. response, solid and stolid. Eventually he got one of those above-and-beyond-the-call-of-duty citations for his day's work — from the governor, I think — and his picture was in the paper. His wife framed the citation and hung it on the wall

355

of the rumpus room. I'm not sure George ever understood what the fuss was about. In his mind he was just doing what seemed prudent and reasonable. If there was ever such a thing as the right man at the right place, it was George Stankowski that day at Poteenville Grammar School.

'Bus'd be better,' he said. 'Faster. This is 14, I'm 7.'

Shortly, Shirley and I would forget all about Poteenville for awhile; we had our own oats to roll. If you're curious, Trooper George Stankowski got into one of the buses he'd seen by busting a folding door with a rock. He started the forty-passenger Blue Bird with a spare key he found taped to the back of the driver's sunvisor, and eventually packed twenty-four coughing, weeping, red-eyed children and two teachers inside. Many of the children were still clutching the misshapen pots, blots, and ceramic ashtrays they'd made that afternoon. Three of the kids were unconscious, one from an allergic reaction to chlorine fumes. The other two were simple fainting victims, OD'd on terror and excitement. One of the crafts teachers, Rosellen Nevers, was in more serious straits. George saw her on the sidewalk, lying on her side, gasping and semiconscious, digging at her swelled throat with weakening fingers. Her eyes bulged from their sockets like the yolks of poached eggs.

'That's my Mommy,' one of the little girls said. Tears were welling steadily from her huge brown eyes, but she never lost hold of the clay vase she was holding, or tilted it so the black-eyed Susan she'd put in it fell out. 'She has the azmar.'

George was kneeling beside the woman by then with her head back over his forearm to keep her airway as wide-open as possible. Her hair hung down on the concrete. 'Does she take something for her asthma, honey, when it's bad like this?'

'In her pocket,' the little girl with the vase said. 'Is my Mommy going to die?'

'Nah,' George said. He got the Flovent inhaler out of Mrs Nevers's pocket and shot a good blast down her throat. She gasped, shivered, and sat up.

George carried her on to the bus in his arms, walking behind the coughing, crying children. He plopped Rosellen in a seat next to her daughter, then slipped behind the steering wheel. He put the bus in gear and bumped it across the soccer field, past his cruiser, and on to the access road. By the time he nosed the Blue Bird back on to County Road 46, the kids were singing 'Row, Row, Row Your Boat'. And that's how Trooper George Stankowski became an authentic hero while the few of us left behind were just trying to hold on to our sanity.

And our lives.

THEN:

Shirley

George's last communication to dispatch was 14, *I'm* 7 — this is Unit 14, I'm out of service. I logged it, looking up at the clock to note the time. It was 2.23 p.m. I remember that well, just as I remember Huddie standing beside me, giving my shoulder a little squeeze — trying to tell me George and the kids would be all right without coming right out and saying it, I suppose. 2.23 p.m., that's when all hell broke loose. And I mean that as literally as anyone ever has.

Mister Dillon started barking. Not his deep-throated bark, the one he usually saved for deer who scouted our back field or the raccoons that dared come sniffing around the stoop, but a series of high, yarking yips I had never heard before. It was as if he'd run himself on to something sharp and couldn't get free.

'What the *hell*?' Huddie said.

D took five or six stiff, backing steps away from the screen door, looking sort of like a rodeo horse in a calf-roping event. I think I knew what was going to happen next, and I think Huddie did, too, but neither of us could believe it. Even if we *had* believed it, we couldn't have stopped him. Sweet as he was, I think Mister Dillon would have bitten us if we'd tried. He was still letting out those yipping, hurt little barks, and foam had started to splatter from the corners of his mouth.

I remember reflected light dazzling into my eyes just then. I blinked and the light ran away from me down the length of the wall. That was Unit 6, Eddie and George coming in with their suspect, but I hardly registered that at all. I was looking at Mister Dillon.

He ran at the screen door, and once he was rolling he never hesitated. Never even slowed. Just dropped his head and broke on through to the other side, tearing the door out of its latch and pulling it after him even as he went through, still voicing barks that were almost like screams. At the same time I smelled something, very strong: seawater and decayed vegetable matter. There came a howl of brakes and rubber, the blast of a horn, and someone yelling, '*Watch out! Watch out!*' Huddie ran for the door and I followed him.

THEN:

Eddie

We were wrecking his day by taking him to the barracks. We'd stopped him, at least temporarily, from beating up his girlfriend. He had to sit in the back seat with the springs digging into his ass and his fancy boots planted on our special puke-resistant plastic floormats. But Brian was making us pay. Me in particular, but of course George had to listen to him, too.

He'd chant his version of my name and then stomp down rhythmically with the big old stacked heels of his shitkickers just as hard as he could. The overall effect was something like a football cheer. And all the time he was staring through the mesh at me with his head down and his little stoned eyes gleaming — I could see him in the mirror clipped to the sunvisor.

'JACK-you-BOYS!' *Clump-clumpclump!* 'JACK-you-BOYS!' *Clump-clumpclump!*

'Want to quit that, Brian?' George asked. We were nearing the barracks. The pretty nearly empty barracks; by then we knew what was going on out in Poteenville. Shirley had given us some of it, and the rest we'd picked up from the chatter of the converging units. 'You're giving me an earache.'

It was all the encouragement Brian needed.

'JACK-you-BOYS!' CLUMP-CLUMPCLUMP!

If he stomped much harder he was apt to put his feet right through the floorboards, but George didn't bother asking him to stop again. When they're buttoned up in the back of your cruiser, getting under your skin is just about all they can try. I'd experienced it before, but hearing this dumbbell, who once knocked the books out of my arms in the high school caff and tore the loops off the backs of my shirts in study hall, chanting that old hateful version of my name . . . man, that was spooky. Like a trip in Professor Peabody's Wayback Machine.

I didn't say anything, but I'm pretty sure George knew. And when he picked up the mike and called in — '20-base in a tick' was what he said — I knew he was talking to me more than Shirley. We'd chain Brian to the chair in the Bad Boy Corner, turn on the TV for him if he wanted it, and take a preliminary pass at the paperwork. Then we'd head for Poteenville, unless the situation out there changed suddenly for the better. Shirley could call Statler County Jail and tell them we had one of their favorite troublemakers coming their way. In the meantime, however —

'JACK-you-BOYS!' *Clump-clumpclump*! 'JACK-you-BOYS!'

Now screaming so loud his cheeks were red and the cords stood out on the sides of his neck. He wasn't just playing me anymore; Brian had moved on to an authentic shit fit. What a pleasure getting rid of him was going to be.

We went up Bookin's Hill, George driving a

little faster than was strictly necessary, headed for Troop D at the top. George signaled and turned in, perhaps still moving a little faster than he strictly should have been. Lippy, understanding that his time to annoy us had grown short, began shaking the mesh between us and him as well as thumping down with those John Wayne boots of his.

'JACK-you-BOYS!' *Clump-clumpclump! Shake-shakeshake!*

Up the driveway we went, toward the parking lot at the back. George turned tight to the left around the corner of the building, meaning to park with the rear half of Unit 6 by the back steps of the barracks, so we could take good old Bri right up and right in with no fuss, muss, or bother.

And as George came around the corner, there was Mister Dillon, right in front of us.

'*Watch out, watch out!*' George shouted, whether to me or to the dog or possibly to himself I have no way of knowing. And remembering all this, it strikes me how much it was like the day he hit the woman in Lassburg. So close it was almost a dress rehearsal, but with one very large difference. I wonder if in the last few weeks before he sucked the barrel of his gun he didn't find himself thinking *I missed the dog and hit the woman* over and over again. Maybe not, but I know I would've, if it had been me. *Missed the dog and hit the woman. How can you believe in a God when it's that way around instead of the other?*

George slammed on the brakes with both feet

and drove the heel of his left hand down on the horn. I was thrown forward. My shoulder-harness locked. There were lap belts in the back but our prisoner hadn't troubled to put one on — he'd been too busy doing the Jacubois Cheer for that — and his face shot forward into the mesh, which he'd been gripping. I heard something snap, like when you crack your knuckles. I heard something else crunch. The snap was probably one of his fingers. The crunch was undoubtedly his nose. I have heard them go before, and it always sounds the same, like breaking chicken bones. He gave a muffled, surprised scream. A big squirt of blood, hot as the skin of a hot-water bottle, landed on the shoulder of my uniform.

Mister Dillon probably came within half a foot of dying right there, maybe only two inches, but he ran on without a single look at us, ears laid back tight against his skull, yelping and barking, headed straight for Shed B. His shadow ran beside him on the hottop, black and sharp.

'*Ah Grise, I'be hurd!*' Brian screamed through his plugged nose. '*I'be bleedin all fuggin over!*' And then he began yelling about police brutality.

George opened the driver's-side door. I just sat where I was for a moment, watching D, expecting him to stop when he got to the shed. He never did. He ran full-tilt into the roll-up door, braining himself. He fell over on his side and let out a scream. Until that day I didn't know dogs *could* scream, but they can. To me it didn't sound like pain but frustration. My arms broke out in gooseflesh. D got up and turned in a circle, as if chasing his tail. He did that twice, shook his head as if to clear it, and ran straight at the roll-up door again.

'D, no!' Huddie shouted from the back stoop. Shirley was standing right beside him, her hand up to shade her eyes. '*Stop it, D, you mind me, now!*'

Mister D paid zero attention to them. I don't think he would have paid any attention to Orville Garrett, had Orville been there that day, and Orv was the closest thing to an alpha male that D had. He threw himself into the roll-up door again and again, barking crazily, uttering another of those awful frustrated screams each time he struck the solid surface. The third time he did it, he left a bloody noseprint on the white-painted wood.

During all of this, my old pal Brian was yelling his foolish head off. '*Help me, Jacubois, I'be bleedin like a stuck fuggin pig, where'd your dumbdick friend learn to drive, Sears and fuckin Roebuck? Ged me outta here, my fuggin dose!*'

I ignored him and got out of the cruiser, meaning to ask George if he thought D might be rabid, but before I could open my mouth the stink hit me: that smell of seawater and old cabbage and something else, something a whole lot worse.

Mister D suddenly turned and raced to his right, toward the corner of the shed.

'No, D, no!' Shirley screamed. She saw what I

saw a second after her — the door on the side, the one you opened with a regular knob instead of rolling up on tracks, was standing a few inches open. I have no idea if someone — Arky, maybe — left it that way

NOW:

Arky

It wasn't me, I always close dat door. If I forgot, old Sarge woulda torn me a new asshole. Maybe Curt, too. Dey wanted dat place closed up *tight*.
Dey was *strong* on dat.

THEN:

Eddie

---

or maybe something from inside opened it. Some force originating in the Buick, I suppose that's what I'm talking about. I don't know if that's the case or not; I only know that the door *was* open. That was where the worst of the stench was coming from, and that was where Mister Dillon was going.

Shirley ran down the steps, Huddie right behind her, both of them yelling for Mister D to come back. They passed us. George ran after them, and I ran after George.

There had been a lightshow from the Buick two or three days before. I hadn't been there, but someone had told me about it, and the temperature had been down in Shed B for almost a week. Not a lot, only four or five degrees. There were a few signs, in other words, but nothing really spectacular. Nothing you'd get up in the middle of the night and write home to Mother about. Nothing that would have led us to suspect what we found when we got inside.

Shirley was first, screaming D's name . . . and then just *screaming*. A second later and Huddie was screaming, too. Mister Dillon was barking in a lower register by then, only it was barking and growling all mixed together. It's the sound a dog makes when he's got something treed or at bay.

367

George Morgan yelled out, 'Oh my Lord! Oh my dear Jesus Christ! What *is* it?'

I went into the shed, but not very far. Shirley and Huddie were standing shoulder to shoulder and George was right behind them. They had the way pretty well blocked up. The smell was rank — it made your eyes water and your throat close — but I hardly noticed it.

The Buick's trunk was open again. Beyond the car, in the far corner of the shed, stood a thin and wrinkled yellow nightmare with a head that wasn't really a head at all but a loose tangle of pink cords, all of them twitching and squirming. Under them you could see more of the yellow, wrinkled flesh. It was very tall, seven feet at least. Some of those pink cords lashed at one of the overhead beams as it stood there. The sound they made was fluttery, like moths striking window-glass at night, trying to get at the light they see or sense behind it. I can still hear that sound. Sometimes I hear it in my dreams.

Within the thicket made by those wavering, convulsing pink things, something kept opening and closing in the yellow flesh. Something black and round. It might have been a mouth. It might have been trying to scream. I can't describe what it was standing on. It's like my brain couldn't make any sense of what my eyes were seeing. Not legs, I'm sure of that much, and I think there might have been three instead of two. They ended in black, curved talons. The talons had bunches of wiry hair growing out of them — I think it was hair, and I think there were bugs hopping in the tufts, little bugs like nits or fleas.

From the thing's chest there hung a twitching gray hose of flesh covered with shiny black circles of flesh. Maybe they were blisters. Or maybe, God help me, those things were its eyes.

Standing in front of it, barking and snarling and spraying curds of foam from his muzzle, was our dog. He made as if to lunge forward and the thing shrieked at him from the black hole. The gray hose twitched like a boneless arm or a frog's leg when you shoot electricity into it. Drops of something flew from the end and hit the shed's floor. Smoke began to rise from those spots at once, and I could see them eating into the concrete.

Mister D drew back a little when it shrieked at him but kept on barking and snarling, ears laid back against his skull, eyes bulging out of their sockets. It shrieked again. Shirley screamed and put her hands over her ears. I could understand the urge to do that, but I didn't think it would help much. The shrieks didn't seem to go into your head through your ears but rather just the other way around: they seemed to start in your head and then go *out* through your ears, escaping like steam. I felt like telling Shirley not to do that, not to block her ears, she'd give herself an embolism or something if she held that awful shrieking inside, and then she dropped her hands on her own.

Huddie put his arm around Shirley and she

THEN:

Shirley

I felt Huddie put his arm around me and I took his hand. I had to. I had to have something human to hold on to. The way Eddie tells it, the Buick's first livebirth sounds too close to human: it had a mouth inside all those writhing pink things, it had a chest, it had something that served for eyes. I'm not saying any of that's wrong, but I can't say it's right, either. I'm not sure we ever saw it at all, certainly not the way police officers are trained to look and see. That thing was too strange, too far outside not just our experience but our combined frame of reference. Was it humanoid? A little — at least we perceived it that way. Was it *human*? Not in the least, don't you believe it. Was it intelligent, aware? There's no way to tell for sure, but yes, I think it probably was. Not that it mattered. We were more than horrified by its strangeness. Beyond the horror (or perhaps inside it is what I mean, like a nut inside a shell) there was hate. Part of me wanted to bark and snarl at it just as Mister Dillon was. It woke an anger in me, an *enmity*, as well as fright and revulsion. The other things had been dead on arrival. This one wasn't, but we *wanted* it dead. Oh boy, did we ever!

The second time it shrieked, it seemed to be looking right at us. The hose in its middle lifted

370

like an outstretched arm that's perhaps trying to signal *Help me, call this barking monstrosity off.*

Mister Dillon lunged again. The thing in the corner shrieked a third time and drew back. More liquid splattered from its trunk or arm or penis or whatever it was. A couple of drops struck D and his fur began to smoke at once. He gave a series of hurt, yipping cries. Then, instead of backing off, he leaped at it.

It moved with eerie, gliding speed. Mister Dillon snatched his teeth into one fold of its wrinkled, baggy skin and then it was gone, lurching along the wall on the far side of the Buick, shrieking from that hole in its yellow skin, the hose wagging back and forth. Black goop, like the stuff that had come out of the bat and the fish, was dribbling from where D had nicked it.

It struck the roll-up door and screeched in pain or frustration or both. And then Mister Dillon was on it from behind. He leaped up and seized it by the loose folds hanging from what I suppose you'd call its back. The flesh tore with sickening ease. Mister Dillon dropped to the shed floor with his jaws clenched. More of the thing's skin tore loose and unrolled like loose wallpaper. Black slime . . . blood . . . whatever it was . . . poured over D's upturned face. He howled at the touch of it but held on to what he had, even shaking his head from side to side to tear more of it loose, shaking his head the way a terrier does when it has hold of a rat.

The thing screamed and then made a gibbering sound that was almost words. And yes,

371

the screams and the wordlike sounds all seemed to start in the middle of your head, almost to *hatch* there. The thing beat at the roll-up door with its trunk, as if demanding to be let out, but there was no strength in it.

Huddie had drawn his gun. He had a momentarily clear shot at the pink threads and the yellow knob under them, but then the thing whirled around, still wailing out of that black hole, and it fell on top of Mister D. The gray thing growing from its chest wrapped itself around D's throat and D began to yip and howl with pain. I saw smoke starting to rise up from where the thing had him, and a moment later I could smell burning fur as well as rotting vegetables and seawater. The intruder was sprawled on top of our dog, squealing and thrashing, its legs (if they *were* legs) thumping against the roll-up door and leaving smudges that looked like nicotine stains. And Mister Dillon let out howl after long, agonized howl.

Huddie leveled his gun. I grabbed his wrist and forced it down. *'No! You'll hit D!'* And then Eddie shoved past me, almost knocking me down. He'd found a pair of rubber gloves on some bags by the door and snapped them on.

THEN:

Eddie

You have to understand that I don't remember any of this the way people ordinarily remember things. For me this is more like remembering the bitter end of a bad drunk. It wasn't Eddie Jacubois who took that pair of rubber gloves from the pile of them on top of the lawn-food bags by the door. It was someone *dreaming* that he was Eddie Jacubois. That's how it seems now, anyway. I think it seemed that way then.

Was Mister Dillon on my mind? Kid, I'd like to think so. And that's the best I can say. Because I can't really remember. I think it's more likely that I just wanted to shut that shrieking yellow thing up, get it out of the middle of my head. I hated it in there. Loathed it. Having it in there was like being raped.

But I must have been thinking, you know it? On some level I really must have been, because I put the rubber gloves on before I took the pickaxe down from the wall. I remember the gloves were blue. There were at least a dozen pairs stacked on those bags, all the colors of the rainbow, but the ones I took were blue. I put them on fast — as fast as the doctors on that *ER* show. Then I took the pickaxe off its pegs. I pushed past Shirley so hard I almost knocked

373

her down. I *would* have knocked her down, I think, only Huddie grabbed her before she could fall.

George shouted something. I think it was 'Be careful of the acid'. I don't remember feeling scared and I certainly don't remember feeling brave. I remember feeling outrage and revulsion. It was the way you'd feel if you woke up with a leech in your mouth, sucking the blood out of your tongue. I said that once to Curtis and he used a phrase I never forgot: *the horror of trespass.* That's what it was, the horror of trespass.

Mister D, howling and thrashing and snarling, trying to get away; the thing lying on him, the pink threads growing out of its top thrashing around like kelp in a wave; the smell of burning fur; the stench of salt and cabbage; the black stuff pouring out of the thing's dog-bit, furrowed back, running down the wrinkles in its yellow skin like sludge and then pattering on the floor; my need to kill it, erase it, make it gone from the world: all these things were whirling in my mind — *whirling,* I tell you, as if the shock of what we'd found in Shed B had whipped my brains, pureed them and then stirred them into a cyclone that had nothing to do with sanity or lunacy or police work or vigilante work or Eddie Jacubois. Like I say, I remember it, but not the way you remember ordinary things. More like a dream. And I'm glad. To remember it at all is bad enough. And you can't not remember. Even drinking doesn't stop that, only pushes it away a little bit, and when you stop, it all comes rushing back. Like waking up with a bloodsucker in your mouth.

I got to it and I swung the pickaxe and the pointed end of it went into the middle of it. The thing screamed and threw itself backward against the roll-up door. Mister Dillon got loose and backed away, creeping with his belly low to the floor. He was barking with anger and howling with pain, the sounds mixed together. There was a charred trench in his fur behind his collar. Half his muzzle had been singed black, as if he'd stuck it in a campfire. Little tendrils of smoke were rising from it.

The thing lying against the roll-up door lifted that gray hose in its chest and those *were* eyes embedded in it, all right. They were looking at me and I couldn't bear it. I turned the pickaxe in my hands and brought the axe side of it down. There was a thick *chumping* sound, and part of the hose rolled away on the concrete. I'd also caved in the chest area. Clouds of stuff like pink shaving cream came out of the hole, billowing, like it was under pressure. Along the length of the gray trunk — the severed piece is what I'm talking about — those eyes rolled spastically, seeming to look in all different directions at once. Clear drops of liquid, its venom, I guess, dribbled out and scorched the concrete.

Then George was beside me. He had a shovel. He drove the blade of it down into the middle of the tendrils on the creature's head. Buried it in the thing's yellow flesh all the way up to the ashwood shaft. The thing screamed. I heard it so loud in my mind that it seemed to push my eyes out in their sockets, the way a frog's eyes will bulge when you wrap your hand around its flabby body and squeeze.

THEN:

Huddie

I put on a pair of gloves myself and grabbed one of the other tools — I think it was a hard rake, but I'm not entirely sure. Whatever it was, I grabbed it, then joined Eddie and George. A few seconds later (or maybe it was a minute, I don't know, time stopped meaning anything) I looked around and Shirley was there, too. She'd put on her own pair of gloves, then grabbed Arky's posthole digger. Her hair had come loose and was hanging down all around her face. She looked to me like Sheena, Queen of the Jungle.

We all remembered to put on gloves, but we were all crazy. Completely nuts. The look of it, the gibbering keening screeching *sound* of it, even the way Mister D was howling and whining — all of that *made* us crazy. I'd forgotten about the overturned tanker, and George Stankowski trying to get the kids into the schoolbus and drive them to safety, and the angry young man Eddie and George Morgan had brought in. I think I forgot there was any world at all outside that stinking little shed. I was screaming as I swung the rake, plunging the tines into the thing on the floor again and again and again. The others were screaming, too. We stood around it in a circle, beating and bludgeoning and cutting it to pieces; we were screaming at it to die and it *wouldn't* die, it seemed as if it would never die.

If I could forget anything, any part of it, I'd forget this: at the very end, just before it finally did die, it raised the stump of the thing in its chest. The stump was trembling like an old man's hand. There were eyes in the stump, some of them hanging from shiny threads of gristle by then. Maybe those threads were optic nerves. I don't know. Anyway, the stump rose up and for just a moment, in the center of my head, *I saw myself.* I saw all of us standing around in a circle and looking down, looking like murderers at the grave of their victim, and I saw how strange and alien we were. How *horrible* we were. In that moment I felt its awful confusion. Not its fear, because it wasn't afraid. Not its innocence, because it wasn't innocent. Or guilty, for that matter. What it was was confused. Did it know *where* it was? I don't think so. Did it know why Mister Dillon had attacked it and we were killing it? Yes, it knew that much. We were doing it because we were so different, so different and so horrible that its many eyes could hardly see us, could hardly hold on to our images as we surrounded it screaming and chopping and cutting and hitting. And then it finally stopped moving. The stub of the trunk-thing in its chest dropped back down again. The eyes stopped twitching and just stared.

We stood there, Eddie and George side by side, panting. Shirley and I were across from them — on the other side of that thing — and Mister D was behind us, panting and whining.

Shirley dropped the posthole digger and when it hit the concrete, I saw a plug of the dead thing's yellow flesh caught in it like a piece of diseased dirt. Her face was bone-white except for two wild bright patches of red in her cheeks and another blooming on her throat like a birthmark.

'Huddie,' she whispered.

'What?' I asked. I could hardly talk, my throat was that dry.

'Huddie!'

'*What*, goddammit?'

'It could *think*,' she whispered. Her eyes were big and horrified, swimming with tears. 'We killed a *thinking being*. That's murder.'

'Bullshit's what that is,' George said. 'Even if it's not, what damn good does it do to go on about it?'

Whining — but not in the same urgent way as before — Mister Dillon pushed in between me and Shirley. There were big bald patches in the fur on his neck and back and chest, as if he had the mange. The tip of one ear seemed to be singed clean off. He stretched out his neck and sniffed the corpse of the thing lying beside the roll-up door.

'Grab him outta there,' George said.

'No, he's all right,' I said.

As D scented at the limp and now unmoving tangle of pink tendrils on the thing's head, he whined again. Then he lifted his leg and pissed on the severed piece of trunk or horn or whatever it was. With that done he backed away, still whining.

I could hear a faint hiss. The smell of cabbage

379

was getting stronger, and the yellow color was fading from the creature's flesh. It was turning white. Tiny, almost invisible ribbons of steam were starting to drift up. That's where the worst of the stench was, in that rising vapor. The thing had started to decompose, like the rest of the stuff that had come through.

'Shirley, go back inside,' I said. 'You've got a 99 to handle.'

She blinked rapidly, like someone who is just coming to. 'The tanker,' she said. 'George S. Oh Lord, I forgot.'

'Take the dog with you,' I said.

'Yes. All right.' She paused. 'What about — ?' She gestured at the tools scattered on the concrete, the ones we'd used to kill the creature as it lay against the door, mangled and screaming. Screaming what? For mercy? Would it (or its kind) have accorded mercy to one of us, had our positions been reversed? I don't think so . . . but of course I wouldn't, would I? Because you have to get through first one night and then another and then a year of nights and then ten. You have to be able to turn off the lights and lie there in the dark. You have to believe you only did what would have been done to you. You have to arrange your thoughts because you know you can only live with the lights on so much of the time.

'I don't know, Shirley,' I said. I felt very tired, and the smell of the rotting cabbage was making me sick to my stomach. 'What the fuck does it matter, it's not like there's going to be a trial or an inquest or anything official. Go on inside.

380

You're the police communications officer. So communicate.'

She nodded jerkily. 'Come on, Mister Dillon.'

I wasn't sure D would go with her but he did, walking neatly behind one of Shirley's brown low-heeled shoes. He kept whining, though, and just before they went out the side door he kind of shivered all over, as if he'd caught a chill.

'We oughtta get out, too,' George said to Eddie. He started to rub at his eyes, realized he was still wearing gloves, and stripped them off. 'We've got a prisoner to take care of.'

Eddie looked as surprised as Shirley had when I reminded her that she had business to deal with over in Poteenville. 'Forgot all about the loudmouth sonofabitch,' he said. 'He broke his nose, George — I heard it.'

'Yeah?' George said. 'Oh what a shame.'

Eddie grinned. You could see him trying to pull it back. It widened, instead. They have a way of doing that, even under the worst of circumstances. *Especially* under the worst of circumstances.

'Go on,' I said. 'Take care of him.'

'Come with us,' Eddie said. 'You shouldn't be in here alone.'

'Why not? It's dead, isn't it?'

'*That's* not.' Eddie lifted his chin in the Buick's direction. 'Goddam fake car's hinky, still hinky, and I mean to the max. Don't you feel it?'

'I feel something,' George said. 'Probably just reaction from dealing with that' — he gestured at the dead creature — 'that whatever-it-was.'

'No,' Eddie said. 'What you feel's coming from

the goddam Buick, not that dead thing. It *breathes*, that's what I think. Whatever that car really is, it breathes. I don't think it's safe to be in here, Hud. Not for any of us.'

'You're overreacting.'

'The hell I am. *It breathes*. It blew that pink-headed thing out on the exhale, the way you can blow a booger out of your nose when you sneeze. Now it's getting ready to suck back in. I tell you I can feel it.'

'Look,' I said, 'I just want one quick look around, okay? Then I'm going to grab the tarp and cover up . . . that.' I jerked my thumb at what we'd killed. 'Anything more complicated can wait for Tony and Curt. They're the experts.'

But calming him down was impossible. He was working himself into a state.

'You can't let them near that fake car until after it sucks in again.' Eddie looked balefully at the Buick. 'And you better be ready for an argument on the subject. The Sarge'll want to come in and Curt will want to come in even more, but you can't let them. Because — '

'I know,' I said. 'It's getting ready to suck back in, you can feel it. We ought to get you your own eight-hundred number, Eddie. You could make your fortune reading palms over the phone.'

'Yeah, go ahead, laugh. You think Ennis Rafferty's laughing, wherever he is? I'm telling you what I know, whether you like it or not. It's breathing. It's what it's been doing all along. This time when it sucks back, it's going to be hard. Tell you what. Let me and George help you with the tarp. We'll cover the thing up together and then we'll all go out together.'

That seemed like a bad idea to me, although I didn't know exactly why. 'Eddie, I can handle this. Swear to God. Also, I want to take a few pictures of Mr E.T. before he rots away to nothing but stone-crab soup.'

'Quit it,' George said. He was looking a little green.

'Sorry. I'll be out in two shakes of a lamb's tail. Go on, now, you guys, take care of your subject.'

Eddie was staring at the Buick, standing there on its big smooth whitewall tires, its trunk open so its ass end looked like the front end of a crocodile. 'I hate that thing,' he said. 'For two cents — '

George was heading for the door by then, and Eddie followed without finishing what he'd do for two cents. It wasn't that hard to figure out, anyway.

The smell of the decaying creature was getting worse by the minute, and I remembered the Puff-Pak Curtis had worn when he'd come in here to investigate the plant that looked like a lily. I thought it was still in the hutch. There was a Polaroid camera, too, or had been the last time I looked.

Very faint, from the parking lot, I heard George calling to Shirley, asking her if she was all right. She called back and said she was. A second or two later, Eddie yelled '*FUCK!*' at the top of his voice. Another country heard from. He sounded pissed like a bear. I figured his prisoner, probably high on drugs and with a broken nose to boot, had upchucked in the back of Unit 6. Well, so what? There are worse things than having a prisoner blow chunks in your ride. Once, while I was assisting at the scene of a three-car collision over in Patchin, I stashed the drunk driver who'd caused it all in the back of my unit for safekeeping while I set out some road flares. When I returned, I discovered that my subject had taken off his shirt and taken a shit in it. He then used one of the sleeves as a squeeze-tube — you have to imagine a baker decorating a cake to get what I'm trying to describe here — and wrote his name on both side windows in the back. He was trying to do the rear window, too, only he ran out of his special brown icing. When I asked him why he'd want to do such a nasty goddam thing, he looked at me with that cockeyed hauteur only a longtime drunk can manage and said, 'It's a nasty goddam world, Trooper.'

Anyway, I didn't think Eddie yelling was important, and I went out back to the hutch where we kept our supplies without bothering to check on him. I was more than half-convinced the Puff-Pak would be gone, but it was still on the shelf, wedged between the box of blank videotapes and a pile of *Field & Stream* magazines. Some tidy soul had even tucked it into a plastic evidence bag to keep the dust off. Taking it down, I remembered how crazy Curt had looked on the day I first saw him wearing this gadget, Curt also wearing a plastic barber's smock and a blue bathing cap and red galoshes.

You're beautiful, wave to your adoring fans, I'd told him.

I put the mask to my mouth and nose, almost sure that what came out of it would be unbreathable, but it was air, all right — stale as week-old bread but not actually moldy, if you know what I mean. Better than the stench in the shed, certainly. I grabbed the battered old Polaroid One-Shot from the nail where it was hanging by the strap. I backed out of the hutch, and — this could be nothing but hindsight, I'll be the first to admit it — I think I saw movement. Just a flash of movement. Not from the vicinity of the shed, though, because I was looking right at that and this was more a corner-of-the-eye phenomenon. Something in our back field. In the high grass. I probably thought it was Mister Dillon, maybe rolling around and trying to get that thing's smell off. Well, it wasn't. Mister Dillon wasn't up to any rolling around by then. By then poor old D was busy dying.

I went back into the shed, breathing through the mask. And although I hadn't felt what Eddie was talking about before, this time it came through loud and clear. It was like being outside the shed for a few moments had freshened me for it, or attuned me to it. The Buick wasn't flashing purple lightning or glowing or humming, it was only sitting there, but there was a sense of *liveliness* to it that was unmistakable. You could feel it hovering just over your skin, like the lightest touch of a breeze huffing at the hairs on your forearms. And I thought . . . this is

385

crazy, but I thought, *What if the Buick's nothing but another version of what I'm wearing on my face right now? What if it's nothing but a Puff-Pak? What if the thing wearing it has exhaled and now its chest is lying flat but in a second or two —*

Even with the Puff-Pak, the smell of the dead creature was enough to make my eyes water. Brian Cole and Jackie O'Hara, two of the handier build-em-and-fix-em fellows on the roster back then, had installed an overhead fan the year before, and I flipped the switch as I passed it.

I took three pictures, and then the One-Shot was out of film — I'd never even checked the load. Stupid. I tucked the photos into my back pocket, put the camera down on the floor, then went to get the tarp. As I bent and grabbed it, I realized that I'd taken the camera but walked out of the hutch right past the looped length of bright yellow rope. I should have taken it and cinched the loop in the end of it around my waist. Tied the other end to the big old hook Curtis had mounted to the left of Shed B's side door for just that purpose. But I didn't do that. The rope was too goddam bright to miss, but I missed it anyway. Funny, huh? And there I was where I had no business to be on my own, but I *was* on my own. I wasn't wearing a security line, either. Had walked right past it, maybe because something *wanted* me to walk right past it. There was a dead E.T. on the floor and the air was full of a lively, chilly, *gathering* feeling. I think it crossed my mind that if I disappeared, my wife

386

and Ennis Rafferty's sister could join up forces. I think I might have laughed out loud at that. I can't remember for sure, but I do remember being struck humorous by something. The global absurdity of the situation, maybe.

The thing we'd killed had turned entirely white. It was steaming like dry ice. The eyes on the severed piece still seemed to be staring at me, even though by then they'd started to melt and run. I was as afraid as I've ever been in my life, afraid the way you are when you're in a situation where you could really die and you know it. That sense of something about to breathe, to *suck in*, was so strong it made my skin crawl. But I was grinning, too. Big old grin. Not quite laughing, but almost. Feeling humorous. I tossed the tarp over Mr E.T. and started backing out of the shed. Forgot the Polaroid entirely. Left it sitting there on the concrete.

I was almost at the door when I looked at the Buick. And some force pulled me toward it. Am I sure it was *its* force? Actually, I'm not. It might just have been the fascination deadly things have for us: the edge and the drop, how the muzzle of a gun looks back at us like an eye if we turn it this way and that. Even the point of a knife starts to look different if the hour's late and everyone else in the house has gone to sleep.

All this was below the level of thinking, though. On the level of thinking I just decided I couldn't go out and leave the Buick with its trunk open. It just looked too . . . I don't know, too getting ready to breathe. Something like that.

I was still smiling. Might even have laughed a little.

I took eight steps — or maybe it was a dozen, I guess it could have been as many as a dozen. I was telling myself there was nothing foolish about what I was doing, Eddie J. was nothing but an old lady mistaking feelings for facts. I reached for the trunk-lid. I meant to just slam it and scat (or so I told myself), but then I looked inside and I said one of those things you say when you're surprised, I can't remember which one, it might have been *Well, I be dog* or *I'll be switched*. Because there was something in there, lying on the trunk's plain brown carpeting. It looked like a transistor radio from the late fifties or early sixties. There was even a shiny stub of what could have been an antenna sticking up from it.

I reached into the trunk and picked the gizmo up. Had a good laugh over it, too. I felt like I was in a dream, or tripping on some chemical. And all the time I knew it was closing in on me, getting ready to take me. I didn't know if it got Ennis the same way, but probably, yeah. I was standing in front of that open trunk, no rope on me and no one to pull me back, and something was getting ready to pull me in, to breathe me like cigarette smoke. And I didn't give Shit One. All I cared about was what I'd found in the trunk.

It might have been some sort of communication device — that's what it looked like — but it might have been something else entirely: where the monster kept its prescription drugs, some

388

sort of musical instrument, maybe even a weapon. It was the size of a cigarette-pack but a lot heavier. Heavier than a transistor radio or a Walkman, too. There were no dials or knobs or levers on it. The stuff it was made of didn't look or feel like either metal or plastic. It had a fine-grained texture, not exactly unpleasant but organic, like cured cowhide. I touched the rod sticking out of it and it retracted into a hole on top. I touched the hole and the rod came back out. Touched the rod again and this time nothing happened. Not then, not ever. Although *ever* for what we called 'the radio' wasn't very long; after a week or so, the surface of it began to pit and corrode. It was in an evidence bag with a Ziploc top, but that didn't matter. A month later the 'radio' looked like something that's been left out in the wind and rain for about eighty years. And by the following spring it was nothing but a bunch of gray fragments lying at the bottom of a Baggie. The antenna, if that's what it was, never moved again. Not so much as a silly millimeter.

I thought of Shirley saying *We killed a thinking being* and George saying that was bullshit. Except it wasn't bullshit. The bat and the fish hadn't come equipped with things that looked like transistor radios because they had been animals. Today's visitor — which we'd hacked to pieces with tools we'd taken from the pegboard — had been something quite different. However loathsome it had seemed to us, no matter how instinctively we'd — what was that word? — we'd repudiated it, Shirley was right: it had been a thinking being. We'd killed it nevertheless, hacked it to pieces even as it lay on the concrete, holding out the severed stump of its trunk in surrender and screaming for the mercy it must have known we'd never give it. *Couldn't* give it. And that didn't horrify me. What did was a vision of the shoe on the other foot. Of Ennis Rafferty falling into the midst of other creatures like this, things with yellow knobs for heads under tangled masses of pink ropes that might have been hair. I saw him dying beneath their flailing, acid-lined trunks and hooking talons, trying to scream for mercy and choking on air he could barely breathe, and when he lay dead before them, dead and already beginning to rot, had one of them worked his weapon out of its holster? Had they stood there looking at it under an alien sky of some unimaginable color? As puzzled by the gun as I had been by the 'radio'? Had one of them said *We just killed a thinking being*, to which another had responded *That's bullshit*? And as I thought these things, I also thought I ought to get out of there right away. Unless I wanted to investigate such questions in person, that was. So what happened next? I've never told anyone that, but I might as well tell now; seems foolish to come this far and then hold back.

I decided to get in the trunk.

I could see myself doing it. There would be plenty of space; you know how big the trunks of those old cars were. When I was a kid we used to joke that Buicks and Cadillacs and Chryslers were mob cars because there was room enough for either two polacks or three guineas in the trunk. Plenty of space. Old Huddie Royer would get in, and lie on his side, and reach up, and pull the trunk closed. Softly. So it made just the faintest click. Then he'd lie there in the dark, breathing stale air from the Puff-Pak and holding the 'radio' to his chest. There wouldn't be much air left in the little tank, but there'd be enough. Old Huddie would just curl up and lie there and keep smilin and then . . . pretty soon . . .

Something interesting would happen.

I haven't thought of this in years, unless it was in the kind of dreams you can't remember when you wake up, the ones you just know were bad because your heart is pounding and your mouth is dry and your tongue tastes like a burnt fuse. The last time I thought consciously about standing there in front of the Buick Roadmaster's trunk was when I heard George Morgan had taken his own life. I thought of him out there in his garage, sitting down on the floor, maybe listening to the kids playing baseball under the lights over on McClurg Field around the other side of the block and then with his can of beer finished taking up the gun and looking at it. We might have switched over to the Beretta by then, but George kept his Ruger. Said it just felt right in his hand. I thought of him turning it this way and that, looking into its eye. Every gun has an eye. Anyone who's ever looked into one knows that. I thought of him putting the barrel between his teeth and feeling the hard little bump of the gunsight against the roof of his mouth. Tasting the oil. Maybe even poking into the muzzle with

391

the tip of his tongue, the way you might tongue the mouthpiece of a trumpet when you're getting ready to blow. Sitting there in the corner of the garage, still tasting that last can of beer, also tasting the gun-oil and the steel, licking the hole in the muzzle, the eye the slug comes out of at twice the speed of sound, riding a pad of hot expanding gases. Sitting there smelling the grass caked under the Lawnboy and a little spilled gasoline. Hearing kids cheer across the block. Thinking of how it felt to hit a woman with two tons of police cruiser, the thud and slew of it, seeing drops of blood appear on the windshield like the debut of a Biblical curse and hearing the dry gourdlike rattle of something caught in one of the wheelwells, what turned out to be one of her sneakers. I thought of all that and I think it was how it was for him because I know it's how it was for me. I knew it was going to be horrible but I didn't care because it would be kind of funny, too. That's why I was smiling. I didn't want to get away. I don't think George did, either. In the end, when you really decide to do it, it's like falling in love. It's like your wedding night. And I had decided to do it.

Saved by the bell, that's the saying, but I was saved by a scream: Shirley's. At first it was just a high shriek, and then there were words. *'Help! Please! Help me! Please, please help me!'*

It was like being slapped out of a trance. I took two big steps away from the Buick's trunk, wavering like a drunk, hardly able to believe what I'd been on the verge of. Then Shirley screamed again and I heard Eddie yell: 'What's wrong with him, George? What's happening to him?'

I turned and ran out the shed door.

Yeah, saved by the scream. That's me.

THEN:

Eddie

It was better outside, so much better I almost felt, as I hurried along after George, that the whole thing in Shed B had been a dream. Surely there were no monsters with pink strings growing out of their heads and trunks with eyes in them and talons with hair growing out of them. Reality was our subject in the back seat of Unit 6, that debonair, girlfriend-punching puke, ladies and gentleman, let's give him a great big hand, Brian Lippy. I was still afraid of the Buick — afraid as I'd never been before or have been since — and I was sure there was a perfectly good reason to feel that way, but I could no longer remember what it was. Which was a relief.

I trotted to catch up with George. 'Hey, man, I might have gotten a little carried away in there. If I did — '

'Shit,' he said in a flat, disgusted voice, stopping so quick I almost ran into his back. He was standing at the edge of the parking lot with his hands curled into fists that were planted on his hips. 'Look at that.' Then he called, 'Shirley! You all right?'

'Fine,' she called back. 'But Mister D . . . aw sugar, there goes the radio. I have to get that.'

'Doesn't this *bite*,' George said in a low voice.

I stepped up beside him and saw why he was

upset. 6's right rear window had been broken clean out to the doorframe, undoubtedly by a pair of cowboy boots with stacked heels. Two or three kicks wouldn't have done that, maybe not even a dozen, but we'd given my old school chum Brian plenty of time to go to town. Rowdy-dow and a hot-cha-cha, as my old mother used to say. The sun was reflecting fire off a thousand crumbles of glass lying heaped on the hottop. Of Monsieur Brian Lippy himself, there was no sign. '*FUCK!*' I shouted, and actually shook my fists at Unit 6.

We had a burning chemical tanker over in Pogus County, we had a dead monster rotting in our back shed, and now we also had one escaped neo-Nazi asshole. Plus a broken cruiser window. You might think that's not much compared to the rest, kid, but that's because you've never had to fill out the forms, beginning with 24-A-24, Damaged Property, PSP and ending with Complete Incident Report, Fill Out All Appropriate Fields. One thing I'd like to know is why you never have a series of good days in which one thing goes wrong. Because it's not that way, at least not in my experience. In my experience the bad shit gets saved up until you have a day when everything comes due at once. That was one of those days. The granddaddy of them all.

George started walking toward 6. I walked beside him. He hunkered down, took the walkie out of its holster on his hip, and stirred through the strew of broken Saf-T-Glas with the rubber antenna. Then he picked something up. It was our pal's cruicifix earring. He must have lost it when he climbed through the broken window.

'Fuck,' I said again, but in a lower voice. 'Where do you think he went?'

'Well, he's not in with Shirley. Which is good. Otherwise? Down the road, up the road, across the road, across the back field and into the woods. One of those. Take your pick.' He got up and looked into the empty back seat. 'This could be bad, Eddie. This could be a real fuckarow. You know that, don't you?'

Losing a prisoner was never good, but Brian Lippy wasn't exactly John Dillinger, and I said so.

George shook his head as if I didn't get it. 'We don't know what he *saw*. Do we?'

'Huh?'

'Maybe nothing,' he went on, and dragged a shoe through the broken glass. The little pieces clicked and scritched. There were droplets of blood on some of them. 'Maybe he hightailed it away from the shed. But of course going that way'd take him to the road, and even if he was as high as an elephant's eye, he might not've wanted to go that way, in case some cop 20-base should see him — a guy covered with blood, busted glass in his hair — and arrest him all over again.'

I was slow that day and I admit it. Or maybe I was still in shock. 'I don't see what you're — '

George was standing with his head down and his arms folded across his chest. He was still dragging his foot back and forth, stirring that broken glass like stew. 'Me, I'd head for the back field. I'd want to hook around to the highway

396

through the woods, maybe wash up in one of the streams back there, then try to hitch a ride. Only what if I get distracted while I'm making my escape? What if I hear a lot of screaming and thrashing coming from inside that shed?'

'Oh,' I said. 'Oh my God. You don't think he'd really stop what *he* was doing to check on what *we* were doing, do you?'

'Probably not. But is it possible? Hell, yes. Curiosity's a powerful thing.'

That made me think of what Curt liked to say about the curious cat. 'Yeah, but who on God's earth would ever believe him?'

'If it ever got into the *American*,' George said heavily, 'Ennis's sister might. And that would be a start. Wouldn't it?'

'Shit,' I said. I thought it over. 'We better have Shirley put out an all-points on Brian Lippy.'

'First let's let folks get the mess in Poteenville picked up a little. Then, when he gets here, we'll tell the Sarge everything — including what Lippy might have seen — and show him what's left in Shed B. If Huddie gets some half-decent pictures . . . ' He glanced back over his shoulder. 'Say, where *is* Huddie? He should've been out of there by now. Christ, I hope — '

He got that far and then Shirley started screaming. '*Help! Please! Help me! Please, please help me!*'

Before either of us could take a step toward the barracks, Mister Dillon came out through the hole he'd already put in the screen door. He was staggering from side to side like a drunk, and his head was down. Smoke was rising from his fur. More seemed to be coming out of his head, although at first I couldn't see where it was coming from; *everywhere* was my first impression. He got his forepaws on the first of the three steps going down from the back stoop to the parking lot, then lost his balance and fell on his side. When he did, he twisted his head in a series of jerks. It was the way people move in those oldtime silent movies. I saw smoke coming out of his nostrils in twin streams. It made me think of the woman sitting there in Lippy's bigfoot truck, the smoke from her cigarette rising in a ribbon that seemed to disappear before it got to the roof. More smoke was coming from his eyes, which had gone a strange, knitted white. He vomited out a spew of smoky blood, half-dissolved tissue, and triangular white things. After a moment or two I realized they were his teeth.

THEN:

Shirley

There was a great confused clatter of radio traffic, but none of it was directed to base. Why would it be, when all the action was either out at Poteenville Grammar School or headed that way? George Stankowski had gotten the kids away from the smoke, at least, I got that. Poteenville Volunteer One, aided by pumpers from Statler County, were controlling the grassfires around the school. Those fires had indeed been touched off by burning diesel and not some flammable chemical. It was chlorine liquid in the tanker, that was now confirmed. Not good, but nowhere near as bad as it might have been.

George called to me from outside, wanting to know if I was all right. Thinking that was rather sweet, I called back and told him I was. A second or two later, Eddie called out the f-word, angry. During all this I felt strange, not myself, like someone going through ordinary chores and routines in the wake of some vast change.

Mister D was standing in the door to dispatch with his head down, whining at me. I thought the burned patches in his fur were probably paining him. There were more burned places, dottings of them, on both sides of his muzzle. I reminded myself that someone — Orv Garrett was the logical choice — should take him to the vet when things finally settled back down. That would mean making up some sort of story about how he got burned, probably a real whopper.

'Want some water, big boy?' I asked. 'Bet you do, don't you?'

He whined again, as if to say water was a very good idea. I went into the kitchenette, got his bowl, filled it at the sink. I could hear him clicking along on the lino behind me but I never turned around until I had the bowl full.

'Here you a — '

I got that far, then took a good look at him and dropped the bowl on the floor, splashing my ankles. He was shivering all over — not like he was cold but like someone was passing an electric current through him. And foam was dripping out from both sides of his muzzle.

He's rabid, I thought. *Whatever that thing had, it's turned D rabid.*

He didn't look rabid, though, only confused and in misery. His eyes seemed to be asking me to fix whatever was wrong. I was the human, I was in charge, I should be able to fix it.

'D?' I said. I dropped down on one knee and held my hand out to him. I know that sounds stupid — dangerous — but at the time it seemed like the right thing. 'D, what is it? What's wrong? Poor old thing, what's wrong?'

He came to me, but very slowly, whining and shivering with every step. When he got close I saw a terrible thing: little tendrils of smoke were coming from the birdshot-spatter of holes on his muzzle. More was coming from the burned patches on his fur, and from the corners of his eyes, as well. I could see his eyes starting to lighten, as if a mist was covering them from the inside.

I reached out and touched the top of his head. When I felt how hot it was, I gave a little yell and yanked my hand back, the way you do when you touch a stove burner you thought was off but isn't. Mister D made as if to snap at me, but I don't think he meant anything by it; he just couldn't think what else to do. Then he turned and blundered his way out of the kitchen.

I got up, and for a moment the whole world swam in front of my eyes. If I hadn't grabbed the counter, I think I would have fallen. Then I went after him (staggering a little myself) and said, 'D? Come back, honeybunch.'

He was halfway across the duty room. He turned once to look back at me — toward the sound of my voice — and I saw . . . oh, I saw smoke coming out of his mouth and nose, out of his ears, too. The sides of his mouth drew back and for a second it seemed like he was trying to grin at me, the way dogs will do when they're happy. Then he vomited. Most of what came out wasn't food but his own insides. And they were smoking.

That was when I screamed. '*Help! Please! Help me! Please, please help me!*'

Mister D turned away as if all that screaming was hurting his poor hot ears, and went on staggering across the floor. He must have seen the hole in the screen, he must have had enough eyesight left for that, because he set sail for it and slipped out through it.

I went after him, still screaming.

THEN:

Eddie

'*What's wrong with him, George?*' I shouted.
Mister Dillon had managed to get on his feet
again. He was turning slowly around, the smoke
rising from his fur and coming out of his mouth
in gray billows. '*What's happening to him?*'

Shirley came out, her cheeks wet with tears.
'Help him!' she shouted. 'He's burning up!'

Huddie joined us then, panting as if he'd run a
race. 'What the hell is it?'

Then he saw. Mister Dillon had collapsed
again. We walked cautiously toward him from
one side. From the other, Shirley came down
from the stoop. She was closer and reached him
first.

'Don't touch him!' George said.

Shirley ignored him and put a hand on D's
neck, but she couldn't hold it there. She looked
at us, her eyes swimming with tears. 'He's on fire
inside,' she said.

Whining, Mister Dillon tried to get on his feet
again. He made it halfway, the front half, and
began to move slowly toward the far side of the
parking lot, where Curt's Bel Air was parked
next to Dicky-Duck Eliot's Toyota. By then he
had to have been blind; his eyes were nothing
but boiling jelly in their sockets. He kind of
paddled along, pulling himself with his front

403

paws, dragging his rump.

'Christ,' Huddie said.

By then tears were pouring down Shirley's face and her voice was so choked it was hard to make out what she was saying. 'Please, for the love of God, can't one of you help him?'

I had an image then, very bright and clear. I saw myself getting the hose, which Arky always kept coiled under the faucet-bib on the side of the building. I saw myself turning on the spigot, then running to Mister D and slamming the cold brass nozzle of the hose into his mouth, feeding water down the chimney that was his throat. I saw myself putting him out.

But George was already walking toward the dying ruin that had been our barracks dog, taking his gun out of his holster as he went. D, meanwhile, was still paddling mindlessly along toward a spot of nothing much between Curt's Bel Air and Dicky-Duck's Toyota, moving in a cloud of thickening smoke. How long, I wondered, before the fire inside broke through and he went up in flames like one of those suicidal Buddhist monks you used to see on television during the Vietnam war?

George stopped and held his gun up so Shirley could see it. 'It's the only thing, darlin. Don't you think?'

'Yes, hurry,' she said, speaking very rapidly.

NOW:

Shirley

I turned to Ned, who was sitting there with his head down and his hair hanging on his brow. I put my hand on his chin and tilted it up so he'd have to look at me. 'There was nothing else we could do,' I said. 'You see that, don't you?'

For a moment he said nothing and I was afraid. Then he nodded.

I looked at Sandy Dearborn, but he wasn't looking at me. He was looking at Curtis's boy, and I've rarely seen him with such a troubled expression.

Then Eddie started talking again and I sat back to listen. It's funny how close the past is, sometimes. Sometimes it seems as if you could almost reach out and touch it. Only . . .

Only who really wants to?

THEN:

Eddie

In the end there was no more melodrama, just a Trooper in a gray uniform with the shadow of his big hat shielding his eyes bending and reaching out like you might reach out your hand to a crying child to comfort him. He touched the muzzle of his Ruger to the dog's smoking ear and pulled the trigger. There was a loud *Pow!* and D fell dead on his side. The smoke was still coming out of his fur in little ribbons.

George holstered his weapon and stood back. Then he put his hands over his face and cried something out. I don't know what it was. It was too muffled to tell. Huddie and I walked to where he was. Shirley did, too. We put our arms around him, all of us. We were standing in the middle of the parking lot with Unit 6 behind us and Shed B to our right and our nice barracks dog who never made any trouble for anybody lying dead in front of us. We could smell him cooking, and without a word we all moved farther to our right, upwind, shuffling rather than walking because we weren't quite ready to lose hold of one another. We didn't talk. We waited to see if he'd actually catch on fire like we thought he might, but it seemed that the fire didn't want him or maybe couldn't use him now that he was dead. He swelled some, and there was a gruesome little sound from inside him, almost like the one you get when you pop a paper lunchsack. It might have been one of his lungs. Anyway, once that happened, the smoke started to thin.

'That thing from the Buick poisoned him, didn't it?' Huddie asked. 'It poisoned him when he bit into it.'

'Poisoned him my ass,' I said. 'That pink-hair mother-fucker *firebombed* him.' Then I remembered that Shirley was there, and she never had appreciated that kind of talk. 'Sorry,' I said.

She seemed not to have heard me. She was still looking fixedly down at Mister D. 'What do we do now?' she asked. 'Does anyone have any ideas?'

'I don't,' I said. 'This situation is totally out of control.'

'Maybe not,' George said. 'Did you cover up the thing in there, Hud?'

'Yeah.'

'All right, that's a start. And how does it look out in Poteenville, Shirl?'

'The kids are out of danger. They've got a dead bus driver, but considering how bad things looked at first, I'd say . . . ' She stopped, lips pressed together so tight they were almost gone, her throat working. Then she said, 'Excuse me, fellas.'

She walked stiff-legged around the corner of the barracks with the back of her hand pressed against her mouth. She held on until she was out of sight — nothing showing but her shadow

— and then there came three big wet whooping sounds. The three of us stood over the smoking corpse of the dog without saying anything, and after a few minutes she came back, dead white and wiping her mouth with a Kleenex. And picked up right where she'd left off. It was as if she'd paused just long enough to clear her throat or swat a fly. 'I'd say that was a pretty low score. The question is, what's the score here?'

'Get either Curt or the Sarge on the radio,' George said. 'Curt will do but Tony's better because he's more level-headed when it comes to the Buick. You guys buy that?'

Huddie and I nodded. So did Shirley. 'Tell him you have a Code D and we want him here as soon as he can get here. He should know it's not an emergency, but he should also know it's damn *close* to an emergency. Also, tell him we may have a Kubrick.' This was another piece of slang peculiar (so far as I know) to our barracks. A Kubrick is a 2001, and 2001 is PSP code for 'escaped prisoner'. I had heard it talked about, but never actually called.

'Kubrick, copy,' Shirley said. She seemed steadier now that she had orders. 'Do you — '

There was a loud bang. Shirley gave a small scream and all three of us turned toward the shed, reaching for our weapons as we did. Then Huddie laughed. The breeze had blown the shed door closed.

'Go on, Shirley,' George said. 'Get the Sarge. Let's make this happen.'

'And Brian Lippy?' I asked. 'No APB?'

Huddie sighed. Took off his hat. Rubbed the nape of his neck. Looked up at the sky. Put his hat back on. 'I don't know,' he said. 'But if one *does* go out, it won't be any of us who *puts* it out. That's the Sarge's call. It's why they pay him the big bucks.'

'Good point,' George said. Now that he saw that the responsibility was going to travel on, he looked a little more relaxed.

Shirley turned to go into the barracks, then looked back over her shoulder. 'Cover him up, would you?' she said. 'Poor old Mister D. Put something over him. Looking at him that way hurts my heart.'

'Okay,' I said, and started toward the shed.

'Eddie?' Huddie said.

'Yeah?'

'There's a piece of tarp big enough to do the job in the hutch. Use that. Don't go into the shed.'

'Why not?'

'Because something's still going on with that Buick. Hard to tell exactly what, but if you go in there, you might not come back out.'

'All right,' I said. 'You don't have to twist my arm.'

I got the piece of tarp out of the hutch — just a flimsy blue thing, but it would do. On the way back to cover D's body, I stopped at the roll-up door and took a look into the shed, cupping one hand to the side of my face to cut the glare. I wanted a look at the thermometer; I also wanted to make sure my old school chum Brian wasn't skulk-assing around in there. He

wasn't, and the temperature appeared to have
gone up a degree or two. Only one thing in
the landscape had changed. The trunk was
shut.

The crocodile had closed its mouth.

NOW:

Sandy

Shirley, Huddie, Eddie: the sound of their entwined voices was oddly beautiful to me, like the voices of characters speaking lines in some strange play. Eddie said the crocodile had closed its mouth and then his voice ceased and I waited for one of the other voices to come in and when none did and Eddie himself didn't resume, I knew it was over. I knew but Ned Wilcox didn't. Or maybe he did and just didn't want to admit it.

'Well?' he said, and that barely disguised impatience was back in his voice.

What happened when you dissected the bat-thing? Tell me about the fish. Tell me everything. But — this is important — tell me a story, one that has a beginning and a middle and an end where everything is explained. Because I deserve that. Don't shake the rattle of your ambiguity in my face. I deny its place. I repudiate its claim. I want a story.

He was young and that explained part of it, he was faced with something that was, as they say, not of this Earth, and that explained more of it . . . but there was something else, too, and it wasn't pretty. A kind of selfish, single-minded grubbing. And he thought he had a right. We spoil the grief-stricken, have you ever noticed

411

that? And they become used to the treatment.

'Well what?' I asked. I spoke in my least encouraging voice. Not that it would help.

'What happened when Sergeant Schoondist and my father got back? Did you catch Brian Lippy? Did he see? Did he *tell*? Jesus, you guys can't stop there!'

He was wrong, we could stop anyplace we chose to, but I kept that fact to myself (at least for the time being) and told him that no, we never did catch Brian Lippy; Brian Lippy remained Code Kubrick to this very day.

'Who wrote the report?' Ned asked. 'Did you, Eddie? Or was it Trooper Morgan?'

'George,' he said with a trace of a grin. 'He was always better at stuff like that. Took Creative Writing in college. He used to say any state cop worth his salt needed to know the basics of creative writing. When we started to fall apart that day, George was the one who pulled us together. Didn't he, Huddie?'

Huddie nodded.

Eddie got up, put his hands in the small of his back, and stretched until we could hear the bones crackle. 'Gotta go home, fellas. Might stop for a beer at The Tap on the way. Maybe even two. After all this talking, I'm pretty dry, and soda pop just don't cut it.'

Ned looked at him with surprise, anger, and reproach. 'You can't leave just like that!' he exclaimed. 'I want to hear the whole thing!'

And Eddie, who was slowly losing the struggle not to return to being Fat Eddie, said what I knew, what we all knew. He said it while looking

412

at Ned with eyes which were not exactly friendly. 'You did, kid. You just don't know it.'

Ned watched him walk away, then turned to the rest of us. Only Shirley looked back with real sympathy, and I think that hers was tempered with sadness for the boy.

'What does he mean, I heard it all?'

'There's nothing left but a few anecdotes,' I said, 'and those are only variations on the same theme. About as interesting as the kernels at the bottom of the popcorn bowl.

'As for Brian Lippy, the report George wrote said 'Troopers Morgan and Jacubois spoke to the subject and ascertained he was sober. Subject denied assaulting his girlfriend and Trooper Jacubois ascertained that the girlfriend supported him in this. Subject was then released.' '

'But Lippy kicked out their cruiser window!'

'Right, and under the circumstances George and Eddie couldn't very well put in a claim for the damages.'

'So?'

'So the money to replace it probably came out of the contingency fund. The Buick 8 contingency fund, if you want me to cross the *t*'s. We keep it the same place now we did then, a coffee can in the kitchen.'

'Yar, dat's where it come from,' Arky said. 'Poor ole coffee can's taken a fair number of hits over d'years.' He stood up and also stretched his back. 'Gotta go, boys n girls. Unlike some of you, I got friends — what dey call a personal life on d'daytime talkshows. But before I leave, you want to know sup'm else, Neddie? About dat day?'

'Anything you want to tell me.'

'Dey buried D.' He said the verb the old way, so it rhymes with *scurried*. 'An right nex' to im dey buried d'tools dey use on dat t'ing poisoned im. One of em was my pos'hole digger, an I din' get no coffee-can compensation for *dat!*'

'You didn't fill out a TS 1, that's why,' Shirley said. 'I know the paperwork's a pain in the fanny, but . . . ' She shrugged as if to say *That's the way of the world*.

Arky was frowning suspiciously at her. 'TS 1? What kind of form is dat?'

'It's your tough-shit list,' Shirley told him, perfectly straight-faced. 'The one you fill out every month and send to the chaplain. Goodness, I never saw such a Swedish squarehead. Didn't they teach you *anything* in the Army?'

Arky flapped his hands at her, but he was smiling. He'd taken plenty of ribbing over the years, believe me — that accent of his attracted it. 'Geddout witcha!'

'Walked right into it, Arky,' I said. I was also smiling. Ned wasn't. Ned looked as if the joking and teasing — our way of winding things back down to normal — had gone right past him.

'Where were you, Arky?' he asked. 'Where were you when all this was going on?' Across from us, Eddie Jacubois started his pickup truck and the headlights came on.

'Vacation,' Arky said. 'On my brudder's farm in Wisconsin. So dat was one mess someone else

414

got to clean up.' He said this last with great satisfaction.

Eddie drove past, giving us a wave. We gave him a little right-back-atcha, Ned along with the rest of us. But he continued to look troubled.

'I gotta get it in gear, too,' Phil said. He disposed of his cigarette butt, got on his feet, hitched up his belt. 'Kiddo, leave it at this: your dad was an excellent officer and a credit to Troop D, Statler Barracks.'

'But I want to know — '

'It don't *matter* what you want to know,' Phil told him gently. 'He's dead, you're not. Those are the facts, as Joe Friday used to say. G'night, Sarge.'

'Night,' I said, and watched the two of them, Arky and Phil, walk away together across the parking lot. There was good moonlight by then, enough for me to see that neither man so much as turned his head in the direction of Shed B.

That left Huddie, Shirley, and me. Plus the boy, of course. Curtis Wilcox's boy, who had come and mowed the grass and raked the leaves and erased the snowdrifts when it was too cold for Arky to be outside; Curt's boy, who had quit off the football team and come here instead to try and keep his father alive a little longer. I remembered him holding up his college acceptance letter like a judge holding up a score at the Olympics, and I was ashamed to feel angry with him, considering all that he'd been through and how much he'd lost. But he wasn't the only boy in the history of the world to lose his dad, and at least there'd been a funeral, and his father's name was on the marble memorial out front of the barracks, along with those of Corporal Brady Paul, Trooper Albert Rizzo, and Trooper Samuel Stamson, who died in the seventies and is sometimes known in the PSP as the Shotgun Trooper. Until Stamson's death, we carried our shotguns in roof-racks — if you needed the gun, you just had to reach up over your shoulder and grab it. Trooper Stamson was rear-ended while parked in the turnpike breakdown lane, writing up a traffic stop. The guy who hit him was drunk and doing about a hundred and five at the moment of impact. The cruiser accordioned forward. The gas tank didn't blow, but Trooper Stamson was decapitated by his own shotgun rack. Since 1974 we keep our shotguns clipped under the dash, and since 1973 Sam Stamson's name has been on the memorial. 'On the rock,' we say. Ennis Rafferty is on the books as a disappearance, so he's not on the rock. The official story on Trooper George Morgan is that he died while cleaning his gun (the same Ruger that ended Mister Dillon's misery), and since he didn't die on the job, his name isn't on the rock, either. You don't get on the rock for dying *as a result of* the job; it was Tony Schoondist who pointed that out to me one day when he saw me looking at the names. 'Probably just as well,' he said. 'We'd have a dozen of those things out here.'

Currently, the last name on the stone is Curtis K. Wilcox. July 2001. Line of duty. It wasn't nice to have your father's name carved in granite when what you wanted — *needed* — was the father, but it was something. Ennis's name should have been carved there, too, so his bitch of a sister could come and look at it if she wanted to, but it wasn't. And what *did* she have? A reputation as a nasty old lady, that's what, the kind of person who if she saw you on fire in the street wouldn't piss on you to put you out. She'd been a thorn in our side for years and liking her was impossible but feeling sorry for her was not. She'd ended up with even less than this boy, who at least knew for sure that his father was over, that he was never going to come back in someday with a shamefaced grin and some wild story to explain his empty pockets and how come he had that Tijuana tan and why it hurt like hell each time he had to pass a little water.

I had no good feeling about the night's work. I'd hoped the truth might make things better (it'll set you free, someone said, probably a fool), but I had an idea it had made things worse instead. Satisfaction might have brought the curious cat back, but I could make out zero satisfaction on Ned Wilcox's face. All I saw there was a kind of stubborn, tired curiosity. I'd seen the same look on Curtis's face from time to time, most often when he was standing at one of Shed B's roll-up doors in that sidewalk superintendent's stance — legs apart, forehead to the glass, eyes squinted a little, mouth thoughtful. But what's passed down in the blood is the strongest chain of all, isn't it? What's mailed along, one generation to the next, good news here, bad news there, complete disaster over yonder.

★ ★ ★

I said, 'As far as anyone knows, Brian Lippy just took off for greener pastures. It might even be the truth; none of us can say different for certain. And it's an ill wind that doesn't blow somebody some good; him disappearing that way might have saved his girlfriend's life.'

'I doubt it,' Huddie rumbled. 'I bet her next one was just Brian Lippy with different-colored hair. They pick up guys who beat them until they go through the change. It's like they define themselves through the bruises on their faces and arms.'

'She never filed a missing-persons on him, tell you that,' Shirley said. 'Not one that came across my desk, anyway, and I see the town and county reports as well as our own. No one in his family did, either. I don't know what happened to her, but he was an authentic case of good riddance to bad rubbish.'

'*You* don't believe he just slipped out through that broken window and ran away, do you?' Ned asked Huddie. 'I mean, you were *there*.'

'No,' Huddie said, 'as a matter of fact I don't. But what I think doesn't matter. The point's the same as the one Sarge has been trying to drum into your thick head all night long: *we don't know*.'

It was as if the kid didn't hear him. He turned back to me. 'What about my dad, Sandy? When it came to Brian Lippy, what did *he* believe?'

'He and Tony believed that Brian wound up in the same place as Ennis Rafferty and Jimmy the

Gerbil. As for the corpse of the thing they killed that day — '

'Son of a bitch rotted quick,' Shirley said in a brisk that-ends-it voice. 'There are pictures and you can look at them all you want, but for the most part they're photos of something that could be anything, including a complete hoax. They don't show you how it looked when it was trying to get away from Mister D — how fast it moved or how loud it shrieked. They don't show you anything, really. Nor can we tell you so you'll understand. That's all over your face. Do you know why the past is the past, darling?'

Ned shook his head.

'Because it doesn't work.' She looked into her pack of cigarettes, and whatever she saw there must have satisfied her because she nodded, put them into her purse, and stood up. 'I'm going home. I have two cats that should have been fed three hours ago.'

That was Shirley, all right — Shirley the All-American Girlie, Curt used to call her when he felt like getting under her skin a bit. No husband (there'd been one once, when she was barely out of high school), no kids, two cats, roughly 10,000 Beanie Babies. Like me, she was married to Troop D. A walking cliché, in other words, and if you didn't like it, you could stick it.

'Shirl?'

She turned to the plaintive sound in Ned's voice. 'What, hon?'

'Did you like my father?'

She put her hands on his shoulders, bent down, and planted a kiss on Ned's forehead.

'Loved him, kid. And I love you. We've told you all we can, and it wasn't easy. I hope it helps.' She paused. 'I hope it's enough.'

'I hope so, too,' he said.

Shirley tightened her grip on his shoulders for a moment, giving him a squeeze. Then she let go and stood up. 'Hudson Royer — would you see a lady to her car?'

'My pleasure,' he said, and took her arm. 'See you tomorrow, Sandy? You still on days?'

'Bright and early,' I said. 'We'll do it all again.'

'You better go home and get some sleep, then.'

'I will.'

He and Shirley left. Ned and I sat on the bench and watched them go. We raised our hands as they drove past in their cars — Huddie's big old New Yorker, Shirley in her little Subaru with the bumper sticker reading MY KARMA RAN OVER MY DOGMA. When their taillights had disappeared around the corner of the barracks, I took out my cigarettes and had my own peek into the pack. One left. I'd smoke it and then quit. I'd been telling myself this charming fable for at least ten years.

'There's really no more you can tell me?' Ned asked in a small, disillusioned voice.

'No. It'd never make a play, would it? There's no third act. Tony and your dad ran a few more experiments over the next five years, and finally brought Bibi Roth in on it. That would've been your father persuading Tony and me getting caught in the middle, as usual. And I have to tell you the truth: after Brian Lippy disappeared and Mister Dillon died, I was against doing anything

420

with the Buick beyond keeping an eye on it and offering up the occasional prayer that it would either fall apart or disappear back to where it came from. Oh, and killing anything that came out of the trunk still lively enough to stand up and maybe run around the shed looking for a way out.'

'Did that ever happen?'

'You mean another pink-headed E.T.? No.'

'And Bibi? What did he say?'

'He listened to Tony and your dad, he took another look, and then he walked away. He said he was too old to deal with anything so far outside his understanding of the world and how it works. He told them he intended to erase the Buick from his memory and urged Tony and Curt to do the same.'

'Oh, for God's sake! This guy was a scientist? Jesus, he should have been *fascinated*!'

'Your *father* was the scientist,' I said. 'An amateur one, yeah, but a good one. The things that came out of the Buick and his curiosity about the Buick itself, those were the things that *made* him a scientist. His dissection of the bat-thing, for instance. Crazy as that was, there was something noble about it, too, like the Wright Brothers going up in their little glue-and-paste airplane. Bibi Roth, on the other hand . . . Bibi was a microscope mechanic. He sometimes called himself that, and with absolute pride. He was a person who had carefully and consciously narrowed his vision to a single strip of knowledge, casting a blaze of light over a small area. Mechanics hate mysteries. Scientists

— especially *amateur* scientists — embrace them. Your father was two people at the same time. As a cop, he was a mystery-hater. As a Roadmaster Scholar . . . well, let's just say that when your father was that person, he was very different.'

'Which version did you like better?'

I thought it over. 'That's like a kid asking his parents who they love best, him or his sister. Not a fair question. But the amateur Curt used to scare me. Used to scare Tony a little, too.'

The kid sat pondering this.

'A few more things appeared,' I said. 'In 1991, there was a bird with four wings.'

'*Four — !*'

'That's right. It flew a little bit, hit one of the walls, and dropped dead. In the fall of 1993, the trunk popped open after one of those light-quakes and it was half-filled with dirt. Curt wanted to leave it there and see what would happen and Tony agreed at first, but then it began to stink. I didn't know dirt could decompose, but I guess it can if it's dirt from the right place. And so . . . this is crazy, but we buried the dirt. Can you believe it?'

He nodded. 'And did my dad keep an eye on the place where it was buried? Sure he did. Just to see what would grow.'

'I think he was hoping for a few of those weird lilies.'

'Any luck?'

'I guess that depends on what you think of as luck. Nothing sprouted, I'll tell you that much. The dirt from the trunk went into the ground not far from where we buried Mister D and the tools. As for the monster, what didn't turn to goo we burned in the incinerator. The ground where the dirt went is still bare. A few things try to straggle up every spring, but so far they always die. Eventually, I suppose, that'll change.'

I put the last cigarette in my mouth and lit it.

'A year and a half or so after the dirt-delivery, we got another red-stick lizard. Dead. That's been the last. It's still earthquake country in there, but the earth never shakes as hard these days. It wouldn't do to be careless around the Buick any more than it would to be careless around an old rifle just because it's rusty and the barrel's plugged with dirt, but with reasonable precautions it's probably safe enough. And someday — your dad believed it, Tony believed it, and I do too — that old car really *will* fall apart. All at once, just like the wonderful one-hoss shay in the poem.'

He looked at me vaguely, and I realized he had no idea what poem I was talking about. We live in degenerate times. Then he said, 'I can feel it.'

Something in his tone startled me badly, and I gave him a hard stare. He still looked younger than his eighteen years, I thought. Just a boy, no more than that, sitting with his sneakered feet crossed and his face painted with starlight. 'Can you?' I asked.

'Yes. Can't you?'

All the Troopers who'd passed through D over the years had felt the pull of it, I guessed. Felt it the way people who live on the coast come to feel the motions of the sea, the tides a clock their hearts beat to. On most days and nights we noticed it no more than you consciously notice your nose, a shape sitting at the bottom of all you see. Sometimes, though, the pull was stronger, and then it made you ache, somehow.

'All right,' I said, 'let's say I do. Huddie sure did — what do you think would have happened to him that day if Shirley hadn't screamed when she did? What do you think would have happened to him if he'd crawled into the trunk like he said he had a mind to do?'

'You really never heard that story before tonight, Sandy?'

I shook my head.

'You didn't look all that surprised, even so.'

'Nothing about that Buick surprises me anymore.'

'Do you think he really meant to do it? To crawl in and shut the lid behind him?'

'Yes. Only I don't think *he* had anything to do with it. It's that pull — that attraction it has. It was stronger then, but it's still there.'

He made no reply to that. Just sat looking across at Shed B.

'You didn't answer my question, Ned. What do you think would have happened to him if he'd crawled in there?'

'I don't know.'

A reasonable enough answer, I suppose — a kid's answer, certainly, they say it a dozen times a day — but I hated it just the same. He'd quit off the football team, but it seemed he hadn't forgotten all he'd learned there about bobbing and weaving. I drew in smoke that tasted like hot

424

hay, then blew it back out. 'You don't.'

'No.'

'After Ennis and Jimmy and — probably — Brian Lippy, you don't.'

'Not everything goes on to somewhere else, Sandy. Take the other gerbil, for instance. Rosalie or Rosalynn or whatever her name was.'

I sighed. 'Have it your way. I'm going down to The Country Way to bite a cheeseburger. You're welcome to join me, but only if we can let this go and talk about something else.'

He thought it over, then shook his head. 'Think I'll head home. Do some thinking.'

'Okay, but don't be sharing any of your thinking with your mother.'

He looked almost comically shocked. 'God, no!'

I laughed and clapped him on the shoulder. The shadows had gone out of his face and suddenly it was possible to like him again. As for his questions and his childish insistence that the story must have an ending and the ending must hold some kind of answer, time might take care of it. Maybe I'd been expecting too many of my own answers. The imitation lives we see on TV and in the movies whisper the idea that human existence consists of revelations and abrupt changes of heart; by the time we've reached full adulthood, I think, this is an idea we have on some level come to accept. Such things may happen from time to time, but I think that for the most part it's a lie. Life's changes come slowly. They come the way my youngest nephew breathes in his deepest sleep; sometimes I feel the urge to put a hand on his chest just to assure myself he's still alive. Seen in that light, the whole idea of curious cats attaining satisfaction seemed slightly absurd. The world rarely finishes its conversations. If twenty-three years of living with the Buick 8 had taught me nothing else, it should have taught me that. At this moment Curt's boy looked as if he might have taken a step toward getting better. Maybe even two. And if I couldn't let that be enough for one night, I had my own problems.

'You're in tomorrow, right?' I asked.

'Bright and early, Sarge. We'll do it all again.'

'Then maybe you ought to postpone your thinking and do a little sleeping instead.'

'I guess I can give it a try.' He touched my hand briefly. 'Thanks, Sandy.'

'No problem.'

'If I was a pisshead about any of it — '

'You weren't,' I said. He *had* been a pisshead about some of it, but I didn't think he'd been able to help it. And at his age I likely would have been pissier by far. I watched him walk toward the restored Bel Air his father had left behind, a car of roughly the same vintage as the one in our shed but a good deal less *lively*. Halfway across the parking lot he paused, looking at Shed B, and I paused with the smoldering stub of my cigarette poised before my lips, watching to see what he'd do.

He moved on instead of going over. Good. I took a final puff on my tube of delightful death, thought about crushing it on the hottop, and found a place for it in the butt-can instead, where roughly two hundred previous butts had been buried standing up. The others could crush out their smokes on the pavement if they wanted to — Arky would sweep them up without complaint — but it was better if I didn't do that. I was the Sarge, after all, the guy who sat in the big chair.

I went into the barracks. Stephanie Colucci was in dispatch, drinking a Coke and reading a magazine. She put the Coke down and smoothed her skirt over her knees when she saw me.

'What's up, sweetheart?' I asked.

'Nothing much. Communications are clearing up, though not as fast as they usually do after . . . one of those. I've got enough to keep track of things.'

'What things?'

'9 is responding to a car-fire on the 1–87 Exit 9 ramp, Mac says the driver's a salesman headed for Cleveland, lit up like a neon sign and refusing the field sobriety test. 16 with a possible break-in at Statler Ford. Jeff Cutler with vandalism over at Statler Middle School, but he's just assisting, the local police have got that one.'

'That it?'

'Paul Loving is 10–98 for home in his cruiser, his son's having an asthma attack.'

'You might forget to put that on the report.'

Steffie gave me a reproachful look, as if she hardly needed me to tell her that. 'What's going on out in Shed B?'

'Nothing,' I said. 'Well, nothing much. Normalizing. I'm out of here. If anything comes up, just . . . ' I stopped, sort of horrified.

'Sandy?' she asked. 'Is something wrong?'

If anything comes up, just call Tony Schoondist, I'd been about to say, as if twenty years hadn't slipped under the bridge and the old Sarge wasn't dribbling mindlessly in front of *Nick at Nite* in a Statler nursing home. 'Nothing wrong,' I said. 'If anything comes up, call Frank Soderberg. It's his turn in the barrel.'

'Very good, sir. Have a nice night.'

'Thanks, Steff, right back atcha.'

As I stepped out, the Bel Air rolled slowly toward the driveway with one of the groups Ned likes — Wilco, or maybe The Jayhawks — blaring from the custom speakers. I lifted a hand and he returned the wave. With a smile. A sweet one. Once more I found it hard to believe I'd been so angry with him.

I stepped over to the shed and assumed the position, that feet-apart, sidewalk superintendent stance that makes everyone feel like a Republican somehow, ready to heap contempt on welfare slackers at home and flag-burning foreigners abroad. I looked in. There it sat, silent under the overhead lights, casting a shadow just as though it were sane, fat and luxy on its whitewall tires. A steering wheel that was far too big. A hide that rejected dirt and healed scratches — that happened more slowly now, but it did still happen. *Oil's fine* was what the man said before he went around the corner, those were his last words on the matter, and here it still was, like an *objet d'art* somehow left behind in a closed-down gallery. My arms broke out in gooseflesh and I could feel my balls tightening.

My mouth had that dry-lint taste it gets when I know I'm in deep shit. Ha'past trouble and goin on a jackpot, Ennis Rafferty used to say. It wasn't humming and it wasn't glowing, the temperature was up above sixty again, but I could feel it pulling at me, whispering for me to come in and look. It could show me things, it whispered, especially now that we were alone. Looking at it like this made one thing clear: I'd been angry at Ned because I'd been scared for him. Of course. Looking at it like this, feeling its tidal pull way down in the middle of my head — beating in my guts and my groin, as well — made everything easier to understand. The Buick bred monsters. Yes. But sometimes you still wanted to go to it, the way you sometimes wanted to look over the edge when you were on a high place or peer into the muzzle of your gun and see the hole at the end of the barrel turn into an eye. One that was watching you, just you and only you. There was no sense trying to reason your way through such moments, or trying to understand that neurotic attraction; best to just step back from the drop, put the gun back in its holster, drive away from the barracks. Away from Shed B. Until you got beyond the range of that subtle whispering voice. Sometimes running away is a perfectly acceptable response.

I stood there a moment longer, though, feeling that distant beat-beat-beat in my head and around my heart, looking in at the midnight-blue Buick Roadmaster. Then I stepped back, drew a deep breath of night air, and looked up at the moon until I felt entirely myself again. When I did, I went to my own car and got in and drove away.

The Country Way wasn't crowded. It never is these days, not even on Friday and Saturday nights. The restaurants out by Wal-Mart and the new Statler Mall are killing the downtown eateries just as surely as the new cineplex out on 32 killed off the old Gem Theater downtown.

As always, people glanced at me when I walked in. Only it's the uniform they're really looking at, of course. A couple of guys — one a deputy sheriff, the other a county attorney — said hello and shook my hand. The attorney asked if I wouldn't join him and his wife and I said no thanks, I might be meeting someone. The idea of being with people, of having to do any more talking that night (even small-talking), made me feel sick in my stomach.

I sat in one of the little booths at the back of the main room, and Cynthia Garris came over to take my order. She was a pretty blonde thing with big, beautiful eyes. I'd noticed her making someone a sundae when I came in, and was touched to see that between delivering the ice cream and bringing me a menu, she'd undone the top button on her uniform so that the little silver heart she wore at the base of her throat showed. I didn't know if that was for me or just another response to the uniform. I hoped it was for me.

'Hey, Sandy, where you been lately? Olive Garden? Outback? Macaroni Grill? One of those?' She sniffed with mock disdain.

'Nope, just been eatin in. What you got on special?'

'Chicken and gravy, stuffed shells with meat sauce — both of em a little heavy on a night like this, in my humble opinion — and fried haddock. All you can eat's a dollar more. You know the deal.'

'Think I'll just have a cheeseburger and an Iron City to wash it down with.'

She jotted on her pad, then gave me a real stare. 'Are you all right? You look tired.'

'I *am* tired. Otherwise fine. Seen anyone from Troop D tonight?'

'George Stankowski was in earlier. Otherwise, you're it, darlin. Copwise, I mean. Well, those guys out there, but . . . ' She shrugged as if to say those guys weren't real cops. As it happened, I agreed with her.

'Well, if the robbers come in, I'll stop em single-handed.'

'If they tip fifteen per cent, Hero, let em rob,' she said. 'I'll get your beer.' Off she went, pert little tail switching under white nylon.

Pete Quinland, the grease-pit's original owner, was long gone, but the mini-jukeboxes he'd installed were still on the walls of the booths. The selections were in a kind of display-book, and there were little chrome levers on top to turn the pages. These antique gadgets no longer worked, but it was hard to resist twiddling the levers, turning the pages, and reading the songs on the little pink labels. About half of them were by Pete's beloved Chairman of the Board, hepcat fingersnappers like

431

'Witchcraft' and 'Luck Be a Lady Tonight'. **FRANK SINATRA**, said the little pink labels, and beneath, in smaller letters: THE NELSON RIDDLE ORCH. The others were those old rock and roll songs you never think about anymore once they leave the charts; the ones they never seem to play on the oldies stations, although you'd think there'd be room; after all, how many times can you listen to 'Brandy (You're a Fine Girl)' before beginning to scream? I flipped through the jukebox pages, looking at tunes a dropped quarter would no longer call forth; time marches on. If you're quiet you can hear its shuffling, rueful tread.

If anyone asks about that Buick 8, just tell em it's an impound. That's what the Old Sarge had said on the night we met out here in the back room. By then the waitresses had been sent away and we were pulling our own beers, running our own tab, and keeping our accounts straight down to the very last penny. Honor system, and why not? We were honorable men, doing our duty as we saw it. Still are. We're the Pennsylvania State Police, do you see? The *real* road warriors. As Eddie used to say — when he was younger as well as thinner — it's not just a job, it's a fuckin adventure.

I turned a page. Here was 'Heart of Glass', by **BLONDIE**.

On this subject you can't get far enough off the record. More words of wisdom from Tony Schoondist, spoken while the blue clouds of cigarette smoke rose to the ceiling. Back then *everybody* smoked, except maybe for Curt, and look what happened to *him*. Sinatra sang 'One for My Baby' from the overhead speakers, and from the steam tables had come the sweet smell of barbecued pork. The Old Sarge had been a believer in that off-the-record stuff, at least as regarded the Buick, until his mind had taken French leave, first just infantry squads of brain-cells stealing away in the night, then platoons, then whole regiments in broad daylight. *What's not on the record can't hurt you,* he'd told me once — this was around the time when it became clear it would be me who'd step into Tony's shoes and sit in Tony's office, ooh Grampa, what a big chair you have. Only I'd gone on the record tonight, hadn't I? Yeah, whole hog. Opened my mouth and spilled the whole tale. With a little help from my friends, as the song says. We'd spilled it to a boy who was still lost in the funhouse of grief. Who was agog with quite natural curiosity in spite of that grief. A lost boy? Perhaps. On TV, such tales as Ned's end happily, but I can tell you that life in Statler, Pennsylvania, bears Christing little resemblance to *The Hallmark Hall of Fame*. I'd told myself I knew the risks, but now I found myself wondering if that was really true. Because we never go forward believing we will fail, do we? No. We do it because we think we're going to save the goddam day and six times out of ten we step on the business end of a rake hidden in the high grass and up comes the handle and whammo, right between the eyes.

Tell me what happened when you dissected the bat. Tell me about the fish.

Here was 'Pledging My Love', by **JOHNNY ACE**.

Brushing aside every effort I made — that any of us made — to suggest this lesson was not in the learning but in the letting go. Just bulling onward. Sort of a surprise he hadn't read us the Miranda, because hadn't it been an interrogation as much as it had been stories of the old days when his old man had still been alive? *Young and alive?*

I still felt sick in my stomach. I could drink the beer Cynthia was bringing, the bubbles might even help, but eat a cheeseburger? I didn't think so. It had been years since the night Curtis dissected the bat-thing, but I was thinking about it now. How he'd said *Inquiring minds want to know* and then poked his scalpel into its eye. The eye had made a popping sound and then collapsed, dribbling out of its socket like a black tear. Tony and I had screamed, and how was I supposed to eat a cheeseburger now, remembering that? *Stop it, this is pointless*, I'd said, but he hadn't stopped. The father had been as insistent as the son. *Let's look in the lower gut and then we're done*, he had said, only he had *never* been done. He had poked, he had prodded, he had investigated, and the Buick had killed him for his pains.

I wondered if the boy knew it. I wondered if he understood the Buick Roadmaster 8 had killed his father as surely as Huddie, George, Eddie, Shirley, and Mister Dillon had killed the shrieking monstrosity that had come out of the car's trunk in 1988.

Here was 'Billy Don't Be a Hero,' by **BO DONALDSON AND THE HEYWOODS**. Gone from the charts *and* our hearts.

Tell me about the bat, tell me about the fish, tell me about the E. T. with the pink cords for hair, the thing that could think, the thing that showed up with something like a radio. Tell me about my father, too, because I have to come to terms with him. Of course I do, I see his life in my face and his ghost in my eyes every time I stand at the mirror to shave. Tell me everything . . . but don't tell me there's no answer. Don't you dare. I reject that. I repudiate it.

'Oil's fine,' I murmured, and turned the steel levers on top of the booth's mini-juke a little faster. There was sweat on my forehead. My stomach felt worse than ever. I wished I could believe it was the flu, or maybe food poisoning, but it wasn't either one and I knew it. 'Oil's just fuckin ducky.'

Here was 'Indiana Wants Me' and 'Green-Eyed Lady' and 'Love Is Blue'. Songs that had somehow slipped between the cracks. 'Surfer Joe', by **THE SURFARIS**.

Tell me everything, tell me the answers, tell me the one answer.

The kid had been clear about the things he wanted, you had to give him that. He'd asked for it with the pure untinctured selfishness of the lost and the grief-stricken.

Except once.

He'd started to ask for one piece of the past . . . and then changed his mind. What piece had that been? I reached for it, fumbled at it, felt it

435

shrink slyly from my touch. When that happens, it's no good to chase. You have to back off and let the recollection come back to you of its own free will.

I thumbed the pages of the useless jukebox back and forth. Little pink stickers like tongues.

'Polk Salad Annie', by **TONY JOE WHITE** and *Tell me about The Year of the Fish.*

'When', by **THE KALIN TWINS** and *Tell me about the meeting you had, tell me everything, tell me everything but the one thing that might pop up a red flag in your suspicious cop's mind —*

'Here's your beer — ' Cynthia Garris began, and then there was a light gasp.

I looked up from twiddling the metal levers (the pages flipping back and forth under the glass had half-hypnotized me by then). She was looking at me with fascinated horror. 'Sandy — you got a fever, hon? Because you're just *running* with sweat.'

And that was when it came to me. Telling him about the Labor Day picnic of 1979. *The more we talked, the more we drank*, Phil Candleton had said. *My head ached for two days after.*

'Sandy?' Cynthia standing there with a bottle of IC and a glass. Cynthia with the top button of her uniform undone so she could show me her heart. So to speak. She was there but she wasn't. She was years from where I was at that moment.

All that talk and not one single conclusion, I'd said, and the talk had moved on — to the O'Day farm, among other things — and then all at once the boy had asked . . . had *begun* to ask . . .

436

Sandy, that day at the picnic, did any of you talk about . . .

And then he had trailed off.

'Did any of you talk about destroying it,' I said. 'That's the question he didn't finish.' I looked into Cynthia Garris's frightened, concerned face. 'He started to ask and then he stopped.'

Had I thought storytime was over and Curt's boy was heading home? That he'd let go that easily? A mile or so down the road, headlights had passed me going the other way. Going back toward the barracks at a good but not quite illegal clip. Had Curt Wilcox's Bel Air been behind those lights, and Curt Wilcox's son behind the wheel? Had he gone back just as soon as he could be sure we were gone?

I thought yes.

I took the bottle of Iron City from Cynthia's tray, watching my arm stretch out and my hand grasp the neck the way you watch yourself do things in dreams. I felt the cold ring of the bottle's neck slip between my teeth and thought of George Morgan in his garage, sitting on the floor and smelling cut grass under the mower. That good green smell. I drank the beer, all of it. Then I stood up and put a ten on Cynthia's tray.

'Sandy?'

'I can't stay and eat,' I said. 'I forgot something back at the barracks.'

★　★　★

437

I kept a battery-powered Kojak light in the glove compartment of my personal and put it on the roof as soon as I was out of town, running my car up to eighty and trusting to the red flasher to get anyone ahead of me out of my way. There weren't many. Western Pennsylvania folks roll up the sidewalks early on most weeknights. It was only four miles back to the barracks, but the run seemed to take an hour. I kept thinking about how my heart sank each time Ennis's sister — The Dragon — walked into the barracks under the haystack heap of her outrageous henna hair. I kept thinking, *Get out of here, you're too close*. And I didn't even like her. How much worse would it be to have to face Michelle Wilcox, especially if she had the twins, the Little J's, with her?

I drove up the driveway too fast, just as Eddie and George had done a dozen or so years before, wanting to be rid of their unpleasant prisoner so they could go over to Poteenville, where it must have seemed half the world was going up in smoke. The names of old songs — 'I Met Him on a Sunday', 'Ballroom Blitz', 'Sugar Sugar' — jigged senselessly up and down in my head. Foolish, but better than asking myself what I'd do if the Bel Air was back but empty; what I'd do if Ned Wilcox was gone off the face of the earth.

The Bel Air *was* back, as I'd known it would be. He'd parked it where Arky's truck had been earlier. And it was empty. I could see that in the first splash of my headlights. The song titles dropped out of my head. What replaced them was a cold readiness, the kind that comes by itself, empty-handed and without plans, ready to improvise.

The Buick had taken hold of Curt's boy. Even while we'd been sitting with him, conducting our own peculiar kind of wake for his dad and trying to be his friend, it had reached out and taken hold of him. If there was still a chance to take him back, I'd do well not to bitch it up by thinking too much.

Steff, probably worried at the sight of a single Kojak instead of a rack of roof-lights, poked her head out the back door. 'Who's that? Who's there?'

'It's me, Steff.' I got out of the car, leaving it parked where it was with the red bubble flashing on the roof over the driver's seat. If anyone came hauling in behind me, it would at least keep them from rear-ending my car. 'Go back inside.'

'What's wrong?'

'Nothing.'

'That's what *he* said.' She pointed at the Bel Air, then stalked back inside.

I ran for the roll-up door of Shed B in the stutter-pulse of the light — so many stressful moments of my life have been lit by flashers. A John Q. stopped or overtaken by flashers is always frightened. They have no idea what those same lights sometimes do to us. And what we have seen by their glow.

We always left a light on in the shed, but it was brighter than a single night-light in there now, and the side door was standing open. I thought about diverting to it, then kept on as I was. I wanted a look at the playing-field before anything else.

What I'd been most afraid of seeing was nothing but the Buick. Looking in, I discovered something scarier. The boy was sitting behind the Roadmaster's oversized steering wheel with his chest smashed in. There was nothing where his shirt had been except a bright bloody ruin. My legs started to unbuckle at the knees, and then I realized it wasn't blood I was looking at, after all. *Maybe* not blood. The shape was too regular. There was a straight red line running just below the round neck of his blue T-shirt . . . and corners . . . neat right-angled corners . . .

No, not blood.

The gas-can Arky kept for the mower.

Ned shifted behind the wheel and one of his hands came into view. It moved slowly, dreamily. There was a Beretta in it. Had he been driving around with his father's sidearm in the trunk of the Bel Air? Perhaps even in the glove compartment?

I decided it didn't matter. He was sitting in that deathtrap with gas and a gun. Kill or cure, I'd thought. It had never crossed my mind to think he might try doing both at the same time.

He didn't see me. He should've — my white, scared face filling one of those dark windows should have been perfectly visible to him from where he sat — and he should've seen the red pulse from the light I'd stuck on the roof of my car. He saw neither. He was as hypnotized as Huddie Royer had been when Huddie decided to crawl into the Roadmaster's trunk and pull the lid shut behind him. I could feel it even from outside. That tidal pulse. That *liveliness*. There were even words in it. I suppose I might have made them up to suit myself, but it almost doesn't matter because it was the pulse that called them forth, the throb all of us had felt around the Buick from the very start. It was a throb some of us — this boy's father, for one — had felt more strongly than others.

Come in or stay out, the voice in my head told me, and it spoke with perfect chilling indifference. *I'll take one or two, then sleep. That much more mischief before I'm done for good. One or two, I don't care which.*

I looked up at the round thermometer mounted on the beam. The red needle had stood at sixty-one before I went down to The Country Way, but now it had dropped back to fifty-seven. I could almost see it slumping to even colder levels as I watched, and all at once I was struck by a memory so vivid it was frightening.

On the smokers' bench, this had been. I had been smoking and Curt had just been sitting. The smokers' bench had assumed odd importance in the six years since the barracks itself was declared a smoke-free zone. It's where we went to compare notes on the cases we were rolling, to work out scheduling conflicts, to mull over retirement plans and insurance plans and the GDR. It was on the smokers' bench that Carl Brundage told me his wife was leaving him and taking the kids. His voice hadn't wavered but tears had gone rolling down his cheeks as he talked. Tony had been sitting on the bench with me on one side and Curt on the other ('Christ and the two thieves,' he'd said with a sardonic smile) when he told us he was putting me up for the SC post his own retirement would leave vacant. If I wanted it, that was. The little gleam in his eyes saying he knew goddam well I wanted it. Curtis and I had both nodded, not saying much. And it was on the smokers' bench that Curt and I had our final discussion about the Buick 8. How soon before his death had that been? I realized with a nasty chill that it might well have been on the very day. Certainly that would explain why the vividness of the memory seemed so terrible to me.

Does it think? Curt had asked. I could remember strong morning sun on his face and — I think — a paper cup of coffee in his hand. *Does it watch and think, wait for its chances, pick its moments?*

I'm almost sure not, I had replied, but I'd been troubled. Because *almost* covers a lot of territory, doesn't it? Maybe the only word in the language that covers more is *if.*

But it saved its biggest horror show for a time when this place was almost entirely deserted, Ned's father had said. Thoughtful. Setting his coffee aside so he could turn his Stetson over and over in his hands, an old habit of his. If I was right about the day, that hat was less than five hours from being knocked from his head and cast bloody into the weeds, where it would later be found among the McDonald's wrappers and empty Coke cans. *As if it knew. As if it can think. Watch. Wait.*

I had laughed. It was one of those gruff little ha-ha laughs that don't really have much amusement in them. I told him he was cuckoo on the subject. I said, *Next thing you'll be telling me it sent out a ray or something to make that Norco tanker crash into the schoolbus that day.*

He made no verbal reply, but his eyes had looked a question at me. *How do you know it didn't?*

And then I had asked the boy's question. I had asked —

A warning bell went off inside my head, very dim and deep. I stepped back from the window and raised my hands to my face, as if I thought I could block off that tidal ache simply by blocking off sight of the Buick. And the sight of Ned, looking so white and lost behind the oversized steering wheel. It had taken hold of him and just now, briefly, it had taken hold of me. Had tried to sidetrack me with a lot of old useless memories. Whether or not it had consciously waited for its chance to get at Ned didn't matter. What mattered was that the temperature in there was going down fast, almost *diving*, and if I intended doing something, now was the time.

Maybe you ought to get some backup in on this, the voice in my head whispered. It sounded like my own voice, but it wasn't. *Might be someone in the barracks. I'd check, if I were you. Not that it matters to me. Doing one more piece of mischief before I sleep, that's what matters to me. Pretty much all that matters to me. And why? Because I can, hoss — just because I can.*

Backup seemed like a good idea. God knows I was terrified at the idea of going into Shed B on my own and approaching the Buick in its current state. What got me going was the knowledge that I had caused this. I was the one who had opened Pandora's box.

I ran around to the hutch, not pausing at the side door although I registered the smell of gasoline, heavy and rich. I knew what he'd done. The only question was how much gas he'd poured under the car and how much he'd saved back in the can.

The door to the hutch was secured with a padlock. For years it had been left open, the curved steel arm just poked through the hasp to keep the door from swinging open in a breeze. The lock was open that night, too. I swear that's the truth. It wasn't noontime bright out there, but there was enough glow from the open side door to see the lock clearly. Then, as I reached for it, the steel post slid down into the hole on the body of the lock with a tiny audible *click*. I saw that happen . . . and I felt it, too. For just a moment the pulse in my head sharpened and focused. It was like a gasp of effort.

I keep two keyrings: cop-keys and personals. There were about twenty on the 'official' ring, and I used a trick I'd learned a long time before, from Tony Schoondist. I let the keys fall on my palm as they would, like pickup sticks, then simply felt among them without looking. It doesn't always work but this time it did, likely because the key to the hutch padlock was smaller than all the others except the one to my locker downstairs, and the locker key has a square head.

Now, faintly, I heard the humming begin. It was faint, like the sound of a motor buried in the earth, but it was there.

I took the key my fingers had found and rammed it into the padlock. The steel arm popped up again. I yanked the lock out of the hasp and dropped it on the ground. Then I opened the door to the hutch and stepped inside.

The little storage space held the still and explosive heat which belongs only to attics and sheds and cubbyholes that have been closed up for a long time in hot weather. No one came out here much anymore, but the things which had accumulated over the years (except for the paint and the paint thinner, flammable items that had been prudently removed) were still here; I could see them in the faint wash of light. Stacks of magazines, the kind men read, for the most part (women think we like to look at naked women but mostly I think we like tools). The kitchen chair with the tape-mended seat. The cheap police-band radio from Radio Shack. The videocam, its battery undoubtedly dead, on its shelf next to the old box of blank tapes. A bumper sticker was pasted to one wall: SUPPORT THE MENTALLY HANDICAPPED, TAKE AN FBI AGENT TO LUNCH. I could smell dust. In my head the pulse that was the Buick's voice was getting stronger and stronger.

There was a hanging lightbulb and a switch on the wall, but I didn't even try it. I had an idea the bulb would be dead, or the switch would be live enough to give me a real walloper of a shock.

The door swung shut behind me, cutting off the moonlight. That was impossible, because when it was left to its own devices, the door always swung the other way, outward. We all knew it. It was why we left the padlock threaded through the hasp. Tonight, however, the impossible was selling cheap. The force inhabiting the Buick wanted me in the dark. Maybe it thought being in the dark would slow me down.

It didn't. I'd already seen what I needed: the coil of yellow rope, still hanging on the wall below the joke sticker and next to a forgotten set of jumper cables. I saw something else, too. Something Curt Wilcox had put up on the shelf near the videocam not long after the E.T. with the lashing pink ropes had made its appearance.

I took this item, stuck it in my back pocket, and grabbed the coil of rope from the wall. Then I banged out again. A dark form loomed up in front of me and I almost screamed. For one mad moment I was sure it was the man in the dark coat and hat, the one with the malformed ear and the Boris Badinoff accent. When the boogeyman spoke up, however, the accent was pure Lawrence Welk.

'Dat damn kid came back,' Arky whispered. 'I got halfway home and Yudas Pries' I jus' turned around. I knew it, somehow. I jus' — '

I interrupted then, told him to stay clear, and ran back around the corner of Shed B with the rope looped over my arm.

'Don' go in dere, Sarge!' Arky said. I think he might've been trying to shout, but he was too scared to get much in the way of volume. 'He's t'rown down gas an' he got a gun, I seen it.'

I stopped beside the door, slipped the rope off my arm, started to tie one end to the stout hook mounted there, then gave the coil of rope to Arky instead.

'Sandy, can you feel it?' he asked. 'An' the radio gone all blooey again, nuttin but static, I heard Steff cussin at it t'rough d'window.'

'Never mind. Tie the end of the rope off. Use the hook.'

'Huh?'

'You heard me.'

I'd held on to the loop in the end of the rope and now I stepped into it, yanked it up to my waist, and ran it tight. It was a hangman's knot, tied by Curt himself, and it ran shut easily.

'Sarge, you can't do dis.' Arky made as if to grab my shoulder, but without any real force.

'Tie it off and then hold on,' I said. 'Don't go in, no matter what. If we . . . ' I wasn't going to say *If we disappear*, though — didn't want to hear those words come out of my mouth. 'If anything happens, tell Steff to put out a Code D as soon as the static clears.'

'Jesus!' Only from Arky it sounded more like *Yeesus*. 'What are you, crazy? Can't you feel it?'

'I feel it,' I said, and went inside. I shook the rope continually as I went to keep it from snagging. I felt like a diver starting down to some untried depth, minding his airhose not because he really thinks minding it will help, but because it's at least something to do, something to keep your mind off the things that may be swimming around in the blackness just beyond the reach of your light.

★ ★ ★

The Buick 8 sat fat and luxy on its whitewalls, our little secret, humming deep down in the hollows of itself. The pulse was stronger than the humming, and now that I was actually inside I felt it stop its halfhearted efforts to keep me out. Instead of pushing with its invisible hand, it pulled.

The boy sat behind the wheel with the gas can in his lap, his cheeks and forehead white, the skin there taut and shiny. As I came toward him, his head turned with robotic slowness on his neck and he looked at me. His gaze was wide and dark. In it was the stupidly serene look of the deeply drugged or the cataclysmically wounded. The only emotion that remained in his eyes was a terrible weary stubborness, that adolescent insistence that there must be an answer and he must know the answer. He had a right. And that was what the Buick had used, of course. What it had used against him.

'Ned.'

'I'd get out of here if I were you, Sarge.' Speaking in slow, perfectly articulated syllables. 'There's not much time. It's coming. It sounds like footsteps.'

And he was right. I felt a sudden surge of

horror. The hum was some sort of machinery, perhaps. The pulse was almost certainly a kind of telepathy. This was something else, though, a third thing.

Something was coming.

'Ned, please. You can't understand what this thing is and you certainly can't kill it. All you can do is get yourself sucked up like dirt in a vacuum cleaner. And that'll leave your mother and your sisters on their own. Is that what you want, to leave them alone with a thousand questions no one can answer? It's hard for me to believe that the boy who came here looking so hard for his father could be so selfish.'

Something flickered in his eyes at that. It was the way a man's eyes may flicker when, deep in concentration, he hears a loud noise on the next block. Then the eyes grew serene again. 'This goddamned car killed my Dad,' he said. Spoken calmly. Even patiently.

I certainly wasn't going to argue that. 'All right, maybe it did. Maybe in some way it was as much to blame for what happened to your dad as Bradley Roach was. Does that mean it can kill you, too? What is this, Ned? Buy one, get one free?'

'I'm going to kill *it*,' he said, and at last something rose in his eyes, disturbing the surface serenity. It was more than anger. To me it looked like a kind of madness. He raised his hands. In one was the gun. In the other he now held a butane match. 'Before it sucks me through, I'm going to light its damned transporter on fire. That'll shut the door to this side forever. That's step one.' Spoken with the scary, unconscious arrogance of youth, positive that this idea has occurred to no one before it has occurred to him. 'And if I live through *that* experience, I'm going to kill whatever's waiting on the other side. That's step two.'

'Whatever's *waiting*?' I realized the enormity of his assumptions and was staggered by them. 'Oh, Ned! Oh, Christ!'

The pulse was stronger now. So was the hum. I could feel the unnatural cold that marked the Buick's periods of activity settling against my skin. And saw purple light first blooming in the air just above the oversized steering wheel and then starting to skate across its surface. Coming. It was coming. Ten years ago it would have been here already. Maybe even five. Now it took a little longer.

'Do you think there's going to be a welcoming party, Ned? Are you expecting them to send the Exalted President of the Yellow-Skin Pink-Hair People or maybe the Emperor of the Alternate Universe to say howdy and give you the key to the city? Do you think they'd take the trouble? For what? A kid who can't accept the fact that his father is dead and get on with his own life?'

'Shut up!'

'Know what I think?'

'*I don't care what you think!*'

'I think the last thing you see is going to be a whole lot of nothing much before you choke to death on whatever they breathe over there.'

The uncertainty flickered in his eyes again. Part of him wanted to do a George Morgan and just finish it. But there was another part of him as well, one that might not care so much about Pitt anymore but still wanted to go on living. And above both, above and under and around, binding everything, was the pulse and the quietly calling voice. It wasn't even seductive. It just *pulled* at you.

'Sarge, come outta dere!' Arky called.

I ignored him and kept my eyes on Curt's boy. 'Ned, use the brains that got you this far. *Please.*' Not shouting at him, but raising my voice to get it over the strengthening hum. And at the same time I touched the thing I'd put in my back pocket.

'This *res* you're sitting in may be alive, but that still doesn't make it worth your time. It's not much different from a Venus flytrap or a pitcher plant, don't you see that? You can't get revenge out of this thing, not even a nickel's worth. It's brainless.'

His mouth began to tremble. That was a start, but I wished to God he'd let go of the gun or at least lower it. And there was the butane match. Not as dangerous as the automatic, but bad enough; my shoes were in gasoline as I stood near the driver's door of the Buick, and the fumes were strong enough to make my eyes water. Now the purple glow had begun to spin lazy lines of light across the bogus dashboard controls and to fill up the speedometer dial, making it look like the bubble in a carpenter's level.

'*It killed my daddy!*' he shouted in a child's voice, but it wasn't me he was shouting at. He couldn't find whatever it was he wanted to shout at, and that was precisely what was killing him.

'No, Ned. Listen, if this thing could laugh, it'd be laughing now. It didn't get the father the way it wanted to — not the way it got Ennis and Brian Lippy — but now it's got a damned fine chance at the son. If Curt knows, if he sees, he must be screaming in his grave. Everything he feared, everything he fought to prevent. All of it happening again. To his own son.'

'*Stop it, stop it!*' Tears were spilling over his eyelids.

I bent down, bringing my face into that growing purple glow, into the welling coldness. I brought my face down to Ned's face, where the resistance was finally crumbling. One more blow would do it. I pulled the can I'd taken from the hutch out of my back pocket and held it against my leg and said, 'He must be hearing it laugh, Ned, he must know it's too late — '

'*No!*'

' — that there's nothing he can do. Nothing at all.'

He raised his hands to cover his ears, the gun in the left, the butane match in the right, the gas-can balanced on his thighs, his legs dimming out to lavender mist below his shins, that glow rising like water in a well, and it wasn't great — I hadn't knocked him as completely off-balance as I would have liked — but it would have to be good enough. I pushed the cap off the aerosol can with my thumb, had just one fraction of a second to wonder if there was any pressure left in the damned thing after all the years it had stood unused on the shelf in the hutch, and then I Maced him.

Ned howled with surprise and pain as the spray hit his eyes and nose. His finger squeezed the trigger of his dad's Beretta. The report was deafening in the shed.

'Gah-*DAM!*' I heard Arky shout through the ringing in my ears.

I grabbed the doorhandle, and as I did the little locking post went down by itself, just like the arm of the padlock on the hutch door. I reached through the open window, made a fist, and punched the side of the gas-can. It flew off the convulsing boy's lap, tumbled into the misty lavender light rising up from the floor of the car, and disappeared. I had a momentary sense of it *tumbling*, the way things do when you drop them off a high place. The gun went off again and I felt the wind of the slug. It wasn't really close — he was still firing blind into the Buick's roof, probably unaware that he was shooting at all — but whenever you can feel the air stir with a bullet's passage, it's too damned close.

I fumbled down inside the Buick's door, finally found the inside handle, and pulled. If it didn't come up I wasn't sure what I'd do next — he was too big and too heavy to yank through the window — but it did come up and the door opened. As it did, a brilliant purple flash rose up from where the Roadmaster's floorboards had been, the trunk banged open, and the real pulling began. *Sucked up like dirt in a vacuum cleaner*, I'd said, but I hadn't known the half of it. That tidal beat suddenly sped up to a ferocious, arrhythmic pounding, like precursor waves before the *tsunami* that will destroy everything. There was a sense of an inside-out wind that seemed to pull instead of push, that wanted to suck your eyeballs from their sockets and then peel the skin right off your face, and yet not a hair on my head stirred.

Ned screamed. His hands dropped suddenly, as if invisible ropes had been tied around his wrists and now someone below him was yanking on them. He started to sink in his seat, only the seat was no longer precisely there. It was vanishing, dissolving into that stormy bubble of rising violet light. I grabbed him under the arms, yanked, stumbled backward first one step and then two. Fighting the incredible traction of the force trying to pull me into the descending purple throat that had been the Buick's interior. I fell over backward with Ned on top of me. Gasoline soaked through the legs of my pants.

'*Pull us!*' I screamed at Arky. I paddled with my feet, trying to slide away from the Buick and the light pouring out of it. My feet could find no good purchase. They kept slipping in the gasoline.

Ned was *yanked*, pulled toward the open driver's door so hard he was almost torn out of my grip. At the same time I felt the rope tighten around my waist. We were tugged sharply backward as I resettled my grip around Ned's chest. He was still holding the gun, but as I watched, his arm shot out straight in front of him and the gun flew from his hand. The throbbing purple light in the cabin of the car swallowed it up, and I thought I heard it fire twice more, all by itself, as it disappeared. At the same time the pull around *us* seemed to weaken a little. Maybe enough to make our escape if we went now, just exited stage left with no hesitation.

'*Pull!*' I screamed at Arky.

'Boss, I'm pullin as hard as I — '

'Pull *harder!*'

There was another furious yank, one that cut my breath off as Curtis's hangman's noose pulled tight around my mid-section. Then I was scrambling to my feet and stumbling backward at the same time with the boy still clasped in front of me. He was gasping, his eyes puffed shut like the eyes of a fighter who's had the worst of it for twelve rounds. I don't think he saw what happened next.

The inside of the Buick was gone, cored out by purple light. Some unspeakable, unknowable conduit had opened. I was looking down an infected gullet and into another world. I might have frozen in place long enough for the suction to renew its hold on me and pull me in — to pull both of us in — but then Arky was screaming, high and shrill: 'Help me, Steff! God's sake! Muckle on here and help me!' She must have done it, too, because a second or so later, Ned and I were yanked backward like a couple of well-hooked fish.

I went down again and banged my head, aware that the pulse and the hum had merged, had turned into a howl that seemed to be drilling a hole in my brains. The Buick had begun flashing like a neon sign, and a flood of green-backed beetles came tumbling out of the blazing trunk. They struck the floor, scuttered, died. The suction took hold yet again, and we started moving back toward the Buick. It was like being caught in a hideously strong undertow. Back and forth, back and forth.

'*Help me!*' I shouted in Ned's ear. '*You have to help me or we're going in!*' What I was thinking by that time was that we were probably going in whether he helped me or not.

He was blind but not deaf and had decided he wanted to live. He put his sneakered feet down on the cement floor and shoved backward just as hard as he could, his skidding heels splashing up little flurries of spilled gasoline. At the same time, Arky and Stephanie Colucci gave the rope another hard tug. We shot backward almost five feet toward the door, but then the undertow grabbed hold again. I was able to wrap a bight of slack rope around Ned's chest, binding him to me for better or worse. Then we were off again, the Buick taking back all the ground we'd gained and more. It moved us slowly but with a terrible relentlessness. There was a breathless, claustrophobic pressure in my chest. Part of it was being wrapped in the rope. Part of it was the sense of being pinched and petted and jerked by a huge invisible hand. I didn't want to go into the place I'd seen, but if we got much closer to the car, I would. We both would. The closer we got, the more the force pulling us stacked up. Soon it would snap the yellow nylon rope. The two of us would fly away, still bound together. Into that sick purple throat we'd go and into whatever lay beyond it.

'*Last chance!*' I screamed. '*Pull on three! One . . . two . . . THREE!*'

Arky and Stephanie, standing shoulder to shoulder just outside the door, gave it all they had. Ned and I pushed with our feet. We flew backward, this time all the way to the door before that force seized us yet again, pulling as inexorably as a magnet pulls iron filings.

I rolled over on my side. 'Ned, the doorframe! *Grab the doorframe!*'

He reached blindly out, extending his left arm fully. His hand groped.

'To your right, kid!' Steff screamed. 'Your *right!*'

He found the doorjamb and gripped. Behind us there was another monstrous purple flash from the Buick, and I could feel the pull of the thing ratchet up another notch. It was like some hideous new gravity. The rope around my chest had turned into a steel band and I couldn't get a single inch of fresh breath. I could feel my eyes bulging and my teeth throbbing in their gums. My guts felt all in a plug at the base of my throat. The pulse was filling up my brain, burning out conscious thought. I began slipping toward the Buick again, the heels of my shoes skidding on the cement. In another moment I would be sliding, and a moment after that I'd be *flying*, like a bird sucked into a jet turbine engine. And when I went the boy would go with me, likely with splinters of the doorjamb sticking out from under his fingernails. He would *have* to come with me. My metaphor about chains had become literal reality.

'Sandy, grab my hand!'

I craned my neck to look and wasn't exactly surprised to see Huddie Royer — and behind him, Eddie. They'd come back. It had taken them a little longer than it had taken Arky, but they'd come. And not because Steff had radioed them a Code D, either; they'd been in their personals, and radio communications out of our barracks were FUBAR, for the time being, anyway. No, they had just . . . come.

Huddie was kneeling in the doorway, holding on with one hand to keep from being sucked in. His hair didn't move around his head and his shirt didn't ripple, but he swayed back and forth like a man in a high wind just the same. Eddie was behind him, crouching, looking over Huddie's left shoulder. Probably holding on to Huddie's belt, although I couldn't see that. Huddie's free hand was held out to me, and I seized it like a drowning man. I *felt* like a drowning man.

'Now *pull*, goddammit,' Huddie growled at Arky and Eddie and Steff Colucci. The Buick's purple light was flashing in his eyes. 'Pull your *guts* out.'

They might not have gone quite that far, but they pulled hard and we tumbled out the door like a cork coming out of a bottle, landing in a pigpile with Huddie on the bottom. Ned was panting, his face turned sideways against my neck, the skin of his cheek and forehead burning

458

against me like embers. I could feel the wetness of his tears.

'Ow, Sarge, Christ, get your elbow outta my *nose!*' Huddie yelled in a muffled, furious voice.

'Shut the door!' Steff cried. 'Hurry, before something bad gets out!'

There was nothing but a few harmless bugs with green backs, but she was right, just the same. Because the light was bad enough. That flashing, stuttery purple light.

We were still tangled together on the pavement, arms pinned by knees, feet caught under torsos, Eddie now somehow tangled in the rope as well as Ned, yelling at Arky that it was around his neck, it was choking him, and Steff kneeling beside him, trying to get her fingers under one of the bright yellow loops while Ned gasped and flailed against me. There was no one to shut the door but it *did* slam shut and I craned my head at an angle only raw panic would permit, suddenly sure it was one of *them*, it had come through unseen and now it was out and maybe wanting a little payback for the one that had been slaughtered all those years ago. And I *saw* it, a shadow against the shed's white-painted side. Then it shifted and the shadow's owner came forward and I could see the curves of a woman's breast and hip in the dim light.

'Halfway home and I get this feeling,' Shirley said in an unsteady voice. 'This really bad feeling. I decided the cats could wait a little longer. Stop thrashing, Ned, you're making everything worse.'

Ned stilled at once. She bent down and with a single deft gesture freed Eddie from the loop around his neck. 'There, ya baby,' she said, and then her legs gave out. Shirley Pasternak sprawled on the hottop and began to cry.

★ ★ ★

We got Ned into the barracks and flushed his eyes in the kitchen. The skin around them was puffed and red, the whites badly bloodshot, but he said his vision was basically okay. When Huddie held up two fingers, that was what the kid reported. Ditto four.

'I'm sorry,' he said in a thick, clogged voice. 'I don't know why I did that. I mean, I do, I *meant* to, but not now . . . not tonight — '

'Shhh,' Shirley said. She cupped more water from the tap and bathed his eyes with it. 'Don't talk.'

But he wouldn't be stopped. 'I meant to go home. To think about it, just like I said.' His swelled, horribly bloodshot eyes peered at me, then they were gone as Shirley brought up another palm filled with warm water. 'Next thing I knew I was back here again, and all I can remember thinking is 'I've got to do it tonight, I've got to finish it once and for all.' Then . . . '

Except he didn't know what had happened then; the rest was all a blur to him. He didn't come right out and say that, and didn't need to. I didn't even have to see it in his bloodshot bewildered eyes. I had seen *him*, sitting behind the Roadmaster's steering wheel with the gas can

460

in his lap, looking pale and stoned and lost.

'It took hold of you,' I said. 'It's always had some kind of pull, it's just never had anyone to use it on the way it could on you. When it called you, though, the rest of us heard, too. In our own ways. In any case, it's not your fault, Ned. If there's fault, it's mine.'

He straightened up from the sink, groped, took hold of my forearms. His face was dripping and his hair was plastered to his forehead. In truth he looked rather funny. Like a slapstick baptism.

Steff, who'd been watching the shed from the back door of the barracks, came over to us. 'It's dying down again. Already.'

I nodded. 'It missed its chance. Maybe its last chance.'

'To do mischief,' Ned said. 'That's what it wanted. I heard it in my head. Or, I don't know, maybe I just made that part up.'

'If you did,' I said, 'then I did, too. But there might have been more to tonight than just mischief.'

Before I could say any more, Huddie came out of the bathroom with a first-aid kit. He set it down on the counter, opened it, and took out a jar of salve. 'Put this all around your eyes, Ned. If some gets in them, don't worry. You won't hardly notice.'

We stood there, watching him put the salve around his eyes in circles that gleamed under the kitchen fluorescents. When he was done, Shirley asked him if it was any better. He nodded.

'Then come outside again,' I said. 'There's

one other thing I need to tell you. I would have earlier, but the truth is I never thought of it except in passing until I actually saw you sitting in that goddam car. The shock must have kicked it loose.'

Shirley looked at me with her brow furrowed. She'd never been a mother but it was a mother's sternness I saw on her face right then. 'Not tonight,' she said. 'Can't you see this boy has had enough? One of you needs to take him home and make up some sort of story for his mother — she always believed Curtis's, I expect she'll believe one of yours if you can manage to stay together on the details — and then get him into bed.'

'I'm sorry, but I don't think this can wait,' I said.

She looked hard into my face and must have seen that I at least *thought* I was telling the truth, and so we all went back out to the smokers' bench, and as we watched the dying fireworks from the shed — the second show of the night, although there wasn't much to this one, at least not now — I told Ned one more story of the old days. I saw this one as you might see a scene from a play, two characters on a mostly bare stage, two characters beneath a single bright stagelight, two men sitting

THEN:

Curtis

Two men sitting on the smokers' bench by the light of a summer sun and one will soon be dead — when it comes to our human lives there's a noose at the end of every chain and Curtis Wilcox has nearly reached his. Lunch will be his last meal and neither of them knows it. This condemned man watches the other man light a cigarette and wishes he could have one himself but he's quit the habit. The cost of them is bad, Michelle was always ragging on him about that, but mostly it's wanting to see his children grow up. He wants to see their graduations, he wants to see the color of their children's hair. He has retirement plans as well, he and Michelle have talked them over a lot, the Winnebago that will take them out west where they may finally settle, but he will be retiring sooner than that, and alone. As for smoking, he never had to give up the pleasure at all but a man can't know that. Meanwhile the summer sun is pleasant. Later on the day will be hot, a hot day to die on, but now it's pleasant, and the thing across the way is quiet. It is quiet now for longer and longer stretches. The lightquakes, when they come, are milder. It is winding down, that's what the condemned State Trooper thinks. But Curtis can still sometimes feel its heartbeat and its quiet

463

call and knows it will bear watching. This is his job; he has repudiated any chance of promotion in order to do it. It was his partner the Buick 8 got but in a way, he realizes, it got all of Curtis Wilcox it ever had to. He never locked himself in its trunk, as Huddie Royer once almost did in 1988, and it never ate him alive as it probably ate Brian Lippy, but it got him just the same. It's always close to his thoughts. He hears its whisper the way a fisherman sleeping in his house hears the whisper of the sea even in his sleep. And a whisper is a voice, and a thing with a voice can —

He turns to Sandy Dearborn and asks 'Does it think? Does it watch, think, wait for its chances?'

Dearborn — the old hands still call him the New Sarge behind his back — doesn't need to ask what his friend is talking about. When it comes to the thing in Shed B they are of one mind, all of them, and sometimes Curtis thinks it calls even to those who have transferred out of D or quit the PSP altogether for some other, safer job; he thinks sometimes that it has marked them all like the Amish in their black clothes and black buggies are marked, or the way the priest dirties your forehead on Ash Wednesday, or like roadgang convicts linked together and digging a ditch of endless length.

'I'm almost sure not,' the New Sarge says.

'Still, it saved its biggest horror show for a time when this place was almost completely deserted,' says the man who quit cigarettes so he could watch his children grow up and bear him grandchildren. 'As if it knew. As if it could think.

464

And watch. And wait.'

The New Sarge laughs — a sound of amusement which contains just the thinnest rind of contempt. 'You're gaga on the subject, Curt. Next you'll be telling me it sent out a ray or something to make that Norco tanker crash into the schoolbus that day.'

Trooper Wilcox has set his coffee aside on the bench so he can take off his big hat — his Stetson. He begins turning it over and over in his hands, an old habit of his. Kitty-corner from where they sit, Dicky-Duck Eliot pulls up to the gas-pump and begins filling D-12, something they will not be able to do much longer. He spots them on the bench and waves. They give him a little of the old right-back-atcha, but the man with the hat — the gray Trooper's Stetson that will finish its tour of duty in the weeds with the soda cans and fast-food wrappers — keeps his gaze mostly on the New Sarge. His eyes are asking if they can rule that out, if they can rule anything out.

The Sarge, irritated by this, says: 'Why don't we just finish it off, then? Finish it off and have done? Tow it into the back field, pour gasoline into her until it runs out the windows, then just light 'er up?'

Curtis looks at him with an evenness that can't quite hide his shock. 'That might be the most dangerous thing we could do with it,' he says. 'It might even be what it wants us to do. What it was sent to provoke. How many kids have lost fingers because they found something in the weeds they didn't know was a blastingcap and

465

pounded it with a rock?'

'This isn't the same.'

'How do you know it's not? How do you know?'

And the New Sarge, who will later think It should have been me whose hat wound up lying blood-bolted on the side of the road, can say nothing. It seems almost profane to disagree with him, and besides, who knows? He could be right. Kids do blow off their fingers with blastingcaps or kill their little brothers with guns they find in their parents' bureau drawers or burn down the house with some old sparklight they found out in the garage. Because they don't know what they're playing with.

'Suppose,' says the man twirling his Stetson between his hands, 'that the 8 is a kind of valve. Like the one in a scuba diver's regulator. Sometimes it breathes in and sometimes it breathes out, giving or receiving according to the will of the user. But what it does is always limited by the valve.'

'Yes, but — '

'Or think of it another way. Suppose it breathes like a man lying on the bottom of a swamp and using a hollow reed to sip air with so he won't be seen.'

'All right, but — '

'Either way, everything comes in or goes out in small breaths, they must be small breaths, because the channel through which they pass is small. Maybe the thing using the valve or the reed has put itself into a kind of suspended state, like sleep or hypnosis, so it can survive on so little breath. And then suppose some misguided fool comes along and throws enough dynamite into the swamp to drain it and make the reed unnecessary. Or, if you're thinking in terms of a valve, blows it clean off. Would you want to risk that? Risk giving it all the goddam air it needs?'

'No,' the New Sarge says in a small voice.

Curtis says: 'Once Buck Flanders and Andy Colucci made up their minds to do that very thing.'

'The hell you say!'

'The hell I don't,' Curtis returns evenly. 'Andy said if a couple of State Troopers couldn't get away with a little vehicular arson, they ought to turn in their badges. They even had a plan. They were going to blame it on the paint and the thinner out there in the hutch. Spontaneous combustion, poof, all gone. And besides, Buck said, who'd send for the Fire Marshal in the first place? It's just an old shed with some old beater of a Buick inside it, for Christ's sake.'

The New Sarge can say nothing. He's too amazed.

'I think it may have been talking to them,' Curt says.

'Talking.' He's trying to get the sense of this. 'Talking to them.'

'Yes.' Curt puts his hat — what they always call the big hat — on his head and hooks the strap at the back of the head the way you wear it in warm weather and adjusts the brim purely by feel. Then, to his old friend he says: 'Can you say it's never talked to you, Sandy?'

The New Sarge opens his mouth to say of

467

course it hasn't, but the other man's eyes are on him, and they are grave. In the end the SC says nothing.

'You can't. Because it does. To you, to me, to all of us. It talked loudest to Huddie on the day that monster came through, but we hear it even when it whispers. Don't we? And it talks all the time. Even in its sleep. So it's important not to listen.'

Curt stands up.

'Just to watch. That's our job and I know it now. If it has to breathe through that valve long enough, or that reed, or that whatever-it-is, sooner or later it'll choke. Stifle. Give out. And maybe it won't really mind. Maybe it'll more or less die in its sleep. If no one riles it up, that is. Which mostly means doing no more than staying out of snatching distance. But it also means leaving it alone.'

He starts away, his life running out from under his feet like sand and neither of them knowing, then stops and takes one more look at his old friend. They weren't quite rookies together but they grew into the job together and now it fits both of them as well as it ever will. Once, when drunk, the Old Sarge called law enforcement a case of good men doing bad chores.

'Sandy.'

Sandy gives him a whatnow look.

'My boy is playing Legion ball this year, did I tell you?'

'Only about twenty times.'

'The coach has a little boy, must be about

468

three. And one day last week when I went overtown to pick Ned up, I saw him down on one knee, playing toss with that little boy in left field. And I fell in love with my kid all over again, Sandy. As strong as when I first held him in my arms, wrapped in a blanket. Isn't that funny?'

Sandy doesn't think it's funny. He thinks it's maybe all the truth the world needs about men.

'The coach had given them their uniforms and Ned had his on and he was down on one knee, tossing underhand to the little boy, and I swear he was the whitest, purest thing any summer sky ever looked down on.' And then he says

NOW:

Sandy

In the shed there was a sallow flash, so pale it was almost lilac. It was followed by darkness . . . then another flash . . . then more darkness . . . darkness this time unbroken.

'Is it done?' Huddie asked, then answered his own question: 'Yeah, I think it is.'

Ned ignored this. 'What?' he asked me. 'What did he say then?'

'What any man says when things are all right at home,' I told him. 'He said he was a lucky man.'

Steff had gone away to mind her microphone and computer screen, but the others were still here. Ned took no notice of any of them. His puffy, red-lidded eyes never left me. 'Did he say anything else?'

'Said you hit two homers against the Rocksburg Railroad the week before, and that you gave him a wave after the second one, while you were coming around third. He liked that, laughed telling me about it. He said you saw the ball better on your worst day than he ever had on his best. He also said you needed to start charging ground balls if you were serious about playing third base.'

The boy looked down and began to struggle. We looked away, all of us, to let him do it in reasonable privacy. At last he said: 'He told me not to be a quitter, but that's what he did with that car. That fucking 8. He quit on it.'

I said, 'He made a choice. There's a difference.'

He sat considering this, then nodded. 'All right.'

Arky said: 'Dis time I'm *really* going home.' But before he went he did something I'll never forget: leaned over and put a kiss on Ned's swollen cheek. I was shocked by the tenderness of it. 'G'night, lad.'

'Goodnight, Arky.'

We watched him drive away in his rattletrap pickup and then Huddie said, 'I'll drive Ned home in his Chevy. Who wants to follow along and bring me back here to get my car?'

'I will,' Eddie said. 'Only I'm waiting outside when you take him in. If Michelle Wilcox goes nuclear, I want to be outside the fallout zone.'

'It'll be okay,' Ned told him. 'I'll say I saw the can on the shelf and picked it up to see what it was and Maced my stupid self.'

I liked it. It had the virtue of simplicity. It was exactly the sort of story the boy's father would have told.

Ned sighed. 'Tomorrow bright and early I'll be sitting in the optometrist's chair over in Statler Village, that's the downside.'

'Won't hurt you,' Shirley said. She also kissed him, planting hers on the corner of his mouth. 'Goodnight, boys. This time everyone goes and no one comes back.'

'Amen to that,' Huddie said, and we watched

her walk away. She was forty-five or so, but there was still plenty to look at when she put her backfield in motion. Even by moonlight. (*Especially* by moonlight.)

Off she went, driving past us, a quick flick of right-back-atcha and then nothing but the taillights.

Darkness from Shed B. No taillights there. No fireworks, either. It was over for the night and someday it would be over for good. But not yet. I could still feel the sleepy beat of it far down in my mind, a tidal whisper that could be words if you wanted them to be.

What I'd seen.

What I'd seen when I had the boy hugged in my arms, him blinded by the spray.

'You want to ride along, Sandy?' Huddie asked.

'Nah, guess not. I'll sit here awhile longer, then get on home. If there are problems with Michelle, you have her call me. Here or at the house, makes no difference.'

'There won't be any problem with Mom,' Ned said.

'What about you?' I asked. 'Are there going to be any more problems with you?'

He hesitated, then said: 'I don't know.'

In some ways I thought it was the best answer he could have given. You had to give him points for honesty.

They walked away, Huddie and Ned heading toward the Bel Air. Eddie split apart from them, going toward his own car and pausing long enough at mine to take the Kojak light off the roof and toss it inside.

Ned stopped at the rear bumper of his car and turned back to me. 'Sandy.'

'What is it?'

'Didn't he have any idea at all about where it came from? What it was? Who the man in the black coat was? Didn't *any* of you?'

'No. We blue-sky'd it from time to time, but no one ever had an idea that felt like the real deal, or even close. Jackie O'Hara probably nailed it when he said the Buick was like a jigsaw piece that won't fit into the puzzle anywhere. You worry it and worry it, you turn it this way and that, try it everywhere, and one day you turn it over and see the back is red and the backs of all the pieces in your puzzle are green. Do you follow that?'

'No,' he said.

'Well, think about it,' I said, 'because you're going to have to live with it.'

'How am I supposed to *do* that?' There was no anger in his voice. The anger had been burned away. Now all he wanted was instructions. Good.

'You don't know where *you* came from or where you're going, do you?' I asked him. 'But you live with it just the same. Don't rail against it too much. Don't spend more than an hour a day shaking your fists at the sky and cursing God.'

'But — '

'There are Buicks everywhere,' I said.

⋆ ⋆ ⋆

Steff came out after they were gone and offered me a cup of coffee. I told her thanks, but I'd pass. I asked her if she had a cigarette. She gave me a prim look — almost shocked — and reminded me she didn't smoke. As though that was her toll-booth, one with the sign reading ALL BUICK ROADMASTERS MUST DETOUR BEYOND THIS POINT. Man, if we lived in that world. If only.

'Are you going home?' she asked.

'Shortly.'

She went inside. I sat by myself on the smokers' bench. There were cigarettes in my car, at least half a pack in the glovebox, but getting up seemed like too much work, at least for the moment. When I did get up, I reckoned it would be best just to stay in motion. I could have a smoke on the way home, and a TV dinner when I got in — The Country Way would be closed by now, and I doubted that Cynthia Garris would be very happy to see my face in the place again soon, anyway. I'd given her a pretty good scare earlier, her fright nothing to mine when the penny finally dropped and I realized what Ned was almost certainly planning to do. And my fear then was only a shadow of the terror I'd felt as I looked into that rising purple glare with the boy hanging blind in my arms and that steady beat-beat-beat in my ears, a sound like approaching footfalls. I had been looking both down, as if into a well, and on an uptilted plane . . . as if my vision had been split by some prismatic device. It had been like looking through a periscope lined with lightning. What I

474

saw was very vivid — I'll never forget it — and fabulously strange. Yellow grass, brownish at the tips, covered a rocky slope that rose before me and then broke off at the edge of a drop. Green-backed beetles bustled in the grass, and off to one side there grew a clump of those waxy lilies. I hadn't been able to see the bottom of the drop, but I could see the sky. It was a terrible engorged purple, packed with clouds and ripe with lightnings. A prehistoric sky. In it, circling in ragged flocks, were flying things. Birds, maybe. Or bats like the one Curt had tried to dissect. They were too far away for me to be sure. And all this happened very quickly, remember. I think there was an ocean at the foot of that drop but don't know why I think it — perhaps only because of the fish that came bursting out of the Buick's trunk that time. Or the smell of salt. Around the Roadmaster there was always that vague, teary smell of salt.

Lying in the yellow grass close to where the bottom of my window (if that's what it was) ended was a silvery ornament on a fine chain: Brian Lippy's swastika. Years of being out in the weather had tarnished it. A little farther off was a cowboy boot, the fancy-stitched kind with the stacked heel. Much of the leather had been overgrown with a black-gray moss that looked like spiderwebs. The boot had been torn down one side, creating a ragged mouth through which I could see a yellow gleam of bone. No flesh; twenty years in the caustic air of that place would have decayed it, though I doubt the absence of flesh was due to mere decay alone.

What I think is that Eddie J.'s old school pal was eaten. Probably while still alive. And screaming, if he could catch enough breath to do so.

And two things more, near the top of my momentary window. The first was a hat, also furry with patches of that black-gray moss; it had grown all around the brim and also in the crease of the crown. It wasn't exactly what we wear now, that hat, the uniform has changed some since the 1970's, but it was a PSP Stetson, all right. The big hat. It hadn't blown away because someone or something had driven a splintery wooden stake down through it to hold it in place. As if Ennis Rafferty's killer had been afraid of the alien intruder even after the intruder's death, and had staked the most striking item of his clothing to make sure he wouldn't rise and walk the night like a hungry vampire.

Near the hat, rusty and almost hidden by scrub grass, was his sidearm. Not the Beretta auto we carry now but the Ruger. The kind George Morgan had used. Had Ennis also used his to commit suicide? Or had he seen something coming, and died firing his weapon at it? Had it even been fired at all?

There was no way to tell, and before I could look more closely, Arky had screamed at Steff to help him and I'd been yanked backward with Ned hanging in my arms like a big doll. I saw no more, but one question at least was answered. They'd gone there, all right, Ennis Rafferty and Brian Lippy both.

Wherever *there* was.

I got up from the bench and walked over to the shed a final time. And there it was, midnight blue and not quite right, casting a shadow just as if it were sane. *Oil's fine*, the man in the black coat had told Bradley Roach, and then he was gone, leaving behind this weird steel callingcard.

At some point, during the last listless lightstorm, the trunk had shut itself again. About a dozen dead bugs lay scattered on the floor. We'd clean them up tomorrow. No sense saving them, or photographing them, or any of that; we no longer bothered. A couple of guys would burn them in the incinerator out back. I would delegate this job. Delegating jobs is also part of what sitting in the big chair is about, and you get to like it. Hand this one the shit and that one the sweets. Can they complain? No. Can they put it on their TS list and hand it to the chaplain? Yes. For all the good it does.

'We'll outwait you,' I said to the thing in the shed. 'We can do that.'

It only sat there on its whitewalls, and far down in my head the pulse whispered: Maybe.

. . . *and maybe not.*

LATER

Obituaries are modest, aren't they? Yeah. Shirt always tucked in, skirt kept below the knee. *Died unexpectedly.* Could be anything from a heart attack while sitting on the jakes to being stabbed by a burglar in the bedroom. Cops mostly know the truth, though. You don't always *want* to know, especially when it's one of your own, but you do. Because most of the time we're the guys who show up first, with our reds lit and the walkie-talkies on our belts crackling out what sounds like so much gibble-gabble to the John Q's. For most folks who *die unexpectedly*, we're the first faces their staring open eyes can't see.

When Tony Schoondist told us he was going to retire I remember thinking. *Good, that's good, he's getting a little long in the tooth. Not to mention a little slow on the uptake.* Now, in the year 2006, I'm getting ready to pull the pin myself and probably some of my younger guys are thinking the same thing: long in the tooth and slow on the draw. But mostly, you know, I feel the same as I ever did, full of piss and vinegar, ready to work a double shift just about any day of the week. Most days when I note the gray hair which now predominates the black or how much more forehead there is below the place where the hair starts, I think it's a mistake, a clerical error which will eventually be rectified when brought to the attention of the proper

478

authorities. It is impossible, I think, that a man who still feels so profoundly twenty-five can look so happast fifty. Then there'll be a stretch of bad days and I'll know it's no error, just time marching on, that shuffling, rueful tread. But was there ever a moment as bad as seeing Ned behind the wheel of the Buick Roadmaster 8?

Yes. There was one.

★ ★ ★

Shirley was on duty when the call came in: a crackup out on SR 32, near the Humboldt Road intersection. Where the old Jenny station used to be, in other words. Shirley's face was pale as ashes when she came and stood in the open door of my office.

'What is it?' I asked. 'What the hell's wrong with you?'

'Sandy . . . the man who called it in said the vehicle was an old Chevrolet, red and white. He says the driver's dead.' She swallowed. 'In pieces. That's what he said.'

That part I didn't care about, although I would later, when I had to look at it. At him. 'The Chevrolet — have you got the model?'

'I didn't ask. Sandy, I couldn't.' Her eyes were full of tears. 'I didn't dare. But how many old red-and-white Chevrolets do you think there are in Statler County?'

I went out to the scene with Phil Candleton, praying the crashed Chevy would turn out to be a Malibu or a Biscayne, anything but a Bel Air, vanity plate MY 57. But that's what it was.

479

'Fuck,' Phil said in a low and dismayed voice.

He'd piled it into the side of the cement bridge which spans Redfern Stream less than five minutes' walk from where the Buick 8 first appeared and where Curtis was killed. The Bel Air had seatbelts, but he hadn't been wearing one. Nor were there any skidmarks.

'Christ almighty,' Phil said. 'This ain't right.'

Not right and not an accident. Although in the obituary, where shirts are kept neatly tucked in and skirts are kept discreetly below the knee, it would only say he *died unexpectedly*, which was true. Lord yes.

Lookie-loos had started showing up by then, slowing to stare at what lay facedown on the bridge's narrow walkway. I think one asshole actually took a picture. I wanted to run after him and stuff his shitty little disposable camera down his throat.

'Get some detour signs up,' I told Phil. 'You and Carl. Send the traffic around by County Road. I'll cover him up. Jesus, what a mess! *Jesus!* Who's gonna tell his mother?'

Phil wouldn't look at me. We both knew who was going to tell his mother. Later that day I bit the bullet and did the worst job that comes with the big chair. Afterward I went down to The Country Way with Shirley, Huddie, Phil, and George Stankowski. I don't know about them, but I myself didn't pass go or collect two hundred dollars; old Sandy went directly to shitfaced.

I only have two clear memories of that night. The first is of trying to explain to Shirley how

480

weird The Country Way's jukeboxes were, how all the songs were the very ones you never thought of anymore until you saw their names again here. She didn't get it.

My other memory is of going into the bathroom to throw up. After, while I was splashing cold water on my face, I looked at myself in one of the wavery steel mirrors. And I knew for sure that the getting-to-be-old face I saw looking back at me was no mistake. The mistake was believing that the twenty-five-year-old guy who seemed to live in my brain was real.

I remembered Huddie shouting *Sandy, grab my hand!* and then the two of us, Ned and I, had spilled out on to the pavement, safe with the rest of them. Thinking of that, I began to cry.

Died unexpectedly, that shit is all right for the County *American*, but cops know the truth. We clean up the messes and we always know the truth.

★ ★ ★

Everyone not on duty went to the funeral, of course. He'd been one of us. When it was over, George Stankowski gave his mother and his two sisters a ride home and I drove back to the barracks with Shirley. I asked her if she was going to the reception — what you call a wake, I guess, if you're Irish — and she shook her head. 'I hate those things.'

So we had a final cigarette out on the smokers' bench, idly watching the young Trooper who was looking in at the Buick. He stood in that same legs-apart, goddam-the-Democrats, didya-hear-the-one-about-the-traveling-salesman pose that we all assumed when we looked into Shed B. The century had changed, but everything else was more or less the same.

'It's so unfair,' Shirley said. 'A young man like that —'

'What are you talking about?' I asked her. 'Eddie J. was in his late forties, for God's sake . . . maybe even fifty. I think his sisters are both in their sixties. His mother's almost *eighty*!'

'You know what I mean. He was too young to do that.'

'So was George Morgan,' I said.

'Was it . . . ?' She nodded toward Shed B.

'I don't think so. Just his life. He made an honest effort to get sober, busted his ass. This was right after he bought Curt's old Bel Air from Ned. Eddie always liked that car, you know, and Ned couldn't have it at Pitt anyway, not as a freshman. It would've just been sitting there in his driveway —'

' — — and Ned needed the money.'

'Going off to college from a single-parent home? Every penny. So when Eddie asked him, he said okay, sure. Eddie paid thirty-five hundred dollars —'

'Thirty-two,' Shirley said with the assurance of one who really knows.

'Thirty-two, thirty-five, whatever. The point is, I think Eddie saw getting it as a new leaf he was supposed to turn over. He quit going to The Tap; I think he started going to AA meetings instead.

That was the good part. For Eddie, the good part lasted about two years.'

Across the parking lot, the Trooper who'd been looking into Shed B turned, spotted us, and began walking in our direction. I felt the skin on my arms prickle. In the gray uniform the boy — only he wasn't a boy any longer, not really — looked strikingly like his dead father. Nothing strange about that, I suppose; it's simple genetics, a correspondence that runs in the blood. What made it eerie was the big hat. He had it in his hands and was turning it over and over.

'Eddie fell off the wagon right around the time that one there decided he wasn't cut out for college,' I said.

Ned Wilcox left Pitt and came home to Statler. For a year he'd done Arky's job, Arky by then having retired and moved back to Michigan, where everyone no doubt sounded just like him (a scary thought). When he turned twenty-one, Ned made the application and took the tests. Now, at twenty-two, here he was. Hello, rookie.

Halfway across the parking lot, Curt's boy paused to look back at the shed, still twirling his Stetson in his hands.

'He looks good, doesn't he?' Shirley murmured.

I put on my Old Sarge face — a little aloof, a little disdainful. 'Relatively squared away. Shirley, do you have any idea how much bright red dickens his Ma raised when she finally found out what he had in mind?'

Shirley laughed and put out her cigarette. 'She

483

raised more when she found out he was planning to sell his dad's Bel Air to Eddie Jacubois — at least that's what Ned told me. I mean, c'mon, Sandy, she had to know it was coming. *Had* to. She was married to one, for God's sake. And she probably knew this was where he belonged. Eddie, though, where did *he* belong? Why couldn't he just stop drinking? Once and for all?'

'That's a question for the ages,' I said. 'They say it's a disease, like cancer or diabetes. Maybe they're right.'

Eddie had begun showing up for duty with liquor on his breath, and no one covered for him very long; the situation was too serious. When he refused counselling, and a leave of absence to spend four weeks in the spin-dry facility the PSP favors for their stricken officers, he was given his choice: quit quietly or get fired noisily. Eddie had quit, with about half the retirement package he would have received if he'd managed to hang on to his job for another three years — at the end, the benefits really stack up. And I could understand the outcome no more than Shirley — why *hadn't* he just quit? With that kind of incentive, why hadn't he just said *I'll be thirsty for three years and then I'll pull the pin and take a bath in it*? I didn't know.

The Tap really did become Eddie J.'s home away from home. Along with the old Bel Air, that was. He'd kept it waxed on the outside and spotlessly clean on the inside right up to the day when he'd driven it into a bridge abutment near Redfern Stream at approximately eighty miles an hour. He had plenty of reasons to do it by then — he was not a happy man — but I had to wonder if maybe there weren't a few reasons just a little closer to home. Specifically I had to wonder if he hadn't heard that pulse near the end, that tidal whisper that's like a voice in the middle of your head.

Do it, Eddie, go on, why not? There's not much else, is there? The rest is pretty well used up. Just step down a little brisker on the old go-pedal and then twist the wheel to the right. Do it. Go on. Make a little mischief for your buddies to clean up.

I thought about the night we'd sat out on this same bench, the young man I currently had my eye on four years younger than he was now and listening raptly as Eddie told the tale of stopping Brian Lippy's bigfoot truck. The kid listening as Eddie told about trying to get Lippy's girl to do something about her situation before her boyfriend fucked her up beyond all recognition or maybe killed her. The joke turned out to be on Eddie, of course. So far as I knew, the bloodyface girl is the only one of that roadside quartet still alive. Yeah, she's around. I don't road-patrol much anymore, but her name and picture come across my desk from time to time, each picture showing a woman closer to the beerbreath brokennose fuck-ya-for-a-pack-of-smokes hag she will, barring a miracle, become. She's had lots of DUIs, quite a few D-and-Ds, a trip to the hospital one night with a broken arm and hip after she fell downstairs. I imagine someone like Brian Lippy probably helped her down those stairs, don't you? Because they *do* pick the same kind over and over. She has two or maybe it's three kids in foster care. So yeah, she's around, but is she living? If you say she is, then I have to tell you that maybe George Morgan and Eddie J. had the right idea.

'I'm going to make like a bee and buzz,' Shirley said, getting up. 'Can't take any more hilarity in one day. You doin okay with it?'

'Yeah,' I said.

'Hey, he came back that night, didn't he? There's that.'

She didn't have to be any more specific. I nodded, smiling.

'Eddie was a good guy,' Shirley said. 'Maybe he couldn't leave the booze alone, but he had the kindest heart.'

Nope, I thought, watching her walk across to Ned, watching them talk a little. *I think* you're *the one with the kindest heart, Shirl.*

She gave Ned a little peck on the cheek, putting one hand on his shoulder and going up on her toes to do it, then headed toward her car. Ned came over to where I was sitting. 'You okay?' he asked.

'Yeah, good.'

'And the funeral . . . ?'

'Hey, shit, it was a funeral. I've been to better and I've been to worse. I'm glad the coffin was closed.'

'Sandy, can I show you something? Over there?' He nodded his head at Shed B.

'Sure.' I got up. 'Is the temperature going down?' If so, it was news. It had been two years since the temp in there had dropped more than

486

five degrees below the outside temperature. Sixteen months since the last lightshow, and that one had consisted of no more than eight or nine pallid flickers.

'No,' he said.

'Trunk open?'

'Shut tight as a drum.'

'What, then?'

'I'd rather show you.'

I glanced at him sharply, for the first time getting out of my own head enough to register how excited he was. Then, with decidedly mixed feelings — curiosity and apprehension were the dominant chords, I guess — I walked across the parking lot with my old friend's son. He took up his sidewalk super's pose at one window and I took up mine at the next.

At first I saw nothing unusual; the Buick sat on the concrete as it had for a quarter of a century, give or take. There were no flashing lights, no exotic exhibits. The thermometer's red needle stood at an unremarkable seventy-three degrees.

'So?' I asked.

Ned laughed, delighted. 'You're looking spang at it and don't see it! Perfect! I didn't see it myself, at first. I knew something had changed, but I couldn't tell what.'

'What are you talking about?'

He shook his head, still smiling. 'Nossir, Sergeant, nossir. I think not. You're the boss; you're also one of just three cops who were there then and are still here now. It's right in front of you, so go to it.'

I looked in again, first squinting and then raising my hands to the sides of my face to block the glare, that old gesture. It helped, but what was I seeing? Something, yes, he was right about that, but just what? What had changed?

I remembered that night at The Country Way, flipping the pages of the dead jukebox back and forth, trying to isolate the most important question, which was the one Ned had decided not to ask. It had almost come, then had slipped shyly away again. When that happened, it was no good to chase. I'd thought that then and still did now.

So instead of continuing to give the 8 my cop stare, I unfocused my eyes and let my mind drift away. What it drifted to were song-titles, of course, titles of the ones they never seem to play, even on the oldies stations, once their brief season of popularity has gone. 'Society's Child' and 'Pictures of Matchstick Men' and 'Quick Joey Small' and —

—and bingo, there it was. Like he'd said, it was right in front of me. For a moment I couldn't breathe.

There was a crack in the windshield.

A thin silver lightning-bolt jigjagging top to bottom on the driver's side.

Ned clapped me on the shoulder. 'There you go, Sherlock, I knew you'd get there. After all, it's only right there in front of you.'

I turned to him, started to talk, then turned back to make sure I'd seen what I thought I'd seen. I had. The crack looked like a frozen stroke of quicksilver.

'When did it happen?' I asked him. 'Do you know?'

'I take a fresh Polaroid of it every forty-eight hours or so,' he said. 'I'll check to make sure, but I'll bet you a dead cat and a string to swing it with that the last picture I took doesn't show a crack. So this happened between Wednesday evening and Friday afternoon at . . . ' He checked his watch, then gave me a big smile. 'At four-fifteen.'

'Might even have happened during Eddie's funeral,' I said.

'Possible, yeah.'

We looked in again for a little while, neither of us talking. Then Ned said, 'I read the poem you mentioned. 'The Wonderful One-Hoss Shay'.'

'Did you?'

'Uh-huh. It's pretty good. Pretty funny.'

I stepped back from the window and looked at him.

'It'll happen fast now, like in the poem,' he said. 'Next thing a tire'll blow . . . or the muffler will fall off . . . or a piece of the chrome. You know how you can stand beside a frozen lake in March or early April and listen to the ice creak?'

I nodded.

'This is going to be like that.' His eyes were alight, and a curious idea came to me: I was seeing Ned Wilcox really, genuinely happy for the first time since his father had died.

'You think?'

'Yes. Only instead of ice creaking, the sound will be snapping bolts and cracking glass. Cops will line up at these windows like they did in the

489

old days . . . only it'll be to watch things bend and break and come loose and fall off. Until, finally, the whole thing goes. They'll wonder if there isn't going to be one more flash of light at the very finish, like the final Chinese Flower at the end of the fireworks display on the Fourth of July.'

'Will there be, do you think?'

'I think the fireworks are over. I think we're going to hear one last big steel clank and then you can take the pieces to the crusher.'

'Are you sure?'

'Nah,' he said, and smiled. 'You *can't* be sure. I learned that from you and Shirley and Phil and Arky and Huddie.' He paused. 'And Eddie J. But I'll watch. And sooner or later . . . ' He raised one hand, looked at it, then closed it into a fist and turned back to his window. 'Sooner or later.'

I turned back to my own window, cupping my hands to the sides of my face to cut the glare. I peered in at the thing that looked like a Buick Roadmaster 8. The kid was absolutely right.

Sooner or later.

Bangor, Maine
Boston, Massachusetts
Naples, Florida
Lovell, Maine
Osprey, Florida
April 3, 1999 – March 20, 2002

AUTHOR'S NOTE

I've had ideas fall into my lap from time to time — I suppose this is true of any writer — but *From a Buick 8* was almost comically the reverse: a case of me falling into the lap of an idea. That's worth a note, I think.

My wife and I spent the winter of 1999 on Longboat Key in Florida, where I tinkered at the final draft of a short novel (*The Girl Who Loved Tom Gordon*) and wrote little else of note. Nor did I have plans to write anything in the spring of that year.

In late March, Tabby flew back to Maine from Florida. I drove. I hate to fly, love to drive, and besides, I had a truckload of furnishings, books, guitars, computer components, clothes, and paper. My second or third day on the road found me in western Pennsylvania. I needed gas and got off the turnpike at a rural exit. Near the ramp I found a Conoco station. There was an actual attendant who actually pumped the gas. He even threw in a few words of tolerably pleasant conversation at no extra charge.

I left him doing his thing and went to the restroom to do mine. When I finished, I walked around to the back of the station. Here I found a rather steep slope littered with auto parts and a brawling stream at the foot. There was still a fair amount of snow on the ground, in dirty strips and runners. I walked a little way down the slope to get a better look at the water, and my feet went out from beneath me. I slid about ten feet before grabbing a rusty something-or-other and bringing myself to a stop. Had I missed it, I might well have gone into the water. And then? All bets are off, as they say.

I paid the attendant (so far as I know, he had no idea of my misadventure) and got back on the highway. I mused about my slip as I drove, wondering about what would have happened if I'd gone into the stream (which, with all that spring runoff, was at least temporarily a small river). How long would my truckload of Florida furnishings and our bright Florida clothes have stood at the pumps before the gas-jockey got nervous? Whom would he have called? How long before they'd have found me if I had drowned?

This little incident happened around ten in the morning. By afternoon I was in New York. And by then I had the story you've just read pretty much set in my mind. I have said in my book about the craft of writing that first drafts are only about story; if there is meaning, it should come later, and arise naturally from the tale itself. This story became — I suppose — a meditation on the essentially indecipherable quality of life's events, and how impossible it is to find a coherent meaning in them. The first draft was written in two months. By then I realized I had made myself a whole host of problems by writing of two things I knew nothing about: western Pennsylvania and the Pennsylvania State Police. Before I could address either of these concerns, I suffered my own road-accident and my life changed radically. I came out of the summer of '99 lucky to have any life at all, in fact. It was over a year before I even thought of this story again, let alone worked on it.

The coincidence of having written a book filled with grisly vehicular mishaps shortly before suffering my own has not been lost on me, but I've tried not to make too much of it. Certainly I don't think there was anything premonitory about the similarities between what happens to Curtis Wilcox in *Buick 8* and what happened to me in real life (for one thing, I lived). I can testify at first hand, however, that I got most of it right from imagination: as with Curtis, the coins were stripped from my pockets and the watch from my wrist. The cap I was wearing was later found in the woods, at least twenty yards from the point of impact. But I changed nothing in the course of my story to reflect what happened to me; most of what I wanted was there in the completed first draft. The imagination is a powerful tool.

It never crossed my mind to re-set *From a Buick 8* in Maine, although Maine is the place I know (and love) the best. I stopped at a gas station in Pennsylvania, went on my ass in Pennsylvania, got the idea in Pennsylvania. I thought the resulting tale should stay in Pennsylvania, in spite of the aggravations that presented. Not that there weren't rewards, as well; for one thing, I got to set my fictional town of Statler just down the road apiece from Rocksburg, the town which serves as the locale for K.C. Constantine's brilliant series of novels about small-town police chief Mario Balzic. If you've never read any of these stories, you ought to do yourself a favor. The continuing story of Chief Balzic and his family is like *The Sopranos* turned inside-out and told from a law enforcement point of view. Also, western Pennsylvania is the home of the Amish, whose way of life I wanted to explore a little more fully.

This book could never have been finished without the help of Trooper Lucien Southard of the Pennsylvania State Police. Lou read the manuscript, managed not to laugh too hard at its many howlers, and wrote me eight pages of notes and corrections that could be printed in any writer's handbook without a blush (for one thing, Trooper Southard has been taught to print in large, easy-to-read block letters). He took me to several PSP barracks, introduced me to three PCOs who were kind enough to show me what they do and how they do it (to begin with they ran the license plate of my Dodge pickup — it came back clean, I'm relieved to say, with no wants or warrants), and demonstrated all sorts of State Police equipment. The most informative and patient of these was P.C.O Theresa M. Maker — thank you, Theresa, for your kindness.

More importantly, Lou and some of his mates took me to lunch at a restaurant in Amish country, where we consumed huge sandwiches and drank pitchers of iced tea. They regaled me with an hour of stories of Trooper life. Some of these were funny, some of them were horrible, and some managed to be both at the same time. Not all of them made it into *Buick 8*, but a

494

number of them did, in suitably fictionalized form. They treated me as a friend, and no one moved too fast, which was good. At that time, I was still hopping along on one crutch.

Thanks, Lou — and thanks to all the Troopers who work out of the Butler barracks — for helping me keep my Pennsylvania book in Pennsylvania. Much more important, thanks for helping me understand exactly what it is that State Troopers do, and the price they pay to do it well.

Hodder & Stoughton would not let me close this note without pointing out that certain — ahem! — liberties have been taken with the Buick on the book jacket. GM-ophiles will likely notice that *Eight's* cover-girl is several years younger than the Buick in the story. I was asked if this little cheat bothered me, and I said absolutely not. What bothers me, especially when it's late and I can't sleep, is that sneermouth grille. Looks almost ready to gobble someone up, doesn't it? Maybe me. Or maybe you, my dear Constant Reader.

Maybe you.

Stephen King
May 29, 2002

We do hope that you have enjoyed reading this large print book.

Did you know that all of our titles are available for purchase?

We publish a wide range of high quality large print books including:
Romances, Mysteries, Classics
General Fiction
Non Fiction and Westerns

Special interest titles available in large print are:
The Little Oxford Dictionary
Music Book
Song Book
Hymn Book
Service Book

Also available from us courtesy of Oxford University Press:
Young Readers' Dictionary
(large print edition)
Young Readers' Thesaurus
(large print edition)

For further information or a free brochure, please contact us at:
Ulverscroft Large Print Books Ltd.,
The Green, Bradgate Road, Anstey,
Leicester, LE7 7FU, England.
Tel: (00 44) 0116 236 4325
Fax: (00 44) 0116 234 0205